LAUREN'S
SAINTS OF DIRTY FAITH:
A DIRTY GIRLS SOCIAL CLUB NOVEL
by
Alisa Valdes-Rodriguez

ALSO BY ALISA VALDES-RODRIGUEZ

PUBLISHED BY:
Alisa Valdes-Rodriguez
on Amazon CreateSpace

Paperback Edition License Notes

Dedication the First

This novel is dedicated to all of my loyal readers and fans who found themselves in these six characters back in 2003, and kept asking for more. It is also dedicated to Latina Magazine, and its editors and publishers, for supporting me tirelessly over the years and for always being the first to get the word out about my books. Because of all of you, American publishing changed its view of Latinas in mainstream fiction, no longer just seeing us as stereotypical exotic unfathomable lower-class oversexed "illegal" immigrants, but also as regular, normal American women with hopes, dreams, lives, families, loves, issues, careers and, most importantly, friends -- like any other women. (You have no idea how terrifying and revolutionary such a concept is for some people!) Because of you, this "new" and more realistic image of us leapt off the pages of my books and into the consciousness of American popular culture these past eight years, and into the hearts and minds of a wide variety of people across the nation. Because of you, I was given the opportunity to realize my lifelong dream of being a novelist. Because of you, my son will be able to afford to go to college. Because of you, I have learned and grown, and made thousands of new friends across this great nation and the globe. Because of you, these books exist. Because of you, I write this book. Thank you for everything, for yourselves, and most of all for your time, passion and support.

Dedication the Second

I cannot unleash this book upon the world without first thanking one Mr. Steven Lane, known to many of my Facebook, Twitter and Mamiverse.com readers as The Cowboy. Steve, you are not only the love of my life and my new best friend, you are a gifted writer, editor and thinker, without whom this book would never have happened. Your insights, suggestions and ideas helped shape this book in countless ways, and it simply would not exist without your input. Thank you, too, for giving me those ten wonderful days at the ranch, during which time the bulk of this book was written, for making me coffee and bringing me water, for rubbing my shoulders and neck when the typing got too painful, for listening to me talk about these characters endlessly as though they were real friends, for helping me to understand the heart and mind of a real cowboy. Thank you for your emotional intelligence and maturity. Your fingerprints are all over this story, baby, and you know it. Thank you.

NOTE TO MY READERS FROM ALISA

Welcome to this, the third installment in the *Dirty Girls Social Club* series of novels. Hold on to your seats, because more than the first two books, this third one is a quick-paced, dangerous, sexy ride!

When we first met the "sucias" in book one, they were all about 28 years old and living in Boston. (To refresh your memories, "dirty girls" is meant to be ironic, the name that the studious friends gave themselves in college because it was the opposite of what they actually were!) By the second book, they were in their early 30s and starting to marry, have children and, in some cases, move away to better their careers.

Now, we find them at 36, scattered across the United States, and facing difficulties and dangers unfathomable before.

As I sat down to write this book, it occurred to me that it would be unreasonable to expect the Dirty Girls to all still be as close as they were when they were younger. As those of us who have married, had children, and reached our mid-30s (or older, *cough*) know, life often has a way of getting in the way. Friends end up pushed to the side, and though we still love them as much as ever, we tend to connect less and less the more responsibilities we pick up as life moves on. Friends we used to see every week become friends we see only every couple of months, or once or twice a year. In the eight years since I wrote the first book, the social world of friendship has also changed dramatically, thanks to Facebook and Twitter and other social media sites. Friends we used to actually hang out with have become friends we "tweet" and "update." Everything is different now, and I wanted this new book to reflect those differences.

I meditated a lot on how these women's lives might have played out, where they might have gone, and how they might have handled the various challenges and changes taking place in our nation today. In all, I spent about a year trying to figure out what direction to take with this book. As I did so, only three of the sucias were really speaking to me. The other three were quiet, fading into the background. I realized that this was because that's how it works with real-life friends. Sometimes you are closer to some than others. Friendship is a fluid, ever-changing thing. With this in mind, I chose to focus this third Dirty Girls novel primarily upon one story, of one of the sucias (Lauren), with two others (Rebecca and Usnavys) playing a prominent role in her exciting journey.

As I considered how much our culture had changed in the nine years since I wrote the first *Dirty Girls Social Club* novel, it occurred to me, too, that we had all likely moved past the shallow materialism of the "chick lit" era. I find few things as distasteful in this era of extreme need and desperation as books or other popular culture offerings that glorify materialism, narcissism and consumerism. Those are the sins that got us all into this mess in the first place. I cannot be party to promoting consumption as the road to happiness anymore. It's a lie. We are all ready for something more substantive, aren't we? I know I am.

Because this novel in your hands is self-published (another bonus of the new technology the Internet has to offer, giving authors much more self-determination than ever before) I can honestly tell you all that I have *never* particularly felt like any of my novels fit neatly into the "chick lit" category to begin with. I feel even less so now. I have always been a writer out of synch with the boxes the traditional publishing industry hoped to stuff me into, a writer aching to expand her horizons, and I am extremely pleased to say that self-publishing through sites such as Amazon, Smashwords and Lulu has freed me to do things my way. Among the many small changes I've implemented is my decision not to put Spanish words in italics, for the simple reason that for those of us who think and speak in Spanglish, there is no distinction made, mentally or emotionally, between English and Spanish. I wanted the look of the words to reflect that reality.

All of this means that you will find here a familiar Dirty Girls book that is also quite a bit different from what you've seen before. For instance, I wanted this third book to reflect some of the economic realities of our time. I, like so many of us, have watched the economy of the United States plummet into recession and, some might argue, toy with depression. I have seen many of my friends lose jobs and homes, with little hope of ever recovering, thanks to a banking industry and federal government that have been corrupted almost beyond repair. I have watched as the journalism industry that spawned my writing career, and to which many of the "sucias" initially belonged, self-destructed thanks to media deregulation and monopolies, to the point that it could be argued there is very little true journalism even being done in the country anymore. This book had to reflect all of that, or risk being nonsense. In other words, I could not, and would not, write just another version of the first Dirty Girls book, about fabulously well-off women journalists with lots of nice stuff, living glamorous lives in a nation where regular people can actually get mortgages. That world is unfortunately nearly gone. Imploded. To pretend otherwise would be to turn my back on the harsh new realities that many of us face, myself included.

As a writer, I also wanted to explore the suspense genre a bit, within the confines of a commercial women's fiction book. Many of you know from interviews you've seen with me or from my social media comments that my favorite living writer is without a doubt Dean Koontz. He is a modern master of the craft and art of writing novels. He is our own Charles Dickens. I love the way he is able to mix suspense, romance and pointed social commentary all together in commercial novels that are as beautifully written as they are absolute page-turners. In this third Dirty Girls book, I've tried to capture a little bit of Koontz's approach, creating a sociopathic monster, Jason Flynn, who is out to get Lauren, while still retaining my own signature "Alisa" sardonic humor, relatable American Latino biculturalism and sizzling hot romance. I hope it works for you as well as it worked for me.

I also hope that this new style and take on the Dirty

Girls formula will entertain you, and I have faith that while we all love the classic first Dirty Girls book, we're also all ready for something a little different, a little new, and a lot of fun. I do hope you guys are ready to allow me to evolve a little bit as an artist, and that you'll let me bring you along with me. Thank you for your support, and please, if you can, laugh a little, and maybe cry a little, as you read the rest of this work. Besitos, chiquitas!

LAUREN'S
SAINTS OF DIRTY FAITH:
A DIRTY GIRLS SOCIAL CLUB NOVEL

LAUREN

I'm standing on the red line subway platform at the Andrew station, fresh out of a meeting with a toothless drunk, who knows another drunk who once shared beers and questionable women with legendary Southie mobster Whitey Bulger. I got these leads from my ex-boyfriend, Jason Flynn, who is a detective with the Boston Police Department. Jason grew up in South Boston and went to school with some of today's top mobsters. I don't suppose that's much to brag about for most people, but Jason and I aren't most people. We're adrenaline junkies, addicted to danger and drama. The point being, even though the relationship was crap enough for me to worm my way out of it not too long ago, I *did* get something useful out of it, and this is all the new Lauren talking. The new Lauren is an optimist. The new Lauren actually leaves men before they can leave her, and starts looking for new ones to prey upon. Yes, the new Lauren *still* forgets her dry-cleaning for weeks at a time, and maybe eats too much ice cream, and perhaps doesn't visit the gym nearly as much as she should, but overall there have been improvements.

It is August, and this means Boston is hot and humid. Above ground, the city smells of salty things rotting from the cold dark sea. Below ground, where I am now, the train station is thick with the scent of steamed piss and motor oil. Because the new Lauren is so goddamned bubbly, self-determined and hopeful, I choose to experience this olfactory discomfort as the subterranean perfume of my gritty urban success. It's all in how you look at things. Or sniff them, I suppose.

I got some excellent dirt from the geezer -- I mean, like, Pulitzer-nomination dirt, city-changing dirt, career-defining dirt. You don't think this is a big deal unless you, like I, live in Beantown and understand that there is no mob quite as effective and evasive as the Irish. This kind of thing excites me, unfortunately. It excites me professionally, and also in other ways that I am too ashamed to list. Oh, those bad boys. I've always been something of a sucker for bad boys. I really need to quit that habit, because it's the main reason I am still unmarried and have no kids. It's also the reason I ended up dating Jason Flynn for nearly a year, even though toward the end he was having me followed, and using his position to look at my cell phone records to make sure I wasn't cheating on him. The old Lauren would have tried to figure out how to make a guy like that happy. The new Lauren knows enough to walk away, even if Jason does have the prettiest eyes ever granted by God to a man. I always fall for the kind of guy who's not exactly all about family and home, the kind who makes you anxious and fearful to the point of nausea, as often as he makes you swoon.

I'm also, ironically perhaps, a widely respected prize-winning columnist for the largest daily newspaper in New England. Yes, I know. Like being a fishwife or a gladiator, being a newspaper columnist is not something anyone in his or her right mind *brags* about anymore. It's like going up to someone and telling them with great boastfulness that you are seeking full-time employment as a Cinder Wench. I will fully understand if you fail to be impressed with my job. If you are less than 30 years old, I will also understand if you don't know exactly what a newspaper is, or why people ever found them important. No, really. Don't feel badly. It's okay.

Sad truth is, people don't read (newspapers) anymore. Most people get their news from comedy cable networks and ALL CAPS blogs written by ranting lunatics in their parents' Braintree basements. Or they skim the unpaid "journalism" on the Huffington Post, with brains that science tells us are quickly becoming rewired by the Internet to absorb, retain and comprehend less and less information, for the mere fact that so very much information is now available. Oh, the ironing. Er, irony. Right.

Basically, we are a nation of passive unwrung sponges, drugged by the antidepressants in our drinking water and, thanks to technology, unable to give a rat's ass about anything much anymore. We are the slobbering masses, the babosos. I'd be better off, professionally, writing blogs that list the "Top Ten," oh, *reasons men cheat/places to eat fish/places to eat pussy/cities for angry dentists/sexual positions* (fill in the blank with something quick and easy to understand). I soldier on anyway because I haven't quite figured out what else someone like me, who has only ever *been* a newspaper writer, might do in the modern world. Perhaps there is somewhere an opening for a Jongleur, and all I need do is find myself a lute or a lyre. I've made peace with the fact that I, like the pet rock and the perm-mullet, am a quaint anachronism. Perhaps one of these days I will begin to wear long shorts and socks, and a newsboy cap, and to whistle through my teeth, and to speak like Jimmy Stewart. Yeah, sweetheart. Step. Right. Up.

See, I, like the indoor cat with the feathered-string tied to the bathroom doorknob, still like the thrill of the (mostly futile) chase. I still like digging for real news, even if no one will actually read it. I still take seriously the fact that the only profession named specifically in the United States constitution is journalism, and I agree with Thomas Jefferson that without a free press there can be no democracy. I am aware we not longer possess a free press, thanks to media deregulation under a certain lying cigardildoeur of Monica Lewinsky's, just as I am cognizant of the fact that most of my fellow citizens do not understand the broad implications of mega media monopolies to the future of their country. I am aware that most Americans are more concerned with Kate Gosselin's (admittedly miraculous) tummy tuck than they are with political corruption and, say, organized crime in Southie. So, yes. I am an artifact. A dinosaur at 36.

Which reminds me -- I have to stop off at the package store before I go back to my Jamaica Plain apartment. Don't judge. I know. I stopped drinking once. Then, like the lady says in that movie -- I don't recall which now -- I quit quitting. Makes the extinct news job easier, not to mention the way it fills up that horrible existential abyss that comes with being the only one among my friends who can't seem to find a husband or make a baby. I have five close friends I still keep in touch with, from college, and we still occasionally call ourselves "sucias," which is Spanish for "Dirty Girls" and was the ironic name we gave ourselves because we were all basically really good girls and somewhat nerdy. It's all about balance, and irony, and whatever. The point being -- if there is a point -- that even the sucias aren't as close as we used to be, because we've scattered all over the country in the years since we graduated from Boston University with our degrees in communications and journalism. We used to all live in Boston, but these days the only ones of us who are here are me and Usnavys, who is my plus-sized Puerto Rican friend and thanks to having had two babies has become even more plus-sized, which she calls a "bonus" for her man. She is proud of her curves, even when they start to resemble the curvature of the earth itself. Me? I don't have her confidence; even though many people often tell me I am pretty (in spite of the red curly hair and freckles that come courtesy of my Irish-American mother's side, apparently being made up for my the ample "lady lumps" that come to me courtesy of the Cuban father's side.) I am hopelessly insecure and lacking in self-esteem, rather like Larry David. I can't even find a boyfriend who does not seem to think that the moniker "Lauren Fernandez's man" means "cheat, sir, cheat, with wild monkey abandon" and while I know this is probably related to my own self-loathing attitude, it still fucking sucks.

So, to summarize: I have a terrible love life, a dying career, far-flung evaporating friends whose lives all seem better than mine (Sara is a TV home and cooking host out of Southern California, with a hot and much-younger husband and twin boys who are cuter and smarter than ought to be legal; Cuicatl is a successful recording artist married to her loving and supportive older manager; Elizabeth is married to a woman gallery-owner with a gaggle of Montessori and Waldorf type kids in San Diego; Rebecca is married to a British software mogul and owns her own media empire that she runs out of Santa Fe, New Mexico; Usnavys is a high-ranking executive for a nonprofit in New England and married to her high school sweetheart, with two adorable kids who eat too much). Oh, and I have alcohol. You hang on to what you can. In my case, this is generally the bar in the subway train, because there are rarely seats when you need them. It also generally means the bar in my neighborhood, because, well, they *always* have seats, and I always seem to need one. I hang on. Watch Lauren hang on. Isn't this fun?

See? Here I stand, waiting for a train, texting a long-ago ex-boyfriend, Ed the Bigheaded Texican, about how much I hate him for lying to and two-timing me and how desperately he owes me an apology. I tell him that if he hadn't been such a shit to me, I would never have had reason to get involved with Jason Flynn, the latest man to break my heart. In other words, I blame my latest crap relationship on a distant crap relationship. It's easier that way. I pester Ed now mostly to shove open the door for him to make up with me and do it all again, because that is what I do. Run on the hamster wheel of romance in my fancy Asics *pata*-gear, getting nowhere and worn the hell out at the same time. Some people like to say with great optimism that when one door shuts, another opens. Yeah, well, that never happens for me. For me, when one door slams shut, I'm standing there in the hotel hallway in nothing but a robe and my key is locked inside. Doors don't open for me. I have to force them. That's what I do. I have been known to run around to doors I already went through, testing to see if they'll open again. Like Ed.

There is a name for such behavior, but I don't recall what it is. Crazy? Pathetic? Delusional? No, no, no. While those all sound accurate, they're not quite what I had in mind. Give me a second. Uhm...right! Got. it.

Codependent.

Right. That's the word.

Ed doesn't respond, so I text him again. And again. Because, you know, there is no problem so great that it can't be overcome with a neurotic need to *control* everything by force and lack of impulse control. He hasn't responded for the two days now that I've been reaching out. I hear Ed has a new fiancé, but I don't really care. He loved me once. He'll love me again, if I push hard enough. I like abandonment only slightly less than I might like a Tabasco sauce enema. It is worse than death for me. Anxiety eats at my gut like a hungry lion at the soft, furry belly of a gazelle. For a moment, I consider suicide, and then I realize how bad that sounds. I'd never go there. Except I might if this man keeps ignoring me. That would get his attention, all right.

I give up texting Ed and consider texting Jason, just because he's there. Yes, Jason was a controlling prick. Yes, he hacked my email and constantly accused me of cheating on him. Yes, I overheard some conversations he had that made it sound like he was *maybe* a corrupt cop with ties to the mob that he claimed to be after. Yes, maybe those conversations made it sound like Jason might have been hiring himself out as a hit man to some of his old high school buddies, which seems so far out there that I just kind of stopped even thinking about the possibilities. When confronted with terrifying realities, I have found that the easiest thing to do is pretend you didn't notice. Besides, Jason Flynn is hot. As in, fucking hot. No man with eyes that pretty could kill anyone. That's what I told myself. In the movies, killers never look like Jason Flynn. They look like Anthony Hopkins or Billy Bob Thornton in *Sling Blade*. Jason Flynn is handsome as a model, and in fact was once courted by the Ford modeling agency after he appeared in a "hunky Boston cops" calendar. So you can forgive a lot for the privilege of a guy like that sweating on top of you in your fancy Jamaica Plain condo bedroom. Yes, he threatened my life if I ever left him and said that I was his forever, but he is also given to overstatement and hyperbole, as are many passionate people. Denial is a beautiful thing. I think.

Given all of this, you'd think I'd run, not walk, away from Jason Flynn. But there aren't many women in the world who could or would do that. To understand why, you have to see, smell, and taste Jason Flynn. A finer piece of man flesh there has never existed. Truth be told, Jason is the best lover I've ever had, and it would be very hard to live without his fearless hands all over my body.

I think of Jason and begin to cry.

I stand here now, and remember the last time we were together, physically. It was at his Charlestown loft, in the clean modern living room with the high ceilings. He decorated it without any warmth whatsoever, all black leather and chrome. I liked it. It seemed manly to have an utterly cold interior like that. It was night, and he had not bothered to close the shades. He didn't care if people could see in. I had to have a few drinks to stop worrying. We used toys. Well, actually, he used toys, on me. Slowly, teasingly, in every opening that he could find, with a look of calm, cool, utter fascination on his baby face. He'd push those things harder and harder into me, and his eyes would connect with mine as I made little noises, and the look in them was hypnotic for me. He was in total and complete control, and I guess that for a woman who is always having to be so much in control in her professional life, giving up that control in the bedroom (or living room as the case may be) was refreshing. There was one moment where he asked me to stand in front of him as he stood against the wall, rubbing himself. He wanted me in my skirt and heels, my back to him, facing the opposing wall, bending over slowly, hiking up my skirt. Then he told me to get myself off while he watched. He told me that what I had was his, and that he was giving me permission to make myself come. He'd hand me a toy, and tell me where to put it, and what to do after that. I'd never done anything like that, taking orders from him every step of the way. I should have hated it, as any intelligent and self-respecting woman probably would have, but I didn't. I loved it. Because I'm Lauren. I'm not sure what that says about me, that looking at how turned on he got looking at me from across the room got me turned on, but sometimes the best thing is not to ask too many questions. Sometimes, it's best to just let things be what they are and enjoy them.

I miss the domineering jackass.

I text him, "What's new?" He doesn't reply. This is how it goes in Laurenlandia, by the way. I get pissy and dump men, then I regret it and beg them to come back. If they are foolish enough to indulge me after I have insulted every single thing about them, I dump them again and we start the whole cheery routine over again.

God, I'm stupid. I know I shouldn't text him. I shouldn't even really be very sad that I had to break up with him, even though I don't really feel like we're broken up because I still love him. I should not love him. After all, he wasn't just cheating on me but had also begun to try to isolate me from my friends and tell me what to wear, and once he even raised his fist as though to clock me but smiled and lowered it, saying only, "Be a good girl and don't make me go there." After that particular threat, he fucked my brains out and I liked it. Because I'm Lauren.

I know enough about men to know where that sort of thing might lead, especially when the man in question is a cop, with guns. But he is so freakin' handsome, and really good in bed. I mean, really good. A girl can't live without a thing like that, once she's had it, can she? It might never come around again, with its tongue tricks and chiseled chin. So I watch myself press SEND on the phone and cringe. I know I am an idiot. In fact, I have replaced this man's name in my Blackberry address book with the very clear and well-reasoned words "DO NOT CALL THIS PRICK" but impulse control is not my strong suit. Never has been. I would have made a very bad dog in Pavlov's lab, because I push the level no matter what. If there's a lever at all, I am there, pushing it. I am not stupid, but I play a stupid person quite convincingly in my love life, and often. I am wholly capable of knowing the right thing to do; doing it is another matter altogether. And so it goes.

I get a text back and for a moment I am filled with hope that it is Jason, back from the land of the preemptively dumped. No such luck. It is from my aforementioned best friend, Usnavys. I read it, wishing the train would just come already. Two fingers of rum, two fingers of Coca Cola, some ice, a squeeze of lime. Heaven awaits.

YOU BEST NOT BE TEXTING THAT SINVERGUENZA, NENA. I WILL BEAT YOUR PASTY WHITE ASS.

Yeah. Well, anyway. At least she knows me. She can't help me, granted. Apparently no one can. But she knows me. And knowledge is power, or something like that.

I text back something vague but honest. DON'T WORRY.

The text sound pings again. I expect something from Usnavys, but incredibly, it is from DO NOT CALL THIS PRICK. He wrote back! Jason "pretty eyes" Flynn. Maybe we'll reconcile. Maybe not. Maybe he'll stab me with vibrators again. I'd take that. He doesn't have to love me. Heart racing, I read it.

GOODBYE, LAUREN.

I try to understand what this means. Is the relationship through? That would be too obvious. No, he must mean that we are through fighting and hurting each other. I text back a question mark, and wait.

Mercifully, I hear the inbound train rattling toward the station in the tunnel. Soon, I think, I will be home with the cable remote and a Cuba Libre in hand (though in reality, a free Cuba is nowhere on the horizon of global possibilities, sadly), toggling between a Lifetime movie where you will know the "bad guy" by his slick Andy Garcia hairdo, and something equally banal on the Oprah network. Maybe, if I play my cards right, I'll even have Jason drilling me hard in my bed again. That means I have to shave my legs, and other assorted hairy bits, but, you know, it's worth it.

This is when the three young and very white Irish-looking teen boys approach me. They are dressed like Eminem in rehab, barely out of high school, and staring right at me with cold cruelty that is unfortunately familiar to me from my childhood spent with an "Eight Mile" type of trailer-park mother who had a penchant for beer bongs and Harley dudes. There's a short, fat one, a medium one with what look like burn scars on his face, and a tall one with eyes of palest green, boring right into me. I stiffen, on guard. In a big East Coast city like Boston, it is unusual for anyone to make direct eye contact in public, and even more odd for them to walk right at you. As they get closer, I notice the prison tattoos on the short one, and the mottled massive scar on the neck of the medium one, as though he had his throat slit and survived.

I step out of their way, but one of them grabs me and holds me in place. They surround me. No one else on the platform bothers to look up from their phones, all too busy texting and ignoring the real world. No one notices or cares that I'm being accosted. I'm about to scream when the shortest speaks to me.

"You Lauren Fernandez, or what?"

"Fuck that. It's her," the middle-sized one says. I notice he's trembling.

"Do it, you assholes," says the short one, jumpy as a grasshopper.

The tallest one grabs my free arm now, and together with his pals shoves me toward the edge of the platform. I struggle to escape. The middle one looks me in the eye and says a collection of words that make my blood slow to a cold, thick syrup, "This is from Jason. He wanted you to know."

"Quit flappin' your lips and just fuckin' do it, man," says the short one, who looks scared and nervous. "Fuckin' Flynn will have our asses if we don't."

Jason Flynn. My ex is behind this? I am confused. I don't understand.

The train zooms into the station with a deafening clatter.

"Do it!" shouts the short one.

Then they heave me off the platform and onto the tracks, seconds before the train rolls over me and everything goes black.

USNAVYS

Before I left the house this morning, my husband Juan? He says to me, all fake authoritative and shit - and you know he can't pull that off, m'ija - "You can't wear diamonds to a meeting like that, amorcito. Not advisable."

I shut him up with one hard look of my beautiful brown eye. I might have lost everything else, nena, but I still got power in my gaze.

"I can wear diamonds wherever the hell I damn well please," I reminded his ass.

He answered me all tired as hell sounding, with, "Whatever you say, mi reina," and tossed the latest red-tagged foreclosure notice on top of all the other ones on the entry table. Two weeks to get out, m'ija. Two weeks. Me, Juan, our tomboy daughter Carolina (who I swear to God is going to be the next Chaz Bono, at which point I will have to swan-dive off the Prudential Tower, splatting to death on top of Nieman Marcus) and our loud, destructive son, Dionisio (who just yesterday tried to ride his red wagon off the roof of the garage.) All of this gives me a headache out to here, and sometimes I don't want to get up out of bed at all.

We don't even bother to open them notices from the bank no more. We know what they say. They say, get out. They say, America changed when none all y'all was looking. They say, your man looks tired and you were crazy to marry anything less than a millionaire because look where it got y'all. It got you poor as hell, with two kids of questionable gender. God help me.

Juan acts like he's the only one who's tired. Shit. We're all tired. I'm tired. But you know what I'm most tired of right now? His ass. That's what. This is what I get marrying a poor man. Shoulda known.

Okay, look. The last time I checked, there wasn't no chapter in Miss Manners on what a fabulous woman who just happens to have run up against a temporary rough patch in her family finances should or should not wear to a consultation with a bankruptcy attorney. Any. Any chapter. Fine. I stand corrected. Yes, I know the damn difference between "wasn't no" and "wasn't any," so you can stop looking at me like I'm uncouth because in fact I am elegant and marvelous, even in the middle of all this. I just choose, when my emotions run high, to revert to the language of my upbringing. It soothes me. No, I did not say sues me. You want to sue me, get in line. Go ahead. Sue me, like everybody else and their bill-collector grand-mama.

Now, I might be broke, but I don't gotta look broke, okay? I'm wearing a St. John's suit, diamonds, and Jimmy Choos that are only slightly scuffed on the heels. I look like a millionaire housewife of Roxbury, not a broke-ass bitch on her way to sign the dotted line on Chapter Seven. Don't front, nena. What if I were to see someone I knew as I walked from the subway station to the attorney's office downtown? I'm supposed to dress like little Oliver Twist, in button-down shoes or some shit? Uhm, no. I don't think so. Mores and decorum.

Mira, I don't care how dire things might have gotten - and trust me, we didn't go flat-ass broke because of me alone, okay? Juan had a lot to do with this, being a do-gooder instead of a go-getter. I knew that shit when I married his ass, but I did it anyway, because all my friends sold me on the lie of love before money, and look where it got me. Okay? Then there's the matter of our daughter Carolina, who has until very recently attended only the best schools money could buy, and attended them in only the best clothes a girl might desire. (Not that the little tomboy appreciated any of it, but whatever.) Didn't neither of them appreciate a damn thing. Our son doesn't stop moving long enough for me to tell if he understands anything that's going on at all. Last week, he ran down the driveway naked, screaming "Boy With No Clothes! Boy With No Clothes!" He thought that shit was funny, girl. And you know I can't be chasing him down in my stilettos, or carrying that squirmy filthy mess up in my arms and ruin my blouse. It took me an hour to get that monster child back in the house. I swear, I made me a baby boy out of pure caffeine. Maybe now that it's all getting taken away, the ungrateful people in this family of mine will understand how important it is to have class and quality.

Anyway, the point is, no matter how bad things get, never let them see you sweat. Just like my mama used to say, and it ain't like she said much that made sense to begin with, crazy superstitious bruja with all her espiritismo and little glasses of water behind all the doors in her apartment, so you take what you can get with her. What I'm saying is, if you dress like a fool, the world treats your ass like a fool. Run naked down the driveway of life, and you're on your goddamned own, okay? Dress for success, even when they're pushing your soul under the Mass Ave bus, and you draw success to you. Fake it 'til you make it, m'ija, and, trust me, I'm gonna make it again. Soon. Watch. Te lo juro and pass the ketchup, Amen.

I clip and clop along State Street and find the address for the discount Internet bankruptcy lawyer. You know I am not going to go to any lawyer anyone I know would know for this shit. I got me the shadiest motherfucker I could find.

I look around before I duck into the stairwell, because I don't want nobody to see me going here. None of my friends know about our situation. My family in Puerto Rico doesn't know either. And unless Juan starts to run his mouth like a drippy faucet or some shit, ain't no one gonna know, neither, cuz I ain't about to start advertising this. This shit is private, okay? Serious.

There is nothing more private than money in the world, except sex, and given the way things are headed in that department I'm not eager to talk about it neither. There should be a goddamned Chapter Seven of sex, m'ija. If there was, I can guarantee you 80 percent of all married couples with kids would be filing. No sleep, no money, no job, all adds up to no nookie. Now that I think about it, looks like I ain't got nothing left but my left hand -- and, no, we're not going to discuss *that*.

Usnavys is not a happy camper right now. Don't get

me started. Just - don't. Okay? I am not about to cry, not with these fake fur eyelashes glued to my lids. Just - just don't. Ay, ay, ay. Stop!

I don't see nobody I know - yes, anybody, I know, shut the fuck up already - so I pop inside the building and start up the stairs. Motherfucker doesn't have an elevator. Not even one of them really old deals with the cages and oil oozing everywhere and a creepy old man standing there dressed like Curious fucking George to push the buttons for you. Everybody gotta be downsizing these days, huh? Even the sleazy attorneys. Goddamn.

It is no secret, given the luscious proportions and curves I display, that I'm not exactly a girl who spends a lot of time on the treadmill or stair stepper, and right now my damn feet hurt too much for climbing a mountain of stairs. I cannot believe I have been reduced to hiking up some goddamned stairs to declare goddamned bankruptcy. Who woulda thought? You think you plan ahead you might know what's coming, but you never know, m'ija. You never fucking know.

Up I go, one slow step at a time. By the time I get to this abogado's office I'll be huffing and puffing like Thomas the damn Train Engine. No, m'ija. This can't be happening to me! It can't. Dios mio. I hate my life right now, every single piece of it. Especially this part, having to declare myself legally sorry-ass broke so the IRS doesn't seize my bank account - not that there's anything in there anyway. Ande diablo. This is not dignified, any of this. It's unacceptable.

I stop twenty steps into the climb and give myself exactly twelve seconds to feel sorry for my ass. Then I swallow what's left of my pride, and ready myself to push on - except that I am stopped by the buzzing of my iPhone, which I still cling to thank you very much. It's in the phone pocket of the one Vuitton bag Juan let me keep. Somebody has something to tell me. Maybe it's a job offer. I been applying for everything that comes up for a woman of excellent taste such as myself, but I don't hear back from anybody. Maybe I won the flippin' lottery. Maybe Juan's dead. God, give me some good news for a change.

I look at the text. It's from Lauren. Bitch been trying to call me for the past hour, and I, not wanting to talk to her self-centered overly-dramatic ass right now, in the same way a woman being led to the gallows has lost the urge to chat, pushed her straight through to voicemail. I read the text now, mostly because it gives me something to do while I catch my breath.

IN HOSPITAL. PUSHED IN FRONT OF A TRAIN. CALL ME.

I blow the air out through my pursed lips in a way that pushes the bangs out of my rolling eyes. Like I'm gonna believe *that* shit? Puh-lease. That girl be damn dramatic, m'ija. Push her over to voicemail a couple times, and she makes up some stupid shit like this to get your attention. Temper tantrums R us. There is no setting on Lauren's dial except ten. Zero, and ten. That's it, y ya. Things are nothing, or everything with her. People are great, or they're crap. Good is the best ever, or the worst. No in between. I read me an article at the pediatrician's office the other day, in Psychology Today magazine, about Borderline Personality Disorder, and I swear it was like I was reading a profile of my best friend. She has it, I am telling you. She doesn't want to hear it, but I am telling you, that girl is permeated with BPD. I'm getting sick of her personal seesaw routine. Fuck it, I'm sick of everything. I bet she just got bumped at Park Street by somebody, and thinks her precious little life is over. Thinks the damn world is out to get her. Me, though? The world actually *is* out to get me, IRS first. I delete the text, stare up to the top of the stairs.

It is so, so far away.

Further than I ever imagined.

My once fabulous life? Sucks, m'ija.

Bolas.

REBECCA

Our son Connor is home with the nanny, and I've taken the afternoon off from my post as publisher of a miniature media empire in order to drive from my home in Santa Fe to the home where I grew up, in Albuquerque.

My mother, who still lives in that house with my father, asked me to come speak with her in person today. She said it was urgent. Her voice quaked just a bit when she spoke, and this made me anxious and curious. I hope it's not the diabetes, or something else with her health. She hates going to the doctor, but is sickly. This is a bad combination.

She asked that I come alone, but this is no surprise, considering how much she detests my husband Andre, for nothing other than the color of his skin. For this reason, she has not been much of a grandmother to our mixed-race daughter, either. You don't think it is possible to love and hate a person at the same time, but I absolutely do, in matters related to my mother this is the exact combination of sentiments.

I drive in the right lane, and go precisely the speed limit. People zip past me in the left lane, their old dusty cars all over the road. I shudder. New Mexico has the highest rates of drunk driving deaths in the nation, and the largest percentage of the population that is illiterate. I feel fortunate to be driving an Infiniti QX56, new, because it is one of the largest and safest SUVs money can buy. If I were to be hit by any of these people, I'd stand a fighting chance.

Sometimes I wonder why I decided to move back here from Boston, but then I look out at these endless plains and purple mountains, and remember - this is where my soul resides. I turn up the volume on my Andrea Bocelli download, and will my shoulders to relax. Since getting Connor from the surrogate the day she was born four years ago, I have had to learn some relaxation techniques. I am a naturally high-strung person, and that sort of temperament does not make living with a young child with autism easy at all.

As I breathe in through my nose and out through my mouth, focused on the inhale and exhale as my meditation instructor has taught me, the chime goes off on the speakers to indicate an incoming phone call. I look at the screen on the dashboard and see the number. Usnavys Rivera is calling me from Boston. She is an old friend, from back in my college years at Boston University, and we stay in touch quite regularly, though not as regularly as we once did. With marriage and children and careers have come new responsibilities that have naturally led the members of our once-close group of friends to have busy lives that don't always have room for much else.

I decide to answer.

"Hello, Usnavys," I say, knowing that the microphone built into the ceiling of the car will pick up my voice.

"Becca Baca, girl, are you sitting down?" she asks. I bristle at her ghetto vernacular. I am not a girl, and have not been a girl since I began to menstruate.

"I am driving," I say.

"Well, alright then. Unless you're driving you a gilded Roman chariot I'll assume your skinny ass is in a seat. And knowing you, it's probably a butter-soft leather seat, too."

"What is it you want, Usnavys?" I ask, bristling yet again at her use of the word "ass" as well as at her physical description of me as skinny. Everyone is skinny compared to Usnavys.

"I'll ask you how you're doing in a minute," she says, as though peeved that I'd made such a request when, in fact, I have made no request whatsoever. "We don't got time for that shit right now."

"What is your point?"

"My point is, I just talked to Lauren and she's swearing somebody tried to kill her ass today. Shoved her in front of a subway train, she says. She fell between the tracks, just got a few bad scrapes and bruises, maybe a concussion, but she lived."

I gasp in horror. "Who did it?"

"Look. She says some cracker thugs pushed her, but that's why I'm calling you. We know she fell down in front of a train. We know she's also prone to exaggeration and drama."

"That is true."

"So while I want to be supportive and she is in the hospital, I don't know if I should believe things are as bad as she says. She's hysterical, but she always is, right?"

"That's a tough one. Is she okay?"

"Yeah. She's fine. But do you think some cracked hoods would actually try to kill that girl?"

"Some what?"

"White boys, Southie types, the trash Ben Affleck and his drowned-rat brother glorify in their movies."

"Wait a minute," I say, trying to wrap my mind around what I've just been told. "Some gangster types from Southie pushed Lauren in front of a train? That's what she's telling you?"

"Yep. Red line."

"This is horrible. Even if it isn't certain that what she's saying is true, the fact that she believes it to be true is bad enough."

"Damn straight it is. At first I didn't believe her ass, because you know how she is, always dramatic and so on and so forth, but then she said she was in the hospital, and the fact that her redheaded ass survived being run the fuck over by a train was all over the news, and so now I'm, like, maybe the bitch was telling the truth."

"I see." I cringe at her use of the words that most people in our social circles never use in polite company. I long ago gave up trying to refine her.

"She's saying she thinks it might be Jason. Her latest boyfriend. Remember him?"

"Jason," I say. "The really cute detective?"

"Yeah, fine as shit, right?"

"And very nice, as I recall."

"The first perfect gentleman Lauren ever dated. She broke up with him for no reason, because she said he was spying on her."

"Maybe he was."

"Girl, no. He wasn't. He was the most normal guy she's known. Problem was she didn't know how to handle normal. That's just how Lauren is."

"Okay. Maybe."

"Me, I think if there's any truth to what she's saying, it's gotta be because she's upset the mob. You know? She's been doing these stories about them Irish mafia types lately, like she's gonna crack some code. I warned her that was a bad idea, but she said Jason knew a lot of inside stuff, and she couldn't let it go to waste."

"My God."

"Yeah. So, you know you know, girl. I'm thinkin' it could be some of the mob people she's been investigating, the Irish mafia is not to be fucked with, m'ija, but that's exactly what she did. You know how she is."

"Relentless," I say, with a touch of admiration. I might not approve of everything about our mutual friend Lauren, who has always been a little emotionally unbalanced for my tastes, but I recognize her talent as a reporter.

"The point being," continues Usnavys, "that if it happened the way she says it did, that her ass was pushed by some thugs, and they told her it wasn't over, then far as I'm concerned it really don't matter who the fuck did it. What matters is they meant to kill her and they probably won't stop, because she said the kids who pushed her, when they hauled her away from under the train, one of them was across the platform and they wheeled her past on the stretcher and he was holding up three fingers and mouthed to her 'two more times,' or something. Now, m'ija, where I grew up, you know we know what that shit means. That's prison talk. You go to prison, the guys beat your ass three times, nearly kill you three times, just to keep you in check, and they always make sure to tell you after the first time that you got two more coming."

"Okay," I say uncertainly.

"So I told her, even if this might not be true you have to err on the side of caution, I told her she has to quit her job, like now. Like today. And she has to dis-a-fucking-pear. Immediately. Which is where you come in."

I feel my blood turn cold. What is she saying? I wait for the rest, not wanting to be drawn into the middle of any more of Lauren's dramas. She lives the single most chaotic personal life of any human being I have ever known.

Silence.

I clear my throat. "What is it you want from me?" I ask, point blank.

"One of your houses," she says. "How many you got now?"

The answer to her question is four, but I don't feel like getting into it. "Why do you need one of my houses?" I ask.

"So she can hide there for a while, until we figure this shit out."

I take a deep, slow breath and blow it out quietly. I think before speaking. Then, I say, "I'm not entirely comfortable with the idea of Lauren 'hiding' in one of my houses."

Usnavys reacts angrily. "You see? That's the shit right there. That's the uptight shit I was expecting from you. Here we have a friend whose thinks – I said thinks, okay, I don't believe it – that her actual life is in danger, and all that matters to you is your comfort. Sometimes you gotta help a girl out just because she thinks she needs it."

"Listen to me," I snap, momentarily losing my cool.

"You're selfish, you know that? That's what you are. Always have been, freakin' ice queen."

"Usnavys. Stop."

"Prim and proper and all about herself."

"Stop. I will not let you speak to me this way!" I shout.

Usnavys, to my great surprise, stays quiet.

"What I was trying to say, *if you would let me finish a sentence*, is that if someone is after Lauren, they will likely know who her friends are, and it would be quite easy for them to trace her to one of our properties, especially if the would-be killer is her ex-boyfriend the *detective*. Would you agree?"

Usnavys pauses for a moment, and I can hear her gulping as though drinking something with great enthusiasm.

"Maybe. But I would bet my life on two facts. One, no one's trying to kill Lauren. Two, if someone is trying to kill the girl, it's not Jason Flynn. That boy is a Saint, a hot little altar boy of a man."

"Fine. I understand all that. So what I propose is that you give me a little time to think about this, and to see what else I can come up with. Andre and I are not the only people in the world with empty properties."

"You got someone else in mind?" she asks.

"Yes," I say. "My uncle Turnbull. But I need to check with him first, and see what's going on with his ranch."

"Ranch?" asks Usnavys, as though I might have suggested sending Lauren to the surface of Mars.

"My aunt's husband, he has a little ranch in the southern part of the state here. He never uses it anymore because my aunt says she's done being out in the middle of nowhere with him. They live here in Santa Fe and that place is pretty much empty. It's a nice place, very isolated; no one would find anyone there. It's off the grid and I don't even think it's listed anywhere. I'll let you know as soon as I can."

Usnavys makes a sound like she might be picking something out of her teeth. "Yeah, okay, but don't take too long. Girl gets out of the E.R. in a few minutes, and I'm taking her to my house. She don't got a car, as you know, because she has use of a company car, or she did, and she's all miss little subway - though I bet you she isn't gonna want to go near another one of them things for a while. I'm trying to get Juan to let us give her one of our cars for now, this one he has in the garage that nobody's seen, an old Impala."

"That's nice of you."

"Nice, *shit*. I hate that ugly car. It's a goddamned eyesore. I am happy to have any excuse to get rid of it."

"Does Juan share your views of his car?" I ask.

"Ask me do I care."

I sigh to convey my continued displeasure in the way Usnavys takes her husband for granted. As usual, she doesn't seem to notice.

"Look. I'm gonna tell Lauren she needs to get her ass out of town now. Like, tonight. Late at night. I'm putting her in that car and I'm giving her a road atlas."

"Seems a little extreme."

"Girl, I know. I don't think she's in danger, either -- except from herself, maybe. But this is one of those things where if you're wrong, or you don't assume the worst, then you could end up with a dead Lauren."

"True."

"If she's wrong, then at least she's off her ass out of that nasty-ass newspaper where they don't appreciate her and she can start writing that novel she always dreamed about. A *newspaper*, m'ija. She's still working for one of those things. That's like working for a slave-trader. Not exactly people lining up to buy what you got anymore, know what I mean?"

Usnavys has a point, amazingly. Even in my business, magazines, we're moving into synergistic multimedia platforms. Newspapers are the dinosaurs of our industry. I say, supportively, "She has been talking about writing a novel for years."

"Asi, m'ija. We get her out of here, to your uncle's place, and she can write her a nice little book about her six messed-up Latina friends from college."

"Please. That would never sell."

"You never know."

"Usnavys, you need to think hard about counseling Lauren to quit her job. She's liable to do it, and if she's not actually in any danger then you're basically destroying her life."

"Can't destroy something that's already fucked up."

"That's not fair."

"Life's not fair. Mira, the worst that can happen if she's full of shit and she gets her a nice little vacation and maybe shakes things up for the better a little bit. The best is that if she's right, we save her life."

"I see."

"I don't want to doubt her. She's my best friend. So I say if she got the mob or a dirty cop on her ass, she better go to extremes to stay out of his target hairs."

"I see your point."

"I gotta go pick her ass up. You do what you need to do. Call me back as soon as you can. I'm pointing Lauren toward New Mexico, just so you know. I know you can figure out something for her. But for now, don't go calling any of the sucias and telling them. We need this thing hush-hush for a while. Just in case."

I am offended at her presumptuousness, but as usual I say nothing about it. "I will call you when I know more."

We say our goodbyes and I end the call. I've already made it to the Albuquerque city limits, and my previously relaxed mood, forced on top of the curious anxiety about my mother, is gone. I am nothing now but a ball of anxiety. I try to sit up straighter and to give myself a half-smile in the rearview mirror, because half of the battle against stress is faking it out of your life.

I arrive at my family's large sprawling hacienda in the North Valley, and pull into the driveway. I let myself in with my key, and find my mother sitting at the large oak kitchen table. There is an open can of beer in front of her. I look around for my father, the only one I have ever known to drink beer. My mother notices and makes a bitterly amused face, taking one long gulp before telling me, "El Patron, he's not here. He's at the office." I hate it when she calls my father "the boss," but she has always done it and probably always will.

"Mom?" I take a seat across from her and look at her, worriedly. "What's going on?"

"It's his secretary," she says. "The one with big chichis and the low-cut *puta* shirts down to here."

"Janelle?" I ask.

"*Esa misma*," spits my mother, tears welling in her eyes. I get a cold, sick feeling in anticipation of what I'm about to hear.

"Your father," she says, unable to meet my eyes anymore. "He's been - he's been carrying on with her for a number of years."

"What?" I feel the bottom drop out of my life in this moment. My father? He has been the rock in my life. I've known he wasn't perfect -- he's sexist, and racist -- but I never thought he could betray my mother.

"And now she says all her kids are his."

I feel all the blood drain out of my face. I am dizzy, and grip the table to steady myself. It is worse than I thought. Cheating is one thing, but having a whole second secret family? This sort of thing doesn't happen to people like us.

"Are you sure?" I ask. "Maybe Janelle's just trying to get money. Framing him."

"I knew he was messing around on me for years," she tells me. "That Janelle, she's probably telling the truth. Some of her kids look just like your dad. I always thought so. One of them..." her voice trails off, and she gets a cold, frighteningly distant look in her eyes. "One of them looks like you. She's your same age y todo."

I knew my father was domineering. He was that way all my life. But I had never suspected him of being unfaithful to my mother. This is truly shocking.

"You knew?" I ask, taking a seat because I am suddenly feeling so unsteady.

She nods, almost imperceptibly. "But I didn't know for sure about who he was messing around with, and I never knew until now for sure about those kids. That oldest girl of hers, she looks a lot like you. I always noticed that but I just told myself it was a coincidence. Now that girl went and got her a DNA test and got him involved somehow, and she's sent me and your father the results and she's demanding that he do something to make it up to her. That girl is not right in the head. Your father, I told him I want a divorce. I can't look at him the same anymore."

My jaw drops. My parents have been together since they were in junior high. My mother helped my father start and run his successful Mexican food company. In fact, most of "his" best ideas have been hers, and a source of endless frustration for me has been his inability to acknowledge the important role she has played in the success of the company.

I can't find words. I never knew, until right now, that the only thing worse than discovering that your own spouse is cheating on you is the knowledge that your father has been unfaithful to your mother for your entire life.

My mother drinks some more beer. I try to comprehend what I'm seeing. I've never seen her drink beer. Ever.

"So me," she says, pointing to the Miller Light can. "I been drinking these since last night. I figure, he drank them for years to dull the pain of coming home to *me* night after night. So maybe, you know, maybe they'll make me happy, too."

"Mom, no. It wasn't your fault. Don't."

She goes on. "And now I don't feel so much like I did before. Now I feel like maybe it doesn't matter." She gives a drunk smile, and my heart breaks. She wags an unsteady finger at me. "And it was my fault. There's things you don't know. I'll leave it at that."

"What can I do?" I ask her, the tears welling in my own eyes.

"I'm gonna take that son of a bitch to the cleaners, Rebecca," she says matter-of-fact. "I am going to get what's mine out of this."

"You should," I say, not happy that she's insulted my father or that she's called my grandmother a "bitch," but I suppose it is understandable under the circumstances.

"But until then, I don't want to stay here. I think when there are lawyers and this type of thing it can take quite some time."

"True."

"It drags on forever in the movies, you know."

I nod, and feel terribly, horribly sorry for her. My mother is falling apart, and the only "reality" she has to compare herself to is the movies.

"So, I was hoping to ask you..." Here my mother looks at the floor and frowns as though to hold back her tears. I feel cold, and fold my arms across my chest. My father? My father? How could he? How will I ever be able to look at him again? It is such an enormous betrayal, of my mother, yes, but of me, too.

"Anything," I tell her. "Whatever you need, I'm here for you. You know that."

"I know I haven't been on the best of terms with your...with the person you married."

"Andre is my husband, mother. You can call him that. I'd also like it if you used his name. Andre."

She shakes her head, and chokes out the word "husband" as though it pains her to say it. I know she would rather just call him my "mayate" - the Mexican slang for "nigger" that my parents have liberally used against the love of my life for years. The betrayals against me at the hands of my family are seemingly endless now.

She goes on, "But if you wouldn't mind, I would like to know if I might stay in your guest house for a time. Until this all blows over. I could rent me an apartment maybe, or your father, he offered to move out, said he'd move in with that secretary of his, but I don't want to stay in this house anymore, especially not by myself, too many memories, and I don't think I'd like to have an apartment where I was all alone because that's too much like being a spinster viejita."

She chokes back a sob.

"I understand," I tell her. "You are of course welcome to stay with us whenever you like, for as long as you wish."

My mother looks up from the floor, her eyes wet with tears but her jaw set firm against defeat. I have never noticed the brute strength in her. I realize, with alarm, that all those years I thought she let him walk all over her, she was actually holding up the sky over his head. She is suffering now, but I would bet every dime I have that in the end, my father will be the one who doesn't make it through this in tact. Without her to serve him and prop him up, he's nothing. He must have known that somewhere deep inside, that must be what drove him to seek validation outside the sanctity of his marriage.

"I'm sorry this is happening to you," I tell her. "You don't deserve it."

My mother shrugs, and her eyes search mine. For a flicker of an instant, I see something in them that almost looks like introspection, or shame.

"I don't know," she says. "Maybe, you know, God is good, and he loves all his children the same, that's what they say in church and in the Bible. So, you know, maybe - maybe I do deserve it. You know, for that way I've..." she stops here, and drops her eyes again. She winces. Then she focuses her eyes on mine with fire in them. "Andre. He is your *husband*. I never respected that. And I'm sorry."

"Let's not talk about that now," I say, suddenly overwhelmed with emotions I do not want to address or feel yet. It is all too much. Too much input. I get up, dust my hands together, and say, "Right now, let's just get some things packed, and get you out of here."

"Please," she begs pathetically. "I don't feel good enough to leave tonight. I feel like I have the stomach flu or food poisoning. The room is spinning, Rebecca. Make it stop. I can't get up."

"You're drunk." I pity her intensely, and resent her, and love her, and hate her, all at once. She begins to sob.

"Please, mi'jita. Stay with me the night, Rebecca. Take me with you in the morning. I want one last night in my house. One last night with my broken dreams."

I think about Connor, and my husband, and how I should get home to them, and then it dawns on me that I would actually very much like an excuse to stay away for one night. It isn't a nice thought. But it is real. Just as my mother's dreams for her life did not turn out as she hoped, mine are also different from how I'd imagined. I never imagined I'd be this tired. I never thought I'd stare into my child's face and feel nothing but despair.

"Okay," I tell my mother. "Let me call and tell them

what's happening."

I hold her, and tell her that we'll get through this. And perhaps *she* will.

I am not sure, however, about me.

JASON

Jason Flynn feels fortunate to be a detective, because that means he doesn't have to wear a uniform. Thus liberated, he can go where he wants, when he wants, and he can do exactly what he wants, without anyone knowing who or what he is.

This afternoon, after watching those three fucking inbred no-good punks fail to do the job he'd given them to do, this means that Jason Flynn has walked from the Copley Square subway station to a nearby tavern, where, even though he's on the clock, he has ordered a couple of beers to help settle his nerves and his mind. The bitch survived the fall. Not a scratch. Start over. Figure it out.

Whenever a plan fails to go as he'd expected, it takes Jason a while to get back on track. He has to think about every detail, and run through the situation again and again in his mind, so that he understands. To do this, he must make sure to first channel his anger at the failure, in a positive direction, so that it doesn't pollute the calm he needs to plan the new course of action. For Jason Flynn, few things are as important as understanding. He likes to understand people, what makes them tick, how you can get them to do the things you want them to do. There is nothing more satisfying than working on a plan that uses everything he understands about everyone he has studied, to make them do what he wants them to do. This is the highest pleasure in Jason's life, this control. He is good at understanding, but he cannot understand a thing until he has cleared his mind and body of everything else, every other distraction, which right now means he needs to release his anger in a sexual manner. That is always very helpful for him. Even when anger has his cock hard and eager to destroy, however, Jason Flynn is still calmer than most men, and better at seeing details other people, so worried about their feelings, miss.

For instance, even though Jason Flynn is not looking at the young female bartender, with her mocha skin and long black curls, he understands that she is staring at him. He understands that she does this because, through the coincidence of nature and lucky genetics, Jason Flynn was born looking the way women (and some men) like for a man to look. He is tall, six-foot-one, with broad shoulders and a narrow waist. He has clear peachy skin that has a healthy glow to it. His brown eyes are light enough to be mistaken for green sometimes, and they are shaped in such a way, and rimmed with such long lashes, that a person would have to work very hard indeed to reconcile their beauty with the horrifying truth about what lies behind them. His eyes are his greatest disguise, because they are eyes women call pretty, and so oftentimes women are so busy admiring them that they fail to understand that those same eyes are sizing them up to give them what's coming to them, and what keeps Jason's mind focused on his tasks. Jason Flynn keeps himself in good physical condition for the same reason, to throw people off. If he were a fat bastard, say, or a wimpy, skinny freak, there would be more reason to suspect him of something illegal, especially when he caught a woman in his meticulously crafted trap. When you look great, and boyishly handsome, when you drape your excellent physique in the finest clothes money can buy, when you smell like fine cologne and are clean, no one ever stops to wonder something like how a police detective might afford an Armani suit. When you look as good in such as suit as Jason Flynn, no one thinks to question it. No, the sheep that we call people would all just rather be near Jason Flynn than understand him, the complex, beautifully gift-wrapped, explosive package of him. Jason Flynn understands, without looking at her at all, that this bartender wants to be near him, as near as a woman can get to a man. She wants him inside of her. He knows this the way a bird knows how to migrate without being taught. Some things are instinct.

Jason finishes the beer, keeping watch on the bartender in his peripheral vision. He does not smile outwardly, but inside he is on fire with thoughts of all the ways he will violate her. He will hurt her and in her pain he will see the smallest corner of the potential power he holds within himself. She will not like what he does, because he derives no pleasure from the pleasure of others, his only pleasure coming in making them do things they don't want to do. She will hate it, and it will make her sob and beg, but she is the type too weak to fight. He enjoys understanding what makes people tick. He doesn't care what they feel. He has never cared about feelings, and in fact he does not have the capacity to even know what they are. He cares about orchestrating behavior, the way a puppet master uses his hands to put on a show. Only instead of his hands, Jason Flynn, who has an IQ of 150, uses his mind. He uses his body to hurt, because that is a great pleasure as well.

Now, for example, he is testing his understanding of the bartender to see whether she is the pliant sort who pays attention and is servile to his needs, or whether he will need to flatter her and lie to her to get her to do what he's decided she must do. Either way, it will work. He understands people and how to move them to action.

An idea occurs to him now. Jason takes his phone out of his inside jacket pocket, and dials his secretary.

"Boston Homicide, District C-6," she answers. "Roseanne speaking."

"Hey, Doyle, it's me."

"Hello, Lieutenant Detective Flynn. What can I do for you?"

"Listen. I need you to start a trace on credit card and bank card purchases on a perp for me."

"Sure thing."

"Name's Lauren Fernandez," he says, also giving Roseanne a social security number and bank. Roseanne's silence indicates that she might be putting two and two together, that the name of the "suspect" is the same as the name of Jason Flynn's most recent girlfriend, a famed local columnist who often called him at work.

"Common name," he says. "Don't worry. Not the same. That's what I thought, too."

Roseanne Doyle laughs, trusting him as she always

does. "Sure thing, Lieutenant. I'll get right on it."

Jason Flynn asks Roseanne about her kids, small stupid people as ugly as their pig-nosed mother and about whom he could not care less. He does this because he knows that the sheep of humanity are moved by such gestures, to trust you. He needs Roseanne's trust. Roseanne is not the kind to ever rock the boat, though. He could do just about anything to her, and she would accept it. His favorite kind of people. He says goodbye now, and tucks the phone back into his pocket.

Jason Flynn feels good now, because he will at least be able to know where she is. The beer is relaxing him, centering him, making him fly. She isn't where he wanted her, but she will get there soon enough. Before she knows it. Jason Flynn is not a religious man, but sometimes he knows things happen for a reason. He woke up this morning regretting the previous plan a little bit, for the simple fact that he would not himself be able to see the life leave her body. He would enjoy that. He wants her to know that you cannot just do what you want; you cannot just make your own decisions, not when you've learned too much about Jason Flynn, not when there are secrets of his that you carry. Not when he needs you cooperative at the newspaper, chasing leads he gives you that will lead nowhere at all. You don't leave Jason Flynn at all, much less taking secrets with you. It simply isn't done. A smart women would see that. She should have known that. She was strange, that woman, because she refused to do what he expected her to. She was difficult, more difficult than she should have been, more difficult than most women. She'll get hers. And he will be the one to give it to her. If he knows anything about her at all, she will leave town. She will run from him. She's been talking about moving to Mexico, or France, or whatever, anyway. She is tired of Boston. And now that she knows it was Jason Flynn who sent those three lowlife fuckups to botch the job on her, she'll understand. She'll finally understand. She's not stupid. She will know.

The chase is on.

This makes anger and adrenaline rise in his body, and that makes other parts of him throb and swell for release. He lives for this combination of sensations. Fury and sex are related in Jason Flynn. There is no separation. Why should there be? Survival of the fittest. People like Jason Flynn have survived, and evolved, because they win. At all costs.

He sets the empty bottle down, and gently pushes it away from him a couple of inches, indicating that he'd like it gone. The bartender, busy with another customer, notices, and as soon as she can she rushes over to take the used bottle away. She has not finished serving the other customer. She doesn't want the other customer inside of her. All people are greedy and self-centered, to some extent. All people are looking out for their own needs, their inner compass set toward fulfilling their own desires – even a "saint" like Mother Theresa was only looking to get lauded for her actions, to go down in history, and she succeeded. That is one of the best tools you have to control people, self-interest. This bartender chick is looking for any excuse to be near him. She will be very easy, indeed.

"Can I get you anything else?" she asks, with that certain playful purr in her voice that some women get. She is one of the ones who revert to a childish state around men. It's almost too easy.

Jason Flynn turns his magical eyes towards her now, looking at her straight on for the first time since he got here. He wanted her to agonize over it a little, the fact that he wasn't looking at her before. He understands that the more a woman longs for something, the easier it will be to catch her when you use it for bait. He would not care if she were not attractive, though it does not hurt that she is, either. His need is not to conquer something beautiful, as theirs is. His need is simpler than that. It is to dominate something with brutality. There is pleasure in that. It is not about love, or longing. For Jason Flynn, it is about control. For Flynn, beauty is in the clockwork he builds, winds, and sets in motion.

As his eyes connect with hers, he flips the mental

switch that enables him to affect facial expressions he has seen on other people, the sorts of people who feel things, the people other people trust. You cannot just be a puppetmaster. You must look, outwardly, just like these other kinds of people, the ones Jason Flynn always knew he was different from, better than. They are weak, the ones who feel things. They let their emotions get in the way and that screws everything up for them. Life is so much easier when you know what you want and instead of sorting through your tangled feelings about it, you understand how to get it. You understand how to make things happen.

"I'll take another," he tells her, with his most charming, dazzling smile. He can almost hear her gasp. She freezes in the beam of his gaze, a suckling fawn in headlights.

"Okay," she says.

Jason understands from the way she hesitates, from the way the small smile plays upon her lips in response to his own, that this is the moment to reach out and touch her hand as though he felt something.

"I am sorry," he says, uttering words that have never been true for Jason Flynn and never will be. "I hope you don't mind me saying this, but you are very attractive."

The bartender blushes and thanks him.

"I can't take my eyes off of you," he tells her.

She stutters, something about how he's not so bad himself. This makes the Jason Flynn lurking just beneath the surface of those falsely charming eyes laugh. Jason Flynn is bad, he thinks. Very, very bad. And that is what makes life so good.

After he finishes the next beer, and after asking the sorts of questions the people who are weak and feel things always seem to ask one another – where does she go to college, what is she studying, where did she grow up, how does she stay in such great shape, does she have a boyfriend – Jason Flynn asks the question that is the trap.

"Have you ever been in a room at the hotel across the street?" He looks at her suggestively, and knows from her earlier attentiveness that she will understand him perfectly.

"No, but I would like to."

"When are you off work?" he asks.

She looks at her watch. Jason Flynn understands that it is a cheap watch and from this he knows that there is no one in this woman's life with the kind of money you'd need to catch and convict a man like him.

"In about another hour," he says with a roll of her eyes. "I feel like I've been here for a year today."

"You must be tired. I bet you could use a back rub."

She lights up at this. He will not give her a back rub, of course. He has never given a woman such a thing, and never will. He only knows that the others, the people who feel things, say this to get women to want to be near them.

"God, that'd be nice," she says. "You look like you have strong hands for it, too."

Jason Flynn understands that she will leave work early this afternoon, because of what he is about to say next. He also understands that she will not be coming to work tomorrow, or any time soon, because she will be too traumatized by what he is about to do to her.

Jason Flynn slips a business card from his pocket, in a name that is not his own, but whose cell number is a phone he carries on him. He tells her to call him when her shift is over, and he will give her the number of the room where he is staying. He tells her he will leave a key for her at the front desk, and then he apologizes because she has not spoken a word in reply.

"I am sorry, I hope I haven't offended you. I'm usually not this forward. It's just that I have never seen a woman as beautiful as you in real life. You see them all the time in movies or magazine, but you're the first one I've ever come across right in front of me."

"No need to apologize," she says, flattered, as they all are, by these well-worn and utterly insincere lines.

No need to apologize.

Nope, he thinks, there isn't.

MARTIN

Martin Bernstein is sitting at his rusty metal desk, pouring over some new evidence on a murder down in the E Street projects, when his phone rings. He's been working on this case for a couple of months, without much luck because you know how the people in Southie are, tight-lipped, angry-eyed. Everybody knows who did it, but nobody's talking. They're like the freakin' Amish, or the Hassids down south in Brooklyn, or the Mormons in those compounds. The Southie Irish protect their own against the outside. Martin knows the drill. He might be from Dorchester, one neighborhood over from Southie, but to the locals in his district he's a Jew and that's about as outside Southie as you can get. Unless, say, you were a black Jew.

"Detective Bernstein," he says.

On the other end, a source tells him to expect an email in a minute, on the case. Bernstein's face brightens in a smile. He's getting close to solving the killing, and God Bless Him for it. The victim was a teenaged boy with good grades, a good kid who didn't want to get into the local gangs, a kid whose winning smile haunts him at night, keeps him up pacing the apartment where he lives alone. The kid deserves justice. Damnit.

That's why Martin Bernstein does this job, so that he can speak for those who can no longer speak for themselves, so he can get the bad guys off the streets, so he can bring the families of this endless parade of victims that the city spits out some solace in their time of loss. Martin Bernstein knows about loss. His own brother was killed in a drug war drive-by in Mattapan. He resolved then that he would be on the right side of the law, that he would stop the madness from ever happening to another kid.

Martin gets the email, and presses the print button to send it to the departmental printer. You'd think that for something as important as homicide investigations that they might be able to get money for their own individual printers, but no. The detectives all share one. He stands in front of it now, as it whirs to life, slowly pushing out a document. At least, he thinks, it ain't dot freakin' matrix. Small blessings. He waits patiently, wondering when the city will start to take dead kids in Southie as seriously as it takes dead people in Beacon Hill or Newton.

Probably never.

The poor, when they die, never die as loud as the rich.

Martin takes the sheet off the printer, and looks at it. It's not his. It's addressed to the attention of his colleague, Lieutenant Detective Jason Flynn. If it were addressed to anyone else in the department, Martin might have put the document back down out of respect for privacy. But Jason Flynn has always rubbed Martin the wrong way. Put simply, Martin doesn't trust the guy. And it's not just the obvious stuff, like the way Martin, left to himself, is considered tall and handsome and charming by just about every woman who crosses his path, but in the company of Jason Flynn, the uber-male, he becomes invisible, a wingman. (Before Jason Flynn, Martin had never been the wingman. Ever.)

No, it's not that. It's something visceral, something Martin can't quite put his finger on. The deadness to Flynn's eyes. The way he never forgets a detail, or a date. The way he is too charming and perfect to be true. The women in the department accuse Martin of being jealous, but that's not it. Well, maybe a little. But it's more that Martin, who grew up hard, in a place where you had to have a good radar to tell you who you could trust, has never quite trusted Jason Flynn the way everyone else seems to. Call it instinct.

Martin holds the document, and squints to make sure he's read it right. He reads the page as the printer feeds him the second page. His heart rate increases as his investigator's antennae go up, and his internal alarm starts to blink hot red. Something ain't right. Flynn is investigating his ex-girlfriend? Credit card and bank records? Why? This is the same ex-girlfriend, Martin realizes with a horrible chill, that the news was reporting had "fallen" in front of a red line subway train and survived.

Too damned weird to be a coincidence.

Martin is aware that Flynn and Lauren split up, because he is unusually attentive to issues with Lauren Fernandez, a woman he has long admired and could probably have even dated if she hadn't met Jason Flynn first. He has long thought that Lauren was too good for Flynn. Now, here it is in his hand, proof that she's not only too good for Flynn, he's freakin' crazy.

Martin reads all five pages. Then he sees Roseanne, the departmental secretary, standing behind him with her eyebrow cocked.

"Bernstein," she says. "I'll take those."

"This about the girl that fell in front of a train?" I ask her.

She shakes her head, disdainful of me. She never liked me. Pretty sure it has something to do with Mel Gibson. "He says it's another one with the same name. You know how it is around here. Place is crawling with effin' spics."

Martin tries to look blank, tries not to reveal his true reaction to her words. He tries to look bored, rather than deeply offended and concerned for Lauren's safety. He considers asking her why she's helping Flynn do something that seems a bit dirty, but he thinks better of it. Even if Roseanne *knows* the truth, and she probably suspects it, she's already making excuses for it, covering her tracks, too. Like every other woman around here, she's in love with Flynn, under his spell.

You like to think that an institution like the Boston Police Department is full of the best and most honest men and women in the city, that everyone working there has the best interests of the community in mind, but Martin knows better. He's young, only in his late twenties, and he's not politically connected like so many of the guys around here. Frankly, he was surprised they hired him. He resolved as soon as he took this job and began to see the corners that some people cut, and worse, that the best thing he could do would be to keep his head down and just do the best job he could.

He quickly memorizes a couple of details from the records on Lauren, then hands the papers to Roseanne, and mumbles something about how he's waiting for a printout and thought this was for him.

"Is Flynn coming in tonight?" he asks, running his hands through his red-brown hair in a way he hopes will make him look more like a little boy than a suspicious man. "I'd like to ask for his help with something." This, of course, it patent bullshit, but Martin Mullen knows how highly Roseanne, like all females, thinks of Jason Flynn.

"He said he might be in later," she says, looking at him suspiciously. "He has some work to do first."

I bet he does, thinks Martin.

But what the hell kind of work is he up to?

LAUREN

It is two o'clock in the morning, and I am in the last place I'd ever want to be at such an hour - behind the wheel of 1959 Chevy Impala, on Interstate 90 outside a town called Mohawk, New York. And, yes, for the record, it *is* as depressing as it sounds.

The world is completely dark, and the road is pretty much empty. Now and then I see headlights, either coming toward me or in the distance behind me. I like it better when I don't see them at all. I would like it best if I were the only person on earth for a while. Then, I could relax. Or at least not be killed.

Killed? Seriously?

Seriously.

Jason Flynn is *seriously* trying to kill me. For what? Breaking up with him, yes, but also because of that conversation I overheard and asked him about. He said it was nothing, and I believed it, but he didn't believe that I believed it, and so I stopped believing it, and that's when it hit me that he was probably into some dirty cop shit. Like, hiring himself out to do hits on people. I didn't want to believe it, because it seemed so James Bond, so unreal, so not like anything I had ever faced in my own life, except that as a reporter and columnist I had been steeped in the corruption of cities and people most of my professional life. You just like to think that you yourself are able to smell that kind of rot. I didn't see it coming, not with Jason. Jason was the hottest, prettiest, sweetest, most thoughtful man I had ever known. After so many failed relationships, it was nice to have one that was so low-conflict, so gratifying. He did everything right. He was amazing. Then that conversation. And the beginning of the end. He didn't trust me. I didn't trust him. He started having me followed. He started looking up my phone records and asking me who I was talking to and what I was talking to them about. You know it never gets better when it reaches that kind of craziness.

The old me, the Lauren I used to be, would have stuck it out and hoped that it would get better, but I was finally healthy enough to walk away. The old me didn't do that. I mean, I wasn't doing it well. I was still pining, still regretting, but at least I had been the first to go. When he told me, with a stone-cold look in his beautiful eyes, that I would never be allowed to leave him, I laughed because I thought he was kidding. I didn't think men actually said things like that to women. I mean, I know they do. But I didn't think men said that kind of thing to women like me, because women like me know better.

Until we don't.

Usnavys didn't seem to believe me about being pushed in front of a train, and she absolutely thought I was insane to believe it was orchestrated by Jason Flynn, even though those kids told me as much before they shoved me off the platform. I don't blame her for not believing me. Over the many years I've known her, I've come running to Usnavys with no shortage of personal problems, many of them exaggerated or just my own damn fault. She is sick of my drama, and I don't blame her. I'm sick of my drama, too.

The small part of Usnavys that believed me – and she was the first to admit that she didn't completely discount the possibility that what I was saying could be true – convinced me to leave at midnight, six hours after I was pushed in front of a subway train. I was nearly murdered, and would be dead or maimed but for the happy mistake that I fell exactly between the tracks and managed to lie flat enough to avoid being sliced in two. Or three.

I'm bruised, tired, sick and scared, and all I've got with me is my cat, Fatso, who is old and won't stop mewling in a panic at the fact she is in the car. My best guess is that every time she blinks she forgets she's in a car, only to rediscover this terrifying fact the minute her eyes pop open again. I also have my desktop and laptop computers, because you never know when someone might hack into them and discover the kinds of crap I actually look at online. (I'm not sure what's worse, the porn or the celebrity gossip sites.) And I have a couple of suitcases filled with clothes that I am quite certain will be of no use to me whatsoever in whatever sort of new life I find myself in mere days from now when I officially go into hiding in a place where no one knows me, and where I have no job and therefore will be completely useless and miserable.

I quit my job at the Boston Gazette with an email around ten o'clock. I have worked there since I was first out of J-School, and now I am no longer a reporter or columnist. I am surprised by how large of an existential abyss this has opened within me. They say men are the ones who identify primarily with their occupations, but I am here to tell you that is not necessarily so; many women do, too. And I have never until now truly understood how large a part of me, or who I believed myself to be, was attached to the fact that I worked for a newspaper.

My email said I'd had enough and was leaving the country. That's all it said and it is all anyone at that paper will ever know about me from now until God knows when. Usnavys, who grew up in the projects and knows her fair share of miscreants, assured me that if someone was out to get me, regardless of who was out to get me, they would try again, and after the day I had, I agreed. We resolved to keep this thing quick, to the point, and as bulletproof as possible. That means pretty much no one can know where I am, and the people I meet when I get to where I'm going cannot really know who I am, either. I feel like an international spy, except that I'm not anywhere near that interesting. Yet. Something tells me I'm working on it.

I'm on my way to New Mexico, to a ranch near the town of Quemado, New Mexico. Quemado means "Burned," and I'm not sure whether this is a good omen, or a bad one. The ranch is owned by my friend Rebecca's uncle, a wealthy older oil baron named Jasper Turnbull who married her mom's sister. Other than directions on how to get there I know absolutely nothing about it.

My BlackBerry is somewhere in the Charles River, where we tossed it off the Mass Ave Bridge to, you know, swim with the fishes. I'll go into a T-Mobile place and cancel it officially, eventually. But until then, you know, better safe than Lauren. Hey, better that the phone be sunk down under water than me. Usnavys has promised to take care of selling my condo and putting my things in storage. I sense things are tight for her, moneywise, so I'm not sure how she's going to do all that, but right now I can't worry about my furniture or mortgage. I have bigger problems.

I have a prepaid and therefore untraceable cell phone in my purse, and I have not told anyone other than Usnavys and our other friend Rebecca where I'm going. Not even my family knows, and this is *not* just because they probably wouldn't much care. I haven't told them because Usnavys has rightly advised me to stay quiet and invisible for a while, until this thing is sorted out.

Mostly I feel numbed out, and very alone. I am not good at being alone. I never have been. It has me in a state of panic that I can no longer text my ex-boyfriends, including, sadly, Jason Flynn. I realize with a smirk that this is what it takes for me to finally cut a man completely off – that he try to kill me. Great.

Rebecca, when she called to give me directions to the ranch, told me that I need to see a therapist as soon as I get settled. She said she recently ran a series on personality disorders in one of her magazines, and that while she is no doctor she is fairly certain I am afflicted with one of them. I forget which one. It's amazing how good people are at diagnosing the afflictions of others, while being utterly blind to their own shortcomings, but I didn't tell her that. I was too numb to say much of anything at all, and the last thing I needed was more reason to doubt myself.

The road rolls on. A light drizzle hits the windshield. I try the wipers. They leave the glass smeary. The entire car smells of gasoline and makes a god-awful racket of pistons and metallic things I know nothing about. If you were hoping to make a nice anonymous getaway, this would not be the first choice for a car. It is old, gaudy, and was on its way to being turned into some sort of low-rider when Usnavys and her husband Juan gave it to me. She thought it would be the last car anyone would expect to find me in, and in that regard she is probably correct. No one has seen it, she said, because it has been sitting in her garage, where her man and his friends work on it every weekend.

I drive on.

I am getting hungry.

Hunger will have to wait.

I pass an exit for Dyke Road and this, sadly, makes me think of my lesbian friend Elizabeth Cruz. She was my best friend in college, and yet I had no idea she was gay until we were in our late 20s. She's very good at keeping secrets. I have wanted to talk to her very badly about all of what is happening, but I think Usnavys is right that I have to wait until I'm settled at the ranch before I start contacting people. Even Elizabeth. I can't risk getting them worked up or having Jason or whoever is after me contact them. I don't want to put my friends in a position to lie about me to keep me safe. I guess I'll have to keep up with her on Facebook, but not in any way she'd know I was watching. Her, Sara, and Amber. All three of them. I'll check their status updates and leave it at that for now.

Elizabeth is so sensible and grounded; I know she'd have good advice for me about the mess I've made of my life. Her life is perfect. She is married to a woman who owns a gallery, and they live in Encinitas, California, along the border with Mexico. I wonder for a brief moment if I'd be better off hiding in Mexico, then I remember that Mexico is a disaster. This is why, in spite of all my threats to move there a few years ago, when I was feeling a ridiculously romantic impulse to run away and write novels, I decided against it. As Usnavys rightly says, not even the Mexicans want to live in Mexico anymore. The world is a mess.

New Mexico, second best option. Maybe. Who the hell knows? I wasn't all that impressed with the place the last time I was there, when my college friends and I went to a resort between Albuquerque and Santa Fe a few years back. It was okay. I'm from the Deep South, so the whole arid landscape thing is hard for me to fathom. Now I'm off to Quemado. Quemado? Oh, how quickly a life can change.

I drive on and soon I'm passing though a slumbering Syracuse. I eye the roadside motels with heated desire. I'm not only hungry but also extremely sleepy. When I fall asleep for a moment and the car drifts onto the shoulder of the road, I realize that I am going to have to stop and sleep somewhere. Usnavys wanted me to chug Red Bulls and drive straight through, but I can't do it. I'm too tired.

I pull over at a Motel Six. I go inside and ask for a non-smoking room.

"Here you are, Ma'am," says the girl behind the counter, probably a college student. When did that age of girl start calling me ma'am? I don't like it, but I better get used to it.

I take the key, and go back to the Impala for my cat, her litter box and food, and a suitcase. I manage drag them up the outdoor stairwell to the second floor, find my room and let us in. I pee, and then open the paper top on the disposable litter box, which Fatso promptly makes good and disgusting use of. It's not like the smell makes things *worse*. The room before she dropped her bomb smelled cheap and wet, its unclean state masked by an industrial strength cleaner. Gross. This whole thing is just fucking gross. But there's a bed, and even though it's probably caked with invisible dried bodily fluids, and filled with bedbugs, it is a beautiful sight. I peel back the comforter, kick off my shoes, and fall face first onto the mattress, ready to fade away. It doesn't take long. Soon, I am asleep.

But just as quickly, the phone in my room rings. My thought is that it has to be the front desk. Who else could it be? No one knows where I am. Not even me, really. So I answer.

"Hello?"

"Lauren? Lauren Fernandez?" says the familiar man's voice with the thick Boston accent.

I say nothing as I take a moment to understand what I've just heard. My skin prickles with goose bumps. "Who is this?"

"That's not important," he says. "I can tell you that I'm on your side, that I work in the police department, and I know that Jason Flynn has gotten hold of your financial records. That's how I know you're staying at this motel. It showed up on our department printer, and I saw it. He's got the same records. You need to be really careful about covering yourself now. He's got it in for you."

"Who *is* this?" I ask again, the blood in my veins slowing and cooling, my head spinning with fear.

The man sighs. "Look. You have to trust me. He had you pushed, didn't he? The thing with the train."

"The kids who pushed me said it was from him."

The man on the other end whistles. "Not good. That's what I thought. He's probably pissed you didn't die. He's trying to figure out where you are, through your credit cards and bank use."

"How do you know all this?" I ask.

"I work closely with him. He's slick. He's clean. He never leaves a trail. There's nothing I can point to specifically to make me think he's dangerous, except what you just told me – and that's enough. I didn't like the way he looked at you, or any woman, and I didn't like the look in his eyes when he talked about you after you left him."

"You've seen him look at me?" I ask, going through in my mind all the times Jason and I were in the company of his colleagues from work. Then, as though it were a lightning bolt, it hits me whose voice this is. "You're that other detective," I say. "From the Christmas party."

"Listen to me," he says. "Whatever you do, don't call him. Don't speak to him, and do not – I repeat, do not – tell him that I called you. Please."

"Bernstein," I say. "Right? Martin Bernstein."

"I am begging you to be smart about this. Do *not* use my name."

"Why are you calling me, Martin?"

"Because I have a really bad feeling. I went into this line of work to keep people safe. That includes you."

I think about this for a moment. He does sound sincere, but then again I thought Jason Flynn was sincere, too.

"What do you want?" I ask.

He tells me that he wants me to leave the hotel immediately, and take out as much cash as I can, and stay somewhere else, somewhere Jason Flynn can't trace. Then he tells me to stop using credit cards completely, if I can, and to live on cash only.

"Except," he says, "Hang on. Let's think about this. Don't stop completely. Okay? Use them a little. Leave a trail for a time. I would suggest you go to the nearest major airport, and use your credit card to buy yourself a one-way ticket to a city really far from Boston. Seattle. Get yourself a ticket to Seattle. Unless that's where you're going."

"No. I'm going to New Mexico," I say.

"Jesus," he says with a deep sigh. "That, right there. That has to stop. Quit telling people where you *are*, where you're going, especially someone like me. You don't even know this isn't someone Jason sent to find out where you're going."

I feel myself begin to cry. "I can't do this. I just want my life back."

"Yes, you *can* do this. You *have* to. Get a ticket to Seattle. Then, if you can access the Internet, buy yourself a couple of weeks at a hotel there."

"That's expensive."

"So is being dead."

"Good point."

"Please do what I've said. Do not check out of the motel you're in, okay? That will only make him start looking elsewhere for you. Just leave. Go. Now. He could have people coming to your hotel right now. Get out."

I thank him, and hang up, and do as he's asked, my hands shaking the whole time. Everything is a blur, and I am completely numb, except for a constant terror that scrambles my guts. Part of me sits back, apart from myself, and watches in disbelief. How does a life turn upside-down so quickly?

At the new hotel, I spend ten minutes pushing the

dresser and the table up against the door, my eyes burning from exhaustion. I am nauseated, but when I lean over the toilet to throw up, nothing but bile rises. I crawl into the bed, and tremble, listening for unusual sounds, more afraid than I have ever been, until, finally, I can't hold on any more, and against my better judgment, I fall asleep, hoping this is all just a very, very bad dream.

USNAVYS

Juan and I had our light summer dinner -- arroz con gandules, pollo guisado and buttered bread, followed by a pineapple coconut flan with cafe con leche -- and now the kids are in bed. I've been listening to some Daddy Yankee on my headphones and to be completely honest with you, I'm feeling ready for some good, hard loving. If I weren't a married woman, and if I were just a little bit younger, girl, I could sit myself up on Daddy Yankee's lap for a good long time, bouncing up and down, or Pit-bull, even though he's Cuban and everybody knows Boricua men are the best lovers. I hate to admit it, but there ain't a sexier man to me in all the world than Pit-bull, but don't you be telling my husband any of that, because you know how he feels about that little fake gangster rapper from Miami. Juan's musical tastes run more toward feminist singers from Spain, like that flaquita loca del diablo Bebe, who must've had her ass kicked up and down her whole life by men. Ain't a woman in the world who hates men more than Bebe, except maybe Rosie O'Donnell, and so of course *that's* the bitch my husband wants to listen to day and night. I blame him for our daughter's gender confusion.

Dios mio, sometimes I swear my man needs to grow him a new set of cojones. I wish they sold Chia cojones at the drug store. Just add water, and out they pop. But, no. We're not so lucky.

Juan seemed droopy and tired the way he always does after he goes to that "financial management" class we're supposed to be taking in order to officially declare ourselves *quebrados*. He's in the home office right now, getting himself even droopier over the latest eviction notices coming from the bank. His eyes keep sinking deeper into his head, with big-ass dark circles all around them. I don't know why he has to obsess on it, m'ija. He should be more like me and be all, yeah, I know, moving on, feeling good. Some people don't understand that you attract what you manifest, and if you act rich you will be rich again. It's that simple.

I change into some enticing lingerie because there is no lazy droop in a man so lazy and droopy that a beautiful curvalicious woman in a white teddy and thigh-high stockings with stilettos can't fix it. I am clean and sweet smelling, and my curves are scrumptious as a buttered crumpet. I turn myself on just looking in the *mirror* at me. Most women when they have two children lose all desire and stop trying to seduce their man, but me? Ay no, nena. Me? I'm going to be a sexy bon-bon *hasta la muerte* and that's just how it's going to be so if you don't like it too bad for *you*. Sexy isn't something you *find*, loca, it's something you create, you earn it, you become it. Usnavys is sex, okay? That's my essence. Being sexy takes willpower, just like being rich. And right now I'm-a will my man to drop his pants and lick my coochie until I say his name all breathless and beautiful, and that's that.

I push my feet into some high-ass stiletto pumps, red, and clickety-clack my way across the hall from the bedroom to the home office. I don't knock on the door, because when a sexy woman is coming into the room to seduce your ass, ain't a man in the world who is going to say "come back later, bitch" okay? I learned that from a lifetime of reading men and their wants and needs, and so on and so forth and what-have-you. I open the door, and I step through it like I'm the greatest gift the world has ever seen, all wrapped up in lace.

Juan is hunched over the desk whispering into his mobile phone like he's conspiring with the C-I-effing-A. At first he's so engrossed in his conversation that he doesn't notice that a spectacular living Venus has just pranced into his orbit in a see-through nightie with her delectable chichis out to here. Probably talking to his mother, which he does way too much for a grown man if you ask me, but he never asks me, so there you go. Once a week, maybe. Talk to that woman once a month, better. But this man? Three times a day, like meals. I watch him and wait for him to notice me. His eyes are clenched shut as if someone's about to slap his face -- which, and I must be honest with you, I am tempted to do if that boy doesn't look up in a minute. At first, all he can do is say, over and over, urgently, "I don't know what to do, I just don't know what to do. This is so hard." Yeah? I think. I know what he can do. He can look at my ass and hang the phone the fuck *up*.

I clear my throat, ladylike but loud enough to catch his attention. I bat my eyes at let my gaze settle on a distant wall, kicking one hip out and putting a hand behind my head to elevate the girls. I am arranged like a fifties pinup girl in a calendar. I flit my gaze to his face quickly, to see if just exactly how greatly he has been aroused by the magnificence that is me. Juan's eyes pop open in surprise, and he looks at me like he's scared, then angry, and then resigned. Oh, no. Huh uh. Girl, let me *tell* you. Ain't a *one* of those three emotions I was hoping to see on him right now, but you work with what you've got when you decide to make a marriage last.

"Uhm, hey, can you hang on a second?" says my husband to his phone, his voice squeaky and awkward. "Usnavys just came in."

"Hola, papito," I purr as I slowly, deliciously turn my eyes toward him. M'ija, you must never forget how to work it, not even when you're married. Especially not when you're married. You need to stay on your toes, and make that man crumble to his knees for you. I thrust my chest out, and lick my lips. Then I order him with a dirty look and a hand motion to hang up the damn phone.

"Mami chula got something I think you want," I say. "*Algo delicioso que a ti te gustaria muchisimo.*"

"Look," he says into the phone with a weary-ass sigh. "I have to go. I'll call you later. Thanks for listening. You're a true friend."

True friend? Probably not his mother, then. That's good. I wonder whom he was talking to all top-secret and painful-faced in here, but now's not the time to start interrogating the man. No man on earth got himself more weird-ass messed-up friends than my husband, and the last thing I want to do right now is hear about one of them scruffy-assed ex-addict dudes. Alls I want is for him to be naked and hard, and up to the task of scratching all my itches, ya know, ya know.

"I was wondering when you might be *coming*...to bed," I say, with a wink.

Juan doesn't react like I hoped. He frowns. This makes me mad.

"What the hell's wrong with you, boy?" I ask him, snapping out of my mood and into another mood altogether. Do *not* reject me, okay? *Don't*. If I'm going to go out of my way to keep that flame ignited, you better damn well hold up your end of this sinking barge, too.

"Nothing." He removes his eyeglasses and rubs the bridge of his nose with his fingers.

"Don't lie to me boy," I snap. "If a red-blooded man is presented with a beautiful and lustful woman in lingerie, winking and waiting for him, and he frowns, then he's either gay or his ass has something *wrong*."

"It's late," he says.

"It is never too late for love," I remind him.

"Fine," he says, in the exact put-upon way a stubborn little kid might finally agree to clean her room in order to, oh, I don't know, go play in the mud outside.

Excuse me, but I am not *mud*. Motherfucker.

He slouches himself up out of that chair and walks in the most world-weary way you can imagine, over to where I'm still displaying myself like a preening hen in front of a doodling cock-house.

"Damn," I say. "Don't break a bone getting too excited."

Juan halfheartedly brings me into a tepid embrace that makes me feel sick and lonesome.

"I love you," he says like a trained parrot that don't understand the meaning of his own words.

"Don't *feel* like you love me," I say. "Normally, you'd be all *over* this."

"I know," he mopes. "And you're beautiful. It's not that. You look amazing. You know I think so. I love your body, and your confidence, Usnavys, you are the sexiest woman I have ever known."

I reach down and touch him through his jeans, where it counts, and my hand tells my brain what my heart already suspected. My husband's junk is as limp as a bruised brown banana at the bottom of a grocery bag.

"Oh really?" I ask, suspicious. "Then explain *that*. You're squishy."

"I told you, I'm tired."

"It's barely ten o'clock!"

"Maybe if you, I don't know," he says, taking me by the hand and leading me back toward the bedroom.

"Maybe if I what?"

He brings me to the bed and sits me down upon it, facing him as he stands over me. "Maybe if you, you know, used your mouth for a while."

"Ugh, no," I say, looking at the zipper of his jeans as though it housed a slimy slug instead of the rock-hard unit I was hoping for. "Usnavys don't beg or cajole, okay? You're either ready, or you're not. If you're not, *pero bueno*. I can't help you. Men be lining up hard as diamonds for a taste of this *biscocho*, and he wants me to slurp on his wilted daffodil for a while. *Huh* uh. I don't *think* so."

I turn away from him, feeling hurt. How could he not get an instant erection just looking at my glorious curves and fabulous physique?

Juan sighs miserably, and sits down on the bed next to me.

"Why do you do this?" he asks.

"Do what? What did I do? You are not going to blame your flaccidity on moi."

He looks at me with very sad eyes, and shakes his head, refusing to answer.

"What?" I insist. "As far as I can tell, I did what most men would love their wives to do. I got my pussy all shaved up smooth, and washed and waxed and polished like a damn race car, and I put on sexy things, and I came to seduce you."

"That's not what I meant," he says. "That's all very nice. I meant, why can't you just let things be the way they are? Why do you always have to expect things to be a certain way and then get mad at me when they're not?"

"Well, excuse me, but I am pretty sure that when a man sees the woman he loves naked and all laid out before him and willing, he's supposed to get a hard-on."

"Not always. I'm not eighteen anymore. It doesn't mean I don't want you."

"Bullshit."

"Usnavys."

"Look," I say, storming up and wrapping myself in my robe. "Forget it, okay? You done had your chance."

"Don't be like this."

"What? Be like what? Like me?"

Juan sighs again, and drops his head in his hands.

"You gave her my *car*," he says miserably.

"Who? Lauren?" I ask as I start to smear cold cream all over my face to remove the makeup, using the mirror over my dresser for guidance.

"Well, unless I have some other car that you gave to some other of your friends, yes. Lauren."

"Y que? She needed it."

"You didn't even ask me, Usnavys."

"You would have said no."

"Exactly. And you don't see anything wrong with this situation?"

I look at him. I am getting sick of his attitude, m'ija. Juan used to be so easy to get along with, but lately he's been acting like he's got the right to make all my decisions for me.

"You'll get it back," I say. "What else was she going to do?"

"Oh, I don't know. How about she goes to therapy, for starters?"

"She needs that, too."

"She's fucking insane, Usnavys! And you just indulge her. And now you gave her one of the only valuable things we have left, at a time when we could really use the money. Your BMW is about to be repossessed, in case you haven't been reading the letters from them. The only car we have that we own outright is that Impala, and you gave it away. It's like you don't think about anyone but you!"

"I was thinking about her when I gave it to her, wasn't I?"

"I mean in this family. You have children to take care of, Usnavys. You can't just go around like this anymore, living like you're rich."

"It's just a car."

"*My* car."

"We'll get it back."

"When? Before the bank comes to throw us out? Did you even think about that? How maybe we'd need to sell that car to pay the overdue mortgage?"

"We'll be fine," I tell him. "Quit acting like you're poor. When you act like you're poor, the universe conspires to make your ass poor."

"Stop!" he shouts.

I spin angrily to face him, my face covered in night cream. "Keep your voice down," I admonish him. "This children are sleeping."

"Lucky them," he says. "I can't remember the last time I got a good night's sleep."

"What the hell has gotten into you?" I ask.

Juan looks at me for a long moment, and says, "You really don't know, do you?"

"Know what?"

"You really have no idea what I'm upset about."

"You make your own hell," I tell him.

Juan laughs bitterly, to himself. "You haven't gone to a single one of these financial management classes with me, do you realize that?"

I shrug, bored with this topic already. "I *know* how to manage money. But I'm sure it's good for *you*."

Juan laughs angrily now. "*You* know how to manage *money*? Is that what you just told me? With a straight face?" I don't answer, so he keeps running his big Boricua yap. "Our instructor, Sandra, she has a lot to say about partnerships, marriages, and how money can often become the main reason people get divorced, Usnavys."

I shrug like I don't understand the point he is trying to indelicately to make. "And?"

Juan stares at me, his lips parted as if to say something more. Then he closes his mouth, and gets up, and grabs his pillow, and the chenille throw off the foot of our bed.

"Good night, Usnavys," he says, passing me on his way to the door.

"And just where the hell do you think you're going?" I demand.

"I'm sleeping on the sofa."

"Why?"

"Because," he says, giving me one last, miserable look before he walks away. "I'm just not feeling very close to you right now. I feel like sleeping alone."

LAUREN

The next morning, I wake up in a remarkably dingy motel room, still steeped in a nightmare. I'm trapped between two worlds, the terrifying dream that smells of sulfur, and the depressing room that smells of ineffectual industrial disinfectant.

I'm not sure which is worse, frankly.

Somewhere in the motel, someone is listening to reggaeton. Of course they are. You can't escape the rickititickitita of that shit anymore. It's everywhere. And wherever it is. Before I understood enough Spanish to know what the guys were singing about in most reggaeton songs, I actually sort of liked how the music sounded. Fun to dance to, all that. But now? Well, once you realize how misogynistic something is, it's hard to love it anymore. This list includes Jason Flynn now. Jason and reggaeton, sitting in a tree...

Suddenly, there is hard, impatient knocking on the door. I panic, in a flood of adrenaline remembering last night -- the warning phone call, the quick move to this dumpy motel near some train tracks. It all comes back in an unwelcome rush.

I'm going to die. He's come for me.

"Housekeeping!" a woman's voice calls through the door. Then, before I've had time to respond, she's trying to come in. The engaged deadbolt stops her.

"Hang on!" I call out, stumbling toward the door. "I'm still in here. Come back later, please!" What the hell is *wrong* with hotel maids? They barge in like they own the place.

Meow, says Fatso, my cat. She's not supposed to be in the motel, but judging from the mouse feces I saw in the bathroom, you think they'd be grateful. I give the cat a harsh look with my finger to my lips, as though this will do any good for a creature that possesses not language, fingers or lips that I know of.

Meow, Fatso replies, twirling to be fed. She really is an

incredibly simple creature. It doesn't take much to please her. Food, scratching behind the ears, a ray of sun to sleep in. That's about it.

"You in there?" asks the maid, ramming the door against the lock again in a way that indicates hotel maids' kinship with prison guards. I do suspect this motel has armed their maids with battering rams as well as mops.

"Yes. Come back later," I call, adding, under my breath, "You intrusive bitch."

She stops struggling with the door and I hear her muttering to herself as she ambles along to the next room.

I look at the clock on the nightstand. It is ten in the morning.

"Fatso! Why didn't you wake me up? It's late!"

Meow.

I should have been on the road by now, headed toward New Mexico and whatever it is that Rebecca might have waiting for me there.

But on the bright side, at least I'm still alive. Alive, and starving. My stomach growls as I begin to shove the desk and dresser away from the door, where I'd hoped they'd keep any would-be killers at bay, back to where they belong.

I sit down on the edge of the bed, drop my head in my hands, and allow myself to feel pitiful for a moment. Why me? Why is this happening to me? Then, I tell myself, that's enough.

I force myself to action. I don't know what to do, exactly, but I do have a pretty good idea of what I should not be doing, and that's wallowing in self-pity. I need to move. Keep moving. Move, or die.

I feed the cat, and as she's contentedly crunching her kibble I hop into the dank mildew palace that is the shower. I wish I had flip-flops, because I am would wager I'm about to get some kind of flesh-eating fungus from the bottom of this tub. I can almost feel it creeping along the bottoms of my feet, nestling itself up between my toes. Eew. I hurry through the motions, wash my hair with the awful radioactive detergent the hotel calls shampoo. I decide to just leave the unruly wavy mess of my curls pulled back in a ponytail today, even if by so doing I voluntarily expose the world to the half inch of somewhat gray roots. When did this happen? Sometime in the last couple of years, my red hair started to go gray, and I began to attack the problem with verve and vengeance, getting the color filled in at a top Newbury Street salon every three or four weeks, dropping a few hundred bucks each time. It is worth it – except that now I don't know where I'm going to get my hair done. I make a mental note to stop at a drug store somewhere and get some hair color.

This should, of course, be the least of my concerns, but even in the throes of running for her life, a modern successful girl before a mirror will always find some fault to indulge. Anyway, it's all a moot point, my hair is I mean, because in the absence of conditioner and straightening serum, with a heedful of wavy red hair that left to its own devices enjoys impersonating that of Robert Plant or Billy Squire, there is no point in even trying.

Dressed in forgiving black yoga pants, a yoga top and a heavy Columbia University sweatshirt, and my expensive running shoes in case I have to, you know, actually *run*, I pack up my stuff, and then dial the front desk.

"Road's End Motel, how may I help you?"

"Can someone come help me to my car?" I ask.

"Uhm. This is the *Road's End Motel*," the receptionist replies, in a sardonic deadpan. "We don't have bellmen. And before you go asking, we don't have fresh waffles, fairies or pink zebras either."

Great. A wiseass underemployed motel receptionist. Must be a college town. Probably a journalism major.

"I know. But I was hoping..."

"He that lives upon hope will die fasting. That's Benjamin Franklin. The grandfather of electricity, which, you might have noticed, we only *have* sporadically here at the Road's End Motel."

"Okay, well in that case could you just do your job and tell the maid to come back? I am ready for her to clean my room now."

"In spite of what you might think of me, it is not my job to tell the maid what to do. I'm not a feudal overlord, though some have mistaken me for such. I'm not sure why. I should probably stop smoking cigars."

"I'd like my room cleaned."

"The maid, I fear, is on another room right now. Much as she would have loved to wait for your acceptance and love, she's moved on. I suggest you do the same."

"Look, wiseass," I snap. "There's someone following me, and I would really rather not have to walk out to the car on my own. That's the truth."

There is an awkward silence as this information sinks in on the other end of the line. "If your outrageous claim of danger is true – and I am not, by saying this, admitting that it is true – then you probably don't need to be talking to me. You need to call the police."

"I can't." I feel tears come. I don't want to cry. Not for this. Not now.

"Okay, well, that's just way too much information for me. I took this job for a little extra money to indulge my World of Warcraft habit, and maybe to have a place to sell pot and used iPods and maybe a little dope without getting caught. I must be truthful and say I had no aspirations at the time of joining the witness protection program. I'd like to keep it that way. But I hope you have a nice day, insofar as someone living on borrowed time can have a nice day. Goodbye."

Click.

I put the receiver back in the cradle and tiptoe to the window. I peel back the mildewed curtain just a little, and peek outside. Nothing unusual, and to my joy I see that the maid's cart of cheap soaps and threadbare white towels is parked just next door.

I open the door just a little, almost as though to test it, and to my horror Fatso runs out into the parking lot. I scream at her, and this naturally does nothing whatsoever to inspire the cat to return to me. She runs underneath a car. The car starts, and then I watch in horror as Fatso runs into the street. This is when a man in a dark coat steps out of a black Lincoln Towncar, and grabs her. For a moment, I am relieved, grateful that there are still nice people in this world. Then, I realize that the man who now stands on the sidewalk a block away from me, petting my cat and staring at me with cold, dead eyes, is none other than my ex-boyfriend, Jason Flynn.

"Oh, my God," I gasp. How did he find me? How long has he been out there?

I watch in horror as Jason takes a few slow steps toward me. I almost don't recognize him because of the look on his face. Gone is the overboard charm that drew me to him; it has been replaced by a demonic clarity, an evil calm. I am face to face, I realize, with the devil. And he still looks fucking great. I do not like the way my heart pings for him, as though it just got a Facebook comment. I should not still want this man, and yet I do. I am an idiot.

I am about to call out to my cat one more time, when Jason puts his hand on her head, as though to pet her, his eyes fixed upon mine with cold, calculated cruelty. He doesn't pet her at all. Instead, he clamps his fingers down over her head, and in one horrifyingly quick motion, he twists it so hard and so fast that it snaps her little neck. My beloved cat goes limp and dead in his arms, and he drops her into a nearby trashcan as though she were nothing but a used napkin.

"No!" I scream.

Jason's eye blaze into mine, and he smiles, putting his fingertips to his temple with a slight bow at the waist, as though tipping an imaginary hat. Then, he gets back into the black car, and drives away, careful to use his turn signal and obey the speed limit.

JENNIFER

It's supposed to be a wedding shower for my younger sister Bonita, but the best description I can come up with for what's going on in her friend Maggie's small living room in the South Valley right now is torture.

I don't just mean the red, penis-shaped lollipops one of my sister's friends has just handed out to everyone, including my mother, either. And I don't mean the polite way my mother, sitting on a kitchen chair next to where I'm seated at the end of the sofa, has actually unwrapped hers and begun to suck on it like it's delicious. Bonita's friends (and my mother, horrifyingly) tend to find this sort of humor appropriate at all times, just like they seem to think it's great when a guy takes them out for a first date to Hooters. Bonita and I might be full sisters, but we're worlds apart. She's more like our mom, with her low-cut blouses and high heels. My mother is in her fifties, but still shops at Charlotte Russe with Bonita, and they share clingy outfits. I prefer to shop at Talbots and Ann Taylor, and always have. Leave something to the imagination, you know? If these two women weren't related to me, I would not know them at all, at least not willingly, unless it was in my capacity as a therapist for children with autism, pertaining to my brother Esteban (who is afflicted with the disorder and was my inspiration for trying to do something to combat it). What I'm trying to say is that I would certainly not be here, pretending to care about the blender from Wal-Mart that Bonita just opened, except for blood, which some say is thicker than water and which I am certain is only meaningful to some people.

My mother's heavily made-up eyes bore in upon me disapprovingly. This is why I've decided the party is hell on earth, that glare of hers, all outlined in dark black liner. It has been often said of my mother than she is beautiful, but I don't see it, mostly because her beauty has so frequently been put ahead of us, her children. That sort of beauty, the desperately seductive kind that takes priority over family and children, is to me the definition of ugly. The look she throws now could melt paint off the side of a car. She's been looking at me like this ever since I arrived. She'd asked Bonita to call to disinvite me to the party, and I'd asked my dear little sister if that was her own wish. "No," she'd said. "I think you're right about this thing, mom's wrong, and you're welcome to come." It was one of those rare moments when Bonita and I agreed upon something other than our favorite food, which for both of us happens to be the huevos rancheros at the Flying Star, scrambled, green.

"What?" I ask my mother, confronting her. Sometimes I hate her. "You have something you want to say?"

I am the only one of my siblings who have ever had the courage to defy this woman. Bonita is too insecure, and Esteban is barely able to talk. I'm not sure what he makes of our mother, being locked in his own world as he is. To Bonita, our mother is the rock upon which the foundation of our lives was built, a devoted single mother who held the sky up over our heads, the dear, self-sacrificing, woman who suffered for us all the way Jesus is said to have suffered for humanity. The three of us siblings are as close as we could be under the circumstances of our lives, which is to say not at all. I have always felt alone and misunderstood.

Three? I suppose I should say four, because from what I understand now, I have a half-sister somewhere in this state, some big-time magazine mogul, married to a software millionaire, and she's my same age. From the pictures I've found of her online, she looks a bit like me, too. I like her clothes, and her hair, and her style. Her name is Rebecca Baca, and I do not know her at all though I have seen her a few times at company parties. I always used to envy her because she was in my same grade but seemed so much better dressed and more polished. We were apparently born only two weeks apart, she to the woman my biological father is married to, me to that man's other woman.

I cannot tell you why I feel that I must connect with

this woman, my half-sister, my almost-twin, but I have a compelling need to look at her, to see her face to face. I've been cheated on before by a man I loved, and the curiosity I feel about this sister of mine is almost like that feeling I had then, the one that compelled me to look up my boyfriend's lover on Facebook and compare her to myself. I wanted to know if she was prettier than I was, fitter than I was, if she was smarter and funnier than I was. I wanted to understand, by looking at her, what it was about me that didn't quite measure up, what flaw I had that had sent my man into the arms of this other woman looking for something better. I want to know the same thing about this sister of mine. Why was she the one our father loved more? Why was she the one with the nice house, and the college back east, and the family dinners at holidays, the one that he always rushed home to while I was left alone with a mother who was much more interested in her own reflection or workout routine than she was interested in us? What was it about that girl, that other daughter, that made her better? What was it about her mother than kept him home with her, while I was stuck with his other woman for a mother? Or one of his other women. I have no idea how many he has, but something tells me it didn't all start and end with my mother. I am interested less in knowing about my father than I am in knowing about the other daughter, my sister Rebecca.

"I am so disappointed in you," my mother whispers as Bonita begins to rip the pastel yellow paper off the next gift.

"Why?" I ask.

"How could you *do* this to me?"

"Do *what*?"

"You shouldn't have done it. What were you thinking, eh?"

"I was thinking I'd like to know who my father was," I snap, a little more loudly than I'd intended to. A few of the women turn their attention from Bonita's joyous moment to me now, and they scowl in hopes I'll pipe down. They clearly don't know me very well.

"Enough," my mother hisses.

"You should have told us," I say, losing my temper with her now. "You knew all along." I am vaguely aware that I am ruining the party and airing our dirty laundry, but I can't help it. I have always had issues controlling my temper around issues of justice, and this is perhaps the most unjust situation I have ever confronted.

"It wasn't important," she says, in that annoyingly dismissive way of hers. Wasn't important? Knowing the identity of my father? Knowing who he was?

"You're insane," I tell her. "What could be more important?"

"Me! I'm the one who gave you everything, you could have done the right thing out of respect for me."

"It is very hard to respect a woman who doesn't respect herself," I say, hating myself as I say it, but also hating her. How could she have been so weak? How could she have set such a terrible example for the rest of us? How could she have thought so little of herself?

"Not now," she says, her eyes filling with tears. "Don't ruin your sister's shower."

"I'm amazed she's getting married at all," I said. "I mean, you must be furious that she would be so demanding of a man."

My mother seethes and stares me down. "You don't understand," she says. "I was never the marrying kind. It worked for me the way it was."

She has always been the strangest mix of powerful and weak, and I see those two sides of her battling behind her eyes now.

"How could you just live like that, like his other woman all those years, mom?"

"I knew he'd leave her, eventually, if it was the right time," she says. "He was good to us. You might not know it, but he gave us everything we needed. I was never the kind to want a man around all the time. I like my freedom, too. You had everything you needed, m'ija. I made sure of that."

"Except a dad," I say, finally unable to control my

anger.

"Our house, our car, your school clothes, all those things that a man would give to a wife, he gave to me, all the things a father gives to his children, he gave you those things. He loved us like his family."

"You are insane," I tell her again, my heart thundering with fury.

"Why? Because I didn't live like a little old Mexican lady from a hundred years ago with a *mantilla* on her head?"

"You guys, please," says Bonita now, to us. "Not now."

I look at my sister, and mouth "I'm sorry," and I get up to leave.

I cannot stand to be here another minute, with that sanctimonious woman who was so tight-lipped all those years, who had that disgusting man over to our house as a "friend" to play cards and games with us, who never told us who he actually was, with his fine suits and wedding ring, and us living in a small house in the North Valley, struggling to make ends meet. All we knew was that he was her boss, and he was concerned for our welfare, and he brought us stuff. I thought maybe every mom's boss was nice like that. I thought they all sang the "sana sana colita de rana" song to their employee's children when they, like I did when I was six years old, fell off the bike he'd just bought me for my birthday, and skinned my knee. He'd smoothed the bandage over the broken skin for me, with a smile, and kissed me on the top of my head, and my mother had beamed standing next to us in the summer sunlight and told me that he was a very kind and wonderful man and that I should thank him.

Thank him.

I remember one Christmas when he came by the house with a bag of gifts for us kids, and how he kept looking at his watch, telling her he had to get back before "they" noticed he was gone, and how she kissed him on the lips and thanked him profusely, how they whispered for a moment like co-conspirators, then later how she cried on her knees as she put the presents under the lopsided tree, like they were the greatest things she'd ever seen. I was twelve by then, old enough to know that most employees did not kiss their bosses on the lips when they thought no one was looking, and I suppose that was the day I began to wonder why my eyes looked so much like his.

I hear the door to Maggie's house slam. To my surprise, my mother gets up to follow me out the door now. I hurry toward my car, a new Lexus coupe, to get away from her, but she stops me as I pull the door open.

"M'ija," she says, angrily.

"Stop." I shrug out of her grasp.

"Listen to me."

"What." I stop cold, and stare at her.

"He wanted to marry me. I was the one who said no. He would have left that frigid bitch a long time ago if I didn't stop him. I didn't *want* him. He wasn't a good father to his other kid, and I knew you'd be better off without him around."

I look at her and try to figure out whether she's telling the truth. She looks sincere.

"His wife, she was cold, sabes? You know what I mean by that? Frigid. They were roommates. Business partners. He wasn't happy, but I didn't want the responsibility of having to take care of him like she did. I could never have put up with him all the time, around the clock, the way she did. She called him 'boss' and he liked that."

"But you had three kids with him! Why'd you do that if he was so awful?"

"Pues, he was good in the sack."

"I'm going to throw up."

"Do what you want. You say you want to know the truth. But look at you. You can't handle the truth."

"He was her *husband*, mom. At the very least you should have respected that."

"You are so naïve," she says.

"Oh, my God," I say, sick to my stomach by the whole

conversation.

"I know you're upset. But you have to think about everyone else, too. Think about how hard this is on him. You should know you've ruined his life with this DNA testing, and telling his wife. Why did you have to go and do that, Jennifer? My God. No he don't got no place to live, and that bitch is going to take him for everything he has, which means less for us, understand?"

My jaw drops and I find no words to tell her. I look at her familiar face, and my brain recognizes it, but there is nothing in it that I love right now. I hate her. I hate her for settling, for accommodating a man who couldn't have cared less about her, I hate her for thinking that being his "otra," his kept woman, his hobby, was enough. I hate her for thinking so little of herself that she was incapable of thinking much of us, her children.

"I ruined *his* life?" I ask, finally. "You sure you got that equation right, mom? I could have sworn he ruined *yours*."

She looks blankly at me, actually unable to comprehend my meaning – which is to say that it was our lives that were ruined by him. "I like my life," she says. "Even if it doesn't work for you. It's going to get worse now, because he doesn't have the money he used to if the courts decide to give it to her."

"What about us? Didn't we have a right to know who he was? He gave us nothing! And you just kept opening your legs for him again and again."

"He gave you nothing, eh? Okay. Answer this. Who do you think paid for your fancy college degrees in social work?" she asks me, tears dripping down her cheeks. "Me?"

I hold my breath, trying to understand what she's telling me. "That's what you told me, that you had saved for it."

My mother laughs. "On a receptionist's salary? And how was I going to do that, for all three of you kids?"

"Esteban couldn't go to college, mom. Just me and Bonita, and I'm pretty sure beauty college doesn't count.

That's your problem, right there. you lie about everything, and exaggerate, and you seem to believe it. You can't fool me."

My mother scowls at me, because I've not gone along with the lie she's been telling herself and anyone else who will listen for decades. She is adept at lying.

"I'm so proud you girls, that you went to college and did better than me. Especially you. Who knew that a social worker could make almost a million dollars a year helping autistic children?"

She says this not as a compliment, but to let me know she thinks I'm ripping people off for my services. She has never thought I was worth my three-bedroom townhome next to the Tanoan golf course, or my Lexus convertible.

She blinks at me with a fake smile that is more like a snarl. "I am so proud of you. And you wouldn't have none of that if el Jefe didn't help with your tuition and all that."

"El Jefe? Is that what you call him? The boss? You just criticized his wife for calling him that! And now you're doing it?"

My mother shrugs. "That's what he likes. I don't do it all the time. Sabes. Just whenever. Ni modo."

"Oh, my God. I'm going to throw up."

"He's been very good to us."

"Right. Because, let's see. What did he do, again? On top of knocking you up, cheating on his wife, and ignoring his kids, well, his illegitimate kids, he paid you a shitty salary, too?" I ask. "My *God*, mom! He was your boss! And you want me to feel sorry for him? Can you even hear what you're saying, mom? It's ridiculous? It's worse than ridiculous. It's disgusting."

My mother shakes her head at me, her eyes betraying her feelings. She thinks I'm ungrateful. She thinks I just don't understand. She pities me. I never thought it might be possible, but there it is. My mother, the ultimate willing fucking victim, feels sorry for me, who has never needed a man, and never will.

"I have to go," I tell her, trying to move my mind away from this train wreck, back to the stack of paperwork in my home office that needs to be handled.

"He loves you, in his own way," she says. "Some men, you just have to understand how they are. They're not like us, men aren't like us at all."

"Oh, I understand him," I say, pushing my mother out of the way so that I can get into my car. "I understand him perfectly well. I understand that he's a class-A asshole! Now, if you'll excuse me."

And with that, I slam the door, fighting back my own tears, and drive toward my office, where I will bury myself in work, the only thing that makes any sense to me anymore.

USNAVYS

Nena, this headache is going to be the death of me. They'll have to take my ass to the cemetery and bury me in Puerto Rico, like they did for *esa poeta tan loca* Julia de Burgos. *Ya tu sabes.* It don't matter that I got my feet up on the arm of the leather sofa and a cold washcloth on my forehead, or that I took three of them Advil before I turned the TV to a *novela* that makes my life look easy because of everything those fake-looking women go through. I'm sorry, m'ija, but there are no real women in this real world who look like those robots they mass-produce for novelas in Mexico. It's like they made this Thalia factory that churns them out, pouty-lipped, perky-chichis, perfect legs, big eyes like a freakin' Pokémon doll. This headache pounds and pounds like I got me a bunch of evil Pikachus trying to get out of my head with electric thunder bolts. Pokémon. Do not ask me why I know so much about the Japanese animated show and game based upon capturing adorable made-up animals by force and then pitting them against each other in a brutal battle so that you, the trainer, get a boost to your weird-ass ego, okay? You'd think it was my son who liked that cute little Asian answer to Michael Vick, but no, nena. It's my daughter, the future Chaz Bono.

I feel like throwing up. I guess it's one of them migraines everybody always talks about, because I don't like looking at the light, either. I cover my eyes with my hands, and then I remember the sorry state my hands are in. My nail tips and pedicure are raggedy because I can't even go to the nail salon without feeling guilty about it. Juan's all, "Luxury expenses are not allowed right now, we have to get our feet back on the ground," and he thinks keeping my hands and feet looking right is a luxury. What's the point of putting *ugly*-ass feet on the ground, tell me that. Juan does not get it. He has it all backwards. You look the part, then the rest will follow. No pedicures, he says. Can you believe that? Que tonteria.

This isn't how it was supposed to end up. I grew up poor, in the projects, and I have worked damn hard all my life to keep from going back there. I got myself out, and I don't ever want to go back. Hard work is the key, nena, except that now there aren't any jobs that I can find to work hard at, and that's the whole problem. What can you do in a situation like that? You can get you a headache, that's what. There has to be a way to fix this. I have got to figure it out.

I keep thinking about how I can't buy anything, and can't get a call back on any of the jobs I have sent out resumes for, about how we're going to have to apply for public assistance pretty soon here if things don't ease up, unemployment and food stamps and all of that nonsense and whatnot. I wasn't born for that, m'ija. You know I wasn't. When I left the projects, I never looked back – except to come around the old neighborhood sometimes to show all them people my nice clothes and car and let the kids know that if they want to, they can be like me. I have been a great example to my barrio about how to escape, and now what do I have? Notices on the door saying I have to vacate my own house in two weeks or the sheriff is going to have me removed. Can you stand it? I can't. I cannot believe any of this is happening to me.

I have worked too hard to come to this place in my life, and so the headache is my body's way of rebelling. It's stress. I know it's stress. Before he took Carolina to the library to rent some books the way you do in those plebian places – and books of women's field hockey and the WNBA, off all things, because my daughter continues to morph into a man with her interest in sports and her lack of interest in dresses and pretty things and her father continues to encourage it -- Juan told me he thought the headache was due to my negative outlook on life in general and the fact that I couldn't see the blessings God had given me right before my eyes. Be grateful for love and health and life, he told me. Be happy we're all still together and that we have friends and family who love us, be grateful that Lauren is safe, blah blah blah.

"Money's not everything," he said as he adjusted our daughter's messy ponytail into something only slightly less messy. The girl was wearing a tank top and basketball shorts, like some teenaged boy. Juan tried to smile but he didn't look no happier than me. Any happier. *Yes*, I know the difference, and *yes* I can speak the Queen's English if I so desire and so on and forth, but listen to me. When you have a headache this monumental the last thing you want to worry your ass about is if you're talking right to please some English teacher somewhere. To hell with English teachers, and education, and all them other lies they tell you about how if you go to college and work hard and do good – well, okay? I know, I know – at your job that you will be rewarded with economic stability and a home and a car and all that other jive. I had me all that stuff, nena, but where is it now? You got bankers getting greedy and the world is falling apart, and there ain't an education or a job in the world that can prepare you for fucked up planning by a bunch of sorry-ass selfish bastards in the government. And don't get me started on this latest president of ours, even if he is the only one who ever went to visit Puerto Rico. He's just as bad as the one before him, and I'll be damned if all of this doesn't add up to make me suspect that the real people in charge of the sinking ship we call America are shadows we know nothing about, and the rest of these dumb Harvard-bred fuckers are just puppets and decoys.

What I really need? What would really make me feel better? To go shopping. Back in the day, back when every girl watched Sex in the City and mortgages were as easy to get as an STD on Lansdowne Street, when I was rolling flush with cash, there wasn't a terrible headache so bad that a trip to Neiman Marcus or Bloomingdales didn't fix me right the hell up. But times have changed. Just walking into those soothing stores with the fresh, flawless scent of the perfume counters and the unmistakable smell of new clothes – nena, it was heaven. Heaven. I am *telling* you. What I wouldn't give to drop me a few thousand in one of them joints right now, come home heavy with shopping bags and hat boxes and shoes.

And a goddamned *pedicure*, thank you very much.

A girl never feels better than when she's struggling to carry all her shopping bags, te lo juro. What I really want is to get me a new perfume. The last thing you want in a new and distressing epoch of your life is to go around smelling like your former happy self, because all that shit does is remind you how you aren't that woman no more. Scent memory. They say it's the strongest memory we got. I want to be the way I used to be, but I can't, so I need to smell new. Something hopeful. Berries, maybe. Berries and cream. I need to find me some new products, hair, skin, fragrance, to usher in a new phase in the Life of Usnavys.

I turn onto my side, feeling very sorry for myself, and I start to cry. I don't like to cry in front of people, okay? That's one thing I learned from growing up in the projects and the ghetto, that you never let them see you sweat or cry. You suck it up, machista style, and put on a strong face for the world, because this is a cruel-ass goddamned world that looks for weakness in order to bring you down. Survival of the fittest and all that shit. Show the world you're hurting at all, and the only thing it does it keep on pushing you further down, m'ija, until ain't nothing left of you but a memory that doesn't nobody want to remember no more.

You know that poem? I can't remember who the fuck wrote it right now. Ow, my head. Why does thinking hurt right now? Who wrote that stupid poem? The one that starts about how all the world loves a winner, but lose and you lose alone? Some shit like that, I remember reading it in high school and I was all, like yeah, baby, that's exactly right, bitch. That's how it is. Laugh and the world laughs with you, that's what it was. Cry and you cry alone. People are attracted to success, not to failure. When you let the world see you fail, you start to draw more failure to you like a gooddamned magnet. So you fake success, even when you're failing. But it ain't easy.

The phone rings. I do not feel like answering it, but what's left of my pride and self-control tells me that I need to. It's probably a motherfucking bill collector with an East Indian accent, getting fifty cents a week to harass people in

America while our own country goes to shit. I hope it is, m'ija, because I think I'll give him a piece of my mind about how fucked up shit is around here right now, and about how his ass is part of the problem because that job he has should belong to someone over here.

I look at the caller ID and it says UNKNOWN NUMBER.

"Hello?" I answer, sitting up and trying to stop crying. "This is Usnavys Rivera." I always gotta add that last bit, to sound like an executive with style and grace because you never know when the person on the other end is maybe going to be someone to give you a job.

It's Lauren on the other end, babbling about how Jason Flynn showed up at her motel and killed her cat with his bare hands, like some kind of a crazy-ass caveman. I ask her is she sure it was him, and is she sure her cat is dead, and she insists that it is *completamente* true. I ask her has she been drinking and she says she had a few drinks but that it's nothing serious. Whatever, chica. Okay? I am up to *here* with this girl. Up. To. Here.

I sigh and feel the headache getting worse. "Girl," I tell her. "You're talking some stupid shit right now. I am not in the mood, okay?"

"You have to believe me. He's going to kill me, Usnavys."   "Where are you now?" I ask, because I am a good friend.

"Just outside of St. Louis," she tells me. Then she tells me she bought a ticket from that city to Seattle, to throw him off.

"You're going to Seattle?"

"No! I want him to *think* I am. He's looking at my credit card records."

Dios mio, she's paranoid on top of everything else. It's that Borderline Personality Disorder, te lo juro. Those people think everyone's out to get them.

I tell her she's driven a long way in one day and she says she's been going fast to see if anyone was following her.

"And?"

"So far, no one I can identify. I'm starting to feel like I'm losing my mind."

I tell her what I think, which is that she needs to buy herself a gun at a pawn shop and figure out how to shoot somebody.

"You'd feel a whole lot better if you knew you could go all Rambo on somebody," I say.

"I don't want a gun," she says. "I want Fatso. I loved that cat. She was my best friend. Other than you, I mean."

"Get you a new cat. It's not like there's a cat shortage."

"Usnavys! It's not that simple. There's no replacement for Fatso."

Yeah, I think. Ain't no way girlfriend is going to find herself another cat that licks itself and sits in the sun and shits in a litter box. Those are super rare. Seriously, I got no patience for Lauren right now. Girl is half-lit and off her rocker. I should mention I am not a pet person. Why would you want a stinky fur-machine in your house? The only good fur is a dead fur, over my shoulders.

"What you need is to get your ass a gun. You should be packing, m'ija. It's not safe. If you're telling the truth, it's not safe at all."

"No shit."

"So get a fucking gun already."

"Fine."

"How did you manage to get into this mess?" I ask her. "I mean, you always been crazy, but this is off the deep end, even for you."

"By being me. I did it by being me." Lauren is crying.

"Got that right."

We sit in silence for a moment, and it sounds like there's rain on the other end. I can hear the wiper blades in back of Lauren's sniffling and crying.

"Just get you a gun," I say.

"I can't. I don't know how to shoot one. I might hurt myself."

"Girl, what is there to know? You put the goddamned bullets in, you aim it, and you pull the trigger. You use a flat iron and a tampon, right? That right there, that's more complicated than a motherfucking gun."

"I guess you're right," she says. "I should get a gun. Oh, God. What's happening to me? I'm not supposed to be this person. I used to have a life, a life where I didn't need a *gun*."

That's when I hear the gasp of a desperate sob, and realize she's got a hell of a lot bigger reasons to be crying that I do.

"I'm sorry you're going through this, nena," I tell her. "I know it seems bad now, but we got some people here working on it, we'll figure out who is doing this to you."

"And then what?" she asks, despondent.

"Then you lay low until we take care of his ass old-school style."

"How?"

"Girl, do you not know me and where I'm from? Do you not remember the kind of people I knew growing up? I got people."

Of course, I do not have people at all, not any more, because I don't like the people where I came from and I've gone out of my delicate way to avoid them or at least let them know I'm better than them, for most of the past twenty years. But it don't hurt to let Lauren think I know people. I'm trying to help the girl feel better. I don't talk to the people I grew up with, precisely because to do so would end up putting me into a predicament not unlike the one Lauren finds herself in at the moment.

"People, huh?" she asks.

"I know me a couple of guys, don't you worry about it. Just get your ass to Rebecca's and figure out what to do next. That is the plan, right?"

Lauren confirms for me that the plan is for her to take a bunch of No-Doze pills, wash them down with Red Bulls, and keep driving through to Santa Fe, where Rebecca is going to hand her off to her uncle, some old-school cowboy man who married into her family and has him a ranch. That's going to be Lauren's hideout. I try to picture Lauren's half-Cuban, half-Irish ass in some cowboy boots and hat, and it isn't pretty.

"Chica, this is some surreal shit right here, what we got going on in your life."

"Talk to me," she says. "Tell me about your life. What's new? Make me feel normal."

"Nothing," I lie. If only she knew. "Work, family. The usual. Same old same old."

"How's work?"

"Good," I lie again.

"And Juan and Carolina?"

"Fine. Had me some great sex with Juan last night." In my dreams, I tell myself. "Boy's on *fire*, nena. Sound the alarm *fire*."

"Lucky you."

"Yeah, I know. I got it like that."

Never let them see you sweat. Fake it til you make it, etc. and so forth.

I reassure the girl some more, and talk her down out of her panic and depression, and remind her that sometimes change is good. I don't believe any of the shit coming out of my mouth right now, because God knows this latest change hasn't been very good for me at all, but it's the right thing to say. In life, you fake it til you make it, and that's all there is to it.

By the time we hang up, my headache is raging again, so I decide to do something I know I should not do. Me and Juan, we have a little stash of emergency cash that we've been keeping in a Bustelo coffee can up on the top shelf of our closet, because we're both paranoid that maybe the banks are going to fail and then what the fuck would we do? It's not much, just a couple thousand dollars, our escape pod Juan calls it. For when things get so bad that maybe we all just have to buy us some tickets to Puerto Rico and go live off his mom for a while, and by a while I mean until I get me the urge to kill her because that woman is crazy and I can't stand her any more than she can stand me.

But the point is, I go to the closet now because I have a craving for shopping and I have to do it. Juan has been very clear to me that I am not to touch this damn money, he's told me that he can forgive me everything else I did to him – I am not proud to say I cheated on him a while back, and he forgave me but still has trust issues – but that if I spend this cash he might never get over it. He just doesn't understand me, sometimes. It's not like I'm not out looking for a job or something. I do it all the time. I'll get back in my game, but to do it I have to feel like myself, m'ija, and I can't feel like myself in old clothes and without shopping.

I go to the closet and take the can down. That money is sure pretty, te lo digo. I tell myself it will be okay because I won't let Juan see anything I get, and I'll return it all for cash in the next day or two anyway. It's just medicine. Just something to do until my headache goes away. That's all.

I take the money, stash the coffee can back behind some winter clothes, and get dressed up in my Gucci dress and heels, and do my makeup, and I look fabulous because I got it like that. And then I start to sneak out of my own damn house like a burglar. I should feel guilty for taking the money, but I don't. I feel guilty only because I don't feel guilty. It should not feel wrong to pamper yourself, m'ija, and this is the part of my life right now that pisses me off the most, the way I just can't even be me anymore.

I take my BMW out of the garage and try not to think about how the bank has been sending notice that in a few days they're going to come and repossess it. I keep hoping something will change and that I'll be able to save it. With my head held high, I drive to the Back Bay and leave it with the valet in front of the Neiman's. I stride through the doors of the elegant retail establishment and instantly feel better. The cool, sterile air of the store, the elegant people out shopping and not having to look at price tags. I read somewhere not too long ago, I think it was in the Los Angeles Times online, an article Cuicatl sent me, about how even though most of the country is going through this deep-ass recession and can't find a place to live or a job or anything that the people who are super-rich are just getting richer and richer, so that the only sector of the retail market that's growing is the one that caters to the mega rich. I see them here now, out in force, and I hate them. I only got me two thousand freakin' dollars in my purse, and I know these women in here, some of them anyway, could spend that on one shoe without blinking. That's power. I want that for me.

I start at the perfume counter and get me a new scent to go with this new era in my life. Something citrusy and bright, that will lift my mood and bring good fortune back to me. It feels so good to buy it, you have no idea, nena. I just feel like I'm flying. I'm back to my old self, and the throbbing in my head goes away. It's beautiful.

I move on to the clothing department and get myself a blouse and then I go get me a handbag and a pair of shoes. Then, just like that, all the money is gone. I take the opportunity to put my sunglasses on and go prancing around the mall for a while, wielding my bags like weapons against the destruction of my dreams. I still got it. It's not much, but I still got it. I think I'll return everything in the next day or two and then use the same money to go shopping again. I realize with a thrill that if I do this shit right, I could keep shopping with this same money almost indefinitely.

The good mood doesn't last long, however, because as soon as I get home what should greet me but Juan, sitting there on the sofa with the empty coffee can in his lap.

"Usnavys," he says, looking up at me with them wet eyes of his. Motherfucker's been crying.

"What?"

"Where is it?" he asks, looking at me like I done whipped his ass with a two-by-four. "What did you do with it?"

"Do with what?"

"The money, Usnavys."

I shrug and tell him I don't know what he's talking about. This is when a young woman who is thin and pretty, with a dark black bob that reminds me of some elegant princess, comes out of the kitchen with one of our red apples in her mouth as she takes a bite like Eve in the

Garden.

"Who the fuck are *you*?" I ask, stunned.

"Usnavys," repeats Juan. "This is my friend Sandra, the one I told you about."

I search though my brain for some memory of a bitch named Sandra, and I remember that Juan has been going to some credit counseling classes so that we could declare bankruptcy, and that some chick named Sandra was teaching it and giving Juan tips on how to rebuild his credit and his life. Right. He was going around for the past month saying "Sandra says this, Sandra says that." Now, here she is, in my house. Or what's left of my house. The house that is going to be taken from me by the bank in another couple of weeks. Juan said she was an accountant but he failed to mention that she looked like a goddamned Playboy bunny princess type. Funny how he left that part out. Now I know why he was always so eager to go to that damn class.

"What is she doing in this house?"

Juan sighs. "I've been – we've been meaning to tell you this for a while. Usnavys, I can't do this anymore. Sandra's here to offer me emotional support."

"What the fuck are you talking about?" I ask, and the blood rises in my face. I get that pit of fear in my gut because I know what's coming and I don't want to hear it.

Sandra comes and sits down next to Juan on the sofa and looks me dead in the eye. She is a strong woman, I realize. She is not messing around. Ain't many people in this world that scare me, or that I don't think I could kick ass on, but this woman has that certain defiant look in her eye, like the mean girls back in middle school. She's pretty as hell, but she could cut me.

"The kids are over at Liam's house," Juan tells me, referring to our daughter's friend down the street. Most girls? They have girls for friends. Not ours. She prefers little boys, and guns, and trucks, and sports. "I took them there so that they wouldn't have to watch this conversation we're having right now. I'm going to go get them as soon as we're through here, and I'm keeping them for a while."

I look around the room now and notice that there are suitcases by the front door. Juan's. Packed and ready to go.

"What the fuck is going on?" I ask, the tears coming against my will and my voice choked back with tears. "What the fuck is wrong with you, boy?"

Sandra shoots him a look, feeding off my harsh words. She clearly doesn't use harsh words with men, but that just tells me men probably walk all over her ass. If you don't keep men in line like dogs, you're in trouble. They need to know their place.

"I want a divorce," says Juan, looking at me as steadily as Sandra does.

"You can do this," Sandra tells him in a soft but firm voice, and I hate that bitch, m'ija. I mean, I really hate her.

"You," I tell Sandra, pointing one of my newly manicured fingernails at her. "Get the fuck out my house."

"It's not your house anymore," she tells me. "It's the bank's."

I look around for something, a weapon, something to cut this bitch with.

"Usnavys, stop," says Juan, who knows what I'm doing. He leans protectively in front of Sandra. "It's not her fault. She's just here to help me."

"Because you're too big a pussy to tell me all this to my face by yourself," I taunt him. M'ija, I know it's not nice to go for the boy's jugular, but when you piss me off, when you attack me like this, there's nothing else to do but let it all hang the fuck out.

I feel dizzy, and the headache comes back. I sink to my knees without realizing what's happening to me.

"I'm sorry," says Juan, not even getting up to help me, so tough now, like he don't feel a goddamned anything for me anymore.

"How long have you felt like this?" I ask him.

"For about six months," he says. "It's over."

"Home wrecker," I tell Sandra. "You come up in here and take this man away from his wife and child."

"I am not romantically involved with your husband,

Usnavys," she says. "I am here as his counselor and confidante."

"Yeah, whatever," I say. "You're so full of shit."

"I want custody of the children," he tells me. "I have the papers, and I have a lawyer."

"We don't have money for a lawyer! How you got you a lawyer all a sudden?"

"It's her brother," he says, indicating Sandra. "Me and Carolina are going to be living with him for a while out in Newton. I left the number and address on the fridge."

"Why are you doing this?" I cry, struggling to get to my feet but only falling to the floor, where I sit, defeated. More defeated than I have ever been.

"Because you took the last of our money, and I knew you would. I told you that'd be the last straw for me." He's got tears running down his face. "I love you, but you do everything you can to push me away, all the time. There's got to come a time when I say enough. It's that time now. Enough. I just can't – Usnavys, it's impossible to raise a family in this kind of instability. You don't even seem to think about what's best for your own kids."

"Me? I'm the one who doesn't think about what's best for them? You're the one encouraging our daughter to be a man."

"She's an athletic girl, Usnavys. That doesn't make her a boy."

"Juan is trying to get things back on track for himself and your children, but he can't very well do that with you continuing to undermine your family's finances," says Sandra.

"Who the fuck asked you?" I shout at her.

"Your husband asked me."

I glare at Juan now. "Get that bitch the fuck out my house, now, before I beat her ass."

Juan's eyes are filling with tears, and I know he's hurting as much as I am. But there's a new look in them, a determination. He says, "Fine. We're going. But let me say this first. You have to focus, and start trying to see the world in a new way, and I just don't think you have what it takes anymore. I'm sorry. I love you, and if and when you're ready to make real changes in your life, I'll be there for you because I've always been there for you and I always will."

"Leaving me isn't being there for me!" I scream. "Are you fucking stupid?"

"Sometimes, leaving is the best thing a person can do for someone they love," he says, moving toward the suitcases.

"I'm going to get it back tomorrow!" I cry. "I just had to shop a little, that's all. I didn't mean it. I'm taking everything back. I wasn't serious about it!"

"You have a problem," he says. "You are out of control. If it's not men, it's money. If it's not men or money, it's food. Usnavys, I love you, but I can't watch you self-destruct anymore. I can't let you drag me down with you, either. That's it. I'm done. I am finally, finally done."

With that, he and Sandra get up, and take his suitcases, and they just leave.

They just leave.

Fuck.

JOHN

Clapton always clears his mind. Reminds him of better times. Today, he's got dog pens to paint, and Clapton's on blast from the workshop. He's built the pens from the ground up, welded, soldered, a labor of love for the three Catahoula Cur dogs who are his only companions and friends these days. The painting is mindless, but anymore John is grateful for mindless tasks, the longer they take the better. Anything to keep his mind off of where he's been. No, more like *who* he's been. And what he's done.

Layla, you got me on my knees, Layla...

Growing up on this ranch in the 1970s and 1980s, music was his connection to the outside world, to all those things that teenagers were doing in places more exciting than the rural, rugged lands outside Datil, New Mexico. Oh, John appreciates having grown up here now. He appreciates this unique and beautiful, empty place. Of course he does. He's been all over the world since college, since his very specialized training with the U.S. Army, for which he worked as a Ranger sniper for almost two decades before retiring last year. Most of the guys who entered the Army struggled with the schedule and discipline, but to John it was relaxing; that's because most of the guys who entered the military weren't raised by John's father, Clayton Smith, a relentless taskmaster cut from old-world cowboy cloth. In those early days in the Army, John's ability to follow orders, his inability to complain, his precise roping and shooting skills, athleticism, stoic demeanor, excellent eyesight, patriotism, psychological stamina and unwavering willingness to carry out orders made him stand out to his instructors as a potentially great sharp-shooter. He lived up to that potential, and went on to become one of the military's top snipers, a job he was allowed to tell no one about, not even his parents. Not even his dad, who would have been proud. John has seen almost everywhere there is to see, often through the crosshairs of an M40. In the end, his mind always returned to this place, this peaceful New Mexico ranch, when he needed peace, solace, a comforting thought -- and there were many times he need all of the above. A large portion of a sniper's life is spend in wait, stiff and quiet, almost in suspended animation. Meditating. You cannot scratch, you cannot make noise, you can barely breathe. It wasn't easy. Often, it was painful. No one knew his feelings, however, because he learned long ago not to complain, and never to display any of his emotions on his handsome face.

He's on the third floor of the building in Falluja, with the dust and the spiders. And the heat. Lord, it's hot in here. He's the only one here. It's all on him. He knows the target, and he knows his job. To take out the insurgents, the terrorists, to pick off their leaders one at a time. He is now one of the world's most highly trained assassins, but because of this he is under orders to reveal his profession to no one, not even to his mother. He lost his father a year ago, and his mother is in failing health now. He is the only son, the one they all expected would return to run the ranch, but his wanderlust, his bravado, that chip on his shoulder, that something to prove, all of it got in the way and now here he is, looking down at a crowded street, waiting for the signal, the sign, the indication that his man is in range. He has known solitude most of his life, but never has he felt so alone as he does now, in this crowded unknown land, with the dark-eyed man at last in the crosshairs of his sniper's machine.

"I beg you darling please stop running 'round," he sings, hoping the melody will move in and displace the memory of the accidental shooting of the wrong man that day. Ah, shit, he thinks. Orders are orders, and yet he suspected they might have been mistaken. Ah, hell. You never really even know, when you've got the right man, if he's truly the right man anyway. These men were supposed to be threats to his country, and for a while he believed it as truly as he believes in hard work as the cure for most anything. But anymore? He's not so sure about the motives of the men who assigned him his tasks, or the men who employ them, or the men above them. He's just not sure anymore. And that's a goddamned shame.

Music is the only thing he's found to calm this madness.

How many did he kill? That's easy. He has kept count. Forty-seven men. Forty-seven men, shot as perfectly as you can shoot a man, shot the way you'd shoot a prize buck, their lives ended instantly, humanely, and done to save the lives of countless others. A noble calling. But at what price to his own soul? Their eyes haunt him. Their last movements, burned into his mind like the symbols he's burned onto the rumps of the cows and bulls who populate this 5,000 acres that his mother left to him when she passed away last year, when he came home, when he retired and came back to try to figure out what to do with the rest of his life. John is only 42 years old.

John stops to wipe the sweat from his brow. Midday, in August, and the New Mexico sun beats down on him. The paint dries as soon as it hits the metal, no time to smooth it out. He needs to call it a day, at least until the sun isn't so high or so hot. What they really need around here is some rain. The goddamned cows are starving, feeding their calves all their fat. He hates to supplement, because that makes welfare cases out of them all. He wants them to fend for themselves, find the grass. But the grass they've got now is nothing but dried newspaper, no nutrition in it, yellow and brittle, death sprung out of the ground, and he's got to give them liquid feed or cake them pretty soon. All the old-timers in the county keep saying they haven't seen it this dry in more than forty years, and as much as John hates to admit to the possibility that climate change is real, he does stop to consider it. He doesn't care if it is real, he's not going to support giving money to the government to fix it, or any other problem. He knows firsthand how that goes. No one wastes money like the United States government, which is accountable to no one and rarely if ever audits itself. He wants to believe in his country, but it's not even recognizable anymore. Everything's changed, changing, and he figures none of us actually know the names of the people who are in charge of the whole goddamned thing, and that is by design. It's all a manipulation. He is a patriot, but anymore he is starting to think that a true patriot...well. He doesn't know.

John glances at his watch. He's been at this for six hours, since six this morning. It's time to head inside the house and take a nap, get rested up for the evening chores. He removes the welding helmet and the gloves, and sets everything back as it should be. No man has ever been more meticulous than John Smith. Even as a young boy his father noticed it. "Other parents have to tell their kids to put things away, but you, son, you just do it." this is because from the earliest age, John has never been comfortable with things out of place. It is in his nature to put things in order, to repair, to fix, to protect.

The main house is on the top of the hill, overlooking the southern side of the ranch lands. If he'd built the house himself, John would have put it low in a canyon somewhere, out of sight. When John's grandfather built the house, he owned all the land surrounding it, including the lowlands to the south where old Jasper Turnbull has his place now. John doesn't like that his own house is now visible from the Turnbull house, just the other side of the fence line down the canyon. He likes a life of solitude, where he can control who comes in and who goes out, and who watches him. Now that John knows the sorts of reasons men watch one another, he is not comfortable being exposed in any way at all. Thankfully for John, old Jasper is at his house up in Santa Fe most of the time and only rarely comes to his ranch. Like too many of the newcomers to the area, Jasper is a recreational rancher, an oilman who grew up in Texas thinking it would be manly and cool to own a ranch, but not to have to do any actual work on it.

John walks from the shop area near the barn, across the spacious lawn and up the steps to the 4500-square-foot stone house with the classic New Mexico pitched metal roof. The house is wrapped around on all sides by a large covered porch, which John's mother had decorated with comfortable yet rustic wooden chairs and tables. Her many pots of perennials bloom in a riot of color because John has been meticulous in their care, both for her memory and also because he likes to be surrounded these days by hopeful things. That's why he longed to come back to this place almost as soon as he left for college, because it is beautiful in every direction, a wide open land of rolling hills and clear blue skies that, this time of year, grow bulbous and moody with thunderstorms every afternoon. In this part of the country, thunderstorms are also hopeful things. Too bad these ones lately have only been building, and building, and never dropping anything but great forked tongues of lightning.

He stands on the porch for a long moment, surveying the land, looking for smoke. Fires are common this time of year, because the same thunderheads that sometimes bring rain more often than not bring lightning. City people talk about the tragedy of the fires, but John knows what all ranchers know, that nature sends fires to these grasslands each summer to burn off the old dead stuff from last year, and to fertilize the ground so that new green grasses will sprout up furiously when the rains finally come. It's nature's way, intended for buffalo but now used by cattle. Now all the ranches are getting bought up by celebrities who pay their cowboys menial wages to do the honorable work that used to be done by the ranch-owners themselves. Times have certainly changed since John's grandfather's era. John's not sure that it's all for the better. He's also not sure he needs to figure out anything else to do with his life, other than carry on this ranch, as his father and father's father did. He would like to have a son of his own to carry on after him, but in his line of work it has been hard to meet the sort of woman he'd like, and now that he's isolated out here, well. He's dating, through an online site, but hasn't found anyone he likes enough for that. There are nice enough gals around, but not The One. John is not the kind of man to settle. He'd rather be alone than compromise.

He opens the enormous wooden door, and locks it behind him. His mother and father would have been heartbroken to see him bolt the door. They would roll over in their graves to know he'd installed an alarm system not only on the house but on the entire property, complete with video cameras. They were proud of the fact that this was one of the last safe places in America, where you didn't have to lock your neighbors out. But given how John has spent the past fifteen years of his life, even though he has been careful to leave no trace or sign of where he went or is, he exercises prudence and caution at all times. He is alert, but not paranoid. He is protective, but not a recluse. If pressed, and after a couple of glasses of Kinclaith single-malt on ice (he developed a taste for it after sampling it on a visit to Scotland and can't shake the habit, even though it runs him $1500 a bottle) he might even admit to feeling, at some level, as though he deserves to be found and held accountable. Mistakes were made. He knows that. He lives with the fallout from that knowledge every day.

The house is spacious; everything a luxurious Western ranch house ought to be, with wide-plank maple floors, pale wooden walls, high ceilings and walls of windows connecting the two. Those parts of the house that were inhabited mostly by his father, such as the library and home theater, are done in dark woods and ruby-tinted, gold-studded leather, with mounted heads of various prize animals hung in strategic places, such as the longhorn steer that graces the wall high above the rocky mantle of the library's fireplace. His father's spaces still bear the faintest hint of the old man's prized Cuban cigars, which he brought in twice a year from the Cayman Islands. The rooms that had been frequented by his mother are airy and bright, like the country kitchen that is done in white granite with stainless steel appliances, and the sewing and crafts room, which is done in palest yellow and faintest lime. His father was always adding on, and improving the place, and now its five bedrooms are just too much for John. He keeps four of them closed altogether, and spends his nights in the bedroom that was his when he was a child. His mother told him she wanted him to take the master suite after she passed away, but he cannot bring himself to do that yet. To sleep there, where his parents slept for so many decades, would be to accept they are gone, and he's not quite there yet. A man can only process so much loss at one time, especially if there's nothing new to hold on to in its place. Sometimes, he has to put some of it on hold.

He goes to the kitchen, and immediately notices the blinking red light on the answering machine. This is extremely unusual, because there is are few people who ever call John, and no one whom John calls with any regularity at this number. The gals he dates contact him via Internet, where he set up a special Google voice account strictly for that purpose. He doesn't want any woman to have his home phone number until she is the woman who will share the home with him. He hasn't had a true friend in a very long time. Years. Which is not to say John is antisocial. He will go to town on occasion, for a drink, to chat with the bartenders and find out what's happening in the area. He will also, when warranted, step in and help a person in need, as was the case when the lady who owns the convenience store was robbed and John found the punks who did it and settled the matter outside of the law. They will not be back to this area for a while, and they won't be telling anyone what happened. In other words, when John has something to say to someone, he does it in person.

Curious, he presses the machine on and listens to the recording.

"Hey, Smith, Jasper Turnbull here. Sorry to miss you. Wanted to let you know I'll be bringing a gal out to stay at my place for a while, friend of Rebecca's, a writer from back East who decided to come out someplace quiet to write a book. I'm letting you know so's you won't be surprised to see her out and about. Hope you're doing well. I think about your mom and dad a lot, sure do miss them. No need to call me back unless there's a problem with the writer. Like I said, this old gal's a friend of my niece's and I'm told she's real quiet. Take care now, son.

Let us know if you need anything. Bye."

Great, thinks John bitterly. An East Coast writer, coming to live on a ranch. The Turnbull place is on well water, a septic tank. The electricity out this way is wholly unreliable and goes on and off all the time. John highly doubts any East Coast writer is going to know anything about generators or power supplies or, if she's here into the fall and winter, how to heat that place. There are rats overrunning the barn out at Turnbull's, he bets, because the coyotes have taken all the cats Turnbull had at one time. Turnbull himself doesn't know the half of what's wrong with his ranch. To have heard John's dad tell it, he was always having to go down there to help fix something for those people.

John pours himself a stiff drink, hoping to numb down the agitation that the phone message has aroused in him. This was the last thing he needed to hear. Since moving back, he's been blissfully isolated, just the way he likes it. Now he's going to have to watch as some city slicker gets herself in over her head in the land of rattlesnakes and mountain lions, thinking she's communing with goddamned nature. No doubt she'll be knocking on his door for help with one or another thing, because Turnbull's likely to give her John's name and number as the nearest neighbor.

No.

He will not help her out. She's on her own.

While John is more than happy to help people who have truly been victimized, like the convenience store owner, he'll be damned if he's going to help uppity privileged East Coast people who screw themselves over by neglected to consider things from every possible angle. Failure to plan ahead is not his problem. The problem with the country anymore is that there's this goddamned sense of entitlement everywhere you look, especially with people back East. People expect things to be given to them. They expect things to work without doing anything to facilitate that themselves. People have to take responsibility for their actions, and be held accountable for what they decide to do with their lives, he thinks.

Then he realizes, with a sickening lurch through his gut, that he is a hypocrite for this very thought. There are things he himself was never held accountable for, and probably never will be. Things, like fathers who will never hold their children again, sons who will grow up with their dads. Mistakes were made.

"God damnit," he says, collapsing in a large, dark leather armchair in the family room, and picking up the remote for the television. *Still*, he thinks, as he flips to his favorite network, the Science Channel. *I am sick of city people who don't know the first goddamned thing about the country. They underestimate us "simple" folks. No. Hell, no. I'm not going to help that woman.*

She's on her own.

REBECCA

By the time I pull into the driveway of my home in Santa Fe, my mother has fallen asleep against the passenger side window. We left her house in the morning, with her still hung-over and seeming to have begun drinking already again, and drove in silence most of the way from Albuquerque, about 45 minutes. She is feeling very sorry for herself, which I understand. But my anger grows as I realize how she thinks this is all just about her. I was betrayed, too. That has not registered with her. And not only was I betrayed by my father, but I have been living without my parents' approval for years now, since falling in love with Andre and divorcing my white husband Brad for him. My mother for a long time seemed as though she'd never forgive me for "marrying down" in such a way. And yet, here I am, helping her pick up the pieces of what's left of her life, and she doesn't stop to consider how many times she herself tried to shatter mine.

I look over at her now, and try to understand my feelings. To say they are mixed would be an understatement. She looks small and frail, and even though she is 64 years old there is something decidedly childlike about the set of her brow. Her mouth is open, and I can smell the alcohol. I have never known my mother to drink. I have always thought she was so strong she could handle anything, and now I'm not so sure. Now, I realize she might have been suffering quietly for many years. This angers me. She should have told me, instead of knowing the truth yet letting me live a lie. After all, she has been so honest about her feelings about me and my black husband, and our mixed-race child, right? She never had trouble voicing the 'truth' about that. I guess it's different when the truth hurts her instead of someone else.

I press the button and the garage door whirs up. Morning has come to the mountain foothills where we live, and with it the calm quiet that I love so much. Sometimes I miss the excitement of living in a big East Coast city like Boston, where I lived from the age of 18 to my early 30s.

But Santa Fe, in spite of only having a little more than 40,000 people, is a cosmopolitan small city in its own way, and there's always something going on in the arts here. It's a good place to live, and a good place to raise a child – even a child like mine. As soon as the negative thought about Connor moves through my head, I will it away. A mother should not feel such ambivalence toward her own child, I remind myself. A real mother, a good mother, does not allow herself to feel trapped and depressed just because her boy is out of synch with the rest of the world. She pushes forward, advocates for him, does what she can to love him even though every doctor has said it is unlikely that he will ever tell her that he loves her back.

I pull the car into the garage and cut the engine. There was a time when I dreamed I'd have the sort of child who looked up from his playing when you got home, and called out to you with excitement, wanting to share some detail of his life with you. Autistic children in general are incapable of sharing joy or pointing out things they've done, and in fact this is one of the first signs we had that our son was autistic. He never pointed to things, or brought things to me and Andre to share his joy in them. This is because autistics lack what is called a "theory of mind," meaning they do not understand that people other than themselves are not having exactly the same experience that they are having. Why point out the pretty red bird if everyone can see it? Why tell someone about something if you automatically assume, from your biological lack of empathy, that they are exactly like you and must already know it?

"Mom," I say softly, touching her arm to rouse her.

My mother's eyes flutter open in surprise, bloodshot and weary. When did she get so old? My God. She blinks, and looks around in confusion for a moment before remembering what's going on.

"We're home," I tell her. "Let's get your things to the guest house."

My mother says nothing. She rubs her eyes with her hands, and runs her fingers through her short, messy hair.

She refused to shower this morning, saying "What's the point?" It hurts me to see her like this. She is usually so well groomed, but not today. Today she looks like she might have been sleeping under a bridge for a week. She has given up appearances. She just doesn't care anymore.

I hop out of the car and take my mother's two suitcases from the cargo area before leading her out the side door that takes us to the red brick path winding across the northern yard. I'm not going to take her into the main house just yet, and told her as much when we left her house. I need time to tell Andre what's going on, and to prepare him for my mother's presence. I suspect he won't agree with me that we should shelter her for the time being, given the way she has treated him and our child.

My mother plods unhappily along behind me, stopping as I do when we get to the front door of the smaller house. It is a three-bedroom adobe home set back off a sprawling green lawn, the outside walls covered in creeping ivy, a home with a full kitchen and a soaring loft over the living room that I have used as a bit of a miniature art gallery. I have my Pola Lopez oil paintings here, and as my mother walks in and glances up at the brightly colored painting of a nude angel staring out the doorway at the other naked angels flying, I can see her mouth tighten with disapproval. My mother has never been what you might call a sensual or passionate person, and in fact I cannot recall ever having gotten a sex talk from her at all. Everything I learned about sex, I learned from my foulmouthed friends in college.

"There's food in the fridge," I tell her. "Clean towels in the bathrooms and fresh sheets on the beds. Make yourself at home."

I look at her as she teeters unsteadily across the room and almost misses the large soft chair she has aimed to sit in.

"Would you like me to make you a pot of coffee?" I ask her.

"Got a beer?" she asks, reminding me for a moment of George Lopez's sitcom mother in his self-titles TV series.

"Yes, we have beer, but I'm not letting you have any more of that today. In fact, I can't believe I'm even having to tell you that you shouldn't drink beer for breakfast. Don't give him this kind of power over you, mom. You're stronger than this."

I go to the kitchen, which is really part of the great room that includes the living area and art loft, and I begin to brew a pot of strong coffee. I like the countertops here, blonde granite with black flecks.

"I don't want coffee," my mother gripes.

"Well, that's fine. It's up to you. It'll be here in case you change your mind." She looks pale and clammy. "When's the last time you ate, mom?"

"I don't know," she says with a shrug and a faraway look in her eyes. "Yesterday. Maybe the day before. I had me some mushrooms. Raw, out of the container. I pretended each one was a penis, and I bit their heads off."

"Mom!"

"What, Rebecca? How do you think you got here? Immaculate conception?"

"Stop it, please."

"His is almost as small as a mushroom, too."

"Mom! Enough."

"Blame me for us never doing it, but he's the one you couldn't even feel it when he did it to you."

I spin around and glare at my mother. "If you don't stop talking like this in my house, I will ask you to leave. Am I making myself clear?"

"Yes, Rebecca."

I take a plate out of the cabinet, and put some cheese and ham slices on it, with a piece of thick multigrain bread. I pull some green grapes off the bunch in the bowl on the counter and rinse and dry them before setting them on it, too.

"Eat this," I tell her as I set the plate on the part of the counter that serves as a bit of a breakfast bar. "You'll feel better."

"I will never feel better," she complains, but I am heartened to see that she gets up and shuffles over to the food anyway. She's hungry. That's a good sign.

"Okay," I say as she sits in front of the food. I get her a glass of iced water, and then tell her that I have to go up to the house for a while. "I'll be back after I've spoken to my husband and let him know what's going on."

My mother stares down at the plate of food and I realize that my spine has hardened in anticipation of an insult from her about my husband. It doesn't come. For the first time in many years, she doesn't have something racist and disgusting to say about him. I am sure this has nothing to do with her having had a change of heart about him, and more to do with the fact that she knows I am pretty much the only person she has to turn to right now, and I won't tolerate her insulting the love of my life.

"Do you need anything else?" I ask her.

My mother shakes her head. I take the remote control from the coffee table in the living area and set it next to her.

"There's cable in here. There are TVs in all the bedrooms, and there in the great room on the wall right there. It looks like a painting, but when you press this button here, look, like this, the painting slides back, like this, voila, and you can see the screen."

I demonstrate it for her. My mother watches, annoyed. She has always been afraid of new technology, and critical of anything she deems overly showy.

"The intercom by the door?" I say, pointing to the small white digitized box by the front door. "If you need me, just press the red button on the bottom. That rings the main house. I might answer it, but it might be Judy. She's our housekeeper and cook. We have a nanny, Paula, who might answer, too. Just so you know."

"I'm fine," she says unconvincingly. "I don't need TV or anything. Just leave me alone. I won't bother you. Just go."

"You're not a bother," I say. I notice there are tears welling anew in her eyes.

I know that in many families this might be the time to kiss your mother on the top of her head, or give her a hug, but we've never been a touchy-feely bunch, and I am not sure yet how I feel about any of this. I have a lot of questions for her, but this isn't the time. Some questions are best not answered by a drunk. So it is that I merely tell my mother I'll see her in a bit, and I walk out the door, leaving her to her misery alone.

I find Andre in his home office, sifting through some paperwork, taking care of the world as he always does, so expertly and efficiently, so unflinchingly. He looks up as I rap lightly on the open door and ask him if I may come in.

"Of course," he says with a loving smile that seems just a tiny bit rote. "You know you're always welcome in here."

I smile and walk over to him. Per habit, I give him a peck on the lips before sitting down on one of the two plush chairs opposite his large shiny walnut desk. I try to remember the last time we actually had sex.

It was at least six weeks ago.

Six *weeks.*

We are both so busy, and the stress of our son's needs often take priority over everything else. We are both usually so tired at the end of the day that sex is the last thing on our minds. Or at least it is the last thing on *my* mind. For a time, after Connor was born, Andre would try to make love to me, but after our son's birth I just didn't ever feel like going there. My womb had failed to get pregnant, and then, after Connor was born autistic via a surrogate, it felt as though God were telling me that I should have heeded his wishes to begin with, and remained barren. I was incapable of producing a normal child, broken, only half a woman, if even that. I lost all desire for sex, because my sex had betrayed me. Now and then, I will allow Andre to make love to me, because it seems cruel to always reject him, but it is clear to me that he is requesting it less and less, slowly letting go of his own desires for me as well. The last time we did it, we did it in a perfunctory sort of way, in the dark, and my mind wandered. Andre didn't climax, either. He just sort of stopped, and kissed me on the forehead and told me to sleep well. I wanted to ask him about it, but I did not know how to bring it up. Maybe, I thought, this is just what happens to married couples after children come. Life gets in the way.

I wonder why we haven't talked about it, and whether we ever should. Do couples talk their way out of this kind of stagnation? Or does it just ebb and flow over time? I wonder if he still finds me attractive, but am too afraid to ask because I don't want to know if the answer is negative. I do not know how any husband could find such a sexually inadequate wife attractive, honestly. I am unworthy of my husband's seed.

The room smells faintly of fine cigars and coffee. My husband wears just an old ratty college t-shirt with sweatpants, his "I'm home from work and need to relax now" outfit, and wire-rimmed glasses, but manages to still be one of the most elegant men in the world, with his beautiful face and intelligent, compassionate eyes. He knows me very well, and his face registers concern as he looks at me.

"What's wrong, darling?" he asks. "How's your mother?"

Before I answer about myself, I ask about Connor.

"Paula's bathed him and put him to bed," says Andre, in a tired sort of way that tells me he, too, is worn down by the task of parenting an autistic child. We don't talk about this, either.

"How was his day?"

Andre shrugs with a bittersweet smile. "I'm not sure any of will ever know the answer to that question." I see the pain in his heart, and know that he is as exhausted as I am by our situation.

I feel my heart lurch again with the sorrow of being a parent to an autistic child. It doesn't matter how long you have lived with the diagnosis, it never gets any less painful. You want life to be easier for your child, but autism is like a prison my son is locked inside of and I am helpless to get him out. Connor's autism feels like a constant reminder of my own inadequacies, as a mother, as a woman.

"Tell me what's bothering you," says Andre. "You look upset."

I take a deep breath to compose myself, before sharing the news of my parents' separation and my father's secret other woman and her children. All I said last night was that my mother was having some personal problems and needed me to stay with her. Then, I let it fly. Andre listens intently, taking time to understand everything I've said before reacting.

"I'm very sorry to hear of their marital problems," he says carefully, working hard not to let his own feelings of rejection at their racist hatred of him get in the way. "But I am primarily sorry that you are now faced with yet another betrayal of your core values and your life at the hands of your father, a man for whom I have very little sympathy or affection. I cannot say I am surprised, though you likely still held onto some illusions about the man. I am very sorry you're going through this."

"Thank you," I say, marveling yet again at how astute my husband is. He is so in tune with my feelings and emotional state that I find it impossible to believe he is unaware of our own marital woes. Nonetheless, I am impressed because Andre is remarkable for always taking the high road, in everything, and one of the main reasons I fell for him was that he was always measured and diplomatic. Sometimes, however, I just wish he'd actually lose control. Sometimes you just can't be sure what he's actually thinking or feeling.

"It must be very hard. I am here to listen, if you wish to talk about it."

"Thank you. I'm still letting it sink in."

"I'd imagine."

"I'm not sure what to think, yet."

I want to yell, or cry, or throw something. I want to call my father on the phone and ask him just who the hell he thinks he is to destroy our lives in this way. I want to know who this other family is. I want to beat that other woman to a bloody goddamned pulp, and I know this is wrong, that it isn't her fault as much as it is my own father's. I am overcome with emotions that I cannot share with my husband.

"My mother is in the guest house," I tell him, flinching just a tiny bit because I don't know how he will take this. I watch him closely. He keeps his face quite still, and takes a long, slow breath. He says nothing.

"Andre," I say. "I know I should have asked you first, but I didn't want you to say no, and she needs me right now."

"My darling," he says with that beautiful English accent of his. "I am not sure what to say."

"I know you probably don't want her here."

"You are correct about that."

"But she's my mother."

"I am aware."

"She doesn't have anywhere else to go."

"She has other relatives."

"She asked me," I say.

"Rebecca."

"Please, just, let's try to figure this out. Try to be nice."

He fights his anger, and I realize it is absurd to ask him to be nice, given how unkind my parents have been to him. He measures his words. "Over the years, your mother has disrespected you, and us, and our family, in myriad different ways."

"I know."

"She has said and done things that I would not have expected even from your worst enemy, much less from your own mother. Yet you have forgiven her, again and again, at cost to me, to us, to Connor."

"Andre, she has her limitations. There's nothing we can do about that. But she's my mother, and she needs me. I don't like her actions any more than you do, but blood is thicker than water and sometimes you have to step up and do the right thing, even when someone probably doesn't deserve it."

He considers what I've said.

"I admire your unconditional love for your parents,"

he says carefully. "It is only natural that a child should always love her mother. You have parents who do the worst things to their kids, and those kids still love them, so at an intellectual level I certainly understand how you'd want to help. Maybe even prove to her that we are better than she is, being there for her in her time of need where she has never been there for you, not when you couldn't get pregnant, not when you miscarried, not when we discovered we were going to be raising an autistic child. You needed her then."

"I know."

Andre sighs, and takes the glasses from his face before rubbing the bridge of his nose in exhaustion.

"What's happening to us?" he asks me, surprising me by the frankness of his words, and the sorrow in his eyes.

"What do you mean?"

"Us. We're not the same. We don't communicate anymore. I feel..." his voice trails off.

I don't want to hear the rest of what he's about to say, so I pretend not to realize he's just tried to steer the conversation away from my mother and over to us, the married couple.

"It's not going to be forever," I say. "She was drunk, Andre. I've never seen her drunk. She's been drinking again this morning. She was talking in this fatalistic way I've never heard her use, and I was worried for her safety."

I don't want to cry, but it happens anyway. It's as though suddenly all the feelings I'd been pushing back and down came washing up over me.

"I can't believe any of this is happening," I say.

Andre gives me a soft but somewhat defeated look, and walks over to wrap me in his big, strong arms. His embrace feels hollow, insincere. And what is that scent on his shirt? It doesn't smell like he usually smells, and it doesn't smell like me. Is it perfume? Really? I feel my blood run cold. Is he like my father? Is this what all men do? Are they actually incapable of keeping that thing in their pants? My God, what is happening to me? How am I doubting him? Andre has never been anything but reliable and honest with me, understanding and faithful. He couldn't be cheating, could he? But that's what I thought, too, of my father. What *is* happening to us? Where did we go? We used to be so in love with each other, unable to keep our hands off each other. When did that change?

"I'm sorry," he says. "I'm being selfish. I should have thought about how this would make you feel, this news about your father. It must be terrible. The last thing you need right now is criticism from me. I am sorry."

"She said he has three children by his receptionist."

"And here you thought you were an only child," he tries to joke.

"It's not funny."

"I know it's not, darling. I know. I'm sorry." Andre sits down in the other plush chair and leans forward, his elbows on his knees. "We'll figure this out. Okay? I just want to make sure we establish some ground rules with her if she's going to be in our home, and first among them is that no one will disrespect my wife, my child, or me in my own house."

"Of course."

"And if she fails to live up to that requirement, she will be asked to leave immediately."

I nod.

"I'm not messing around with her anymore, Rebecca. There will be no wiggle room on this. She is to be respectful, or she must go."

"I understand. I'll talk to her."

At that moment, I hear the doorbell chime. Andre and I look at one another in surprise.

"Are you expecting someone?" I ask. For a moment, I imagine that there will be a woman here, the source of that scent on my husband's shirt. He looks nervous, as though he might be thinking the same thing -- but I could be imagining it. I don't know what to think. It never crossed my mind, until now, that my husband would ever cheat on me. I just didn't think him capable. I never thought my father capable, either. For a moment, I fear my mother's life will simply repeat itself in my own.

He shakes his head and I tell him that I am not expecting anyone either.

"Maybe it's your mother?" he suggests.

"I told her how to work the intercom," I say in frustration, as I realize she has probably been wandering drunkenly around the yard. I hear Judy's sneakers squeaking across the dark hardwood floors as she walks toward the door from the kitchen, to answer it. I get up to join her in hopes of thwarting my mother's efforts to offend someone, anyone, everyone.

To my surprise, it is not my mother waiting outside the front door on the porch. Rather, it is Lauren, my longtime friend from college. The emotionally unstable one who has left her job and apartment, and is running from a supposed killer. I have not yet gotten around to telling Andre about her predicament, mostly because he's had enough to worry about with the latest business deal he's been working on. I forgot she'd be here so soon, having gotten so wrapped up in my mother's drama, and now I feel like a deer caught in headlights.

"Uhm, hello?" says Lauren. I realize I'm standing there smiling like a stepford wife as I try to figure out how to handle the situation.

"Lauren, welcome, come in," I say. I introduce her to Judy and they shake hands. I ask her how her drive from Boston has been, and she says it was fine all except the part where her ex killed her cat in the parking lot of a cheap motel. Judy looks at me in shock. I blink slowly to let them know she might be exaggerating.

I say, "Lauren's going to be staying with us tonight. Is that right?"

"If that's cool, yes." I notice how tired Lauren looks. How ghostlike and shaken up, too, and I draw her into an embrace. She smells gamey, like she hasn't showered in a while.

"Shall I prepare the guest house?" asks Judy.

"No, actually, there's already someone in it. Can you just make sure the guest suite here in the main house is ready?"

"Yes, ma'am."

"Thank you, Judy."

Judy closes the door, and as I release Lauren from my embrace I see my husband standing by, watching with a look of curiosity on his face. I catch him watching Judy's rear end as she walks away, and my breath catches in my throat. No. Not the housekeeper. That would be maudlin, especially for someone as refined as Andre. Did I imagine it? Was he merely watching her go? I feel like I'm losing my mind, and quickly work overtime to compose myself and carry on as though nothing were bothering me.

"Andre, you remember Lauren?"

He says he does, and steps forward gallantly to shake her hand. He asks what brings her here to Santa Fe, and she looks quizzically at me.

"You haven't told him?"

Andre gives me a look. "You haven't told 'him' what, darling?"

"I'm running for my life," says Lauren, and Andre laughs. She tells him she's not kidding, and looks at me to fill in the blanks for him.

"I meant to mention that Lauren will be staying with us tonight before heading off to spend some time on a retreat at my uncle's ranch down by Quemado. Tio Turnbull will be by in the morning to get her."

"I see," says Andre. He smiles at Lauren, and then gets in a dig at me. "I guess Rebecca and I don't talk as much as we used to."

I hear Connor begin to shriek from down the hall, a nightly occurrence. Often it is because his socks are bunched up wrong, or the tag of his pajamas is still on and rubbing him the wrong way. Many times, the irritation is of an unknown origin, something in Connor's world that only Connor can see, hear, or feel. Never has a child been more wrapped up by ghosts than is my poor, dear Connor. Andre and I exchange a knowing, tired look.

"I'll handle it," he says, walking toward our son's room. I watch him go for a moment, and turn toward my friend.

"Rebecca?" asks Lauren, clearly surprised to see whatever it is she sees in my eyes. "Are you okay? You seem depressed."

I smile as best I can, and raise my chin a little. "Yes, of course. The real question is how are you holding up?"

Lauren proceeds to tell me a horrible tale of being chased and almost killed. I am uncertain whether to indulge her, because this could all be fantasy or it could be terrible truth. Lauren has always made poor decisions in her life, and it seems that they are finally coming back around to teach her the lesson she has failed to learn.

"Am I imposing?" she asks, still seeming to search my eyes for something. The truth is, of course, that this is not a very good time for Lauren to bring her drama into our lives. I have plenty of drama enough as it is.

"You're fine," I tell her. "As long as you weren't followed here."

She laughs awkwardly. "I haven't seen anybody on my tail since New York State. I think I finally lost them."

"Good."

I lead her to the wing of the house that is designated for guests, and settle her into the larger of our two guests suites. She runs her fingers over the surface of the dresser, and turns to look at me, impressed.

"How do you do it?" she asks me.

"Do what?"

"Manage to be so perfect."

I laugh a little. If only she knew. "I'm far from perfect, Lauren."

"You're about as close as I think it gets," she says as she flops down on the bed, her eyes shutting almost before she hits the mattress. "I mean, from where I stand, your life looks about as good as a life can look."

I watch her as she almost instantly drifts off into sleep, and I feel a tear come to my eye. Lauren has no idea that, if I could, I would switch lives with her right about now. At least the demons she's running from can be outrun, or stopped.

Mine are my own flesh and blood, and my broken

vows to God to be a good wife and mother.

LAUREN

I leave Rebecca's house early in the morning, after sleeping better than I have slept in weeks, in her luxurious guest suite. I'm no longer driving the Impala Usnavys gave me because Juan wants it back and, according to Rebecca's uncle, Jasper Turnbull, it would never survive the thirteen miles of rough dirt road that awaits us at the end of our journey. Tio Turnbull, or "Plain White Tio" as Rebecca calls him, assures me that there is a pickup I can use at the ranch, after he leaves me there. He also insists that I call him "Tio," which is odd, but who am I to complain? My real family members are too embarrassed to claim me, you know, because I'm not a Harley chick or meth head, so it's a pleasant change of pace to have someone actually wanting to pretend to by my uncle.

We're on the porch at Rebecca's now, me and Tio Turnbull, saying our goodbyes. Tio is tall and thin, wiry even, in his early sixties, and reminds me of a cigarette. He has a full head of shockingly thick white hair, and a large mustache. He wears expensive-looking cowboy clothes, jeans with a button-down shirt with embroidered designs on it, and colorful cowboy boots. He carries himself in a way that reminds me of Ted Turner. There's something very comforting about being in this man's confident presence. I don't know him, but I feel like he could probably take care of me.

Tio carries my bags with ease to his shiny red four-door Chevy pickup truck, and places them in the back seat. Then he tells me to hop in, and I realize that as high off the ground as the vehicle is, he must mean this literally. I hoist myself up into the passenger seat, and Tio closes the door with a secure snap for me from outside. A gentleman. The interior of the truck is beige leather, and extremely clean, as though it is brand-new, though I know it probably isn't. I am not a truck kind of girl, and don't know exactly what to do this high up off the ground.

"Might as well get comfortable," he says as he starts

the engine. "We've got about five hours in here."

"I really appreciate this," I tell him.

Tio looks at me as though sizing up my intentions. "Any friend of Rebecca's is a friend of ours," he says, referring, I assume, to himself and whatever woman is attached to the other end of that wedding band on his left hand.

"Well, it's very nice," I say.

"Rebecca tells me you're out this way to write a book," he says, though his sideways glance implies that he probably knows the real reason I'm here, too. He's just far too polite to say so.

"Something like that," I tell him.

"Dangerous business, book-writing," he says, pulling the pickup smoothly into traffic now. "You never know who's going to read it, or how they're going to react."

"This is true." I watch Santa Fe slide past outside the spotless windows. The ride is the pickup is softer that I had assumed, having never ridden in one before, and I say as much.

"What do you mean, you've never ridden in a pickup?" asks Tio.

"I haven't."

"Really?"

"You're my first," I say.

"Well, the honor's all mine."

Tio asks me if I've had breakfast, and I tell him that I have. He stops off at a Starbucks to get himself a cup of coffee for the drive, and asks if I'd like anything. I have already had coffee, but in my universe there is no such thing as too much of the brown poison, so I take him up on the offer. He tells me to wait in the pickup, and in he goes. I look around, and marvel at this odd little city.

Santa Fe is pretty, in a strangely brown and uniform way. I'll give it that. Rimmed on a couple of sides by purple mountain ranges, it looks like something out of a fairy tale. The buildings are all adobe, beige and brown, and rarely more than two stories high. The sky is huge here, and a shocking shade of bright blue. I try not to think about Fatso, and how I'll never see her again. More than the loss of my home and my job, I miss that damned cat.

I need a tissue for the tears. I look around the cab of the pickup, and find a small package of Kleenex in the glove box, along with a pistol. Tio is packing. This comforts me, even as I feel embarrassed for having invaded his privacy in this way.

Tio returns with our coffee, eyes the tissue and the glove box, but says nothing. Then away we go, through the curving roads of the city toward the Interstate. He turns on the radio, satellite radio. It's set to WSIX, a country music station out of Nashville.

"This work for you?" he asks.

I shrug, because I am fairly unfamiliar with the genre. It has never held my interest, and therefore have no opinion that would be worth sharing.

"If there's something else you'd rather hear, help yourself," he says. "As long as it isn't death metal or disco."

"This is fine."

On we go. The land unfolds vastly, and I feel myself relaxing just a little. I actually like the song that's playing. The digital readout tells me it's called *Dirt Road Anthem*, by someone named Jason Aldean. It's kind of like country rap. I like unexpected music. Much respect, I think. I don't much like the first name anymore, but, hey, not all Jasons are evil. This one sounds earnest and good.

Tio doesn't talk much, so I ask questions to draw him out. In this way I discover that he is married, and retired, that he grew up in Odessa, Texas, that his family made a fortune in the oil business, and that his grandparents always talked about the good old days when their land was used for cattle instead of black gold.

"That's why, when I had a chance, I bought this place where we're going. I named it Spotted Dog Ranch, after my grandpa's best friend. I wanted to keep a little part of that tradition alive, in their honor."

"That's nice," I say, because I don't know how else to respond.

"My wife would have liked to come with us," he tells me. "But she has a brother in hospice out in Colorado, dying."

"Wow. I'm sorry."

"It happens. With much greater frequency the older you get. She's there with him now. That's why I have to just drop you off and head back this evening. I'm headed up that way."

"I'm sorry to be an inconvenience."

"You're not," he says. "From what I understand, this...'book' of yours is fairly urgent as well."

From the way he's said this, I realize that he does in fact know the circumstances of my fleeing Boston.

"I never thought he had it in him," I say, watching the road. Tio stays quiet, and listens as I tell him the entire story of my relationship with Jason Flynn.

"Sounds like a sociopath."

"How could I be so stupid?" I whine.

"You're not stupid," says Tio. "You're human. And have a conscience. My wife's a therapist. The thing with sociopaths is they're extremely charming, and that makes it hard for people like us to know when they're lying -- which is pretty much all the time. And this man is handsome on top of that. I don't think anyone suspects them. That's why so many of them reach such high positions in government and entertainment. They're everywhere. My wife says one in twenty-five people are born without a conscience in this country. Isn't that something?"

"You think he doesn't have a conscience?"

"How else could he do that to your cat? Any person with a conscience would find something like that unthinkable."

"My friend Usnavys thinks I need to get a gun," I say, my eyes darting toward the glove box.

"Only if you know how to use one."

My eyes flit to the glove box. "Maybe you could teach me. I don't like the idea of being all alone in the middle of nowhere. What if he finds me?"

"Tell you what. That gun in there? I'll give it to you."

"You don't have to do that."

"I know. You need it more than I do."

"Thank you."

"No worries. We'll teach you how to shoot it before I leave. That way you'll rest a little easier. But I have to tell you, there's no way anybody can get out to my place without the codes to the locks on my gates, and a good four-wheel-drive vehicle, and even then they'll make enough racket that you'll hear them coming. There's no safer place for you right now. That I promise."

Four hours and several rest stops later, we drive through the small town of Datil, and on to Quemado.

"Hungry?" he asks.

"Starving."

"I know a pretty good place. Let's get some lunch, then we'll stop at the market to stock up for the house. My wife always says to never shop on an empty stomach."

"Wise woman."

"That's why I married her. Well, that and her legs."

I laugh and he winks in a way that makes me hopeful. There are men in this world who love their wives.

Tio stops at one of what appear to be three restaurants in the entire town, and we go in and take seats at the bar. People say hello to him by name, but they stare at me. Tio introduces me around, saying I'm a writer from "Back East" and that I'll be out at the ranch working on a book for a while. He suggests that they all "look out" for me, and be sure to alert me right away if anything strange happens, like if someone comes through town who maybe doesn't belong there.

"Writing books is a risky business," he says, and everyone seems to understand what he means. He tells me that people around here are very independent-minded and self-reliant, and have a great admiration for people who write books.

Tio suggests the green chile burger, so that's what I order, with a cold beer. He gets the same, and we chat a bit with the bartender, a nice enough man by the name of

Larry. Tio asks about the weather, and the surrounding ranches, and they talk about the difficulty posed by the current drought.

Suddenly, all eyes leave off staring at me and turn toward something coming through the door.

"Oh, boy," says Larry. "Here we go."

I notice the female waitress lift her hand to her hair to make sure it looks as good as it can, with that oven-fried mullet perm she's got going on. I turn to see what's captured their attention, and spot the frighteningly handsome cowboy instantly.

He's about six foot two, wearing tight, faded jeans, dusty light-brown cowboy boots, a neatly ironed white button-down shirt, and a sweat-stained beige felt cowboy hat. When he whips the expensive-looking sunglasses off, I am confronted with what is perhaps one of the strongest and most handsome faces I have ever seen. This is saying quite a lot after having been with the likes of Jason Flynn, who is by far the best-looking (and, apparently, most insane) boyfriend I've ever had. This guy here could give Jason a run for his money in that department. He, like Jason, looks sort of like a model, if models were actually cowboys. No, wait. He looks like a more rugged, manly, sun-kissed Kevin Costner, with the kind of attractive crow's feet that only men can pull off. He has a serious look on his face and an intensity of concentration that unnerves me.

"Wow," I say, before I can stop myself.

"That," says Tio under his breath to me, "is John Smith. He's the nearest neighbor to my place. His family owns the Eagleview Ranch. I'm glad he's here, because I need to introduce you. I was going to bring you by his place later, but this is just as good."

"Good-looking guy," I say.

Tio laughs. "Yeah, well, he's tough as nails. Don't let the pretty face fool you. He's as hard as they come."

Tio continues to eat, as John Smith scans the room as though looking for something or someone in particular. I watch the handsome cowboy, and feel my heart squeeze.

He is breathtaking. The chin is square, the cheeks chiseled, the blue eyes flashing with focus and intelligence.

"This isn't going to be good," muses the bartender.

No shit, I think. *I could fall for a guy like that. And the last thing I need is to fall for anyone.*

"Why?" I ask, curious about Larry's trepidation. "What's wrong with him?"

"Nothing. He's just...I don't know. You'll find out soon enough."

John Smith spots Tio now, and his eye flicker over me unsmilingly for an instant before refocusing upon Larry. John makes a beeline for the bartender.

"Hey, Johnny," says the bartender. "What can I do you for?"

"Hey, Larry," he says, leaning up against the bar near us. "Crown Royal with a splash of water. On ice." He looks over at Tio, and nods. "Turnbull." He looks at me, but does not smile.

"You get my message, Smith?" asks Tio.

"Yup." John takes his stiff drink from Larry, and sips it.

"How are things?" Tio asks him.

Smith shrugs. "Same old same."

"Well, this is the writer gal I was telling you about," says Tio, motioning to me. "Lauren Fernandez. She'll be working on a book out at my place for a while."

John looks me up and down for a second, perhaps disapprovingly but more like poker-faced, then addresses Tio. "So you said."

"Nice to meet you," I say as I push my hand into the space between me and John Smith. I will not let yet another man be disgusted by me, without even knowing me. Reluctantly, he takes it, and squeezes with bone-crushing strength, giving me a steady look in the eye, but one that is impossible to read. I have no idea what he's thinking.

"How long you planning to be around?" he asks me.

"Uhm, I'm not sure."

"As long as it takes to get the job done," Tio answers

for me. "She's welcome as long as she needs to be there. Might as well get used to her."

"That so," says John Smith disinterestedly. I'm disappointed. I was hoping he'd at least find me cute, or that I'd pique his interest in some way. He is impossible to read. He turns his attention away from us, and toward Larry now. "Where is he?" His voice is deep, and his accent is Western, rural, a little twang but not too much so.

"Now, Johnny, we don't need to start getting ugly this early in the day," says Larry.

"Who said anything about ugly?" asks John. "All I want is to have a civilized word with the man."

I turn away from the cowboy, uncomfortable with his beauty. Tio raises an eyebrow at me, to indicate that he finds the conversation interesting.

John finishes his drink, and pays with a twenty-dollar bill he does not require change for.

"Guess we're not feeling cooperative today, Larry."

"Ah, Jesus, Johnny. It ain't that."

"When you *do* see him, you let him know I'd like to have a little chat."

"Will do, Johnny," says Larry.

"Turnbull," says John, tipping his hat toward us. "Miz Fernandez."

"We'll see you around, Smith," says Tio.

"Nice to meet you," I say.

"The pleasure's all mine," John tells me with what I suspect is a touch of sarcasm, before walking straight toward the door, and out.

"What's his problem?" I ask Tio in a whisper. Tio smiles in admiration of the younger man.

"He's just Smith. He's a good kid. Just hasn't been the same since the war."

"Oh."

"Rumor has it he was Special Forces. No one really knows. He's real secretive. But he's a good guy, and if you need anything out at the ranch, you let him know. He can fix damn near about anything."

"Or anyone," adds Larry, polishing the counter where

John had set his glass down. "Scary son of a bitch."

"Ah, he's all right," says Tio.

"He's got it in for Hammond Regis. That's who he's asking about."

"Well, good," says Tio with a smile. "Regis is a pain in the ass."

"He's a county commissioner, Jasper."

"So what? Still a pain in the ass. What's Smith got it in for him about?"

Larry sighs. "Some folks saw Hammond talking rude to his wife and kids down at the post office in Quemado the other day, and John got word of it."

"Well, good," says Tio again.

"After what he did to those kids that robbed the store, we're all a little worried he'll go overboard, do something stupid."

"Nothing he could do to Regis would be stupid, if you ask me," says Tio.

Larry smiles at him, and notices that our plates are empty. He clears them, and gives us the bill.

"Welcome to the area," Larry tells me. "Stop by anytime you start to feel lonely out there. We've got some real nice people here, though you might not know it to look at us all today."

I laugh, and thank him. Tio pays the bill, and we leave.

From Quemado, Tio drives about another 30 minutes, to the turnoff for a dirt road. After an hour of this bumpy ride, and after passing through four locked gates, innumerable cattle, stock tanks and windmills, we arrive at a pretty brown house with a silver pitched roof, in a clearing, surrounded on all sides by high, green, rounded hills. The land is covered with grasses, juniper brush, sage, and a few cactus plants.

"Well, this is it," says Tio Turnbull, clearly relishing the sight of the place. "Where'd I'd spend all my time if the wife didn't hate it out here so much."

He cuts the engine.

"It's beautiful here. Why does she hate it?"

"Oh, you know. She likes her Pilates and her yoga studio, her fine restaurants and fancy boutiques. Don't have much of that out here."

"No, I guess not."

With the engines off, the silence of this place is enormous. I hear a few birdcalls, and that is all. I have never, I realize, been in a place this quiet, so quiet you cannot hear a road, a car, or anything but the wind.

Tio exits the pickup, and I follow suit. He leads me up the stone steps to the front door, and opens it with a key, telling me that the house is built in "traditional New Mexican territorial style," meaning it's an adobe house with a metal roof. The air inside the house is still and musty, not dirty exactly, just unused. No one has been here in a while. Tio notices, and starts opening windows, and shades, and he turns on the swamp cooler.

"Make yourself at home," he tells me. "I'll go get your things, and the groceries."

I offer to help, but he insists that it is a man's job to bring the stuff in, and my job to relax.

"Thank you," I say.

"Get acquainted with the place," he calls out over his shoulder. "Have a look around."

The great room living area is very comfortable, with shiny dark wood floors and overstuffed white furniture that I am instantly convinced I will spill something on and ruin. There's a big stone fireplace, with large picture windows on either side of it. A spacious modern kitchen shares this area, and I love the way whomever decorated it has painted one of the walls a dark brown. There's art all over the place, mostly Southwestern, Indian-looking art, and Western cowboy-type art. Sculptures or men riding bucking bulls or sharing meals with dogs over a nighttime fire, paintings of Indian women baking bread in an outdoor oven, that kind of thing.

An alcove off the living area appears to be some sort of study, with a desk and computer, a plush purple sofa and dark red walls, a large flat screen TV, and walls lined with bookshelves. I absolutely love this cozy cocoon or a room, and vow to spend as much time in it as I can. I plop down on the sofa, and look out the enormous window beyond the desk. This is when I notice there is a huge house sitting atop a hill not too far away. It is gorgeous, stately, and imposing.

"There you are," says Tio, peeking his head into the study.

"I love this room!"

"Isn't it great? My wife's study."

"She has good taste."

Tio smiles. "In everything but men, I hear."

I laugh. I like this guy.

"She loves movies, all kinds of movies, and in that cabinet there you'll find just about any DVD you might ever want to watch. Help yourself to all of it. That computer has satellite Internet, too, so use that freely."

"I really appreciate all this. When Rebecca said I'd be staying at a ranch, I imagined something a little more rustic."

"Thought you'd be camping?"

"Pretty much."

"Yeah, well, we don't come here much, but we keep it up to date, and we've got a cleaning girl who comes in once a month to make sure it looks lived in. We also ask Smith to check on the water and electric. That's his place up the hill there."

Tio points at the massive house in the distance.

"So that's where he hides the bodies," I joke.

Tio shakes his head. "Smith's a good kid. People around here get to talking and making things up when a man is too private, and that's what happened with him, I reckon. You'll learn pretty quick that gossip is the main pastime around here. Soon enough they'll be concocting a story for you, too."

"Great."

"Well, how about you come pick out your bedroom?" he suggests.

"Sure." I push myself up from the sofa.

"About Smith, if you need anything at all, he's almost

always around."

"Okay."

I follow him down a hallway, and he shows me three bedrooms, all with their own bathrooms attached.

"We designed it that way for guests," he says. "We wanted three master suites."

"Nice."

"Take your pick."

Each of the bedrooms is decorated in a distinct fashion, and with its own color scheme. There is a room that is very cowboy, with light wood paneled walls, and thick rustic wooden furniture. The lamp bases are iron sculptures of men on horseback with dogs. It's nice, but a bit masculine. The next room is done in more of a flowery feminine style, with gingham and even a collection of handmade rag dolls on a shelf in the corner. I like it, but it's still not quite me. The third room, though, as in the baby bear's bed to Goldilocks, is just right. It is spacious, with a fireplace, and warmly painted earth-tone walls, decorated with what Tio tells me are Navajo runs and Indian pottery. The feeling here is open, clean, and timeless.

"This one," I say.

"Good. I was hoping you wouldn't pick the cowboy room. That's mine."

I laugh, and Tio tells me that one of the secrets to his successful marriage is that he and his wife each have their own bedrooms, even at their main home. "I visit her in hers, she visits me in mine, and we keep our own space and sanity."

As I unpack my suitcases in "my" room, I almost forget, for a moment, that I am running for my life. This place feels like another planet, so remote and protected, so filled with good energy, that I am almost convinced that no one will ever be able to find me here.

Tio takes me out to the large, barn-like detached garage now, and shows me the flatbed pickup that makes its home there. He shows me how to drive it, and shows me the huge tank of gasoline behind the barn and says I am welcome to use as much as I need. There is a guy to call when the fuel level gets low, who will replenish it.

Then, he shows me how to load, aim, shoot and store the pistol, directing the bullets at some trees in the distance. I am trembling and nervous, but do what I can to master this new skill. Tio doesn't seem all that convinced about my abilities, but tells me to keep practicing, every day. He also tells me he's got plenty of ammunition for the thing stocked away in the workshop, which is apparently the small white building next to the barn.

After all that, Tio makes sure I've been briefed on the various systems in the house -- water, electrical, sewage, satellite TV and internet, (extensive) DVD collection, kitchen appliances, telephone, and a list of neighbors' phone numbers -- before apologizing and heading out to return to Santa Fe.

"Are you sure you don't want to rest?" I ask. "It's been a long drive."

"I assure you, I cannot," he says. "You'll be fine here. Keep in touch with us. Call every day, just so we know how things are going."

"Okay."

After he's gone, I settle in to watch a movie in the little study, on the purple sofa. I pick *Bringing Up Baby*, starring Katherine Hepburn -- something uplifting and old, a classic in black and white, from when things were less complicated and women could take care of themselves. I fix myself a sandwich and some microwave popcorn. Sometime while the film plays, the sun goes down, and I can see the lights going on in the house on the hill, and feel unnerved by the proximity of that beautiful, mysterious man.

Then the movie ends. I am sleepy, and afraid, and utterly lost. I have no idea what to do with myself next, and it hasn't hit me yet that this is it, I'm here, I've reached the end of the journey that adrenaline has been pushing me through for the past few days. My God, my life has changed. What am I doing here?

I know Tio locked the gates, and no one was coming

behind us, and that even if they were they wouldn't know the combinations or how to get in. I know I'm probably safe now, but at the deepest and most visceral level I also know now that nowhere is safe, and no place is free of the threat of death.

I go to the gun locker, and take out the black box that holds Tio's pistol. I release the safety and hold the gun the way he showed me. Then I re-engage the safety and sit alone with the firearm on my lap, on the puffy white sofa in the great room. I see stars coming out in the sky, more stars than I ever imagined were possible to see with the naked eye. This place, I think, is as beautiful as it is unforgiving.

This is when I hear a noise outside, a rustling, as though there were someone walking around out there, and I feel my grip tighten around the weapon. My mind tells me it's just the deer Tio told me come out in the evenings, or another animal, or the wind.

But my gut tells me it's something else, something human. I hold my breath, and I wait. I have never felt so uneasy in my life, nor so convinced that if I had to, I, too, could kill a man.

You have no idea how good that feels, until you need to feel it, and do.

JENNIFER

I am not proud of myself as I walk from the long driveway where I've left my Lexus, to the enormous heavy wooden front door of the luxurious adobe house that is home to Rebecca Baca, the half-sister I have never met. Of course her home is nicer and bigger than mine, even though I have worked hard for every penny I have and live quite well compared to most people.

I thought I'd be filled with conviction when I got here, bearing an invitation for Rebecca to come and meet her siblings at my house, but the truth is, I feel strange being here, ashamed. I don't know why. It's not *my* shame, it's his. My father's. *He* should be ashamed of how much more Rebecca got than I did. He should have treated us the same, but he didn't. I was the throwaway child. She was the one he loved.

I ring the doorbell, and wait. No one comes, and so I ring it again. This time I hear someone trying to unlock the door, over and over, without success. I hear a child's voice muttering something, something repetitive whose cadence is familiar to me, so familiar that at first it doesn't register as to why.

After a minute or two, the door opens, and there stands a little boy who appears to be light-skinned black, five or six years old, with his hair cut short and close to his head. He has a handsome, symmetrical face, and is lean. He wears jeans and a plain red t-shirt, and is barefoot. He looks past me, his eyes loosely focused somewhere near my knees, behind me, distant and utterly, completely isolated. Disconnected. I recognize this expression well.

"Hello," I say, my heart sinking as I realize this child is very much like my own brother, and very much like so many of my clients. The world is filled with these incredible, special human beings, with their secrets and their lonesomeness.

"Rain Bird sprinklers," says the boy, rocking back and forth on his feet. "Rain Bird sprinklers have the strongest spray. Rain Bird sprinklers."

"You like sprinklers?" I ask in a quiet tone of voice, instinctively kneeling down so that my face is at the same height as his own. He avoids my eyes.

"Rain Bird sprinklers," he repeats, and the rocking intensifies until it cannot contain whatever feeling he tries to keep at bay, and he must soothe himself by spinning in a circle. "Rain Bird sprinklers have the strongest spray. Toro has good rotors. Hunter has good valves."

"I like sprinklers, too," I say.

"Toro has good rotors. Hunter has good valves."

With my own brother, it was cars, the makes and models and years of all the cars in the world. He knew them all, and still does.

"Is your mother home?" I ask.

"Rain Bird sprinklers have the strongest spray," he says with a distant stare, and my heart breaks.

I reach out to touch this boy's arm, and he screams as though I've burned him. I hear feet running now, and then I see a young woman with blonde hair in a ponytail, a dishtowel in her hands, her face tired and worried.

"Connor!" she cries out to the boy. "Connor, it's okay. I'm here now."

"Does he have a safe spot?" I ask, referring to the quiet place autistics should always have for retreating to when they get overly agitated.

"A what?" she asks, and I realize that this young girl is not prepared to care for a child like this.

"Hello," I say, standing up.

"Hi," she says, surprised.

"My name is Jennifer Contreras," I tell her, holding my hand out professionally. "I'm sorry to alarm you. I rang the doorbell, and this charming young man answered."

The woman relaxes a little, hands the boy what appears to be a black sprinkler valve. The boy seems to take comfort in the thing, because his screaming and twirling scale back to the rocking once more.

"Toro has good rotors," he says.

"I'm Paula, Connor's nanny. This is Connor."

"Hello, Connor," I say. "Paula, it's nice to meet you. I'm here to see Rebecca."

"Is she expecting you?" asks Paula, concern in her eyes.

"Uhm, no. Not exactly. I'm not sure she'll even know who I am, but it's quite important. It's a family matter."

Paula's brows knit together with concern. "I think she's on a conference call right now, but I can interrupt her if you like."

"No, I don't want to bother her work. This is a personal matter, not urgent."

"Will she know what it's about?" asks Paula.

"I'm not sure. Well, no. Probably not. It's about – it's about her father."

At this moment, a very tall dark-skinned man, stunning-looking, walks up behind Paula in a navy blue suit with very subtle pinstripes. He wears a pink shirt with a beautiful patterned silk tie. I am shocked by how attractive I find him. He looks like a movie star.

"Paula?" he asks. "Is everything alright? I heard Connor screaming."

"He's fine. Just a little thrown off his schedule. He answered the door just now. I've never seen him do that before. It means he knew what the ringing bell meant. He was...connecting."

I am appalled that she is speaking of the child as though he were not there or could not hear her.

She continues, and my skin crawls. "I found him here with this woman who came to see Rebecca, something about her father."

The man looks closely at me, interest on his face, and then forces a smile through what appears to be slight unease.

"Hello, I'm Andre Cartier," he says, shaking my hand. His is warm and feels very good. It has been a long time since I felt drawn this powerfully to a man. "I'm Rebecca's husband. You've already met our son, Connor, and his nanny, Paula."

"Yes," I almost stammer, my eyes focused upon his gorgeous face. If he notices me blushing and staring, he doesn't let on, except for a brief second where his eyes seem to linger on my lips. I cannot be sure.

"Is there anything I can help you with?" he asks me.

I feel dizzy with nerves now. What am I doing here? I came here set to hate this woman, but already I have compassion for her because she has an obviously autistic son, an inept caregiver for the child, and a kindhearted husband. Of course she has a perfect husband. That's what happens when you're father loves you. When your father ignores you, you end up alone, like me. You end up afraid of men because they are a complete mystery to you.

"I'm Jennifer Contreras," I tell him, thinking your sister-in-law. "It's nice to meet you. I'm not sure you can help me, but maybe you can. Is there anywhere we could talk?"

I eye the boy and the nanny, and think to myself that the woman is not competent to care for Connor. The child knows this every bit as much as I do. There are so many charlatans out there, posing as autism experts, who know nothing about the disorder. There is a lot of money to be made off autism these days, it being the fashionable disorder. So many children are misdiagnosed with it, and so many who have it are improperly treated or not diagnosed. It is a crisis. Having grown up with my brother, I have almost a sixth sense for autism. I understand instinctively that this boy, Connor, is more present than any of the adults around him recognize. He's not as far gone as they treat him. He'd be easy to get through to, if only these people knew how.

"Mister Cartier, is there any way I might speak to you in private for a moment?"

Andre's eyes widen a little, then narrow as he steps back to make room for me in the grand foyer. "Yes, of course. Please, Miss Contreras, come in."

"I'm going to get Connor his lunch now," says Paula to her employer. "Connor? Lunch, honey."

"Rain Birds make the best arcs," says Connor, his

shoulders sinking in disappointment. He was actually curious about me, but these adults did not notice. This could have been a big learning moment for the child, meeting a stranger, but they don't know what they're doing. Connor looks at my knees, addressing me in his own way, and says, "They spray like rainbows."

"I like rainbows very much, Connor," I tell him. "I would like to learn more about sprinklers from you. Tell me about the Rain Birds. Next time I see you we will talk about it, okay?"

Connor rocks back and forth for moment, and then says, "Okay. Rain Birds and rainbows."

"Yes," I say, and my heart soars. Already, I've gotten through.

Paula and Andre look at me in astonishment.

"Shall we?" I ask Andre, not wanting to get into the discussion about their child right now. I came here for another purpose.

Rebecca's husband speaks to the nanny. "Thank you, Paula. I'll be by in a little while to say goodbye to you both before I leave for the office." He turns his attention to me. "Please, come right this way."

I follow him through the foyer, across a large and luxuriously furnished living room, and on into a bright hallway with dark, hardwood floors, to the end, where he steers me into a spacious home office and library. It is manly, decorated in dark wood and red and purple jewel tones, the home office of a very wealthy man. The kind of man who has never been interested in me.

"Please, have a seat."

I take a seat in one of the soft armchairs facing the desk. He surprises me by taking the seat next to me, rather than the one behind the desk.

"How may I help you?" he asks.

I feel my face reddening, as I try to come up with the right words to say. I stumble over my thoughts, stutter a bit, and choke down the feelings that just won't appear as words. I feel tears come, confused tears of anger and envy. This, I think, should have been me, living here, married to someone like this. But I got the throwaway mom. The absent dad. The lonesome life.

"I'm sorry," I say. "I don't know how to say this."

"I understand. You know something? You look a lot like her," he tells me, his dark eyes, so dark they are almost black, smile kindly at me.

"I'm sorry?" I ask. "I look like whom?"

"You look like Rebecca. My wife. You even have her same mannerisms, the way you fold your hands in your lap, and the way you look down at the floor when you're uncertain what to say. It's uncanny. You know, I never thought she took after her father, but to see you here now, it's clear that you both do."

He knows? I look at him and wipe a tear away. He jumps up and grabs a box of facial tissue from the desk, and hands it to me.

"Please, know you're among friends," he says. "Family."

"How did you know?" I ask.

"She told me."

"Rebecca?"

He nods.

"So she knows?"

"Yes. Her mother told her."

I nod, and try to stop crying. "I'm so sorry. I didn't think I'd get this emotional. It's just, I've actually just come here to invite Rebecca – to invite you both, really, now that I know about you – to come to brunch at my house and meet my sister and my brother. I don't know why I feel so nervous about it now. I was hoping to get past the ugliness of what our father did, and build bridges knowing that we are all in this together, and that we are siblings. I guess it just hurts, even though I try to get past it, knowing that he loved her more."

Rebecca's husband gives me a curious look now, as he tries to understand what I've just revealed. Too much, I think. You've told him too much.

"How much do you know about Rebecca's upbringing, Jennifer?" he asks me.

"I know that he'd drop presents off for us on Christmas like he was running some secret operation for the government, like he was a spy, then he'd leave us there and go running back to his real family."

"And how did that make you feel?"

"Terrible. I never really knew he was my dad, because she never told us, my mother didn't. But I feel terrible now that I know, and I remember how he acted."

"Your mother kept this from you?"

"Yes."

"That must have been very hard." His eyes are beautiful, and I feel like he's looking at me with more familiarity than I deserve. Probably the fact that I look like his wife sets him at ease with me. It also must mean that if he found her attractive, he also...but, no. I cannot be thinking like this. I came here to find my long-lost half-sister, not to seduce her husband.

"It was. It is."

"You feel a double betrayal now, I suppose. One from the father who never acknowledged you, and another from the mother who carried on with him and knew he was your father but never told you."

"Exactly."

"I am very sorry you've had to go through this. Rebecca's been having a very hard time of it as well. This is difficult for all of you, I'm sure."

"She got the best of him. She got his love."

Rebecca's husband looks at me as though I were very naïve. "Ah," he says. "Is that what you think?"

"Yes."

"Then I must respectfully say that you are correct in saying you did not know your father at all."

I think about what he's said and try to comprehend. "What do you mean?"

"I mean that sometimes, even if a father is in a house, or near a child, it doesn't mean that he loves that child as you seem to think he would."

"He didn't love her?"

"Perhaps he did, in his own exceedingly limited way."

Rebecca's husband tells me now about how my father has never spoken to him, in spite of his being madly in love with Rebecca and giving her the life she had always dreamed of. He tells me that both my father and his wife have never acknowledged or paid any attention to their grandson, Connor.

"I'm sorry," I find myself saying.

"Perhaps you're approaching this the wrong way," he suggests, with a warm smile.

"What do you mean?"

"I mean, might it be that a man who chooses to have children that he never acknowledges might not be a man to adequately love the children he does acknowledge?"

I consider his words.

"I am sorry you had to grow up without a father," he tells me, reaching out to me now to touch my hand. His touch is electric, and I recoil from it. He is looking at me in a certain way -- but perhaps I've misunderstood. He continues, "But sometimes I think it might be better to grow up without a father than it would be to grow up with a controlling and abusive father. What do you think?"

"He's autistic, your son?" I say, trying desperately to change the topic.

Rebecca's husband nods. "Yes. High-functioning, we are told."

"He's a beautiful child."

"Thank you."

"I have an autistic brother. Esteban. He reminds me a lot of him."

"Runs in families, perhaps."

"It can. I am a therapist for autistic children. That's my job."

Rebecca's husband's face lights up. "Are you really?"

"Yes. Down in Albuquerque."

"And how did you come to do that?"

"I guess it felt like a calling," I tell him, honestly, wondering as I do what it is about this man that makes him so very easy to talk to.

"That's quite admirable. It also explains why you

handled Connor so well earlier, when you came to the door. I've never seen him react the way he did. It was almost as though he conversed with you."

"He did converse with me, Mister Cartier. He can. He just needs some help to draw him out."

"Amazing." He shakes his head, and touches my shoulder now. This makes me quite uncomfortable, but I also like the attention.

"The local paper did a profile of me once, and dubbed me the Autism Whisperer, because they say I can get through to these kids when no one else can, sometimes."

"That's great. Good for you. I don't suppose, that if things smooth over between your respective families, that we might bring you in as a consultant for Connor?"

"I'd be honored. He's my nephew, after all."

"Yes, he is, isn't he?"

I know I shouldn't say what I'm about to say, but the impulse is too strong. "He's a handsome boy. He looks like his father."

My half-sister's husband smiles at me appreciatively, shyly, as though it has been a very long time since any woman paid him any attention, much less a compliment. It is a shame that in a world with so many despicable men in it, that any woman who happened across a gem like this wouldn't know what to do with him. I would absolutely know what to do with him. Repeatedly.

Perhaps, I think unkindly, frigidity runs in Rebecca's family. Like mother, like...

At that moment, a woman appears in the doorway, wearing a beautiful black suit that seems to be Chanel, with gold jewelry. She looks exactly like me. Her eyes are lasered in on mine, and I can see that she is thinking that I look exactly like her. She is also wondering why her husband's hand is on my shoulder, and probably why he is looking at me with such affection. From the look on her face, she has been expecting as much from him, but did not expect it now.

Men. Who can trust them?

"Andre?" she asks, and her wavering voice betrays

worry.

"Rebecca," says her husband, standing up nervously, guiltily, to greet her. He coughs, as though his conscience has gotten stuck in his throat, and says, "Please, come in, darling. There's someone here I'd like for you to meet."

LAUREN

I wake up in the complete darkness, to a loud thud outside. It takes me a few seconds to remember where I am, and even *who* I am. I'm in the house on Tio's ranch, on the white sofa in the living area, with a gun still in my lap, and a wet spot on my cheek where I've been drooling against the armrest. I guess I was exhausted and slipped down into sleep. Holding a gun. Great. For the record? This is not advisable. For anyone. Actually, nothing about my life right now is advisable for anyone. Just don't be me. Ever. That is all.

There are two enormous picture windows in front of me, without any sort of covering on them, and the expansive grasslands and distant rounded hilltops outside are bathed in a soft and eerie blue light from the full moon. The room is completely silent, which strikes me as weird. I could have sworn there was noise before, like the refrigerator humming at least. Maybe it was the air conditioner. I don't know. I just know I don't want to be here. I am not happy.

My heart is racing as my ears strain against the silence for a hint of the sound that roused me. I reassure myself that there are probably all sorts of things that go bump in the night out here. Tio had told me about the deer that come in to graze at night, and the coyotes that prowl around. I'm much safer here, I remind myself, than I would be in my apartment back in Boston.

As soon as I remember my home, I begin to feel sorry for myself. Then I remind myself that I'm at least alive, which would probably not be the case back in Beantown. This is only temporary, I tell myself. It's going to get better.

Thud.

The sound comes again, something bumping hard against the front of the house, just outside those picture windows. I can feel the sound in the floorboards every bit as much as I hear it with my ears. Whatever is out there, it is close. My heart feels like it's about to burst, or beat itself to a stop. What the hell *was* that? I hold the gun with shaking hands and try to calm myself down.

I see something moving outside, out of the corner of my eye. I turn toward the motion, and see that it is a dark blue shadow, tall like a man or a bear, against the woodpile near the porch. I gasp as it moves again, slowly, methodically. I see it raise what appears to be a hand, or a paw, and wipe its face. The grace of the movement, and the slightness of the body, make me realize with a feeling of sickness that this is not a bear.

It is a man.

My first impulse is to hide, to run back to one of the bedrooms and bury my head under the covers until this whole nightmare ends. But this is life or death. I am going to have to rise to the occasion, or die. I have to fight back. I knew this would happen. It was stupid to come somewhere this isolated in trying to get away. I would have been better off in a big city like Chicago, where I'd blend right in. This is nonsense. What is wrong with me?

"Oh, God," I whisper, sharp hot tears stinging the backs of my eyeballs.

I watch the man. He is tall, about the height of Jason Flynn in fact, and moving slowly. Creeping, really. Up to the window. I stay very still, wondering if he is able to see inside. It is much lighter out there, so chances are he cannot see me.

Yet.

I sit very still, and aim the gun as well as I can, following Tio's advice, and hold it steady, my sites set on the man's head. I want to squeeze the trigger, but what if I'm wrong? What if it's *not* the guy? What if it's a bear? What if there's nothing there at all? What if I'm losing my stinkin' mind?

Thud.

I hear it again, and this time the man moves with speed, out of view. Where did he go? It was horrible to see him, but it's even worse not to see him anymore. Oh, God. I can't take this. I'm in a panic. I don't want to die. Not here. Not like this. I want my mommy. Well, yeah. I know.

Pathetic. But you can't control the kinds of things that come to your mind in moments like this.

Just then, I hear a loud boom, and the picture window shatters. It takes me a moment to register that the kickback from the gun in my hand has mashed me hard against the back of the sofa. My finger is still squeezed against the trigger, and my ears ring from having been so close to a fired weapon. I did it, I realize. I shot the window out. I wasn't even thinking about it, and it happened. I was so scared that I just panicked, and pulled.

I hear feet on the porch now, moving fast, and then a rattling as someone tries to open the front door. I point the gun and try to squeeze the trigger again, but nothing happens. Just a click. In horror, I watch as the door creaks open, and a man steps through.

"Hello?" calls a familiar voice. "Miz Fernandez? Are you okay?"

The lights flip on, and I am momentarily blinded and disoriented, too scared to move, frozen in shock on the sofa with the gun in my hands. I hear the sound of the refrigerator humming back to life. And the air conditioner.

"Miz Fernandez?" comes the man's voice.

I blink and squint, and recognize him as the cowboy from the bar earlier in the day. Smith. John Smith. The guy who lives up the hill. He is without his hat now, and I see that his hair is dark brown, peppered with white. I scream as I instantly assume he is somehow associated with the people who are out to get me in Boston. They must have gotten to him and sent him here.

"Please don't kill me!" I shriek.

"Put the gun down," he says calmly. "Get ahold of yourself."

He appears unarmed, but I'm not about to relinquish my weapon to anyone. I should not notice this, but he is every bit as attractive with his hat off as he was with it on. I know. I'm a stupid girl. This is the last thing that should occur to me, but the mind does its own thing sometimes.

"Please put the gun down," he tells me. He takes calm, large steps toward me, his eyes roving over me and the gun in my hand, sizing it all up.

"No," I say. "I'm not going to let you kill me. Don't come any closer, or I'll shoot you."

John looks at the gun in my hand, smiles at me and shakes his head. "Seriously doubt that," he says, still coming closer.

"I will!"

"You'd have to reload," he says. "And you'd have to stop trembling. And you've have to know how to hold that thing. And you'd have to have good aim."

"I know all that."

He frowns at me, almost upon me now. "Put it down before you hurt yourself."

"It's you I'm going to hurt."

He seems to sigh, and this angers me. I have no idea how to reload this gun, of course, but I was at least hoping to bluff my way out of this.

The cowboy keeps walking toward me, relaxed.

"Stay back!" I shriek.

"Are you alone here?" he asks, still moving toward me. He is almost upon me now.

"Yes," I say. "But I'm armed."

Before I realize what's happened, he has calmly and gently squeezed my wrist in such a way as to open my fingers, taken the gun out of my hand and into his own. He engages the safety lock, and tucks the weapon into his waistband.

"You okay?" he asks. "What's going on here?"

"Please don't hurt me," I say.

He looks offended, and a bit angry. "Lady, why would I *hurt* you?"

"Why are you here?"

"Well," he says. "It's called being neighborly around here. I don't suppose you'd know much about that. Listen. You and I are on the same power grid. Wind knocked out some lines over on my place, and I saw that the electric was out over here, too. I got the system working again, and I was being helpful and making sure all your breakers were working. I didn't want you to wake up without electricity and freak out. Out here it's not like you can just call the power company. You have to take care of these things yourself."

"Oh," I say, feeling foolish now, but still suspicious.

"Why on earth would you go shooting at me?" he asks.

"I thought..." I start to tell him the truth, but think better of it. "I don't know."

"Look, this ain't the city. You're not going to have peeping Toms or whatever around here, okay? All you're going to have is me, or maybe some animals. That's about it. And you're a lot more likely to get hurt by an animal than you are by me."

"Please don't lecture me. I didn't ask you to come over in the middle of the night," I remind him.

John looks insulted, but patient. "No, but Turnbull asked me to keep an eye on the place while you're here, including the power and water, so I was fixing the electric for you. Most people would be grateful someone was looking out for them."

"Thank you."

John looks at the shattered window, and whistles through his teeth. "You did a number on that thing. God *damn*."

"I know."

"How the hell are we going to get that window fixed?" he muses to himself.

"I don't know. Put new glass in it?"

He laughs at me. "You have any idea how hard it is to get glass out here, over that rocky road?"

"I can imagine."

"Were you actually trying to *shoot* me?"

"No. I mean, yes. I think so. But I didn't know it was you. I thought it was..." I stop myself short, before I tell too much.

John looks at me for a long moment. Then he shakes his head like he thinks I'm crazy.

I say, "I'm sorry. I don't know what I was doing. I just kind of panicked."

"You do that a lot? Panic?"

"Lately, yes."

"That's good to know" he says. He looks at me as though figuring something out. "Were you always this jumpy?"

I shake my head. "Just so you know, I have good reason. I can't talk about it. Just know I'm not paranoid. I'm not stupid. And I'm not crazy. Well, not for that reason, anyway."

"Ain't none of my business," he says, looking at the window still. "We gotta get that hole patched up here pretty quick. I'm not sure it's smart for anyone to sleep in a house that coyotes and snakes and bears can come into any old time they feel like."

"Snakes?"

"Rattlesnakes, darlin'. We got 'em by the truckload out here. They like to come out at night during these hot summer months."

He stands up and goes to get a closer look at the broken window.

"Good lord," he says. "Yeah, I'd say you did a number on it. Jesus. Guess I have to go get some plywood and come fix this thing up now." He looks at me with great annoyance. "Not like I have anything better to be doing. Shit."

"You don't have to do that," I say.

"If I don't, who will? *You?*"

I can't think of an answer. I shake my head.

"Christ," he gripes. "Well, I'd rather patch it up now than have to deal with you when you get snake bit."

"I can call Jasper," I suggest.

John shakes his head. "You have to call him, but there's not a hell of a lot he can do right now."

"Can it wait until morning?" I ask.

John looks at his watch. "Darlin', it's five already. Morning's here. We don't wait for the sun to come up to get to work on a ranch. I'll be back in a bit to patch this up. Then I'll get on the phone to the glass guy and see what we can work out for later in the week."

"Thanks."

"You bet," he says, sarcastically. "Welcome to the neighborhood."

Then, he turns to leave, without another word. I sit there helplessly on the sofa, watching his backside as he walks out the door, and hating the fact that it looks *so* very, very good in those jeans.

USNAVYS

When the big, angry knock comes on my door the next morning, I am not prepared, m'ija. I knew the bank letters and the sheriff's letters said they'd be here, but I thought something might happen. I thought it might have just been empty threats to make me pay up. I don't know what I thought. I didn't think they'd actually come, though. I'm in bed with my curlers in when they knock. And when I don't answer right away, they just open the door themselves and walk right in like they owned the place, which I guess they do.

I run out of the bedroom in my robe and slippers, with my eyes all puffy from crying all night. Juan is gone, and he didn't even help me pack any of our things. I look at the wall of people coming through the door, and I scream. I don't know what else to do.

"Please!" I tell them. "Give me one more day to get organized. I forgot you were coming."

I didn't even do the dishes from last night. They're all still dirty in the sink. And the bathrooms are a mess. Everything is falling apart, and I am embarrassed for all these people to see the house like this, to see the way I've been living in the few days since Juan left. I haven't had the energy to do anything but lay in bed. Two days ago, the bank came for my car. I don't even have a car anymore, and now I'm losing my house. This can't be happening. But it is.

"Sorry, ma'am," says the policeman, handing me an eviction notice. "This property is being foreclosed upon today, and you have to vacate the premises immediately."

"But I'm not even dressed."

"You can get dressed. Have you made arrangements for moving or storage?"

"No."

"Then you might want to start thinking about that now. Your belongings will be removed whether you have made other arrangements or not. I'm sorry, but you should have had plenty of warning and time to prepare."

I watch in horror as moving men begin to take my things and put them in common household trash bags. There must be ten moving guys here. Some are already carrying the furniture down to the street.

"Where are you putting it?" I ask of the furniture.

"On the curb," says one of the moving men, without looking at me. I can tell he's afraid to look me in the eye, because of the pain he might see there.

"Look at me, you coward!" I demand. He ignores me. "How can you live with yourself?" I ask him. "How can you look at yourself in the mirror doing this to people every day."

"We all have to make a living, ma'am," he says, still unable to meet my eyes. "You don't know nothing about me."

"You can't!" I shriek.

No one answers me, and the forced removal continues. I have never felt so violated in my life, so misused and so disgusting.

I rush to what used to be my bedroom, and throw some clothes on. I look out the window at the front sidewalk downstairs, and sure enough these motherfuckers are just leaving my furniture and the open trash bags of my stuff there, on the street, like garbage. The neighbors have already started to stand on their porches to watch, and not a single of them is coming over to ask what's going on because they know, it's obvious.

"Oh, my God," I cry, shoving myself into a dress and zipping it up the back. I put on some heels, and try to get the rollers out of my hair. It's a mess, nena, so I pull it back in a ponytail and tie a scarf over the whole thing. I find my largest sunglasses and put them over my face. I don't want anyone to recognize me. Or at least to see my eyes. I want out of this life. I hate myself. My life. Everything. The world. This is the worst day of my life. None of my friends live in Boston anymore, and I don't know who to call to help me. I can't let any of the sucias know about what's going on. They'd be shocked and think less of me, and I can't stand to think about it. They'd know I have been lying to them.

I go back to the living room, and watch. These guys are fast. The living room is already empty. They've started on the bedrooms now.

"Where is it going to go?" I ask the sheriff's deputy.

"That's up to you. We're attaching the cost of moving to what you already owe."

"This is my house!" I scream.

"Not anymore. You should call someone for other arrangements."

I go back into my bedroom, and try to stop the tears. Where is Juan? I call his cell phone, but he doesn't answer. I leave a message for him, telling him that all of our stuff is being thrown onto the street. Before I know it, the movers are in my room, taking my things, treating them terribly, bumping and crashing them around.

"Stop it!" I cry, but it's like they can't even hear me. They keep moving, like robots. "Please! I've got job applications out. I know I'll find something soon!"

Everyone ignores me, and so I just grow numb, and terrified, and I stand back to watch helplessly as my life is dismantled and tossed away. Soon, the house is empty and the officer is coming to remove me.

"Let me make one more call," I beg.

"Go ahead," he tells me. "But make it quick."

I pick up the phone and struggle for a moment to remember the number. I haven't called her in nearly twenty years, not since I left, but I know she's still in the same housing project apartment where I grew up, because like everyone else there she has never considered for a moment that there might be something better waiting for her out there and so she's never seen any reason to leave. She probably still has the same phone number. I haven't called her, but she has called me, every holiday, just to see how I was doing. I've gone over there, of course, to drop off expensive gifts and to brag about how great I was doing.

I can't believe I have to do this. I can't believe it has

come to this.

I punch in the number, and she picks up on the second ring.

"M'ija?" she asks, without saying hello. "Are you okay? How are my grandbabies?"

My mother has a sixth sense about these things, sometimes, either that or she realizes that the only reason I'd call her was if there were a problem.

I tell her what's happening. I don't sugarcoat it. I say it directly and matter-of-fact, because my mother has always been poor, and this sort of nightmare is nothing new to her. I tell her, "I lost my job. Juan left me. He took the kids. They're taking the house today. The repossessed my car last week. I don't have anywhere to go, and I'm out of money."

"Do you have money for a cab?" she asks me.

"All my shit is on the damn front yard, mami," I tell her. "It's not going to fit in a cab."

I hear her sigh. "Let me make some calls, mi vida," she says, using her pet name for me, "my life," and without a trace of judgment or disappointment in her voice. "I'm sorry this is happening, but you're strong and you'll get through it."

"I don't have time for you to make calls, mami, they're throwing me out right now."

I feel my voice crack as the tears come, in spite of my effort to hold them at bay.

"Listen to me," says my mother. "You have to be stronger than this. Usnavys, do you hear me?"

"Yes."

"All that stuff, the fancy house and the nice furniture, it's just things, m'ija. It doesn't matter."

"Of course it matters! It's my home."

"Nothing matters more than family," she says. "And home is where the heart is, not a building."

"It's all gone," I whine. "I'm so scared, mami."

"I know, mi vida. I know. But I know you. You are a fighter, hija. You can do this."

"But I'm so alone. I've lost everything."

"Stay right where you are, hija," she says, in a way that cracks my world open like an egg. "You haven't lost everything. You haven't lost me. I'll be right there."

REBECCA

Judy is setting the table in the formal dining room. I've dressed for Sunday dinner, in a white linen shift that hits mid-calf, and a pair of beige sling backs. Paula is getting Connor ready for his evening routine of purple dinner, bath and bedtime, and I'm not sure where Andre is. My husband of course knows that this is the big night, the night my mother has actually finally agreed to come out of the guesthouse and join us for dinner in our home. All of us. She has agreed to sit down with my husband and me, and share a meal with us, and she has given me her word that she is not going to cause a scene or do anything stupid. She was reluctant, but I told her that if she wished to continue to stay with us that she was going to have to make an effort to at least pretend like she was part of the family. I reminded her that my husband was the man who had built these houses, that it was his brainpower and hard work that was providing the shelter she needed now, and I also reminded her, perhaps unkindly, that it was the philosophy of hatred espoused by my father that also led him to believe women were inferior and therefore enabled him to mistreat her for so many years.

The dining room looks perfect, with a custom-designed centerpiece. The house is redolent with delicious smells, too. We are having lamb chops with a minted cucumber salad and rice pilaf. Well, most of us are. Connor refuses to eat anything that isn't purple. This is his latest obsession. Judy is a fantastic cook, and has so far been able to disguise many healthy foods in purple coloring. I stand at the head of the table and look around. This room, this whole house, it could be in an architectural or interior design magazine. It is perfect. But I feel so tired of it all. I feel that this is someone else's life. I can't recall the last time I had a good, long laugh.

I hear the garage door, and am relieved that Andre has come home. The way he's been acting lately, still friendly enough and supportive but just the slightest bit chilly and preoccupied, has had me worried, silently of course, that he might be considering...a *change*. I have resolved, in the throes of this nightmare my mother is living through, that I should do all I can to try to rekindle the romance with my husband. I'm not blaming myself for the frost between us, but I am also not ruling out that I might be to blame. My mother has been here a week, but he still hasn't seen her. He avoids her. He says that when they meet, it will be because she has come to him, and not the other way around.

I wait in the mudroom off the laundry room, for my husband to come through the door from the garage. He appears, in a suit, holding a paper cup from Starbucks.

"Well, hello there," he says, surprised to find me here.

I step toward him, and brush his cheek with my hand. I look at his mouth, which was always my favorite part of him, and then at his eyes.

"Kiss me," I say, trying to sound seductive.

He seems taken aback, and does as I have asked. There is nothing to the kiss, though. No spark, no heat, no willingness on his part. There is, however, the hint of a taste of...what? Lip-gloss? It can't be.

I try to kiss him harder, and he withdraws. He doesn't want me anymore. I have suspected it, but I feel it certainly now. My heart is crushed, but I don't know how to bring it up, not here, not now, not before our dinner with my mother. I was hoping I'd been wrong, that Andre still felt it for me, that we could reconnect now before having to face her together.

"How was your day?" he asks, on autopilot. No, I think. There's nothing really wrong. There's nothing major. He hasn't been cheating on me. He doesn't have a secret family. But there is this wall between us, unspoken, unnamed. But real.

"Productive," I say. "And yours?"

He moves past me with a polite pat to my back. "Oh, you know. The usual. Meetings and more meetings. All good, though."

I follow him into the kitchen. Judy is taking the lamb

from the broiler.

"Smells great," says Andre to her.

"Thank you."

Andre finds the stack of mail in the basket by the kitchen computer and sorts through it, scowling. He won't even look at me. It seems like forever since he looked at me at all, much less the way he used to.

"Andre," I say.

He continues to examine the mail in his hands, and answers without looking up. "Yes, darling?"

"Can you come upstairs for a minute?"

This catches him off guard, and he looks at me. "Why? What's wrong?"

Judy, to her credit, pretends not to hear any of this.

"Nothing's wrong," I tell him. "It's just that I'd like to speak with you for a minute before dinner."

"Is your mother still joining us?" he asks.

"Yes."

He looks at his watch. "In that case, if you don't mind I'd like to put off this conversation you'd like to have, unless it's urgent, in favor of a quick shower and change of clothes."

I smile sadly, but nod. "Sure," I say. "A shower would probably be refreshing right now."

"Pretty hot out there," he says, loosening his tie and walking toward the back stairs off the pantry. "I'll be down in a bit."

Fifteen minutes later, I walk to the guesthouse to retrieve my mother. I would like to have brought Connor with me, the way you could do with a neurologically typical child, but Connor is thrown off terribly by any major changes or deviations to his rigid routine. Children like Connor do best when things are predictable. Then again, I think bitterly as I knock on the door to the guesthouse, so do we all.

My mother opens the door. She is fresh-scrubbed, and dressed nicely in a pastel peach pantsuit. I tell her she looks lovely, and she returns the compliment, shutting the door behind her. I see from her face that she is worried, though. I would like to be able to reassure her, but we're not that kind of family. I'm not sure how I'd say something to set her at ease.

"The roses are looking good," I say, nodding toward the small rose garden Andre had put in for me back when he built this home for us.

"They're beautiful," says my mother.

"How are you holding up?" I ask her.

"That girl came to see me," she says.

"Which girl?"

"Jennifer Contreras."

"She did?" I ask in astonishment. I stop walking, and look at my mother in disbelief.

"She's got a lot of nerve," says my mother.

"I think she's just got a lot of resentments," I say, remembering my own meeting with her earlier that week. "And a lot of questions. I feel sorry for her, actually."

"She wanted to know why I never reached out to her," my mother spits.

"And what did you tell her?" I ask.

"I told her the truth. That I didn't know about her being his until she sent me those papers about his DNA."

"How did she take that?"

"She has his temper," my mother says unhappily. "Honestly, I'm a little bit afraid of her."

"She's harmless."

"She told me your husband told her she could start consulting as an autism expert for Connor," my mother tells me, and I stop walking, in shock.

"She what?"

My mother repeats herself.

"I can't believe that's true," I say.

"Sometimes we don't know what our husbands are doing when we're not around," she tells me bitterly. "But if I were you, from the way that Jennifer's eyes got all soft when she talked about your husband, I'd watch out."

"I beg your pardon?"

"I think she is in love with your husband. There, I said it."

"That's ridiculous," I say.

My mother looks like she's fighting back tears again. "That son of a bitch," she says softly, not talking about Andre anymore. "He took the best of me. The best years of my life. Wasted."

"Have you talked to him?" I ask.

"No. I haven't called him, and he hasn't called me."

"I'm sorry."

"I'm not. If I never talk to him again, I'll be a happy woman," she says as we reach the back door to the main house.

Andre is already standing in the dining room when I lead my mother in, and I know this is by design. He wants to make sure that she is aware at every moment that she is coming to him on his terms, in his house, and that he is in complete and utter control. I feel sick as we all converge in the dining room, because I don't know how to do this. I don't know how to put all of us together, to try to find peace, if we can. I don't know how to be this woman's daughter and this man's wife, at the same time. I've never been able to do it before, and it is completely new territory.

"Mrs. Baca," says Andre. He flashes her a charming yet defensive smile, and holds one hand out to her as a challenge.

My mother swallows hard, takes a deep breath, and reaches for his hand. The look on her face resembles that of a woman being forced to clean a dog kennel after a very sick dog has been in it. It's as though she thinks blackness will wear off, like it's contagious.

"Hello," she says.

"Welcome to our home," he says. He looks at me critically now, and I realize instantly why. Over the years, you learn to understand what someone's facial expression means, and this one means that he is disappointed that I've chosen to stand at her side rather than at his. I move myself, so that I am next to him. I try to take his arm, to loop mine through his, but he subtly resists. This hurts me more than you might think, because there is so much unspoken in the gesture. The wall is up, and it is staying up.

"It's a beautiful house," my mother tells him. "You have very good taste."

She says this last part as though she is surprised by it, and I know that the subtext is "for a black man," as does Andre. He winces and I can tell he's biting his tongue.

Judy comes in now, and tells us the meal is ready. I can hear Connor and Paula at the kitchen table, talking about sprinklers. How I despise sprinklers now. I know they have nothing to do with my son's disorder, but they are the means with which he connects to the rest of the world from his place of solitude. I hate them because they are a poor bridge to my son's heart and mind. It would be nice, in a perfect world, to have Connor join us, but he is so set in his routine that to bring him to this room to eat would potentially set him off. My mother has never met her grandson, and that is not likely to change tonight.

"Please," I say to my husband and my mother. "Have a seat."

Andre takes his place at the head of the table, and I take mine directly next to him. My mother takes the seat opposite mine, and does not wait for his cue to put her cloth napkin in her lap. She knows better. She does this to defy his authority over her, and it makes me angry. Andre's body language is stiff and defensive, as he catches the slight, too.

"The paintings look very expensive," muses my mother. "Are they replicas?"

Andre smiles slightly to himself, and looks down at the table, breathing slowly and deliberately in order to keep himself calm.

Mercifully, Judy sashays in and serves us now, setting the plates before us with grace. My mother's face remains impassive and I cannot tell whether she approves of the meal or not. I realize logically that it is ridiculous to care so much what she thinks, but I still desperately yearn for her approval of the life I've built for myself.

"Wine?" Judy asks us.

Andre and I agree. My mother shrugs as though she

doesn't care. Judy pours a small amount of red wine into Andre's glass. He swirls it to test the legs, sniffs it, and then samples it.

"It will do," he tells our cook.

My mother's mouth tightens as though she found his display of wine expertise disconcerting. Of course she does, I think. In her mind, black people should be drinking from pig troughs.

We begin to eat, in silence. Awkward silence. I watch, and wait. We are halfway through the meal, and each of us down two glasses of wine, before anyone speaks.

"What did you do today, mom?" I ask as Judy pours more wine for us. I don't tend to drink much, if at all, but I could really use the liquid courage right now.

"Watched TV, sat around," she says with a poignant sigh. "The usual things depressed people who've wasted their lives on lying bastards do."

Andre seems annoyed by this. My husband can be very compassionate, but one thing he cannot stand is when people wallow in self-pity. Life, he likes to say, is not fair, and the best way to handle it is to take the hand you've been dealt, and make the most of it. He is not fond of complainers.

"I am very sorry for what you're going through, Mrs. Baca," says my husband, sincerely. The wine has loosened him up a bit. His shoulders have relaxed, and his brow is smooth.

I watch in amazement as my mother gulps down her entire glass of wine. She has the mouth of a snake, as though she's unhooked her jaw. I have never seen her so desperate to get something down her throat. She looks at him, and smiles. It isn't a big smile, but it is a smile. For the first time in my life, I watch my mother smile at a black person as if they were just people, like herself.

"Let me ask you something, Andre."

My husband awaits what comes next, with diminishing patience.

"Do you love my daughter?" she asks.

Andre looks at me, and smiles in a sad sort of way

that makes me want to cry. "More than life itself," he tells my mother.

She looks at me. "Does he make you happy?"

I feel a pit yawning in my gut. He used to, I think. He used to make me very happy.

"Yes," I say. "Andre makes me happy." It is not entirely untrue; we have a comfortable life, and we don't fight or scream like some couples do. Maybe this dull homeostasis is simply what happens in a marriage after a while.

Andre turns his eyes from whatever he's seen in my own, and my mother speaks to him again. "Do you cheat on her?"

Andre seems shocked by the question, and offended. "Excuse me?" he asks. "You have not just come into my home and accused me..."

"Oh, don't go getting all pissed off," says my mother, using a term for angry that I've never heard escape her lips before. She's drunk. "It's just a question. Answer me honestly. Do you cheat on my daughter?"

Andre looks at me, indignant but with a bit of defensiveness that I find upsetting. What is he hiding? "Of course not," he says. "Why would you even ask such a thing?"

"Because I think all men cheat," says my mother, grabbing the wine bottle herself without waiting for Judy this time, and filling her glass nearly to the top.

"Mother," I chide.

"No," says Andre to me, before turning his attention to her again. "It's okay. I can understand, after what she's been through, why your mother might have some doubts about my gender."

"It's in your DNA," she says, her eyes narrowing sadly as she stares into the dark red of the wine.

"It is in man's DNA to make choices and control his actions," says Andre. "That is what sets us apart from the rest of the animal kingdom, this ability to act selflessly because it is the right and moral thing to do."

My mother laughs bitterly.

"Do all men live up to their potential as ethical beings?" he asks rhetorically. "Unfortunately, no. But just because some of us fail to love and care for the women in our lives as we should, this is not reason to blame the entirety of our group for the transgressions of a few."

"It is more than a few."

"Perhaps," he says. "But I am not among them. This I assure you."

"When is the last time you had sex with my daughter?" my mother asks, and I find myself so astonished by the question that I've spit wine out in a coughing fit.

Andre looks at me, as astonished as I am.

"Mother, please," I say as I wipe my mouth with my napkin.

"I know it's nosy," she tells me. "But one of the things I should have done better as a mother is prepare you for marital life, for a man's hungers and needs. I never spoke about it. I don't know if you understand the needs a man has, physical needs, that is different from the needs we women have."

"I am aware of my husband's needs," I say, knowing as I do that my statement is hollow, because we haven't had sex in a very long time.

My mother observes me for a long moment, her brow furrowing deeper and deeper. "You were always cold, just like me," she says. "I watched it, and I felt good about it, because I knew you were a good Catholic girl without too many appetites. But now I understand that God gave us appetites to please our husbands. He wanted her because she wanted sex. I wanted it too, but I didn't feel like he would respect me if I showed him that side of me. He needed me chaste, sabes. And now I ruined you by sending you those signals, by making you ashamed of your own God-given lusts."

I gasp, and clap my hand over my mouth to keep from saying something I might regret. My own mother, calling me frigid? I might have been at one time, I admit that, but Andre changed all that. Loving Andre, in the beginning, it was remarkable. My first husband, Brad, was not exciting to me, physically, but Andre, with his confidence and sparkling eyes, that changed me.

"I don't want to talk about any of this," I state. "This is completely inappropriate."

"One of the things I should have done better as a wife was make sure he was satisfied in the bedroom," says my mother, talking as though to herself. I feel my cheeks blaze red. I don't want to hear about her sex life with my father. I cannot believe she is even discussing it, in polite company, at the dinner table.

"Mother, stop. This isn't the time or place."

My mother waves me away. "If not now, when? It's too late for me, but I don't think it's too late for you. Men have their needs." My mother looks at Andre. "And your kind, their needs are even stronger than our kind."

"Mother!" I shout.

"My *kind*?" asks Andre, insulted and amused at the same time. "What does that mean, *exactly*, Mrs. Baca? *My kind*?"

"The blacks."

Andre laughs, and I am so mortified I want to hide beneath the table.

"Oh, yes, that's right," says Andre. "We're animals, aren't we? We have to have it ten times a day, with different women every time, because no one woman would be enough for our enormous…"

"Andre!" I stop him.

"She started it, love," he tells me. He tries to affect a calm demeanor but I can tell he's furious.

"Mother, Andre is faithful to me, and we have a wonderful married life. Now, please, stop insulting us in our own home or we will both be forced to ask you to leave. You knew the parameters when you came here."

"I was only trying to help," she says, incredibly. She truly does not see anything wrong with her racist attitudes.

"Well, stop," I say.

"How was your lamb?" Andre asks me, his face still

flushed with the anger he stifles. "Mine was excellent."

"Very good. Probably the best she's done yet."

"Agreed."

I look at him with a deep apology in my eyes. I am so sorry, I think. For so many things. I am sorry for not being able to bear him a child. I am sorry that the child we worked so hard to bring into the world via our surrogate came into the world broken. I am sorry that the brokenness seems to have come from my side, from my father, because otherwise why would my half-sister Jennifer have an autistic brother? I am sorry that life since Connor has been nothing as we had imagined life as parents would be. I am sorry that the stress of it all has driven a wedge between us that I am not sure can ever be removed. I am sorry he is probably seeking affection elsewhere. I am sorry I cannot recall what it was like to feel my husband's longing for me, his hands on me, his mouth...

"Andre," I say, aching to tell him my sorrows but unable to find a way to do it. I want that flame in my belly for him to rekindle, but I can't find it. Why can't I feel anything for him anymore? Why does this happen?

He turns his eyes toward my mother. "And you?" he asks her. "How was your lamb?"

My mother looks at me, then back at him. "She's lonely, my daughter," my mother tells him. "If you'd look at her close, you'd see that. But she loves you. I know her well enough to see it."

"Mother, stop! That's enough."

"Perhaps a little less wine, Mrs. Baca? From what Rebecca tells me, you've never been much of a drinker. I think it's having a very strong effect on you now."

"I need it for now," she says.

"Why is that?"

"To get through this pain."

"Time will heal you," he offers as he gets up to clear his place. He walks behind my mother and, astoundingly, places a reassuring hand on her back. "I know it is incredibly difficult now. Just keep breathing, put one foot in front of the other, and carry on with life. Before you know it, the pain will have begun to dissipate. I promise. You will emerge from this a happier woman, and a stronger one."

"You know what? I deserve it. We all get what we deserve in life," she tells him, point blank.

"Now, I don't know about that," says Andre, taking her plate for her. "I don't think anyone deserves what you're experiencing."

My mother sets her knife and fork down, and swigs down her entire glass of wine. Then she reaches out, and takes my husbands forearm in her hand.

"For being a frigid wife," she tells him as tears pour down her cheeks. "And I was. I never had sex with my husband, except to try to make a baby. Isn't that a shame?"

"Mother!"

"Do you like sex with each other? Is it enjoyable?" she asks us.

"I think you need to get to bed," I tell her.

"Because I never did. I didn't try. I knew he had appetites. I didn't meet that need. She did. She was always dressed provocatively. She made him feel like a man. I couldn't do that. Not like she did. I wanted to, but I didn't know how. It seemed sinful."

"You cannot blame yourself," says Andre.

My mother shakes her head. "I deserve every minute of what I'm getting, and you know it. If for no other reason than how I've treated you. And," her eyes stray to the door leading to the kitchen. "And my grandson."

Andre, always the most in-control person I have ever known, seems completely thrown off by this display of remorse from my mother. He blinks at her, unmoving, unable to think of a response. Finally, he shakes himself, and regains composure.

"We are what we are," he tells her kindly, as he walks away from her, slowly, toward the kitchen. He calls out over his shoulder as he goes. "And I suppose the best that any of the rest of us can do in life is to understand that people are what they are, and accept them anyway. I can accept you. It isn't easy, but I can."

My mother begins to cry. She calls out to stop him from leaving the room.

"Andre. Son. You are wise," she tells him. "And you are right. But accepting someone as he is does not mean liking him."

Andre stiffens again, offended, until my mother clarifies her statement.

"I am not talking about you, mi hijito," she says, wiping a tear from her eye. "I accept you, and I think I just might even *like* you. No. I am talking about your father-in-law. I was his wife, yes. But you know what? I don't think I ever liked him very much. I accept him now, and I accept what he did. But I hate him."

LAUREN

I shower hurriedly in the spacious and elegantly-appointed master bathroom, and get dressed in low-rise jeans, a padded bra that is very flattering, and a form-fitting tank top before digging around for some breakfast things in the kitchen. I make a pot of Starbucks coffee in the Italian silver coffee maker, and put some bread in the somewhat too complicated toaster. Then I find a broom in the laundry-room closet and start to sweep up the broken glass while I wait for John to return to fix my window. And, yes, I have dressed this way because he's coming back here. It isn't honorable. Nope. It's not. But it's Lauren, and it's habitual, and he's hot.

The sun is coming up now, and with it rises a symphony of birdsong. So many birds! Granted, they're probably louder now that I've, you know, *shot* the *window* out, but still. It's a beautiful morning, and I'm happy to be alive. I've also got a bit of a crush on John Smith, and that's a bad thing but a thing that gives me hope nonetheless. Crushes do that. This is probably why I am somewhat addicted to falling in love. Love is hope. At least until you actually get it. Then, as far as I can tell, it is pain.

Beyond the walls of the house, the sun is glowing in pastel shades of tangerine and pink upon the grass and hills. I look at the room and breathe deeply. It smells of cedar, and is decorated like something out of a Ralph Lauren advertisement. If I weren't here because I was running for my life, and if the window weren't destroyed, it would be the perfect vacation.

The silence is cut now by the sound of a loud motor driving up in the near distance. John Smith, I think with a little thrill. John Smith and his firm ass, in those cowboy jeans. I rush to the bathroom again and dab on a little mascara and lip gloss, try to do something with my mess of tangled red curls, realizing I still need to cover the roots. Oh well, if I muss it a bit the roots sort of disappear. I look sort of windswept, which is probably just right considering that I've, you know, shot out the window. I look sort of bed-headed and like I just, well, you know. That's not always a bad look. Men sort of like that look. Oh, God. Why am I even *going* there? Mentally? I need to *not* do this. This is the *last* thing I need, in fact. When will I learn to stop looking for love and just give up?

I will not become obsessed with the hot, manly neighbor, even if my body would be perfectly happy to have a visitor or two. I return to sit on the sofa, listening to the motor as it draws closer, and louder, and cuts out completely next to the house. I hear voices, a man's and a woman's, and my heart falls. There's a woman with John Smith? I shouldn't care. But I do.

I hate her.

I hear a knocking on the front door. I open it to find John Smith standing alone. He wears a long-sleeved denim shirt, and the white stained cowboy hat and sunglasses. The rest of him is encased in the form-fitting jeans, and boots. He's got a wicker basket in his hands, covered with a red and white checkered towel.

"I'm back," he says, taking off the dark glasses so that I can see his sparkling blue eyes. They make my heart skip, even if they do look a bit annoyed by me and the situation.

"Yes, you are." I try to sound disinterested.

"We brought these for you," he says, handing me the basket.

"What is it?" I ask. What I really want to ask, though, is "We?"

"Homemade biscuits, with a little pot of local honey."

I take the basket and thank him. The biscuits smell wonderful.

"You should actually thank *her*," he says, gesturing with his thumb toward the pickup truck that is now parked in the driveway. Is it my imagination or did he roll his eyes just a little as he said "her"? "She made them for me, but I'm not hungry after the morning we've had."

A very shapely young woman with long, shiny, straight blonde hair leans against the pickup. She wears tight short-shorts with cowboy boots and a snug white t-shirt over her ample breasts. She has a flat tummy, and a cowboy hat with sunglasses. My heart drops as she waves and smiles. She looks like she belongs in a beer commercial, or at a Hooters carrying a tray of hot wings.

"I didn't realize you were married," I say, the words coming out a little more obviously disappointed than I'd expected.

John grins almost imperceptibly, seeming to enjoy the look on my face. "She's just a friend."

"Bet you got a lot of those," I say before I can stop myself.

"No more than I need," he replies. "But fewer than need me." His eyes stray to my chest for a moment, and his mouth twitches almost imperceptibly, as though he is amused that I'm trying so hard.

"Modest," I joke.

"Truthful." He pauses, and looks closer at my face, this time letting the corner of his mouth rise up a little. "You look nice. For a Bostonian."

"Yeah, great. Thanks. Whatever. Uhm, so, can I get you guys some coffee?" I ask. I try very hard not to seem interested in this beautiful man.

John shakes his head. "I'm just going to get these boards up as fast as I can. Lots to do today."

Yeah, I think jealously, looking at the hottie. I bet she's at the top of the "to-do" list.

I busy myself unpacking and arranging my things in the master bedroom while John hammers away at the window. I sneak some looks at the girl, and see her filing her nails and looking bored, not offering to help her boyfriend, or whatever he is to her. If it were me, I'd be helpful. But it's not me, and it's not going to be me, so I need to stop fretting about it and focus on something else, like actually writing a book.

About an hour later, he knocks on the front door to tell me he's done. Sure enough, the enormous window is now covered neatly with large pieces of plywood, and the great room is significantly darker. He tells me it's a temporary fix, that in two days a guy will be by to replace the glass, but that the wood will do the job of keeping the wildlife out for now. I thank him for his help, and apologize again for shooting at him.

"As long as you're still a lousy shot, you can shoot at me whenever you like," he jokes, his mood improved significantly since earlier.

"Well, maybe next time you come peeking in my windows you could call first," I joke back.

"What's the fun in that?" he volleys back.

"Well, if you did, I'd be sure to be naked next time."

He seems surprised but pleased by the joke, to the extent that his poker face allows him to express, you know, human emotions. He looks at my hair and face in a way I recognize as admiring now, and this surprises me. Why would a guy with a hot blonde chick waiting in short-shorts waste his time on a chubbier, older woman who tried to shoot him?

"In that case, I will be sure to call," he says.

"Thank you."

He smiles, full on now, and I feel as though I've been stabbed by Cupid's arrow. His smile is incredibly luminous and beautiful.

"All right, Miz Fernandez. I'm heading out to check some water lines, chase a few cows. You need anything else?" he asks.

"Nothing you can provide," I say flirtatiously, looking at the girl. God! What is wrong with me? Even when I want to stop, I can't.

He understands my intent. "She's *not* my girlfriend," he says. "I told you. But I guess most reporters don't listen very well. Let me repeat this: She is just a friend."

"Uh huh."

"In fact, I need to get her back down to the county road pretty quick here. Gets old having her around too long."

"Yeah, I bet her parents are worried."

He grins at me. "You assume too much."

"You assume I've assumed."

"Maybe we both assume too much," he says.

He puts the sunglasses on again, and takes my pistol out of his waistband. Handing it to me he says, "I thought maybe later, after my friend leaves, that I might come by and show you how to actually work this thing."

He looks down at the gun I am holding without any expertise in my hand.

"Why? So I can actually shoot you next time?"

"Well, I was thinking that for my own good, having you around here with a gun, it might be smart to teach you how to handle it."

"I know how."

He rolls his eyes and guffaws. "Yeah. Right. I'll be by at around three, we'll shoot some rounds, get you comfortable with it. Happy to show you what I know."

"I bet that's what you told her, too."

"Assumption."

"I bet she was a fast learner."

"Jealous?" he asks, point blank.

"Whatever."

John turns to leave, seems to hesitate, then comes back, removes the dark glasses, looks directly at me and says, "Look, Lauren. I called Turnbull this morning, to tell him about the window, and he told me the real reason you're out here.'

"I'm writing a book," I say.

"He says you're in some serious trouble back in Boston."

"Yeah. Sort of."

"I think it'd be good for you to learn how to use that gun, under the circumstances."

"I can take care of myself, I told you."

He rolls his eyes again. "Yeah, okay. Well, just in case, I thought I'd give you one of these."

John reaches into his back pocket and produces a yellow and black walkie-talkie.

"There's no cell service out here, but you can usually find me with that if I'm out prowling around."

"I won't need you," I say. "But thanks."

"You won't *need* me?" he asks, perking up as though

he liked nothing better than a challenge. "Sweetest words a woman can say to a man like me, you know that?"

Then, with a tip of his hat, he turns and jogs back down the steps, toward the pickup with the hot babe in it. These people are beautiful. I don't know why I find this surprising. I guess I have this East Coast snobbery going on, where I think that the best and best-looking people are only in big cities where I've been. Who knew there were hot people out here in the middle of nowhere, too?

I watch from the door as he swings himself up into the driver's seat, and revs the engine like it was a motorcycle. The woman leans into him, and kisses him. He glances up at me, awkwardly, as he halfheartedly kisses her back. Just a friend, my ass. Ah, but why do I care? I'm done with men. Right?

Sigh.

He steers the machine back down the driveway, and off over the nearest hill on a little dirt road. I watch it until it's gone over the hill, and then I wander around the house trying to figure out what to do next.

There's a phone in the kitchen. I use it to call Usnavys, to let her know I arrived. I am confused when I get a recording telling me that the cell number I've called is no longer in service. I try her home number, and find that it has been disconnected. This is not normal. I wonder if maybe the phone here doesn't work. I dial Rebecca to check, and she picks up on the first ring. I let her know I got to the ranch in one piece, and she says that she will come down to visit me in a couple of weeks, once she gets some things with her mother straightened out.

"I'm sorry I couldn't be there now," she says. "It's that we're having something of a family crisis."

"Is it something you want to talk about?"

I hear her sigh, and then she asks me to hold on a minute. It sounds like she's walking, and then I hear what sounds like a door creaking shut.

"Okay," she says. "I'm back."

"What's going on, Rebecca?" I ask her. "I can tell something's bothering you."

This is when she tells me about her father having a secret family. I listen and try to understand what she's saying. It's terrible. I always thought of Rebecca as having it all, the perfect intact nuclear family of origin, money, stability, drive, ambition, direction, and tact.

"Did you know?" I ask.

"I had no idea. None. I thought he was the perfect dad."

"Jesus."

"I know."

"Are you okay?"

"I'm okay. My mom's not. She's a mess."

Rebecca tells me her mother is staying with them, and that she is warming up to Andre finally.

"Well, that's good at least," I suggest.

"I don't know. Lauren, Andre and I are moving apart."

"Are you serious? You guys always seem so perfect."

"Yeah. Well, it's not like we're having big fights or anything. It's just like we've slowly drifted apart and now we don't connect at all anymore. I think he might be thinking about other women. I don't know what to do."

She tells me about their child, Connor, and his autism, and how hard it has been on the family to deal with it. She tells me that she and Andre have been sleeping on separate ends of the bed, to the point that if you looked at their mattress from the foot of the bed, she says, "it looks like an inverted V from the fact that neither of us are ever in the middle."

"Wow."

"I wish I could get away and come talk to you about it now. I'm at my wit's end. But listen to me, Lauren. How selfish I'm being. I'm sorry. You're the one who needs to talk right now."

I reassure her that I'm fine, but even as I say it I realize that I'm just numb. Nothing has sunk in yet. I'm pretty sure there will come a time when the barricade holding back my feelings will come crashing down and I'll be flooded with emotion. Right now, I feel nothing much at all.

I ask Rebecca if she's heard anything about Usnavys, and tell her about the disconnected phone numbers.

"That's odd," says Rebecca. "I just talked to her a couple of days ago and she sounded like everything was normal."

"I hope Jason didn't get to her," I say.

"You still think Jason's out to get you?"

"I know he is. He was here. He killed my cat in front of me."

Rebecca tells me that she thinks I need to take all of this to the police. She's probably right, but there is the chance that they won't believe me, because if it is Jason and they find out he's a police officer, there will be that whole police loyalty thing going on. They protect their own. They suspect anyone who attacks one of them.

We say our goodbyes now, and Rebecca promises to call me back as soon as she finds out what's going on with Usnavys' phones. I hang up, and go to pour myself some coffee to go with the biscuits. This is when I realize I forgot to turn the machine on "brew". I put it on now. Stress can make a girl forget all kinds of things.

There's a computer at a small built-in table in the kitchen, and instructions on a post-it note on the screen for how to call up the satellite Internet on it. I do as they say, and go to the Boston Gazette website to read the latest news. I do a search for my own name, to see if they've made any mention of my leaving. There is nothing. My heart is heavy as I read the familiar bylines of all my former colleagues and friends. I should be there now, working. That is my life, my career, the only place I really feel like I belong. Instead, I'm in a stranger's house in an even stranger land.

The chime on the coffee maker finally goes off, signaling the pot is ready. I find some pretty white mugs in a cabinet, and pour myself a nice, hot cup. I drizzle some French Vanilla syrup in, and add some cream. I find a plate, and put a couple of the biscuits on it. I use the microwave to heat them up, and then find some butter in a dish on the counter. I smother the flaky rolls in it, and add some of the fresh honey. It is all delicious, more delicious than anything I can recall. I wonder if facing death helps you to appreciate things like color, texture and flavor more. I have never felt more alive than I do right now.

The phone rings. I dash to answer it -- probably Rebecca, I think. She said she'd call me right back.

"Hello," I say, adding, out of habit, "This is Lauren."

"Hey baby," says a familiar male voice. My blood runs cold.

"Jason?" I ask, in disbelief.

"Wanted to say, really sorry about your pussy," he says. "Such a waste."

"Why are you doing this?" I ask. "Just leave me alone."

"Know where I went?" he asks.

"No."

"I've been in Seattle. Do you know why?"

I say nothing.

"I think you do know why, Lauren."

"Please don't do this."

"I'm not happy, Lauren. I don't like to play game. When I found out you're not actually here, let's just say I got upset."

"How did you find this number?"

"I have ways. Speaking of ways, it was real nice of your friend Usnavys to give you that car. I might just have to thank her personally."

"Leave her alone. She never did anything to you."

"She helped you get away."

"She doesn't know anything about you."

"Don't do this."

"I miss you," he says. "See you soon."

The line goes dead, and with it dies my hope that I'll ever be safe again.

In a panic, and unable to reach my friend Usnavys, I Google the Boston Police Department, and call the only person I think might be able to help her now.

"This is Detective Bernstein," he answers.

"Martin," I tell him, my voice choked with emotion. "It's Lauren Fernandez. I just heard from Jason. He said he went to Seattle, and was pissed I wasn't there. He found my number here in New Mexico."

"Who else has it?" he asks.

"Rebecca knows it, and I emailed it to my friend Usnavys because her phone's not working. She gave me a car to get out here."

"Change your password. Better yet, get a new email account."

"Okay. But listen. He's going after Usnavys in Boston because she helped me get out of town. You have to help her."

I ask him to hold on a second, because I am suddenly overcome with severe nausea, realizing the danger I've put my best friend in. I run to the bathroom, and throw up.

When I get back on the line, Martin Bernstein tells me everything is going to be fine, and asks me not to panic.

"Be alert, and prepared to defend yourself, but don't panic. It won't help you."

USNAVYS

My mother sits on the side of my bed in her thin cotton housedress, looking at me. When I say "my bed," m'ija, I mean my bed. The same broke-ass, sagging in the middle, chipped-white-paint-having, former cheap child's canopy bed, the one I slept in growing up that made me feel like a princess. The same one I couldn't wait to get away from so that I could go to college and get me an education and start a new life. A life that I swore would never lead me back here, to the small, cramped but clean bedroom where I spent my entire childhood, in the Roxbury housing projects my mother has called home for nearly forty years.

"I hate my life," I moan. There is a metal bucket next to the bed on the floor, in case I have to throw up again. Since getting here yesterday morning I have thrown up exactly five times, every single time inspired by thoughts of loss. I don't even have a phone no more, in case one of them headhunters wants to call me about a job I applied for. It's all over for me now.

"Your life is a gift from God," my mother says, fingering the faded fake-gold cross on the chain around her neck.

"Tell God to get me a goddamned mobile phone, then."

"Don't speak that way." My mother crosses herself, like that's going to help. Why is it that all these poor people around here still have faith in a God that doesn't give a rat's ass about them?

"I can't do this," I moan. I feel like a woman on a plane that is falling from the sky toward some saw-tooth jagged-ass mountains.

"Shh, yes you can. You're a strong girl."

She's got a cold washcloth in her hand, and keeps putting it over my forehead. She looks worried but strong, just like she did when she came to my former house with her new man-friend to pick me up in his messed-up

Chrysler hooptie yesterday. He has a white pompadour and wears too much cologne, but she seems to love him and he seems to think she's pretty great. He laughs at all her lame-ass jokes, m'ija. I had no idea my moms had her a new man. You don't think a woman going on seventy is gonna be out looking to get her some, but then there it is. His name is Arturo and he used to play conga with a Boston band that used to open for the Fania AllStars when they played some old nightclub that doesn't exist no more. He's always drumming on his lap, or the steering wheel, on my mother's shoulder blades, whistling melodies through his smiling dentures. That's Arturo's claim to fame, that he once played in a band that once opened for a band most Americans never heard of, in a place that don't exist no more. But it's enough for him, because you look at that viejito and he's pretty full of himself. Sometimes that's all it takes to walk around like you own the world, is to believe you do. Now he can add "saved Usnavys' sorry ass" to this list because he came with mami to rescue me after the movers and bankers and police took all my shit out of my house and dumped it on the street for all the neighbors to see. They changed the locks on me, and told me that if I came near the house again they'd have me arrested. I just hid there on the porch and sat on the hanging swing acting like there wasn't nothing wrong until my mom and her slick old man got there, and then I just walked like a relaxed woman past all my stuff and got into that car with the wire coat hangar jerry-rigged door handle, and left. I knew all them people was staring at me, but I wasn't going to give them the pleasure of seeing me break down about it. Not there. Not then. Not ever, okay?

Since then, my mom says her man went back with his brothers and nephews and cousins to get my stuff and they put it in the back of a moving truck one of his relatives out in Lawrence drives around for a living. They took it to some place out there where another relative of theirs owns a storage facility. My mom said the guy agreed to let me leave my things there as long as I needed to, for free. I guess that's the best thing about being a Boricua in

New England, m'ija. Everybody knows everybody, and everybody got a cousin in some kind of business or another, who will help your ass out in a bind.

"Are you hungry, amor?" she asks. "It's past noon. You slept a long time. You haven't eaten since yesterday. Not that you couldn't stand a few days without eating…"

She's already criticizing me for my gracious curves. Why she's gotta do that? Ever since I was a little girl she stuffed my face full of delicious food to tell me she loved me, and then she went and told me I was fat. That's like throwing someone's ass in a swimming pool then getting pissed off that they're *wet*. You can't have it both ways.

"I could use a little sustenance," I tell her, grandly. Then, because I don't like the pitiful way she's looking at me, like I got my ass run over by a truck or something, I pull the sheet over my head and say, "Stop it, mami. I'm fine."

"I just worry, that's all." She pulls the sheet away from my face and brushes my nappy-ass messy hair out of my eyes.

"M'ija," she says. "Fix this hair. You'll feel so much better if you fix this hair. You can't go around looking like Buckwheat."

"And how I'm gonna fix my hair without any money?"

"I'll pay for your hair."

"No. That's ridiculous."

"What? Who do you think paid for you to get your hair done all those years? Santa Claus? It's nothing."

"No."

"A woman who looks her best, feels her best," says Mami. "And looking at you right now, I can see why you feel your worst."

"Wow. Thanks a *lot*."

"Just being honest. If your mother can't be honest with you, who can?"

"The bank. The police."

"Ay, nena. What's done is done. Stop thinking about it. Get your hair fixed, get yourself dressed, put on some makeup, and get out there and face the world. It's a new day."

"Stop worrying about me."

"It's a mother's job to worry about her kids, and she never stops, no matter how old you get." She pauses a moment then asks if I've heard from my own children.

"No, I have not."

"You should call them."

"I don't have a phone. Remember?"

"Use mine. Estas loca. I have a phone."

"What? And have Juan know that I'm back living here with you? I don't think so."

My mother looks hurt and annoyed. "You'll never change," she says. "I have been praying to God that you will change before it's too late, but sometimes when you talk like this, I just don't know."

"I don't mean it's bad here," I say, annoyed. "I just mean I don't want him to think I can't take care of myself."

"Well, you can't," she says adamantly. "You can't take care of yourself right now. There's nothing wrong with that. It happens to everybody sometimes. He is your husband. He should take care of you, but you, well. You know how you are. You don't let anyone take care of you. Always with that chip on your shoulder."

"I'm doing fine," I insist, but I don't mean it and she knows it. I am lying, and my fresh flood of tears is there to prove that I do actually know the truth about what's happened to my life.

"You need to call your children. You can be too proud for your friends, or for your husband, or for me, Usnavys, but you should never, ever be too proud for your own children. They need you."

"I will. Once I get myself back on track."

My mother looks at me with even more pity now.

"M'ija, you have to accept what's happening. You can't keep pretending anymore. What if you never get back on track the way you were? You have to find a new way to live, let go of the past."

"Pretending what?" I ask.

"That everything's fine. Everything's not fine anymore. And that's okay. God only gives us what we can handle, and what we need to learn our lessons. I think God sent you this hardship now so that you would learn humility."

"Whatever. I'm not using your phone to call Juan. I'll go down to the call place on Center Street first."

My mother balks. "That place where all the drug-dealers go to call Santo Domingo?"

"If you lend me twenty bucks I'll get one of them prepaid phone deals."

She watches me sorrowfully.

"What?" I ask. "What are you looking at?"

My mother sighs. "I'll make some toast and coffee, and some pastelitos."

"Okay."

She gets up to leave, and doesn't close the door behind her. Puerto Rican mothers rarely give their children much privacy. Doors are always open, and your business is everybody's business. There are few secrets in a Puerto Rican neighborhood. Under present circumstances, this scares me, a lot.

I should have remembered the lack of privacy in the barrio before stepping out into my mother's living room in my shiny silk robe and puffy slippers. The viejitas are all here, three ladies my mother's age, who she likes to hang out with, and they all stop whispering when I walk in, and they stare like the holy mother of God just walked in the room. What, they've never seen a woman of style and grace before? I know in an instant that she has told them everything. My mother is in the small kitchen off to one side, putting condensed milk in my cup of coffee and stirring it with a metal spoon that makes a racket to wake the dead.

"You look terrible Usnavys," one of the old women tells me. Velia Vasconcelos. I have known her since before I was born, and she has always been as brutally honest as she was a whore – and the biggest gossip in the projects.

"It's nice to see you, too, vieja," I tell her.

"Sit, sit with us," says Julia Barrientos, another of the old women. "Tell us what's going on."

"I don't feel like talking about it." I plop down on the fake leather love seat my mom probably bought off the back of a truck down at the corner. There's not enough give and padding, and the material feels creepy on my thighs. I look around at the "art" she has displayed – one after another dime store framed portrait of Jesus and scenes from The Bible. She's even got a little Jesus waterfall that stands on an end table and plays a religious song when you put a penny in.

My mother comes into the room with a plastic tray holding five cups of coffee. The tray is painted silver to look like the real deal. She wields it as though it were classy. This depresses me, because even though it's tragic, this tray and this apartment of my mother's are more than I've got to my name anymore. Can you believe that shit, m'ija? How could this happen?

"Here we go, ladies," says my mother as she sets the tray down on the coffee table.

"She say she don't feel like talking about it," Velia tells my mother as though I were unreasonable. Velia adjusts her cleavage, which has settled somewhere near her navel. She still wears hot pants. If I ever get to be all hoochie in my sixties, m'ija, just take me out to Franklin Park in the middle of the night and shoot my ass and let the rats eat my carcass.

"I'll get the toast and pastelitos," says my mother. Then, to me she says, "You're among friends. You can tell us anything. We're here for you. You have no idea how many hard times these ladies helped me get through. They want to help you now."

Yeah, right. They want to help me by running straight to all their friends and telling them what a mess I got myself into. They're here to find out all the dirt and go all over the place telling everyone about me. Chismosas. Ay Dios mio, I can't believe this is happening to me. I bet everyone around here would like nothing more than to hear about how Usnavys Rivera lost all her money, because they've been mad jealous of me and my grace and style for so many years. What they don't understand, of course, is that this shit right here? This shit is *temporary*, okay? I am not falling and never getting up, like those old people in them commercials on TV with the little call buttons. I am falling because somebody done pushed my ass down, and I am wiping my hands off and checking my skirt and then I'm getting back up and I am doing the catwalk on the runway, girl. That's what I'm doing. If you don't like it then you can kiss my Puerto Rican ass.

This is not going to defeat me.

"I'm surprised none of your rich friends are there to help you," says Julia, trying not to sound catty and failing.

"Maybe I didn't ask or assume," I snap. "Maybe some of us don't go around with a sense of entitlement like the world owes us something, and we work for what we have."

The viejitas cluck like hens over my attitude.

"And how is that working hard like a man working out for you now?" Asks Isabel Arias, until now the shyest and quietest of the old ladies. "Your mother tells us you lost your job, your house and your man. I'm not passing judgment, just asking."

She shrugs as though this were no surprise to her, as though I, by losing everything, was merely proving her right about me and laws of the universe.

"I knew it'd end up like this for you," says Velia.

"Oh, *did* you?" I ask. "And how is that?"

"You always acted like a man. So independent."

"Bullshit," I say.

"And talked like a man," says Velia. "So much cursing!"

"I always told her, you can't keep a man if you make more money than him," says my mother, joining in the conversation as she brings another plastic silver tray into the room, this one with plates of delicious flattened French bread toast with loads of butter on it, and fruit-filled empanadas. "Help yourselves."

My mother sits on the sofa and sips her coffee.

"Delicious," says Julia as she digs into her toast, dipping it into her own coffee.

"She looks terrible," repeats Velia, watching me with eagle eyes.

"She's tired. She's had a very rough two days." My mother looks at me with sympathy. "There's a lot going on, right m'ija?"

I am tired. And I'm done arguing with these old bitches.

Velia stares me down. "My youngest daughter," she says, "you remember her? Taina?"

"How could I forget," I muse, remembering a girl who was my same age but very much about displaying her body for boys, even back in the second grade. She wore thigh-high stiletto boots in seventh grade, nena. With pushup bras. She was ghetto tacky, and a whore like her mama, from the start. "I never saw a girl go through so many weaves in my life." And by weaves, I mean boys.

Velia narrows her eyes to slits. "Well, you might like to know that she owns her own salon now, down in Dorchester. You might have heard of it. Taina's House of Hair."

"I'm happy for her," I say, not meaning a word of it. House of Hair? Dios mio. That has to be the worst name I have ever heard of for a salon, m'ija. It sounds like something a desperate Eskimo would build him if the snow ran out from global warming. House of Hair. Pero que disparate. It sounds like something a nomad would live in with his Yak.

Velia continues, "She told me, just the other day she says to me, mom, do you know anybody who can come in here and answer phones for me? She said she lost the last girl to a drug overdose and now she's having trouble finding someone reliable. If you want me to, I could tell Taina that you're looking for a job. She got all those Dominicanas in there that do the fancy blow-dry that all the girls like. Even the black ladies are starting to come in for the Dominican blowout. I think it's because of that Zoe Saldana. Taina, she's making good money. She just got herself a house, a brownstone down by Jackson Square. It's got real pretty furniture and you should see her kitchen, it's like out of a magazine."

I pause, unable to move because the horror of thinking of working as a receptionist for Taina's ghetto hair salon is almost too terrible to envision.

"That's a wonderful idea!" chimes in my mother. "You used to be friends with Taina. Now she'll be happy to help you. You see how God works? God is so good."

Uhm, no, I think. I see that God hates my sorry ass.

"She'll be so happy to hear from you, m'ija!" my mother says, all excited.

My mother clearly doesn't know about the time I cornered Taina and gave her a piece of my mind about what a whore she was and about how I thought she was a walking STD dispenser. "With Pez you pull back the head and get you a candy," I told Taina that day I caught her kissing my boyfriend. "With you, you give head and he gets a disease."

"That won't be necessary," I say.

"It's a very nice offer," says Julia.

"M'ija," says my mother to me. "You *do* need a job, don't you? How else will you get yourself another cell phone?"

"I have resumes out," I tell her. I try to sit up straighter.

"But they can't call you if you don't have a phone, that's what you said," my mother reminds me. "And you can't be caught dead on your mother's phone, from what you said."

"I *know* what I said. I don't need you all quoting me up in here. I *need* a job, but I don't need to be a receptionist. Okay? I did not go to college and graduate school so that I could answer phones for Taina's House of Horrors."

"Hair," Velia corrects me.

"Receptionist is a good job," says Julia. "You get to sit in a nice salon with the air conditioning, and you talk to people on the phone. You look like you like to sit, Usnavys. And God knows you like to talk."

"I'm aware of what a receptionist does, thank you very much," I snap. "And for your information, men enjoy these curves and I am not running to the gym because I'm not going to rob mankind of the pleasure of my Rubinesque self."

"Everyone's always so happy when they go in a beauty parlor," my mother tries to convince me, using an old-ass term for salon that gives me the creeps. "It's not like when I used to answer phones for that gum surgeon who always had blood on his jacket. Nobody was in a good mood there."

"Gum surgeon?" asks Julia.

"Periodontist. Gums." My mother pulls her lower lip out and points to her gums, and I almost throw up again. "People get the gingivitis, and their gums rot out. He cuts them up and sews them back together. You can't believe how much gums bleed. I never knew! So much. You have to floss, that's what I learned there."

"Que asco," says Velia.

"I was not born to be a receptionist," I state.

"And I wasn't born to have an ungrateful daughter," says my mother. "But sometimes, you take what God gives you, and you say thank you, and you make the best of what you have. Que no?"

I don't want this latest statement by my mother to get to me, but it does anyway. She's right. I know she's right, but I can't figure out why this is all happening to me. What did I do wrong to deserve this?

"Beggars can't be choosers," my mother says to me.

"I'm not a beggar."

"You will be," says Velia. "If you don't get a hold of reality. We tried to offer you something nice, and you looked the horse gift in the mouth."

"Gift horse," I say. "The saying is 'never look a gift horse in the mouth.'"

"Especially if he's got the gingivitis," says Julia.

The ladies laugh and I start to think about jumping out the freakin' window.

"Here's what we'll do," my mother says, as cheerfully

as she can. "Usnavys, your hair is a mess. You need to get your hair done. And your nails could use fresh polish. We'll finish up breakfast, get you dressed nice, and take you down to Taina's. We could all use a manicure. Freshen ourselves up."

"Speak for yourself," says Velia. "I got one two days ago."

My mother ignores her and keeps talking to me. "You don't have to tell her about you needing a job. Just get your hair and nails done and see how you like the place."

"Fine," I say. "But first one of you who says something about my situation is going to get a black eye."

"You think you can take me, girl?" says Velia, puffing up like she wants a fight.

"God help me," I say, as I force myself out of the chair and go back to the bedroom to get dressed. "I've fallen into the deepest pit of hell, and it is populated by nightmare creatures from my past. I'm living in a Dickens novel."

An hour later, my mother pulls her boyfriend's gigantic old car up to the curb near Tania's salon in a very ghetto part of Dorchester. There is no sight sadder in all the world, m'ija, than that of my mother trying to parallel park her a big-ass raggedy sedan in the middle of the barrio. I want to just disappear, because you know all them little hoodlum boys who should be in summer school or prison or some shit, but they're all out on the sidewalk just standing around waiting for something like this to come along? Yeah, well, there they are, just standing there against the wall of some old boarded-up shop, leaning back and laughing at my mom because the cochina can't drive, okay? She can't. After about ten minutes of her drawing arcs back and forth on the street, I have just about lost it.

"Get out," I tell her, snapping my fingers in front of my face.

"What?"

"Get your ass out the car and let me do this," I say.

"What are you talking about?"

"Get out of the car, mami. You don't know how to

park."

"Yes, I do. I'm almost there."

"We'll be here all day if you park this boat."

My mother smashes into the car in front of her now, just enough to make a crunching noise.

"Out!" I shout.

I insist that she get out, and finally she does. Then with the ease and grace of an expert driver who used to own the finest German automobile and engineering that money could buy, I park that piece of garbage right up against the curb, and cut the engine. I resist the urge to throw the keys through the windshield.

I hate my life.

Then, together with the viejitas, I walk two blocks to the salon. The hoodlums watch us go and make their usual bullshit comments, until a black unmarked police car slides past all slow and low.

When you grow up in a place like this, you know them unmarked police cars, girl. You'd think the cops might give their detectives something less obvious to drive than big old Crown Vickies with tinted windows, but no. They're so stupid. Just like those boys on the street, who shut the hell up and start walking like they're on their way to the bus stop when the cop drives past. Them boys are so stupid that it's almost a relief when we get to the salon and walk in, except that the cop car stops out front, which makes me wonder what Taina's up to up in here. Money laundering? Maybe it's not a House of Horrors, but a House of Whores.

There's nobody at the reception desk, and three stylists working on three customers, two on hair and one on nails. The stylist at the nearest station is Taina, looking pretty much the same now as she did back in high school, which means she is still curvy and very beautiful, with that fake-ass bleach blonde hair and them green contact lenses clouding up her brown eyes so she looks like some kind of a dead person floating face up in the river. How that girl looks so young after having all them babies and bad babydaddies is beyond me. Her hair is very long and wavy, and her clothes aren't nearly as bad as I thought they might be. She almost looks good. Them other two stylists are talking Dominican Spanish and have that look. I myself am half-Dominican, but the Dominican half is my daddy and I hate him so I don't claim that country.

Taina looks up and sees her mother and the viejitas. She smiles warmly and greets them all with a big waves and air kisses blown across the salon. Then her eyes land on me and her face tightens. It don't matter how many years done passed since you seen a person that tormented you when you were in school, m'ija. As soon as you see that person again, your ass regresses. You go right back to that place.

"Taina, amorcito, you remember Usnavys Rivera?"

"Hi," I say, sheepishly aware of the scarf over my head and the ugly state of my hands.

"I remember her," says Taina, without returning my greeting. She looks pissed off.

Velia tells her daughter that I need to get my hair and nails done, and says I'm back in the old neighborhood visiting my mom for a while.

"She needs her hair and nails good because she's going out on job interviews," blurts my blabbermouth mother, and I have to stop my ass from smacking her down. She's about as subtle as a neon skyscraper. Why she had to go putting my shit on blast like that?

Taina's face twists in doubt and if I'm not mistaken she seems to rather enjoy the idea that I've come upon hard times.

"Have a seat," she tells me, standing up straighter with her own triumph over me. "I'll be done here in a few minutes and I'll get to you then."

The ladies all commence to gossiping in Spanish now with the other ladies who are here, and with the stylists. It's all about baptisms and pregnancies and then there's jacked-up shit, too, like the men who are cheating and the woman who got HIV by her husband who was sneaking around with men. I don't know about you, but me? I think there's a lot of men in this world who need to have their asses just straight up killed or at least have their dicks cut the hell off. With a machete.

I don't have anything to contribute to the conversation, so I just pick up a magazine, a glossy celebrity rag with lots of pictures of people with a lot more money than me. This star is getting divorced. That star overdosed. This star here feeds her babies crickets. That one had his baby taken away. That one over there lost his movie because the director didn't like him anymore. There's even a story about a star from the nineties who just had his house taken away because he couldn't afford it anymore. Guess this disaster is getting to all of us. I take refuge in the fact that even these rich and famous skinny-ass people have their lives all messed up with divorce and stupid nonsense and so on and so forth.

This is when the cop walks in. He's big and tall, and hot for a white boy with curly black hair. He looks all around then settles his eyes on me.

"Usnavys Rivera?" he asks me, taking a seat next to me in the waiting area. All the eyes in the place are on me now.

"Who wants to know?" I ask, engaging him with my grace and charm, even though my heart is about to beat itself to death in fear. What this whiteboy cop wants with me?

"I'm Detective Martin Bernstein with Boston Homicide. May I speak to you outside for a moment?"

"What is this regarding?" I ask.

"Your friend Lauren," he says.

I almost have a heart attack when I hear these words, thinking my girl is dead. I excuse myself from the other ladies and follow the handsome Jewish detective out onto the sidewalk. He asks me to get in his car where we can speak privately, but I know better than to fall for some shit like that.

"Whatever it is you got to tell me, you tell it to me here," I say.

The detective says okay, then tells me that he thinks Jason Flynn actually did try to kill Lauren's redheaded

Cuban ass, and that furthermore he knows where she is in New Mexico and that he's told her he wants to personally thank me for helping her escape.

"I don't mean to alarm you, but you should be aware. Flynn's not a good cop, Usnavys."

"Well, then you should do something about it," I tell him.

"I am," he assures me. "I'm working on it. Until it's resolved, though, you need to be alert. Stay safe. If you see Flynn, get away from him. He's not good for you. He might even wish to harm you."

The detective tells me all kinds of shit now, m'ija, like the kind of car Flynn drives (a Cadillac Escalade, white) so I can be on the lookout for it.

"Are you shitting me?" I ask him, when he's done.

"Not in the least," he says.

"What are you going to do about it?" I ask.

"I can't tell anyone in the department, okay?" he says in a soft hushed voice. "But I can keep watch over you. That's what I intend to do."

"Damn Lauren," I say. "She picked her ass the wrong cop to fall in love with."

Detective Bernstein frowns and says, "I couldn't agree with you more."

LAUREN

I press a few buttons on the walkie-talkie John Smith gave me, until something kicks in and the thing starts working.

"John?" I call into it.

"Lauren? That you?"

"Yes."

"What's up."

"I think I need you to come back as soon as you can," I say, and then the call goes dead. I don't know if he heard me or not.

My thinking in asking him back is so that I can get going on the gun lessons. From the sounds of it, Jason could be very nearby. I don't have any time to waste.

I go out to the shed and dig through the boxes of ammunition Tio told me were there for his pistol. Then I sit down in front of the computer and connect to the Internet. I Google the make and model of the handgun, along with the words "how to load" and "how to shoot". I read as much as I can, and watch a couple of demonstration videos. I'm going to nail this thing. I will not lose to Jason Flynn. Fuck Jason Flynn.

I head outside, and find some open space with a couple of trees to aim at. After making sure there is nothing behind them that might get shot, I return to my spot and take aim. Boom! The first round fires off, and the kickback feels like it's going to rip my shoulder out of the socket. My eardrums are ready to burst. To my dismay, I've landed the bullet nowhere near the tree I was aiming for. I have no idea, in fact, where the bullet when at all.

Great.

I try again, with similar results. This is harder than it looks in the movies.

I shoot again, and again, but can't seem to get the bullet where I need it to go. This sucks.

I stand there in the sun for a long moment, listening to the echo of the blasts coming off the surrounding hills and canyons. Then, there is a complete quiet, a stillness as deep as any I've ever known. Is that what it's like to be dead? This peace, this silence? I don't want to be dead. I don't want to find out. I will never, if I live through this, allow myself to get involved with a dangerous man again. I will never again overlook the obvious red flags. I will stop making excuses for men. I will stop seeing them as better than they are.

The silence is broken now by the sound of a motor. I look up and see the pickup coming back over the hill again, kicking up a trail of beige dust behind it. The vehicle seems to be going a lot faster this time than it was before. I stand and watch it come. I am sad to see the girl is still with him.

Moments later, John Smith pulls up next to me, and slides the truck to a skidding stop. He jumps out of the pickup, comes jogging up to me. He snatches the gun out of my hands.

"Give me that."

"Hey!" I cry. "That's mine."

"Yeah, and my life is mine. Until you know how to handle this thing, you're not going to come anywhere near it. I told you I'd teach you how to use it. You can't just go around here squeezing the trigger."

"I can if there's someone after me."

"You all right?" he asks. He's not exactly worried. No. Rather, he seems perturbed.

"Yeah."

"You called me on the two-way?"

I tell him about the phone call I got, and his eyes grow narrower and narrower.

"Okay," he says, when I've finished.

"Okay? That's all you can say? This is sort of scary."

"Nothing's scary if you know how to handle it," he says. Then to my great surprise he smiles, as though he relishes the news that a psychopathic killer might be showing up here any minute.

"That's why I'm trying to figure that thing out," I say, indicating the gun.

"Look, go back in the house and wait for me. Let me get this girl back down to the highway, and then I'll come back and help you."

"What if he comes when you're gone? I need the gun."

"Nobody's coming on this property without me noticing. There's only the one road in, and I'm going to be on it. Just try to relax."

"Right. Because that's so easy when people are trying to kill you."

"It can be done," he says, simply.

"How would *you* know?"

"I just do. Trust me."

"Have you ever had anyone try to kill you?"

John Smith laughs now. "No comment. Just turn around, get yourself back in the house. Watch some TV, eat something, just wait a little bit. I'll be back by here in about an hour."

I do as he says, but cannot relax completely. I try to call Usnavys again, and get the same disconnect message. I flip through the paper address book in which I collected all my assorted phone numbers before tossing my phone into the Charles River, and find her husband's cell. I dial Juan, and he picks up with that curious sort of hello that we all deliver when we see a number we don't recognize on our caller ID. I tell him it's me, and ask if there's something going on with Usnavys's phone.

"She hasn't told you?" he asks, incredulous and irritated.

"Told me what?"

Juan sighs, and then tells me about Usnavys losing her job almost a year ago and burning through all their cash. He tells me they fell behind on their housing payments and that Usnavys was overspending his meager salary like mad, often behind his back. He says that the house was taken back by the bank, that Usnavys lost her car, and that he has left her and wants a divorce. I am so shocked I have to sit down.

"How could she not tell me any of this?" I ask. "I'm her best friend!"

"I thought I was her best friend, too," he says bitterly. "And there was lots she didn't tell me. Don't blame yourself. Usnavys has issues, Lauren. She's in denial about a lot of things."

"Where is she now?"

"I'm not sure. I talked to my mom last night, and she knows some people back in the old neighborhood. She used to live in the same building with Usnavys' mom? She's in Puerto Rico now, but she got a call from somebody there saying they saw Usnavys back at her mom's."

"Oh, my God. Really?" While I'm shocked by this news, I am also relieved because it means Usnavys will be much harder for Jason Flynn to find, should he actually be trying to find her. I consider telling Juan about the threat from Jason, but it sounds like he has enough to worry about right now. Besides which, Martin Bernstein is supposedly going to handle protecting Usnavys.

"It's probably the best place for her right now," says Juan. "She needs to get her head right."

"You don't sound very worried."

"Look, I have worried about that woman long enough." His voice cracks with emotion. "Since we were kids, you know? I've done everything I could. I've tolerated everything I could. I had one last request from her, that she not spend the last of our money, the little bit of money I was holding out in case we needed an escape hatch, in case we had to do something drastic, and you know what she did?"

"I can guess."

"She went shopping and Nieman Marcus, Lauren."

"Wow."

"We have children. She doesn't seem to care about that at all. She just thinks about herself and that's it. It's always been that way with her, and I just kept hanging around hoping it'd get better. Well, guess what? It got worse. I can't help her anymore."

"I'm sorry."

"How are you doing?" he asks. "I've been thinking

about you. How's my car?"

"It's fine. It's in storage in Santa Fe, at Rebecca's."

"I'd like to get it back. That's another thing. She just gave you my car, like it was hers to give."

"Why didn't you say something? You were there. If you didn't want me to take it you could have stopped it."

"That's just it, I couldn't have. She'd never have let me. Do you have any idea how hard it is to stand up to that woman?"

"Yes. I know. She's sort of scary. But still, you could have said something."

"I know. I think by that time I'd already pretty much checked out, emotionally. There wasn't any fight left in me. I've been in survivor mode all this past year, just trying to make sure that my kids have what they need. It has been so hard. But listen to me. I'm going on and on about this and meanwhile, you're scared for your life. I'm sorry, Lauren."

"It's okay."

"What's happening with everything?"

"Well, I'm here hiding out at a ranch in the middle of nowhere. The only other person around is this womanizing cowboy who everybody in town is apparently afraid of."

"Jesus, out of the frying pan..."

"I know. And then this morning I got a call here from Jason Flynn. My ex who's trying to kill me. Guess he knows where I'm at."

"Fuck."

"I know."

"Why is he doing this to you?"

I sigh, and think about my answer. Juan and I have never been as close as I am to my female friends, but he's always been a decent, upstanding, honest man. And now that he has shared his own personal hurts with me, and now that I realize how enormously his wife has been lying to us both, I feel drawn closer to him.

"I know some stuff about him," I say. "Dirty cop stuff. Plus, the more I got to know him, the weirder he got with sexual stuff. Domination stuff. He's messed up, controlling." I fail to mention that I actually liked the domination sex stuff.

"You need to go to the police."

"I can't."

"Why not?"

"Because Jason *is* the police, that's why. They protect their own."

"It can't be all the police in the whole world."

"No. But there are people really high up involved in this. The best thing I can do is just disappear."

"That doesn't sound like a good plan at all. Do you know stuff you shouldn't know? Are you a witness or something?"

"Sort of. Jason's in with the mob. I think he's actually like a hit man or something."

"Damn, girl! There's got to be a way around this. What about the FBI? Somebody national?"

"I don't know. Right now I just need to stay out of his way."

"You need to keep moving, sounds like, if this guy knows where you are."

"How does he keep finding me?" I ask.

"I don't know. It's so scary."

"I guess I'm numb or something. I just feel like whatever happens, happens. I got a gun."

"What?"

"I'm learning to shoot it. I feel like Ted Kaczynski out here. But you know what? If someone shows up, they're going to get a fight now. I'm not just sitting back and taking it anymore."

"I know what you mean."

"I should hang up," I say. "The cowboy is coming by to teach me how to shoot my gun in a little while."

"How well do you know this guy?"

"I think he's okay, as long as he's on your side."

"What if he's on *their* side, Lauren? Have you considered that?"

"Him?" I ask, my blood running cold. I hadn't

thought about that possibility. "How would they get to him?"

"Well, they know where you are, right?"

"I think so. Jason knows the phone number here."

"Well, how hard would it be to give the neighbor some money to get him to do something for them?"

"I don't know about that."

"Lauren," says Juan, as though he were disappointed in me for being so naïve. "Not to scare you, but how hard do you think it might be for some mafia types to get to a guy like that, with some cash and promises, and get him to do their business for them?"

"Oh, my God," I say. "Maybe you're right."

"Well, good thing you're armed, anyway."

I remember that John Smith took my gun away earlier, and my pulse escalates. "Actually," I tell Juan, "I'm not."

"I thought you said you have a gun."

"I did. The cowboy guy took it from me a little while ago."

"Lauren. And you don't think he's one of them?"

"It's because I have bad aim."

"So he says."

"Well, but he's right."

"I think you need to get out of there. Maybe this cowboy is a good guy, but maybe he's not. You thought Jason was a good guy. I hope you don't mind me saying this, Lauren, but sometimes your radar for men is a bit off."

I realize Juan is right. With a shock of fear, I understand. I say goodbye, hang up, pack my things, and run, not walk, to the pickup truck.

USNAVYS

Taina motions me over to the newly empty chair at her station. I feel sick thinking that Jason Flynn is actually probably trying to kill my friend Lauren, and even sicker that he's out to get me, too. What the hell is wrong with Lauren? Why she's always gotta be screwing up her life and the lives of those around her? I'm sick of it. That's all. Sick of it.

It doesn't help that I'm about to submit myself to be styled by a woman who has every reason in the world to hate me. If it were me, you know I wouldn't be going out of my way to make a bitch look good, not after what I used to say to her. I notice now that there are quite a few religious icons around here, too. I don't remember everybody in the neighborhood being so Holy Roller back in the day, but I guess things change.

"Well, go on," says my mother, noticing that I haven't budged from my seat in the waiting area. I told my mom and all them other women that the detective was here about something to do with the foreclosure. My moms is worried enough about me as it is. I don't need to give her any more reason to get all stupid on me.

I do not want to get letting that woman get her hands all up on me. Is it my imagination, or does she have a gleam in her eye? I bet she's gonna accidentally cut me. Or worse, give me a rainbow weave.

"I'm okay," I say, pushing the scarf a little lower on my brow. "I don't need a fix that bad. I'll wait til I got me some money to go to my girl on Newbury Street."

"Usnavys!" my mother scolds me. "Get over there. Taina's very busy, mi vida. She's squeezing you in before her next appointment, to be nice. Don't embarrass me. We asked for a favor for you, and you should be more grateful."

Reluctantly, I set down the gossip magazine and plod over to Taina. She's taller than I am, and smells like strawberry bubble gum. I've seen that shirt she's wearing somewhere before, I think. Then I realize I just saw it at Nieman's when I was shopping the other day. That horrible day. I liked that damn shirt, too, but they didn't carry it in plus-sizes so I didn't get it.

"You get that at Nieman's?" I ask her.

"Hello to you, too," she says.

"I meant hello. Then I meant did you get that at Nieman Marcus."

"I did."

"It's nice."

"I appreciate that," she says with a smile. She looks all like she's trying to come off as sincere, but I'm not falling for it, m'ija. That's the thing you have to understand about the ghetto, girl. People who grow up fierce can charm the hell out of you when they want to. They know how to get what they want. They know how to manipulate you.

"You're welcome," I say, with a bored expression.

"Have a seat."

I plop down in the chair. Taina wears a large gold cross pendant on a gold chain. It has diamonds in it. I wonder if they're real. If they are, that thing cost a prettier penny than this girl's got. I wonder if she's laundering money through this place or some shit like that. Around here you always gotta ask, is the business legit or is it a front?

"How you been doing?" Taina asks me as she whips a clean smock out of the closet nearby. "It's been forever since I saw you. Last time I saw you I think was senior year or high school. You doing good?"

"Things have been better," I tell her honestly, because I don't give a rat's ass what this woman thinks of me and so there's no reason to deceive her.

"I'm sorry to hear that." She unsnaps the smock, shakes it open, and drapes it over me, snapping it in the back when she's through. She pulls all my hair up out of the collar area, and asks me if it's okay for her to remove the scarf from my head.

"You can't do my hair with it on, can you?" I ask. Tonta.

"I could," she says, smiling. "You might not like it much when I was done, though. Even if I do got mad skills."

With hands that are deceptively gentle – I know she's going to start yanking my hair at some point, nena, she totally has it in for me – Taina unwraps my head. She knows as well as I do that what she finds up under that cloth isn't pretty. I look like I stuck my finger in a socket and that when I got electrocuted half my hair turned white. I do not like what I am seeing in this mirror, m'ija. I look a damn mess. I need a color, and a treatment, and a trim. Bad. But if you looked at Taina's face you wouldn't know I looked a raggedy mess. She has a poker face to rival the best card sharks in Las Vegas, girl. She looks like we're just two old friends, chatting it up.

"So," she says, looking me in the eye through the mirror. "What are we going to do here today?"

There are so many things I'd like to say by way of answering her, m'ija, but I bite my tongue. I want to tell her what she's not going to do, which is fuck me up.

"As you can see I need color, and a trim," I say.

"When you style it, do you do it straight?" she asks.

"Most of the time."

"Okay. We have some great treatments here."

"So I've heard."

"Really?" her eyes brighten. She's doing a damn good job pretending she likes me. "You heard about this little place?"

From your mother, I think. "Yeah, sure," I say. "You're getting famous." Two can play at her flattery game.

"That's amazing! Here you are, the big-shot executive with your fancy degree and all that, and you've actually heard about my salon."

"How long have you had it?" I ask, because she's going too far over the top now and I'm not in a mood, okay? She keeps laying it on that thick I'm gonna have to get in her face and shut that shit down.

"We've been here in this spot for about six years now.

We started out with just that front part of the store, there, and then business got better and better and I was able to buy the rest of the floor."

"You own this place, or lease it?" I ask, knowing I done caught her ass in a lie. She didn't buy this building. No salon ever buys their own building unless they're raking in the dough, and there is no way that any shop in this rundown neighborhood is making that kind of plata. Please.

"Bought," she says. "We got a really good deal, too."

"Who's we? I thought this was just your business."

"It is. I just say we because I don't want to sound conceited."

She makes eye contact with me again in the mirror, and I know she thinks I'm conceited, or that at least I used to be. Fine. Let her ass think what she wants. Just because I used to floss back in the day when I had money rolling in doesn't make me a bad person. You got it, flaunt it. That's what I say.

"I'm thinking we do a warm chocolate brown for your all-over color, that will really make your eyes pop, with some red and caramel highlights," she says. My stomach growls at the mention of chocolate and caramel.

"That sounds fine."

"Can I get you some bottled water?" she asks. "Or coffee? We have a latte machine in the kitchen out back. I can make you an espresso."

"Coffee would be fine," I say.

"Cream and sugar?"

"Yes."

"Okay. Sit tight, bella."

Taina disappears through a doorway at the back of the room, and returns a moment later with a pretty red mug full of coffee. I wonder just how much poison she put in it.

"Here you go."

"Thanks." I take it suspiciously and consider asking her to taste it for me first.

"Something wrong?" she asks.

"I don't know, is there?" I sniff the coffee for traces of

cyanide.

"I'm sorry, you did say you wanted a coffee with cream and sugar, right? Would you prefer something else?"

"Taste it for me," I say.

"I'm sorry?"

"Just, to see if it's too hot or something."

Taina looks confused, and concerned with my mental health, but being a good stylist and all about service, she obliges my request, taking a delicate sip from my mug.

"Good?" I ask.

She makes a strained smile. "Tastes like Starbucks coffee with organic Horizon cream and sugar."

I wait, and watch. After a few seconds she has not keeled over, so I decide it's safe and snatch my cup back.

"Thank you," I say.

"I'll be right back." Taina moves away from me the way you might walk slowly around a rabid dog you don't want to upset. "I'm just going to run back and mix your color. Can I get you anything else? A magazine?"

"I'd like a new cell phone so I can at least check my email," I gripe, joking but only half-joking. "If you have an extra one of those lying around, I'll take it."

"Would an iPad work?" she asks.

"Excuse me?"

"We have a couple of iPads with wireless for our guests," she says, scurrying over to the reception area and returning with a shiny new tablet. "It's really easy. You just pull up the browser like this, and voila! See?"

I take the iPad and thank her, wondering if it's rigged with explosives.

"Enjoy," she says. "I'll be right back."

My mother is watching me closely, and as soon as Taina is out of earshot, she comes over to me with that "I told you so" look in her eye.

"You see?" she asks.

"I don't see anything but a ghetto salon," I tell her, though that's not entirely true. I also see that Taina is trying to offer the sorts of services here that you might find at the high-end salons in town. Probably because that way, when she kills your ass and pickles you in brine in the basement, people are going to be less likely to suspect her of it.

"She made it real nice here," my mom says.

"Please go sit back down so I can check my email," I say.

"Usnavys. Don't you use that tone of voice with me. I am trying to help you. We all are."

"I appreciate that. Now go sit down."

My mother goes back to the waiting area in a sulking mood, and I start to surf. I check my email. Nothing of any significance. There's an email from a couple of days ago, from Rebecca, asking why I can't be reached by phone, and telling me that Lauren arrived safe and sound in Santa Fe and has gone on to the ranch.

She has included the phone number to the ranch and said that Lauren would probably appreciate a call from her friends so that she knows she's not alone in the world. Good for Lauren, I think. I have yahoo email, and there's a message from them saying that my account was hacked a few nights ago, or an attempt was made to hack into it. They want me to change my damn password. Juan, I think. That little weasel is probably trying to find out if I'm cheating on him again (I'm not, but the way he's been treating my ass I wish I were cheating on him) so he can use that information in a custody battle. I hate that little rat of a man right now, the way JLo hates that Marc Anthony. Maybe I should call Miss Lopez up and suggest to her that we buy us an island somewhere, some little shitty island full of wild carnivores, where we can ship all the no-good, scrawny-assed, ungrateful, control-freak Boricua husbands. I'd like that. I think me and la Jenny would get along great. She's a go-getter, and so am I. She's from the block, and so am I. She's beautiful and voluptuous and curvy and so am I. We are a lot alike.

I go to a career site and start looking at jobs. I'm reading an advertisement for an opening in New Hampshire when Taina returns with the dye mixed up in little plastic bowls. She sets these on a small high table on wheels, and rolls it next to me.

"Isn't that cool?" she asks of the iPad. "I love my iPad. I use it all the time. My oldest, she's thirteen? She's got one, too. Addicted."

"It's very nice."

She peeks at the screen. She pretends she hasn't, but I notice. I know that she knows I'm looking for a job. Sneaky bitch. She'll use it against me, I can guarantee you that.

"These things happen," I tell her. "Even to the best of us."

"I'm sorry? What things?"

"Never mind."

Taina starts to dab a brush loaded with color onto my roots. "Your hair is nice and thick," she tells me. "It's so pretty. You always had good hair."

Now I know the bitch is a stone-faced liar. My hair is not pretty. Not right now. And back in grade school, I had me some of the worst hair you ever saw.

"So, do you ever talk to any of the people from back in the day?" she asks me, trying to make conversation.

"No."

"Except Juan. Right? I heard you two got married."

"We did. That was a long time ago."

"That's beautiful. I always liked him. He was always crazy about you, and you never gave him the time of day. See, that's the key with men, I think. You have to ignore them long enough to get them to feel like the chase to get you was worth it. Men are goal-oriented. They need to feel useful. You give them too much, too soon, and they take you for granted. They think you're not worth anything."

I feel myself starting to breathe faster, fighting back the tears. "Don't take too much length off," I say, directing her attention away from my main source of pain, to my head. "I'm gonna grow it out another inch or two."

"Let me see the condition of your ends. We might need to take just a little off. Not a lot."

"You're the expert," I say sarcastically. She doesn't seem to pick up on my snide remark.

Taina keeps on daubing on the coloring for a while without saying anything, and then she starts in again. I brace for what she's gonna say, all that bottled up resentment and so on and so forth.

I feel guilty for misleading her about Juan. I don't know why, m'ija, don't ask. I just told you, when I don't care what the person thinks of me, I can be brutally honest with them.

"He left me, just so you know."

Taina's brow shoots up. "What? Juan left you?"

"Yep. Took my kids, and just went."

"I am so sorry to hear that. When did it happen?"

"Couple days ago."

"Ay, Usnavys. I am sorry."

"It is what it is."

"I want you to know, I feel you on what's happening right now," she tells me in a lowered voice, without moving any of the muscles in her pretty face.

I sit up straighter to make sure I look dignified, because I don't want to feel like the kind of woman who is left by her husband. Time to talk about something else.

"Girl, what do you put on your hair? It's shinier now than when you were in high school, and I know you're not getting any younger because I'm not, either."

Taina flips her long, lustrous hair over a shoulder, and juts her chin toward a display shelf with a bunch of plastic bottles with homemade-looking labels on them.

"I make my own products," she says with a shrug and a smile. "They're specially formulated for hair like ours, not exactly black, but not white, either."

"You cooking up some mulatta hair serums, or what?" I ask, pleased I've gotten her, for the moment, off the trail of my despair.

She nods. "Mmm hmm. I took a bunch of the homegrown recipes my mom and aunts were using from back in Puerto Rico, and I added some modern elements, made them organic because I'm not big on chemicals."

"You serious?"

"As a heart attack, girl. They smell good, too."

"What do you call your products?"

"House of Hair," she says.

I hold my tongue. If she's stupid enough to think that's a good name, then her products are probably not worth the stress of educating her sorry ass out of its delusional state.

She tells me, "People around here, my clients, they're snatching this stuff up like it's running out. I'm actually making most of my money from the products."

"That's great. House of Hair. Huh."

Taina watches me for a moment, thinking. "I meant what I said, about feeling where you're at and wanting you to know I'm here for you."

"I'm fine. I'll live."

"Oh, c'mon, Usnavys," she says. "Don't front."

"Who's fronting?"

"Everyone knows. I shouldn't have acted like I didn't because I already knew. Everyone's talking, girl. I'm not saying that's right. Okay? It's not right to gossip. The Bible says that. So I don't do it. But a lot of people who come sit in this chair, they do. It's about all the do, and you know how it is around here. Everybody is always up in everybody's business."

"What are you saying?'

"It's okay. It's nothing to be ashamed of. Shit happens, girl."

"Everyone knows what?"

Taina looks in my eyes via the mirror again, this time like she feels sorry for me, but not in a mean way. I am telling you, chica, this girl is a great actress. She is almost convincing me that she likes me or some shit, and I know that ain't true.

"Just cut my damn hair, Taina."

"Usnavys," she says in a patient tone, a little amused. I don't see any trace of the volatile angry girl she used to be. Where'd she go and hide all that?

"But not too much. Like I said, don't cut it a lot. Soon as I'm on my feet again, I'm going back to my salon."

"I'm not going to cut it short, okay? Stop freaking

out."

"Who's freaking out? Me? I'm fine."

Taina keeps going with the foils and the color, painting pieces of my hair root to tip, the folding the piece up inside a little piece of aluminum foil. She works like a real stylist, and it shouldn't surprise me but it does. It makes me feel stupid, but I'm not really sure why.

When she finishes with the foils, she tells me to follow her to a different part of the salon, back behind a little paper wall like you'd find somewhere in Asia. This is where the dryers are. She sits me beneath one, but before turning it on, she kneels down so that we are eye to eye, and looks at me with what appears to be great sympathy.

"I understand where you're at, girl." She puts a hand on my arm in a sisterly fashion that makes me want to smack her face.

"How on earth would you know where I'm at if I haven't told your ass?"

"Because I've been there. My husband left me after our last baby was born, and I was sick with an autoimmune disease, I thought I was dying, and he was tired of hearing me cry and complain about the pain so he just walked out on us and left me like that to care for three kids and a salon on my own. I almost went under with this business. I had to move heaven and earth to make it through, and I got me three kids counting on me."

"I'm happy for you."

"I couldn't have done it without my mom and all the support I got from the people at church."

"That's nice."

"What I'm trying to say is, I know you don't know me anymore, and I know we were never that close, but I am here for you now. I don't have a lot, all I have is this salon, and I make enough to get by but God knows I'm not getting rich. I make enough to employ someone full-time to answer phones for us, I can't pay a lot. I can pay twelve dollars an hour to start, with full benefits."

"Enough," I say.

"I know you had a great job, Usnavys, and believe it

or not, everybody back in the 'hood was really happy for you. No one was happier for you than I was. I know we had our problems."

"I treated you like shit," I say.

"We were kids. Kids are stupid and mean. Trust me. I have three, I see it in them. Girls especially. Gosh, girls can be mean."

I feel the tears come. I don't want to cry. I don't.

"It wouldn't be forever. Just until you find something else. Give you a place to go, some friends to talk to. We talk all day long in here. It's like the freakin' Doctor Phil Show, girl. Free therapy, benefits, and a little spending money."

I don't answer her, not because I don't want to but because I know that if I open my mouth, I'm going to flat start to cry like a damn lunatic, and I don't need to be showing that much vulnerability right now. Taina watches me for a moment and then seems to be embarrassed for me. She pats me on the knee, and says she'll be back to check on my highlights in a few minutes.

"Can I get you a magazine? Some water?"

I compose myself, and take a deep breath before I ask her the question that's foremost on my mind.

"Why are you being so nice to me? I was terrible to you. Pez dispenser? Remember?"

Taina laughs. "At least you were creative with your insults."

"I don't understand," I tell her. "If it were me, I'd be rolling in your misery like the best thing ever happened to me."

"I'm not about that," she says.

"Why not?"

Taina points to a crucifix on the wall. "There's the guy you might have heard about," she tells me. "He turned my life around. His name is Jesus Christ. You should come to church with me sometime."

"I'm not really a church person," I tell her, uncomfortable, as I always am, when zealous people start to push their agendas on me.

"I wasn't either. But the one I go to, they taught me a lot. And one of the best things they taught me was that it's better to forgive people than to try to get revenge. I used to always try to get even."

"I remember."

"It didn't help. It only ever made things worse."

I am not sure why, but I feel goose bumps rising on my arms and on the back of my neck.

"The other thing I learned is that the only way you can reap the rewards that God has in store for you is by being honest."

Her eyes connect with mine again.

"I am not a liar," I tell her. When she doesn't respond, I say it again, adding, "I do not lie to people, okay? I maybe just don't tell them a few things now and then."

Taina smiles, and squeezes my hand with an unguarded love and sincerity that throw me off balance mentally.

"Oh, Usnavys," she says. "You don't have to lie to other people to be dishonest. Sometimes, the worst kind of dishonesty is when you lie to yourself."

Oh, my God, m'ija. No, she *didn't*. She did *not* just say that. I should punch her right in the goddamned mouth for that, you know I should. But it's pretty hard to punch someone when you have your hands covering your face to keep them from seeing you cry.

JASON

Jason Flynn likes the universe. This is because it always gives him exactly what he needs. Some people say the universe is nothing but wrinkles and folds, but Jason Flynn knows that God is adept at controlling this flow. God smoothes the wrinkles out, and sometimes you see the edges of His handiwork and you realize that God is ruthlessly destructive. God also has a very good sense of humor, and a direct connection to Jason Flynn. God talks to him, sometimes. God tells him what to do. Sometimes he is not even aware of what he needs until it comes from God, and then he is often surprised he did not understand the need before.

Today, it is all about Martin Bernstein, a wrinkle in Jason Flynn's plans.

Jason sits at his desk with a pen in his mouth and his feet up, watching the slightly younger, slightly homelier detective. Something about the way Bernstein avoids looking at him -- and indeed, has avoided looking at him all afternoon -- tells Jason Flynn that Bernstein knows too much about him. Usually, Bernstein looks at Jason Flynn now and then, just as he looks at everyone else in the room. But for the past few days, Bernstein has acted as though Jason Flynn weren't there at all. This is unusual, and unusual things are like wrinkles in smooth, fine fabric. They stand out to Jason Flynn in stark relief. Wrinkles of this type are good indications of something new to be understood. So he watches, and waits for God to deliver the understanding, and the orders.

Jason Flynn enjoys understanding things, and he is a very good student of human behavior. He knows how people do things, and he knows their reasons. He does not have the same motivations as other people, but unlike them, he understands others deeply. Most people assume everyone is like them. Jason Flynn knows better. No one is like him, and this is because Jason Flynn alone is as close as a man can get to being *godlike*.

Jason gets up from his desk now, and walks past Bernstein's desk, just to see what he will do. Bernstein pretends to make a phone call when he feels Flynn approach. Jason finds this curious. Extremely curious. Jason Flynn stops in front of Bernstein's desk and looks at the detective for a long enough moment that Bernstein covers the mouthpiece of his phone as though he were talking to someone, and asks Jason if he can help him.

"Just wanted to say hi," says Jason Flynn, with his most charming smile.

Bernstein's face registers alarm, and Jason Flynn is pleased to be capable of frightening the detective. Jason Flynn also notices the scrap of paper on Bernstein's desk with the words "house of hair salon, Usnavys" written on it.

Interesting.

"Hi," says Bernstein, covering his fear with bravado. Without seeming to see it, Jason Flynn notices Bernstein turning the scrap paper with Lauren's friend's name on it upside down, casually, elegantly almost. But still clumsy.

"Wondered if you might want to get a drink after work," says Jason Flynn. He has never invited Bernstein out for a drink. He has never socialized with Bernstein at all. He wonders if Bernstein is good at noticing wrinkles, too, or if he's just one of those feeling men who trip along through life chasing emotions.

"Something up?" asks Bernstein, with more confidence behind his eyes than Jason Flynn expected. This is good. This will be interesting. This will be fun to sort out and understand.

"Oh, you know. Girl troubles. Thought you might know a thing or two about it, being that you're the only other halfway decent-looking fellow around here," says Jason Flynn with a disarming grin.

Bernstein is not impressed or flattered by this, and in fact he returns Jason Flynn's gaze with an expression Flynn recognizes as that of a man trying also to understand. Bernstein notices wrinkles, too.

Good.

"I wouldn't know anything about the sorts of girl troubles you have, Jason," says Bernstein, in carefully measured words.

Jason Flynn hears the unspoken paragraph of arrogant, hateful subtext as though it were sung to him in an aria. Wonderful. Ah, yes. This delights Jason Flynn, because it tells him all he needs to know.

Suddenly, from those thirteen words uttered by Bernstein, Jason Flynn sees the universe open up and deliver unto him a deep and meaningful new understanding of his colleague.

Jason Flynn understands that Bernstein loves Lauren. Interesting. He would not have guessed that one. He also understands that Bernstein has stopped watching Jason Flynn because in the wake of Lauren's "accident" in the train station, Bernstein has begun to watch Jason Flynn more closely than ever before. I

In other words, Bernstein suspects Jason Flynn is behind the attempted murder.

Marvelous! This is rich.

This is exciting, and good, for Jason Flynn enjoys few things more than an adversary worthy of him. Bernstein is smart, handsome, tall -- in fact, when he started out here in the department, more than one person remarked about how similar Bernstein was to himself, Jason Flynn. They are nothing alike, of course, because Bernstein is weak with emotion. He wears it on his sleeve.

Bernstein is nothing like him, but he is similar enough to make the new plan hatching in Jason Flynn's mind absolutely thrilling. Jason Flynn realizes that he could take care of several of his problems at once, with the help of Bernstein. With Bernstein's help, Jason Flynn could get the mob off his ass, he could get Lauren to let down her guard, and he could be rid of Bernstein altogether. With Bernstein's help, Jason Flynn could be rid of this police department and the ruse of being a good guy, and he could go undercover in life, period. He could become rich. He could be free.

Bernstein is like an angel, sent by God, and Jason

Flynn knows now precisely how he will use this man.

"I'd still like to get your opinion on a few things," says Jason Flynn, reveling in all this new understanding, and in all his new plans. Bernstein knows. Bernstein suspects. Bernstein is an idiot, even though everyone seems to think otherwise, because he has just stood up and walked in front of a monster, exposed his soft white underbelly for a ravenous beast. Bernstein suspects Jason Flynn, but he has no clue how godlike Flynn actually is, how completely impassively he is able to stand master of life and death.

"I'm busy," says Bernstein. "Sorry."

"Tomorrow, then," suggests Jason Flynn, enjoying this so much he almost hates to have to go back to his desk.

"Busy."

"When aren't you busy?" asks Jason Flynn.

This is when Bernstein narrows his eyes at him, thinking that such a thing will scare him, that such hints and menacing looks will make Jason Flynn think twice. It is delicious how naive Bernstein is about him.

"I'm always busy, Flynn. We're not friends."

"I see," says Jason Flynn. "And I understand."

Bernstein returns to his fake phone call, and Jason Flynn smiles the biggest smile to have infected his face in days. Things are going so beautifully, he almost can't stand it. Look at the details of how marvelous it all is! He knows where Lauren is. He's determined to find her. And now, the wrinkle of Martin Bernstein is about to be smoothed out with deft and swift godlike skill.

Jason Flynn returns to his desk only long enough to grab his suit jacket. Then he heads out the door, to drive his white Cadillac Escalade home. He is overcome with a sudden overpowering urge to iron every shirt in his closet. There are few things more satisfying in life, he thinks as he drives, than flattening wrinkles beneath metal so hot it might have come straight from hell. Life, thinks Jason Flynn, is good.

But death -- a crushing, flattening, merciless death so hot it will feel as though it has come from hell itself -- is so much better.

LAUREN

I've made it about halfway back down the dirt road that leads from Tio's ranch to the Highway when I see John Smith's pickup truck coming up the same road, toward me.

"Oh, crap," I say, berating myself for not having considered the possibility that I'd run into him this way. I try to think of something to tell him, some lie that he'll believe and let me go past him.

I can't let on that I suspect he's somehow in with the guys who want me dead. I am going to have to act. Act, like an anorexic in search of an Academy Award – or like a twenty-something Playboy bunny who thinks Heff will actually believe she wants to schtup his shriveled old carapace. It's all an act.

Because there is only room for one truck on the road, I gamely move to the side as we approach one another, hoping that he will simply ease on past me and keep going toward home. No such luck.

Instead, the handsome and possibly deadly cowboy pulls his truck right up next to mine, rolls down the window, and motions for me to do the same. I plaster a fake smile on my face, and hope that I look relaxed and not at all like I'm visualizing all the many ways this man might snuff out my life and all the things he might do to me along the way.

"Hi there," I say, with syrupy cheer.

"Where do you think you're going?" he asks, serious.

"To town. I, uhm, I sort of got my period, and I don't have any, you know. Girl stuff."

John shakes his head and narrows his eyes at me, as though he sees right through my ruse.

"I've got supplies for that," he tells me.

"I seriously doubt that. Five o'clock shadow and all that."

"A lady friend left them," he explains.

"Ah. Lady friends again."

He shows no reaction to my lame attempt at a joke. "Come on, turn around and let's get you back. This road's no fun to drive on. Plus, we have a shooting lesson scheduled."

"I'd really like to go to the store and get my own, if you don't mind," I say, my heart skipping beats in fear. Just look calm and cool, I tell myself, and everything will be fine. "I've got a few other things I'd like to get, too."

John stares me down. "I am only going to say this once," he says. "I know you're an independent woman, from the big city, but you have to understand that out here, things are a lot different than what you're used to."

"I am more than aware of that. Thanks, though."

He narrows his beautiful eyes at me. "You can't just go around driving on roads like this. It's bad enough with the coyotes and bobcats, if you got a flat tire or something, but with the problem you've got that you're running from, with them calling you up here, you'd have to be half-stupid and whole-crazy to go running around by yourself."

"I can handle it. I appreciate your concern, though. I really do." Yeah, *right*.

"People in Quemado say a guy's been through, asking about you."

"What?"

"Just heard, down at the store. After what you told me, and knowing your situation, I don't think you can handle it, and I'm not going to let you get hurt. I couldn't live with that."

"I'm sorry," I tell him, "but the last time I checked, you weren't my mother, and you didn't have any right to tell me what to do. So with all due respect, I'd like to wish you a very good day. I'll see you later, when I get back from the store."

"Please don't be foolish," he says.

I roll the window up, put the car in drive, and start off through the scrub brush along the side of the road, past his truck, and go as fast as I can over the rough road, toward freedom. My hope is that he will believe that I'm nothing more than an impetuous girl in need of tampons, and that he'll believe me about me coming back to the house later. But, as your average potheaded motel clerk knows, hope is a foolish thing sometimes.

I look in the rearview mirror, and see John Smith turning his truck around in a cloudy fit of agitated dust, with the intention of chasing me. This is when I feel one of the tires pop underneath me. I keep driving on it, until I simply can't anymore -- this lasts about two minutes.

John stops his pickup behind the one I'm in, and gets out. He comes over on foot, and I am terrified, thinking the worst. When he gets to my window, and stands there looking at me, I finally just lose it. He's going to kill me, I think. It's all over now. Because I am Lauren, and inherently foolish, I break down and start to sob. I cover my face with my hands, and collapse over the steering wheel. It is finally just too much, all of it, everything that is happening. I realize that I am likely having a full-blown breakdown, but am helpless to control it. There's nothing left to do.

After a few minutes of this, I realize I am still alive. I peek out from between my fingers, and see John Smith still standing there next to the pickup, with a look of extreme annoyance on his face. Why hasn't he killed me yet?

"Roll down the window," he calls out when he sees that I'm looking at him.

"No."

"Lauren, c'mon."

Well, I think, what if he's not going to kill me? What if he's not one of the bad guys? What if he's being truthful when he says he wants to help me?

I roll down the window, thinking that I really don't have anything to lose at this point. If this man wanted me dead, he could have killed me by now.

"Are you working for him?" I ask.

"Who?"

"Jason Flynn."

"I don't even know who that is," he says. "What are you talking about?"

"That's my ex-boyfriend's name. He's a bad cop. He's an assassin, actually. For the Irish mob in Boston. That's what I found out about him, and I didn't want to believe it, then he started trying to control me, and I broke up with him, and he pushed me in front of a train. Well, not him, exactly, but he hired some thugs to do it, and then the train just rolled over me, and didn't even touch me. And now here I am."

"And you think he hired *me*?"

"Did he?"

John looks deeply disgusted and offended. "No, of course not. How would he hire me to live in a house next to where you're staying, when that house has been in my family for three generations?"

"Maybe he paid you off," I say.

"And you think I'm hurting for money that badly, huh? Do I *look* broke to you?"

"Are you?"

"No, Lauren. I'm not hurting for money at all. I'm retired military."

"You're too young to retire."

"Not from the army, I'm not. I went in at eighteen. On top of that, I inherited the house and the land, and we run a profitable ranch. Plus my folks had some savings and stocks. I'm more than fine."

"Oh. But maybe he just talked you into it."

"Jesus Christ, Lauren, let it go, okay? I'm not the bad guy here. I haven't met Jason Flynn, and I have no interest in killing you. What you're too pigheaded to see is that I'm trying to help keep you away from guys like that. I don't want to kill you. Truth of the matter is, I don't want to kill *anyone* anymore."

The last word catches me off guard, and I feel the hairs rise on the back of my neck.

"What do you mean, 'anymore'?" I ask.

"Nothing," he says, seeming tired of this conversation, and tired of standing outside in the hot sun.

"Have you killed people *before*?" I ask, completely creeped out now.

"Yes." He says this without hesitating and as though it were the most normal thing in the world.

"What?" I cry.

He raises his voice just a hair now. "I was in the goddamned military, Lauren. Just let it go."

I consider this. I suppose people in the military sometimes have to kill people, and tell him so.

"You think?" he asks, sarcastically. "Even at *war*?" He stares at me as though I were an idiot, which I probably am.

"Sorry," I say. I am trembling uncontrollably, and really am starting to question my sanity.

"I think you need to rest," he says. "Let's go back to the house in my truck and we'll talk about everything, okay? I'll tell you all about the war, and you tell me all about Jason freakin' *Flynn*."

"No. I'm not going anywhere with you."

John looks extremely angry, but like he's controlling it with great effort. "You can't sit out here on the road, and you can't drive your truck like that."

I start to sob again. "Don't yell at me," I say.

"Oh, good Lord. Get out. Come on. I'll take you back, then I'll get a trailer and come back to tow the truck here back to your place."

"Please don't kill me."

John laughs, but he's not entirely amused. He's annoyed and maybe even angry, too. I sense he's got a temper that he rarely shows.

"Come on," he says. "This is ridiculous."

I sit there crying without talking and he waits a minute or two before giving me an ultimatum.

"I'm done standing here on this road. You can either get out and come with me, or you can sit here all alone in that broken truck. Given that there's a guy going around asking about you in Quemado, and given that you actually do have some prick named Jason Flynn trying to hunt you down, I'd suggest you come with me."

I look at him for a long moment, worry all over my face.

"I'm one of the good guys," he tells me, in a tone and with an expression that tells me there is a lot more depth to the statement than I am able to understand yet. "You have to trust me. Okay?"

Without much other choice left, I do as he's asked, and get out, following him to his truck. He opens the door for me, and helps me in. The cab still smells of his "friend's" perfume.

"Your little lady friend certainly smells good," I say in a bratty sort of way. I cough dramatically into my hand.

"She's history. I told you that."

"Whatever. None of my business."

"It's over. I've been meaning to break it off for a while now. Today, I did."

"Why?"

"You want the truth?"

"No," I deadpan. "Lie to me. Girls love that."

He laughs. "Okay. The truth is, she was a nice enough girl, but she bored me."

"With those legs and boobs? You were bored? *Really*?"

"Believe it or not, some guys look for more than that."

"Yeah, okay. Like *what*?" I ask.

John looks at me and shakes his head. "You're a piece of work," he says.

"I am actually probably *several* pieces of work. All patched together. Like a quilt."

"You know what? I don't really need this right now," he tells me. "Any of it."

"Me neither."

"I need a beer," he says.

"Me too."

"Lord. And a movie."

"That would rock."

"Preferably a comedy."

"Monty Python," I suggest.

"Or Seinfeld," he retorts.

"That's not a movie."

He shoots me a sideways glance. "You always so pleasant to be around?"

"Sadly, yes."

We drive in silence, all the way back to Tio's house. When he has failed to try to kill me by the time we get to the door, I start to think he probably won't try at all. But as has been well established by now, I am often (if not usually) wrong about these things.

Once inside the house, John busies himself looking through the impressive selection of DVD movies in the little office with the purple sofa. I, meanwhile, make a beeline for the kitchen, where two six-packs of cold Santa Fe Brewing Company beer await us in the stainless steel refrigerator. I see that the answering machine on the part of the counter that serves as a desk is blinking, and so as I open the dark brown bottles of beer I listen to the message. As it plays, John comes into the kitchen holding a DVD out for me to approve. It is *The 40-Year-Old Virgin*. I nod, and hand him an open beer. John lingers reluctantly, looking at the floor as though this might stop him from overhearing the message.

It is Usnavys, telling me that Martin Bernstein has come to see her and he has confirmed that Jason Flynn is actually trying to kill me. She apologizes for not believing me, and then berates me for getting "her ass" involved in my mess, and tells me that if she ends up dead she will never forgive me. She goes on, saying that Bernstein is following her around to protect her, because "that boy is in love with you, in case you never noticed, and you? Girl, please. *You* went and picked you the wrong damn detective to fall in love with. You should have gone with the nice Jewish boy instead of the Irish bag of garbage, nena, but whatever. Too late now."

Beep. Message over.

"Awkward," John says, when I can't manage to find words to say myself. "I didn't mean to eavesdrop, it's just..."

"Nah, no big deal. I'm an open book now. Right?"

He looks at me as though he feels sorry for me, and really, I can't blame him. I'd feel sorry for me, too. In fact, I do feel sorry for me, right now. The only good thing about being me right now is that I get to look at John Smith, who, in spite of finding me annoying, is still extremely hot.

"She's my best friend," I tell him.

"She sounds, uhm, strong."

I laugh. "She is. And pissed. I don't blame her. I mean, what kind of a best friend gets a psycho after her best friend?"

John sits at the counter on one of the stools, and asks me to tell him the whole story with Jason Flynn, start to finish.

"It's not over yet," I remind him. "I mean, I hope it is, but maybe it's not."

"Well, okay. Up until now."

"Why does it matter? I ask.

"I would like to understand what's going on, because I live next door to you right now. I didn't choose to have you come here, but here you are, and I think I have a right to know what I'm in the middle of now."

"You're not in the middle of it."

"Yes, I am."

"I'm sorry."

"No need. Life is full of surprises, anyway."

I consider this, and guzzle some of the cold, dark ale. I offer to make John a sandwich, and he agrees to it. As I assemble some mozzarella, basil, tomato and olive oil on crusty sourdough bread, I tell him the whole story of me and Jason Flynn. He listens. As I get into the details of Jason's increasing brutality toward me, and ultimately to the moment where he snapped Fatso's neck, John's eyes grow harder, colder, and angrier. His nostrils flare. His poker face wavers sometimes, apparently.

"And that's where we're at now," I say, wrapping up. He sets down his sandwich, and scowls for a moment. He tells me the food is good, but seems to disturbed to eat anymore.

"Guess you must think I'm an idiot," I say.

"Not at all. Guys like that are masters of disguise. I'd say you thought you were falling for a very different man than the one he actually was."

"Well, yeah."

"Do you know why I went into the military?" he asks.

I put my fingers to my temples and close my eyes for a moment, joking, "I wish I were psychic, but no. I don't know why you went into the military. Tell me."

"Smart ass," he says with a grin.

"So I've been told."

"I went into the military because I hate bullies, Lauren. I have always hated a bully. I'm the guy who likes to let bullies get a taste of their own medicine."

"Good to know."

"Jason Flynn is nothing but a bully."

"And a psychopath."

"That goes without saying."

John pauses, and takes a bite of the sandwich, complimenting me on it. I thank him, and watch him chew. His mouth is truly exquisite. A full, well-formed, beautiful mouth. I want to put my mouth on his mouth, but this is obviously not the time or place for such a thing. He swallows, and the Adam's apple bobs in a very masculine way in that most manly of necks.

The cold, hard look in John's eyes is replaced now, by a look of excitement, and an almost Cheshire grin. "You know, I'd really, really like to meet this guy."

"Who? Jason?"

John nods with a viscous grin. "Hell, yeah. Give him a taste of his own medicine. Picking on women and cats. Let's see what he does with a guy his own size."

Upon seeing the extreme confidence with which John says this, I realize that he is possibly as dangerous as Jason Flynn, but it a totally different way. He is dangerous to bullies, to people like Jason. Upon understanding what John means by what he's said -- and I am pretty sure he means that he'd like to beat the shit out of Jason Flynn -- I relax. It feels as though a ton of bricks has just been lifted off of me.

For the first time since I fled Boston in the middle of the night in Juan's weird old car a week ago, I feel myself actually let go of my anxiety enough to truly relax. The knot of horrible anticipation that has been my belly releases. My shoulders lower themselves from where they've taken up residence around my ears. I take a full, deep breath, and feel my pulse slow down.

John notices, and his face softens a bit. I notice the rugged furrows on either side of his mouth now, sort of like dimples, but manlier than that word implies. He is a striking man, his skin kissed by the sun, roughened by it, and he is every bit as physically appealing as Jason Flynn, but with that added bonus of, you know, *not* being a psycho killer.

"Wanna watch the movie?" he asks. "Take your mind off it for a while?"

"I'd love that," I say.

I find some microwave popcorn in the pantry. I pop it, put it in a large yellow plastic bowl, and douse it in red chile powder. Then we both go to the purple sofa to watch the movie. I sit at one end, John sits at the other. We reach for the popcorn on the little rustic coffee table whenever the other one is far from it, careful not to touch. The space between us remains a big, empty question mark. I watch the movie, but cannot quite get lost in it the way you usually do, because I am so focused on the incredible and inappropriate attraction I feel toward this man. If this week has taught me nothing else, it is that Lauren has very bad taste in men and needs to stop trying to taste them for a while.

When the movie ends, I stretch my arms overhead and yawn. For the past few nights, I haven't slept well at all. I am exhausted.

"You go on to bed," he says. "I'll stay right here tonight, if that's okay with you."

"Don't you want to go home?" I ask, my mind wandering to thoughts of how nice it might be to have him sleep with me -- and I don't mean have sex with me, though that would probably be pretty nice, too. I mean, to have him hold me, and wrap me in his big, strong arms. To be protected by this mysterious cowboy about whom I know so little.

"Once a soldier, always a soldier," he tells me. "I took an oath to protect my fellow citizens from harm, and that includes you."

"So you're going to sleep on the sofa?" I ask, hoping he might suggest something else.

"Yes," he says slowly, sizing me up in a hungry sort of way. "Unless you had something else in mind, Miz Fernandez?"

"There are two guest rooms you could use," I tell him as my heartbeat accelerates. I would like to suggest my bedroom, but it doesn't seem wise. At all.

"I see," he says. "I think I'll stay out here, in that case."

"Okay," I say. I linger for a moment, and I see that he is looking at me over on his end of the sofa, in the exactly the way a man looks at a woman he might like to kiss.

"What are you thinking about?" I ask him, and he blinks slowly, an almost imperceptible smile playing on his lips.

"Why do women always ask men questions that they don't actually want to know the answers to?" he asks. "It's incredible how often you guys do that."

"Do we?"

"All the time."

"So I don't want to know what you're thinking? Is that what you're saying?"

"Probably not a good thing for you to know."

"Tell me."

John Smith takes a deep breath, as though composing and controlling himself. He is very good at both. He is also very good at moving his eyes over me in a way that lets me know more or less what's on his mind. But to remove all doubt, he tells me in words, too.

"I am thinking that life is funny," he says. "When I first heard you were coming out here, I was pissed about it. I'm not going to lie. I wasn't happy to have my privacy invaded, to have to deal with some woman from the city who doesn't know which end of a horse is which."

"Wow. You think very little of me. The end with the

tail is the head. Right?"

He grins. "Now, wait a minute. I'm not done yet."

"Sorry. Please go on. Your words flatter me."

"And now, here I am, filled with this...need."

"Oh?" This piques my interest.

"To protect you," he clarifies.

"Oh," I say, slightly disappointed.

He smiles, amused by me. "Now, hold on. I feel a need to protect you, but I also think it'd be pretty nice to...well, let's just say to *touch* you."

His eyes lock on mine, and I feel the breath catch in my throat. He sizes me up for my reaction, and satisfied that I've not been offended, he continues.

"You just seem like the kind of woman who, with the right man, could be very...uhm...let's just say *passionate*."

"You think?"

He laughs softly. "Uhm. Yeah. I do." He sits up straighter now, plants his elbows on his thighs and leans towards me. "Miz Fernandez, let me ask you something."

"Uhm, okay."

"Do you ever think about how nice it might be to have someone kiss you along that narrow muscle on the side of your neck, the one that goes from your ear to your collarbone? Softly, but with determination? Just, right there, stopping right above your breasts?"

I shudder at the directness of his words, and the calm, seductive way he speaks them.

"Sounds fine, I guess," I blurt stupidly.

He nods and narrows his smiling eyes. "I was thinking, and I'm saying this because you asked, in that way that women always do, that it would be very nice to do that to you. And it'd be nice -- well, not nice exactly, but *good* maybe -- to run my hands up under your shirt, and unhook your bra, and just sort of touch you lightly with my fingertips, and learn what makes you...tick."

"Oh."

"Yep. I'd like to do that. That, and a few other things."

"Tell me what they are."

John Smith laughs now, and repeats his question

about women asking for information they can't handle.

"I can handle you," I say.

"Doubt that," he says.

"I can!"

"I'm here to protect you, not take advantage of you," he says. "But you asked me what I was thinking. That doesn't mean it's what I'll be *doing*."

"Why not?" I complain. I always end up getting rejected by the good ones, I think. Only the bad ones are drawn to me.

"Get some sleep, Miz Fernandez," he tells me with a chuckle, taking a gun from the waistband of his pants and setting it on the coffee table before reclining on the sofa in his stocking feet with his hands behind his head. He's got a sly look on his face as he licks his lips in my general direction, then turns his eyes toward the windows.

"You can't do this!" I whine.

"Do what?"

"Start something you don't finish."

"We were just talking," he says. "I didn't start anything. You did. You and your reporter's questions."

"C'mon."

"Sorry, honey. It's late."

"Seriously?"

"Sleep tight, Miz Fernandez," he says, closing his eyes against me. "I'll see you in the morning."

MARTIN

Martin Bernstein has finally come home, dog-tired after spending three after-work hours sitting in his car outside the housing project where Lauren's friend Usnavys Rivera is staying with her mother. There was no sign of Jason Flynn, and that's a good thing. Martin is feeling confident that Jason won't be bothered Usnavys at all. Could be Jason's all talk, just trying to scare Lauren into coming back to Boston to help her friend. The only thing worse than a sociopath is a lazy sociopath.

Martin is wilted and hungry, ready for a shower and dinner. He is trying to stick the key into the lock on the front door of his Dorchester house without much luck because the porch light is out. He's cursing to himself when he sees a smiling Jason Flynn step toward him from behind a bush. The man's height and gait are unmistakable. It could be none other. The smile is chilling.

Martin barely has time to think about how he should have cut that bush down a long time ago (knowing as he did that it could conceal a man but being too trusting and cocky to think it mattered much) before seeing Jason's arm come up. There is a large, heavy black police flashlight in Jason's hand, the kind few policemen use for anything but beating people. Flynn brings it down hard, with a blunt thud, on top of Martin's head. There is a crack. There is a hot, searing pain. Then another blow. Both strikes are done calmly, and are extremely well placed. Snake strikes, really. Martin only has time to think, "Jason Flynn is a human viper" before everything goes dark.

When he regains consciousness, Martin finds himself inside Jason Flynn's white Cadillac Escalade. It smells of cinnamon car freshener, the kind you get in little cakes at a car was to put under your seats. Strangely, Martin is sitting in the driver's seat, even though his wrists and ankles are tightly bound with what feels like wire. In fact, the wrists are affixed to the seat somehow, and Martin cannot raise his hands at all. He tries to move his head, but realizes that it is fastened somehow to the headrest of the seat. It is dark outside, and Martin cannot make out where, exactly, they are. He begins to panic, and tries to talk, but finds that there is a gag in his mouth. It is tight.

"Calm down," says Jason Flynn quietly, sitting next to Martin in the passenger seat of the car. Martin feels Jason's hands on him, adjusting the binds but also tracing delicate lines across him, like a lover. He sees that Jason's hands are encased in dark leather gloves. The kind that prevent fingerprints.

Martin tries to scream, to move, but he can't.

"You think you're valiant," says Jason. "Noble. Prince Charming. Doing the right thing. But the truth is, you don't understand. You don't understand it at all. The universe. God. The way things actually work. The earth is going to burn when the sun explodes, eventually. The sun will die, the earth will die. Everything has to die. That's what I understand that you do not."

Martin's head is throbbing. He looks down, and sees that he's not wearing his own clothes anymore. He's wearing an expensive suit he recognizes as belonging to Jason Flynn. Jason Flynn's class ring is on his own finger. Jason Flynn's wristwatch on his arm.

"The less we fear death, the happier we are," says Jason in a terrifyingly cold, flat voice. "I've heard it has a pleasant quality as the brain dies, not unlike being very high."

Martin smells gasoline. He hears liquid sloshing and spilling, then feels it as it saturates him. Jason is pouring gas on him, all over him. It is in his hair now, dripping down his face, into his eyes. He screams and coughs, and gags. The smell is soon overwhelming, and he realizes that Jason is filling the car with fuel. Martin screams. He hears the passenger door open, and close. He watches through burning eyes, in horror, as Jason douses the outside of the car with gasoline, pouring it from an orange container.

Jason Flynn is going to kill him, in his own car, wearing his own clothes. But why? Martin tries to understand, and then it dawns on him. Jason wants everyone to think it is he himself who has died. He is setting Martin up to pose, in death, as himself. Then he's going to kill Lauren. No. *No.*

Martin tries frantically to get himself lose, but there's no way. The binds are perfect, powerful, rigid, unyielding. This, he thinks, is the end of me.

He hears the passenger door open again.

"Goodbye, Martin," says Jason Flynn.

Then the lit match lands with horrifying certainty on Martin's lap. The flame licks him all over, spreading quickly across his entire body, and then on to the seat, and the steering wheel. It takes mere seconds for the entire car to ignite. At first, he feels nothing, because the surreal quality of the whole thing overrides sensation. This can't be happening, Martin thinks in a panic. And yet, it is.

Then, pain. The pain Martin feels is beyond anything he ever imagined possible, and lasts several minutes, each minute bringing with it a new, horrific suffering, until mercifully, suddenly, the pain simply disappears as though it were a light that someone turned off as they left a room.

Martin finds himself floating now, above the car, looking down upon it from the air. He feels nothing for the car, which seems to be exploding now. He feels nothing for the body inside of the car, either. He feels only happiness, and peace. The flames that have drawn a crowd from the decrepit neighborhood, a crowd of junkies and prostitutes and stray dogs, holds no fascination for Martin. The body charred within the Escalade is just a lump of flesh, a rock, something inanimate. It has nothing whatsoever anymore to do with Martin Bernstein, who is whole and comfortable and free, separate from the misery below.

His attention is drawn now to a bright white light, a warm and welcoming light in the sky. It is more beautiful than anything he has ever seen or felt, and he decides that he is going to go toward it, and as he nears it, he sees his parents inside of it, smiling, and waiting for him with open arms. The both appear to be about thirty years old, and in better health and spirits than he ever remembers them having been before. They welcome him home. It is just as it should be, and perfect. There are colors he has never seen before, and a music he feels in every string. Everyone is there who he has ever known, or would have known, even those he left behind, and some he hadn't yet met in that dimension he just left. Time has stopped and he is aware that it is now all happening at once. The secrets of time, existence, order, this universe, they all come to him like a whisper from God, and it all makes sense. All of time exists, here and now. The fiery darkness closes up behind him, and Martin, engulfed in the light and whisked away by love, peace and forgiveness, is.

REBECCA

I love early mornings because they are the time I have completely to myself. Because I own a media company, I must keep myself up to date on the latest news. This is why I wake at 4:30 a.m., and position myself on the treadmill in our home gym, with five televisions on the wall in front of me, each set to a different news program. One is local to New Mexico, the others are national, via Satellite -- Boston (I must keep up with my old hometown), New York, Los Angeles, Miami and Houston.

I have headphones that I toggle between the various frequencies of the stations. I do this while simultaneously skimming the top stories in four newspapers on my iPad. I like the darkness outside the windows, and the solitude of my ventures in the early morning. It reminds me of the days before I was married and a mother, or even of the days when I was married to my first husband, Brad, who was so busy with his own work that I never really felt all that married anyway. Connor is still sleeping, and so is Andre. I do wonder, sometimes, whether I was cut out for marriage and motherhood at all. It is terrible to have such thoughts, especially after I have given a vow to God that I will be a wife and mother, and so I run faster, and read harder, and try to ignore the nagging feelings that I know will only lead to trouble.

I am rounding into my second mile when the breaking news story appears on the local television morning news show out of Boston. There is footage of the burned-out hull of a car, in a decrepit-looking part of town. The reporter stands across the street, as locals (black and Latino, mostly) mug for the camera behind her. She reports that the car has been identified as belonging to a detective with the Boston Police Department by the name of Jason Flynn, adding that a man's body matching the description of Flynn's was found beaten, bound and burned to death inside the vehicle. She adds that a short time before the fire was estimated to have been set the Boston Police received an anonymous call from someone identifying themselves as a member of a local organized crime outfit, saying they had evidence that Jason Flynn was crooked and involved with criminal activities, including the possible attempted murder of his ex-girlfriend, a former columnist with the Boston Gazette who abruptly left her job and disappeared without a trace last week. The caller said the mob was going to take care of Jason Flynn as a message to others about keeping family business within the family.

I feel my legs grow weak. Lauren wasn't lying. In fact, she was in very serious danger from this man. I press the red "emergency stop" button on the treadmill keypad to halt the belt beneath my feet, and I stand there for a long moment, catching my breath and trying to comprehend what I've just seen. I take a sip of water from the bottle in the treadmill's holder, and then I punch in the number to Tio's ranch. Lauren doesn't answer, and the machine picks up. I hang up and dial again. This time, a man answers. I am thrown for a moment, but then I ask for Lauren.

"She's sleeping. Can I take a message?" says the man.

"Who is this?" I ask.

"John Smith, her neighbor."

Of course, I think. Lauren, who has never been able to live as a single woman for very long, has already attached herself to the nearest man around. This is how she gets herself into trouble, I think.

"Will you wake her, please? It's urgent. This is Rebecca Baca calling."

"Jasper's niece?" he asks.

"Yes. Please put Lauren on the phone."

"Okay. Hang on."

I hear a knocking on a door on the other end of the line, which strikes me as odd. Wouldn't he have been sleeping with her? I tell myself this isn't the time for conjecture about Lauren's private life -- at least not in its newest incarnation with John Smith. I hear some muttered voices, and then Lauren is on the phone.

"Rebecca? Everything okay?"

I tell Lauren what I've just seen on the television

program out of Boston, and she is silent.

"Are you there?" I ask.

"Yes," she says weakly. "They said he's dead?"

"Yes."

"Killed by the mafia?" she asks.

"That's what they said. I thought you should know."

"Have you talked to Usnavys?" she asks me. I tell her that I have been unable to reach Usnavys for several days, and that's when Lauren tells me that our friend is unemployed, in the midst of a divorce, and living in the projects with her mother again. I am dumbfounded by this news.

"I'll call her," Lauren tells me. "He was trying to get to her, too. She'll be relieved to hear about this."

"They mentioned you on the news story. The police think he might have had something to do with pushing you in front of the train. You ought to call them. Tell them what you know now."

"I don't think that's a good idea," she says.

"At least tell them you're alive. There are rumors going around that he might have killed you."

"Good," says Lauren.

"What do you mean 'good'?"

"Rebecca, he wasn't the only dirty cop in the bunch. If they'd kill him for telling me stuff, then they'd probably kill me for knowing stuff. It's best that people don't know what happened to me for now."

I take a deep breath and try to understand. "I'm sorry this is happening to you," I tell her.

"Me too."

"I'd say this is a bad time for you to be alone, but it sounds like you're not," I say, hinting that I'd like to know who the man who answered the phone was.

"Don't worry. He's just a friend. A neighbor."

"Just a friend?"

"He's been hanging out with me, and has it in his mind that he's going to protect me from Jason."

"I guess he doesn't have to do that anymore," she says.

"Apparently not."

"Well, I just thought you should know. I need to get going. Do you need anything else?"

"No. You've done enough. More than enough. I am really grateful, Rebecca. Thank you."

"That's what friends are for," I tell her. We say our goodbyes and I hang up.

I should return to my workout, but I can't. I'm too scrambled up about this thing. Lauren is the second one of my college friends to have found herself involved with a violent man who ended up dead. I know the statistics, I know how common this sort of thing is, but when it strikes so close to home it is disturbing. I wonder if it would be okay now to tell our other friends about what's going on? Surely it would be useful for Lauren to discuss this with Sara, our friend who left an abusive marriage to a charming but violent man named Roberto. She knows a thing or two about this, and about how to recover from it. She's very happily married now, to a much-younger man.

I will let Lauren decide what to do from here. It's not my place to tell anyone about what is going on in her life.

I return to the master suite, where Andre is up and shaving in his boxer shorts at the sink. He smiles tepidly at me through the mirror, and my heart sinks. We have lost the flame we once had, and neither of us has the guts to talk about it.

I tell him about the news, and he listens, rapt. We agree that it is very good news for Lauren that this insane man is dead. We also agree that it is worrisome that she got involved with him in the first place.

"You think she'd know better," he says. "She's a smart woman."

"Maybe she knew, but they never talked about it," I say, giving him a significant look meant to convey that I also mean our situation.

Andre looks at me, and gets it. He understands instantly what I mean. And I, in that moment, understand that life is too short to sit around waiting for things to fix themselves. I have always been excellent at fixing my professional life, a problem-solver. It is time, I think, to make the same effort in my marriage, or risk losing it.

"I miss you," I tell him, simply.

Andre swipes the blade over the last spot of shaving cream, and rinses his face with water before toweling it dry and turning to face me.

"What do you mean?" he asks.

I peel the sports bra off, and let it fall to the floor.

"I mean, I miss you," I tell him. I feel my nipples hardening from the cool air against my damp skin. I remove my shorts next, and then my panties, and I stand in front of him completely nude.

Andre seems surprised. I fight the urge to hide, to run away, to argue, and I step toward him with a small Mona Lisa smile. I remind myself that sometimes marriage is work, just like a job. Sometimes you have to go through the motions until they feel natural again. My mother learned the hard way the costs of not communicating with her husband, of letting the sex part of the marriage slip away without talking about it. I am not about to let that same thing happen to us.

"I miss your touch," I tell him, taking his hand in my own and placing it on my breast. Andre's eyelids flutter a little as he caresses me, and I see his guard, the one he has so careful hidden himself behind, begin to slip.

"You're cold," he tells me. "You have goose bumps."

"I was running. A little sweaty, that's all."

"Don't you want to shower?" he asks, referring to my reluctance over the years to be intimate without being completely clean first.

"Kiss them," I tell him.

"Sorry?"

"My breasts. Kiss them."

Andre's eyes search mine for a moment as though he is trying to understand whether I am joking or not.

"Please," I say. "It's been too long."

My husband looks at me in the strangest way now, as though confused, then mildly pleased, and he bends at the waist, and plants a couple of lukewarm kisses on my breasts. It doesn't feel sincere. I tell myself to ignore that part of it, to keep going.

"Tell me what you need," I say, softly. I touch the soft, curly hair on his head, and caress the side of his face. I run my hand along his strong, solid neck and down onto his upper back, pulling him into me.

Andre looks up at me, sorrowfully.

"I don't know," he says. "I need you. The whole you."

"Tell me what I can do," I say.

Andre straightens up again, and holds me tightly against him. I wrap my arms around him, and kiss his bare chest. He drops his head to kiss me on the lips. It is a slow, gentle kiss, a lingering kiss, that grows hungrier and more intense as it progresses. When we come out of it, I stop censoring myself.

"What's happened to us?" I ask him.

"Life," he says, touching my chin softly with a fingertip. "That's the best I can figure."

"It's not how we thought we'd be, is it?"

Andre shakes his head.

"I was going to ask you if there was someone else, but I don't want to know," I say.

"Rebecca!" He looks offended. I put my finger over his lips to silence him.

"I don't want to talk about it. At all. I don't care. I just want us to be together. The way we used to. I just want you right here, right now. I don't care about anything else, because this is all we have."

"There is no one else."

"Shh."

"I've thought about it. I've been tempted. There have been offers. I've ever planned for a tryst."

My heart lurches, and breaks, but I keep a blank face, and just listen.

"But in the end," he says, "I couldn't go through with it. I was so lonesome, Rebecca. I just wanted, I don't know, someone to care about me, to see me, to be playful, I guess."

"Do you miss me? The way we used to be."

"I do. I don't let myself think too hard about it anymore. I...try to stay busy."

"I understand." I fight the urge to slug him for even thinking about cheating on me. I remind myself that it's not always just the man's fault, that sometimes women enable the men -- no, sometimes they almost force it. "I'm sorry," I say. "Let's make it better. Let's fix this."

I take him by the hand and pull him toward our high California king-sized bed. I push him down onto it, and he sprawls on his back, his feet still on the floor, smiling.

"Who's just a little bit ornery this morning?" he asks.

"I don't hear you complaining," I say.

I climb onto the bed, and straddle my husband's lap. I can feel his excitement though his boxers. I sit just a little harder on him, press myself into him. He seems surprised.

"You're not angry at me?" he asks.

"I don't want to talk about all that, I told you. I just want to be with you. To feel you inside of me."

"Frankly, I didn't think you still wanted to," he says, pushing back up into me, grinding his hips against me. "What's changed?"

"I've decided not to let guilt destroy me," I say.

"Guilt?"

"For giving you an imperfect child, after an imperfect pregnancy."

Andre stops pushing into me and gives me a concerned look. "Is that what did it?"

I nod. "I'm afraid so."

"Rebecca." He takes my hands in his, and kisses each of my knuckles, slowly, sweetly. "Why must you be ruled by such debilitating perfectionism, darling? It destroys everything around you."

"I know. I'm not, anymore. I don't want to be. I want to...I miss connecting with you. I miss *us*."

"I thought you'd lost interest in me," he says. "I felt so alone."

"No, never. It was all about me feeling inadequate and shutting down. I'm sorry. I want you back."

Andre sits up, holding me around the waist with his

large hands, and he smiles at me, all barriers gone, the old Andre back.

"I haven't gone anywhere," he tells me. "I've just been waiting for you to come back, that's all."

"I'm here," I say, loving the way his touch feels, his mouth, the smell of his breath and skin, everything about him that is so powerful and masculine.

He kisses my cheeks, then my neck, working his way down. He kisses my collarbone, and then my breasts. He takes his time with them, using his lips, tongue and fingers to stimulate me almost to the point of climax just from this alone. He was always so very good at this. It hasn't changed.

He reclines again on the bed, on his back, and with his strong arms lifts me up, moving me so that I am on my knees now, straddling his chest. He moves himself down, so that his face is where his chest was, and he begins to do the thing that he is so very, very good at. He works his way around the edges, my perimeter, teasing. A hand wanders up to my breasts, and as he kisses and licks me in my most sensitive of spots, he also squeezes and pinches and thrums my nipples. With his free hand he uses the fingers to enter me, knowing exactly how I like it, and able to read my every sigh, moan, gasp and shudder as though they were his own. Easily, effortlessly, he brings me to the point of explosion, and I ride it like the sea, wave upon wave of pleasure.

When I am finished, he lifts me off of him, and positions me on my back, opens my legs, and removes his boxers. Then, holding himself at the base, he finds my slickness with his stiffness, and enters me. I gasp as he fills me up, and rocks me. His eyes are focused on my own, and he smiles, my best friend.

"I love you," I say, tears beginning to flow from my eyes.

"I love you, too," he says, lowering his mouth to kiss mine, moving ever so slowly in and out of me. "I'm on your side, Rebecca. We're in this together. Never forget that."

"I won't," I say.

"Whatever it is you need from me, tell me. From now on, no more secrets, no more silence."

"Okay," I say.

"Tell me."

"Tell you what?" I ask, aching for him to take me faster, harder, loving the slowness of it, but needing more right now. Andre and I have always had a good sex life, at least back when we had one, but we've always been rather polite about it. I'm tired of being polite. I'm tired of waiting. I'm tired of holding back my true feelings.

"Tell me what you want, Rebecca."

I look my husband in the eyes, and for the first time in a very long while, I smile in a naughty, playful sort of way.

"You sure you want to know?" I ask.

He cocks one brow and waits, liking the look on my face.

"Well, what I *want*," I tell him, without dropping my gaze, "is for the man I love to..." I can't bring myself to say it.

"To...what?"

To fuck me, I think. But I can't say it. He knows I'm holding back.

"What is it you want?" he asks, teasing me by sliding out completely and hesitating at the garden gate, so to speak. I writhe and squirm and wait for him to go back inside of me, but he doesn't.

"Tell me," he says. "Say it."

"Say what?"

"What you're thinking," he says. "Stop censoring yourself."

"I can't," I whine.

"Yes, you can." I feel him rubbing his hard cock along the outside of me, hitting my sensitive spot. It's a great feeling, but I want, I want...more, deeper. Inside.

"I," I stammer.

"Say it."

"I want you to fuck me," I tell him in a whisper.

I feel him grow harder against of me with these

words, and his face registers shock, then determination.

"I'm sorry," he says. "I'm not sure I understood you. Say it again. Like you mean it."

"Fuck me," I tell him in a steady voice this time. "Please."

Andre grins, and plunges himself hard and deep into me, and I scream with pleasure.

"Like that?" he asks.

"Harder," I say. "Faster."

"Yeah?"

"Yes, please, Mr. Cartier."

"I was beginning to think you'd never ask again," he says, before obliging my request, all morning long.

USNAVYS

It is *way* too damn early in the morning, and I walk from the subway station to Taina's House of Hair hoping nobody I know sees me. It's my first day of "work" as the receptionist for this ghetto salon owned by a woman who used to be my high school nemesis, and because so many of her clients have jobs driving city buses and whatnot, she has to open at six in the morning to accommodate their proletariat schedules. It's not worth it, nena, but what can I do? Sit around the house crying over how I don't get to see my babies until the court date because Juan done took out a restraining order on me, saying I'm capable of stealing money from my own children. Can you believe that nonsense? I am heartbroken by the whole thing, and so I keep moving, because when you swim with sharks you can't stop or they eat you alive. Just keep moving, until I get somewhere. That's all. I cry at night, but I try to do it quiet so my mom doesn't come in with holy water and herbs from the botanica to try to cleanse me of my grief. I bet you that holy water she spends all that money on in them little plastic bottles is nothing but Chelsea tap water with babalao spit in it, but you can't tell my mother any of that. She is a true believer, loca del diablo.

I've worn me a St. John's suit, because there is no reason that I have to look ghetto just because I am now officially working in the ghetto -- besides which, you never know who you're going to run into. It's a cloudy day, with a little drizzle starting, and so I've put a scarf over my head. With my big Kate Spade sunglasses, I look something like a finer, Boricua Jackie O. I got some of Taina's smoothing serum on my head, and girl, this stuff smells and works so good. Well. I know. Well, not good. Shut the fuck up and stop correcting a sister. I do not care anymore. I mean, look where I am. I go around here using the Queen's English they all gonna look at me like I'm from another damned planet. It's all about knowing what words to use for the context, okay? That's all.

As I round the corner closest to the salon, I am thinking about how Taina might actually be able to sell those serums she's made with all that Puerto Rican witchcraft and whatnot and what-have-you, if only she got her some nice bottles and changed the brand name, when my train of thought is interrupted by the horrible sight of a charred-out car sitting there in the middle of the street. All the neighborhood people with nothing better to do have circled around it like it's a public hanging, laughing and pointing because they are desensitized to the point of stone-ass crazy. Some of these idiots have even brought their babies to stare in the windows of the burned vehicle to see if there's a body inside. Of course, this is all happening right across the street from the "salon" where I now work, which depresses me more than you can even begin to imagine, okay? Just when you think your headache is going to stop, something like this comes along to sledgehammer your cranium all over again.

I cross the street away from the disaster, because I am not about to go getting my ass all up in the middle of some drug cartel nonsense, or whatever this is. With all them news cameras and reporters swarming around, I am not about to subject myself to having a big microphone shoved in my face so some smug bubblehead can ask me how I feel about this happening in my neighborhood. I feel like I don't care, okay? And it's not my goddamned neighborhood. You think I'd pick this for myself? Girl, puh-lease. I'm just gonna pretend I didn't see none of it, because if you have any sense in your head at all, m'ija, that's what you do. You walk on by.

Taina is already at the salon, because I swear to God that woman lives in the back room or something, and she's standing there all cheerful, fit, pretty and worried at the same time, behind the front counter. She's got Dunkin Donuts all spread out before her, a large coffee she says is for me and a box of mixed donuts that she says are for everyone, even though it's obvious she hasn't eaten any and never will. I unwrap the scarf from my head and exhale a sigh of relief to be off the street and in a place that looks decent. I grab for the coffee and notice Taina's eyes are focused on the ruckus across the street.

"What the fuck happened out there?" I ask her.

"Police were just here. They said it's a cop. He was tied up and torched in his own car. So sad."

"Dangerous job, being a cop," I say, as I daintily select a jelly-filled from the center of the box.

"I guess he was a detective."

I feel time slow down as she says the word "detective" and my face goes ashy.

"Did they know his name?" I ask.

"Yeah, something Irish," she says. "I can't remember."

"Flynn?" I ask her. "Was it by any chance Jason Flynn?"

Taina's eyes light up. "Yes! That's what it was." Then as quickly as they lit up, her eyes darken suspiciously. "How did you know that, Usnavys?"

I look out the window at the cinders of the wreckage with a new attitude, one of relief and excitement. It feels like Christmas.

"I've heard of him," I tell her. "Heard he was crooked."

"Still, he was a human being," she says, making the sign of the cross over her chest. "It's a terrible way to die, being burned alive all tied up like that."

I shrug. "Live by the sword," I tell her.

"Usnavys, how can you be so cold?"

"Honey," I say, nibbling with grace upon the edge of my donut. "Sometimes you just gotta trust me to know what I'm doing, okay?"

"Uhm, okay," she says uncertainly.

"Which reminds me," I say, pointing a newly manicured fingernail at her. "You and me, we need to talk about a few things around here."

"We do?" Taina looks surprised.

"First thing, I need you to understand that even though I'm just the receptionist, I come to you with a wealth of experience in business and marketing."

"Okay," she says, still uncertain.

"The point being, I have been thinking about this place. You have you some great ideas up in here, Taina."

"Thank you."

"But what you lack is common sense."

Taina stares at me in shock, like I'm some sort of insubordinate child.

"Hear me out before your eyes bug out your damn head," I tell her. "First thing, you have to change the name of the salon."

Taina stares at me, still in shock.

"Please, girl. 'House of Hair'? That sounds like the shit itches, okay? It sound like something the big bad wolf would blow the fuck *down*."

"I like it."

"Obviously, you like it. But I am telling you, as a woman of grace and decorum and taste and style, that name is only gonna take you so far. That name might fly in the 'hood, but nena, I have bigger plans for you than that."

"Oh, you do, do you?"

I grab her by the arm and pull her over to the waiting area and sit her ass down on one of them soft chairs. "Yes, I do," I say. "You have a gift, Taina. I can't believe I'm telling you that shit, but yes, you do. You have a good eye for fashion, for design, for hair, I mean, look at this place. It looks like something you'd find over on Newbury Street, girl, and you didn't even hire you an interior decorator or anything like that."

"I did it all myself."

"I realize that. And my hair looks da bomb because of you. And all these hood rat ladies walking all over Roxbury and Dorchester looking like they just stepped out of Beverly Hills or some shit, that's all you, your vision."

"Thank you."

"But listen to me, girl, that's not where the big money is going to be for you."

"I don't want big money. I have what I want right now."

"Okay, well I do, okay? I want big money, and I'm asking you to officially let me be your director of product merchandising and marketing."

Taina laughs out loud and I fight the urge to slap the bitch silly upside the head.

"I'm glad you find that amusing," I tell her. "But I'm dead serious here. You get you a good name, and some fashionable bottles and packaging, and you can sell your potions up in the nicest stores in town."

"You think?"

"Girl! I don't lie, okay? I might cleverly evade the truth sometimes, but I am not someone to want to waste my precious time and energy marketing some shit that I don't think has a chance of doing anything."

"Okay."

"I envision you with your own line of hair and body products at Bloomingdales, or Neiman Marcus."

"Are you serious?"

"As a heart attack. And not just that, Taina. Listen to me. You could get yourself up on one of them home shopping networks, with products for girls of color. You feel me?"

"I think so."

"I got contacts, my college friend Amber, she's a big pop star, Cuicatl."

"You know that girl?"

"She's a friend. She's crazy as batshit, but she's a friend and I bet she'd do us a favor and be, like, your spokesperson or something."

"Really?"

"Hells yeah. We just have to get her up in here to get her hair and nails did. My other friend, Sara, she has her a lifestyle show, kind of like the Latina Martha Stewart. You start there, we can get you anywhere you need to go."

"Wow. You really think you can make that happen?"

"I wouldn't say it if I didn't. You have to think bigger than this place, Taina. I say that to you not as an insult but because I believe in you and your products and your talents."

"I don't know what to say."

"Say 'thank you,' then."

She laughs, and this is good because I was hoping she would.

"I'm going to need some business cards," I tell her. "I'll write out exactly the wording I want. And I'm going to need a budget to get you some real bottles and packaging. I know the buyers at the bigger department stores, and I have some other contacts in the magazine and media world. We need to put our heads together and come up with something that's going to work out."

"How much money do you think this could make?" she asks.

"You ever heard of Aveda?" I ask.

"Of course."

"I see you being like Aveda, Boricua style, okay?"

"Okay."

"Aveda makes about seventy million dollars a year in sales, and those are mostly from just ten products."

"Are you serious?"

"It's all about branding, girl. You gotta get you a good name, a niche market, a pretty and effective product, and you get out there and you make it happen."

"This is your first day," she says with a big-ass grin.

"Damn straight," I tell her, getting up to sashay over to the desk, to answer the damn phone. "Just wait until you see me tomorrow."

LAUREN

I sit at the computer work station in the cozy home office of Tio's wife, reading through the news stories on boston.com about the burned Escalade with Jason Flynn's body inside of it. John Smith, my handsome and mysterious neighbor, stands behind me, leaned over just a bit so that he, too, can read, watch and hear the stories. I am in such a state of disbelief I almost can't speak. I am relieved, yes, of course I am. I feel as though I've just gotten out of prison, in fact. I am giddy with excitement that this man is no longer on the earth to come after me. But I am also strangely conflicted and disturbed by it all. If the mob came for him, does that mean they'll still keep coming for me? Just how dirty a cop was this guy? And, worst of all, how the hell did I end up falling in love with someone who was so clearly not the right guy?

John says nothing. This bothers me. I was hoping he at least would have something to say.

"Well?" I ask him. I swivel my head so that I can see his face. He shrugs.

"Looks like your nightmare is over," he says. "Guy was in with the mob. The mob eats its own."

"I just hate that I lost my job and my whole life because of him, and I probably didn't need to."

"I wouldn't say that," John says, with a comforting (and thrilling) hand to my shoulder. "I mean, didn't you say you were dreaming of leaving that paper to write books anyway?"

"Yeah."

"And didn't you say you've got enough savings to survive for a couple of years?"

"Yes."

"And you have this free place to live, with no distractions, until you finish your manuscript?"

I look at him, his chiseled face, his beautiful eyes. "I wouldn't say *no* distractions," I say.

John seems to understand what I mean, and he gives

me a warm grin. "Yeah, well if it's any consolation, I know the feeling."

"Not my fault you bring perky little bouncy things around to distract you," I say, still bitter about the perfect blonde he claims to have broken up with.

"I wasn't talking about anything I brought around," he says, and the hand that is on my shoulder brushes my upper back now, and comes to rest on the back of my neck, underneath my hair. I feel his finger trace a line to my ear, and back. I am suddenly covered with goose bumps.

"What were you talking about, then?" I ask, playing dumb. My voice has faded somewhat, to a whisper.

"Hmm," he says, taking his hand off of me and moving a couple of steps back. "I'd say that I'll leave it up to you to figure that out. You're a smart woman."

"But not perky," I say.

"Plenty perky, too," he says. "Thus the 'more' in my earlier statement about some men wanting more. I didn't say I don't want perky. I like perky. But I also like smart."

"Is that so?"

"But don't go getting any ideas," he says.

Not wanting to play along right now, I return my attention to the computer screen, and let a TV news clip play. It shows a reporter in front of the burned Escalade, interviewing some local people who describe seeing a bonfire in the middle of the night. As they talk, I see a familiar figure prancing down the opposite side of the street, in a familiar red St. John's suit that was purchased in my presence.

"Oh, my God!" I cry.

John comes back and asks me what's wrong.

"That's Usnavys!" I cry. "Right there. Going into that shop. That's my best friend. What the hell is she doing there?"

"House of Hair?" asks John.

"Sounds like a salon of some kind," I say. "This is too weird."

I Google the House of Hair, and a number comes up. I dial it, and to my enormous surprise, Usnavys answers the phone.

"Thank you for calling Tango, Ms. Rivera speaking."

"Usnavys?" I ask.

"Who wants to know?"

I identify myself, and tell her I just saw her on the news from Boston, walking into House of Hair. "And now you're answering the phone, but you're saying 'Tango' instead."

"You like it?" she asks.

"Like what?"

"Tango. I'm trying out some new names."

"What are you even doing there?"

"Oh, you know, girl. I had some time off before work and I needed to get my hair did. My friend runs this place, so I just answered the phone for her..."

"I talked to Juan a couple of days ago. He told me about you losing your job, and everything else."

Silence.

"Usnavys, it's okay. You don't have to hide it from me. I've been worried about you."

Silence.

"I'm your friend. You can tell me anything. I mean, it's not like I have a lot to brag about these days, either."

"True dat, nena," she says.

"Are you working there?"

"Yes, but it's not what you think." Usnavys now tells me about her big plans to market her friend's beauty products. I actually think it's a good idea, and tell her so.

"So I guess you seen your barbecued boyfriend on the news, then," she says.

"Yeah."

"Never thought I'd see the day where I welcomed the smell of burning human flesh, girl, but today is that day."

"No shit."

"So are you coming back? Juan's asking for his car. Goddamned whiner."

"Actually, no."

"But the fool's dead. You can come back."

"I know. I, I don't know. I guess I kind of like it here.

I'm ready for a change."

"You meet you a man or something?" she asks, knowing me so well.

"Sort of."

"Dios mio, just be careful this time and don't go shacking up with a killer."

"No promises," I say.

"God help me, you are so lucky I'm not right there because I'd have to smack your mouth to shock you back into being sane."

"It's fine. Trust me."

"Tango. What do you think?"

"Beats House of Hair," I say.

"I know, right? House of fucking Hair, girl."

"Not good."

"Tango, though."

"It's okay. You can probably think of something better. Something more mainstream, universal."

"You think?"

"Yeah, like a made-up word."

"Like Aveda," she says.

"Exactly."

"Like what?"

"What's your friend's name, who owns the salon?"

"Taina. Like the Indians."

I take a pen and a piece of scrap paper and write TAINA, then I write it backwards: ANIAT.

"How about Aniat?" I ask. I tell her it's Taina backwards. She is quiet for a minute.

"Girl, I think you nailed it!" she says.

"Aniat, right? It's elegant, original, almost regal, exotic."

"Aniat. I like that."

"Good."

"So who's this latest crazy bastard you've fallen for?" she asks.

"Can't talk about that right now," I say.

"Motherfucker's over there?"

"Sort of."

"Dios mio."

"It's not like that. I want to stay here because it's time for a change and I think I'll stick around for a while and try to actually write a book like I've been telling everyone."

"Whatever."

"I will. You'll see. Actually, we should have a race to see who can get her new project off the ground first. You with Aniat, and me with my book."

"What's it going to be about?" she asks me.

"I don't know. I was thinking of something like what you said, about six Latina friends, all really diverse, who met in college and end up having lots of drama in their lives."

"I'd read it. Just don't base none of them on me, okay?"

"No promises."

"What's with you, girl? You're all 'no promises' today."

"It's a really good fucking day," I say. "Jason's dead."

"Okay, but if you do base a character on me, make sure she's glamorous and employed. You want it to be aspirational fiction, not the shit that wins Pulitzers and makes everyone who reads it want to slit their fucking wrists. Whatever you do, promise you won't go all E. Annie Proulx on me, because ain't nobody actually likes them books of hers."

"Deal."

"Is he hot?"

"Who?"

"Your latest psychopath."

"Yes. Very."

"Hotter than the dead fucker?"

"Yes. Well, about the same. But nicer."

"Charles Manson was nicer than Jason Flynn, Lauren."

I laugh. "I miss you, sucia."

"I miss you, too."

"I can't believe he's gone."

"Believe it. I smelled his cooked ass, okay? That boy will not be bothering you again."

"Thank God."

"Yes," she says, solemnly. "That's something Taina's helping to teach me."

"What's that?"

"God. We need to thank God for what we have. Even when we don't think we have anything. Because God doesn't make mistakes, and even when it seems like we lost it all, there's probably some other door waiting for us to open it."

"Wow. Profound. When did you go all Miss Holy Roller?"

"Shut the fuck up."

I laugh again, for what feels like the first time in decades.

"Nena, it's good to hear you happy again," she says.

"Thanks. It's good to feel happy."

"Now, if you'll excuse me, my boss, Miss Taina, is giving me the evil eye, and you know she's all up in that island voodoo. I better hang up and attend to this business before my hair starts to fall out or something."

"Okay."

"Use condoms."

"It's not even there yet."

"Yet, you say. So that means it will be."

"With any luck."

"No such thing as luck, m'ija," she says. "But I am here to tell you, prayer works."

"Then I'll pray for it."

"And I'll pray you use you some condoms," she quips.

"Thanks."

"You know, I bet you God gets sick of those kinds of prayers. 'Dear Lord, help me find a coochie to stick my dick in.' Or 'Dear God, please don't let my crazy-ass friend get her a disease from her new man.'"

"Wow. That was beautiful. Church has turned you into a poet."

"Thank you."

"Most welcome."

"Aniat," she says again. "No, m'ija, I'd say you're the poet."

"Bye, Usnavys. I love you."

"I love your crazy ass, too, bitch. Now, if you'll excuse me, I have to call my children and tell them I love them even if their daddy is a fucking pig."

"Wow. That's got to be the worst parenting through divorce advice I've ever heard."

"I call it like I see it."

"It is amazing," I say, "that you and I can be so good at some things, and so really truly incredibly bad at others, isn't it?"

"You can't win them all, sucia," she says. "Peace out."

And she hangs up.

JASON

Jason Flynn leaves.

He's got cash, because you don't work as a hired gun for the mob for a decade and get paid in shiny marbles. He's got fake papers showing him as someone else altogether, because he knows a guy who will make you whatever you want, for the right price. Everyone, you see, is for sale. Martin Bernstein sold his soul to impress a woman who wasn't worth impressing. People are sheep. Jason Flynn couldn't care less that he now must answer to another name. Shakespeare was a punk, but he got one thing right. Names are just sounds, temporary and random. Jason Flynn never felt any affection toward his parents, and so why should he give a fuck about the sounds they affixed to his person? Meaningless. What's in a name? Nothing. Then again, there is nothing in everything, if you think about it. Nothing is always waiting just around the bend. Jason is a broker for the big black nothing. He knows it well. He sends people there all the time. This brings him pleasure.

He flies to Aruba. Why does he do that? It makes no sense to the people who feel things because they don't realize the energy that a place like that holds for a man like Jason Flynn. Women have been hurt in Aruba, and they disappear in Aruba. This makes Aruba a beautiful place to the man formerly known as Jason Flynn. Yes, that happens in other places, too. But when so much attention is paid to Aruba for these crimes, the collective energy of the people focuses itself there. Aruba has become synonymous to the sheep, to the followers, with fear for its women. It is a fear magnet. Jason Flynn feeds on fear. He loves it, insofar as he is capable of love. No, love, no. Need. He needs it. Fear. It is fuel.

There is a woman who is no longer afraid, but she should be.

She will be again.

And he will be there.

Soon.

Vacation first. A man needs to organize himself before a performance this grand. He must practice first. He is an artist of death.

He flies to Aruba with his cash, some of it. In Aruba he pays for a very nice hotel suite, and he hits the bars in his finest clothes. Heads turn. Women smile. They all want him inside of them. Women are predictable in this way. He finds women. Two of them should be adequate for one night. They are friends, and they are horny, and they are drunk and this combination makes them phenomenally stupid. Just the way he likes them. Jason Flynn is flying high on his own power, on the adrenaline that was released when he burned Martin Bernstein and smoked him into the blackness. He has more positive energy than he knows what to do with. If fills him from the middle out, from the middle out, from the middle out, yes, just like that, mmm, he likes how it feels to be pulsating, pulsating, pulsating with life force and to have a humming and wild sort of blood filling him up, making him hard, from the middle out, and he just wants to stab someone with it, stab someone in the middle, out, fucking show them what he can do, get it out, and so he picks these two and they are as good as any. He charms them, says the sorts of things men that women like say to make them like them. It is all bullshit. They lap it up because they are the shit-eaters. They are the mice, and he is the pretty Persian cat. Life is all about the chain, the food chain, the bigger things that swallow up the smaller ones, the stronger things that take and take and take from the weak. Nature designed it thusly and only the sheep people try to force it all another direction. The sheep people are unnatural. Jason Flynn is a nature boy, and king of the jungle.

They follow him sloppily to his room, leaning into each other and giggling because they are both married, this is what they've told him, and they think this is incredibly sneaky, what they're doing, having a threesome with a hot guy in Aruba, a guy they think is a nice, lonely, recently-divorced Canadian named Thomas Pike. If only their husbands knew, they giggle, and fuck the husbands because they cheat all the time, and if they didn't we wouldn't need this girl's weekend away in Aruba, Aruba, where all manner of bad things happen to all manner of stupid fucking women. Jason Flynn does not pity the husbands at all, because those men were stupid enough to marry this trash. They deserve what's coming to them. Jason Flynn is doing them a favor.

He lets the whores into his room.

He closes the door.

He sits on the chair, and tells them to give him a show. When there are two of them, and they are friends, and they are stupid and soft and drunk and past their prime by just a few years, sagging a bit, wrinkled a bit, they always forget how ugly they are and they always want to give you a show. They live to give men shows. He puts a song on, a song from his iPod, on the hotel stereo, a song by Bush. "Machinehead," and he tells them to strip for him.

"Give me a show, girls. Show me what you're going to give me."

And they stagger and stumble, pathetic in their scuffed high heels and cheaply made short skirts, he thinks: These are women with children, acting like idiots. It's so much better when they clearly deserve what's coming to them. It is so much better when you know exactly where the damp sinkhole is in the ground of Aruba that will swallow their bodies up and leave no trace, because the jungle will close over them and grow itself back together like a green scab.

He watches them and he poses the way men with feelings pose for women, as though he's never seen anything so erotic, so perfect, when in truth his blood has been ready and coagulating in his cock for this since the flame dropped into Martin's lap. If he hadn't run the risk of being incinerated himself, he would have liked to stick his cock in Jason's mouth as the fucker burned. That would have been rich. He's bottled the victory and the rage, and channeled it down, down to his middle, where it has filled him up, rock hard, ready. Fuck these bitches.

The women's tongues dance together, and Jason Flynn yawns into his closed fist. He is bored by this disgusting exchange of their thick and boozy fluids, but he cannot let them know. He has to let them think it's just a threesome with a lonely Canadian businessman, and so he smiles when they look at him and he tells them, "Yeah, baby, just like that," though inside he thinks he might try to take this a little further than normal. Normal for him. Do something new. Something beautifully brutal.

"Take off your clothes," he says. The women take off their clothes.

"Suck my dick," he tells the taller one. "You're next," he tells the shorter one. The tall one falls to her knees with a dirty smile on her puffy, drunken face. She opens her mouth. He lets her lick and suckle the way women do, but soon he becomes annoyed by her enjoyment of it. She isn't supposed to like it. He doesn't want her smiling and thinking she's in control. He wants her crying and afraid. Jason Flynn grabs her by the back of her head, and he pushes himself deep into her throat, so deep he cuts off her airway. At first she opens her eyes to look at him with that longing women get when they actually like a little pain, thinking maybe she's in for a little role-play, but no. She is not. Soon enough, as he pushes further, further, almost to her fucking stomach, almost into her damaged smoker's lungs, as she heaves and vomits against him and begins to choke on her own spew, as her face starts to turn blue and she claws at his legs with her hand little hands, she realizes she is going to suffocate.

Pleasure is Jason Flynn's.

The friend is too busy masturbating like a truffled pig on the bed to notice, waiting her turn. Jason Flynn holds the head in place, feels himself growing harder the longer she goes without oxygen. Power belongs to him. He wonders if he should just kill her now, or wait.

He waits.

He lets her up for air. She gags, coughs, sputters, spits. Her makeup is smeared all around her eyes, giving her the look of a tragic harlequin. It is a good look on her, and

Jason Flynn likes her better this way.

"Jesus Christ," she says, wiping vomit from her chin. "I couldn't breathe."

"I know," says Jason Flynn. "It was wonderful."

"What's wrong with you?" she asks, getting up, no longer in the mood.

"Absolutely nothing," he tells her as he uses a tissue from the box on the desk to wipe his dick off.

She starts in a panic toward the door, and calls her friend to come. The friend is confused. Jason finds the sharp, small hunting knife in his jacket pocket, and takes it out. Thick blade, efficient, a beautiful tool that curves like a smile.

"Sit down," he tells her.

The tall one is streetwise. He did not see that in her earlier. He saw a frustrated housewife, but now he understands that she married up. She wasn't always this well off. She knows a few things. She has fought her fair share of fights. Jason Flynn is upset with himself for not understanding what he was getting himself into. He is usually so very good at understanding things. He must be more careful. He must not let freedom and success make him stupid.

"Fuck you, ya fucking derelict," she says. "Lisa, let's go."

"What?" asks the masturbating oinker whose name must be Lisa.

"Don't make me get the gun," says Jason Flynn, his excitement growing only more powerful with their resistance. Oh, this, he thinks, this will make it so good. So good.

"He's fucking nuts," the tall one says. "Fucking sadistic rapist fuck."

"You're fucking right," answers Jason Flynn, mocking her tone and accent. Energized by her fear. Disgusted by her face. He is overcome with a need to cut her head off. Moving fast as a panther, before she has a chance to scream -- for she is undoubtedly the brassy, screaming type -- he grabs her and sinks the knife into her throat, efficient, clean. Quick. He keeps her chin down long enough to see that her face registers what he's done. The ripping sensation sinks in. Her eyes are filled with dread and terror, and, most deliciously, with an admission that he has won. Her hand comes up to where the hot blood has begun to seep out of the deep, direct wound. She tries to scream, but the air pushes through the flap in her neck and the only sound in her bubbling impending doom.

"Fuck," he whispers in her ear, licking her cheek. "You."

Bush sings on the stereo: *Breathe in, breathe out, breathe in, breath out, breathe in...*

On a strong downbeat, like a conductor, Jason Flynn pulls her head back, opening the wound wide. Blood pulses out in time to the music, and this confirms for Jason Flynn that the moment is holy. Synchronicity. The one that is called Lisa is about to scream, but Jason Flynn drops the tall one as the chorus begins, and puts his bloody finger to his lips, tasting the metal of a wasted life.

"Shh," he tells her. "Be quiet, beautiful. Trust me, sexy. You don't want to do that."

Lisa watches her friend fall to the floor with a thud, where she writhes for a moment and then dies. Jason Flynn is vaguely aware that he didn't get to sodomize her, as he would have liked to have done, but that's okay because there is this other one left here, and that's fine.

"Please," the woman pleads.

"It's okay," he says. "I'm not going to hurt you."

She wants to believe this. And that is what amazes him about the sheep people, the way their faith and hope remain, even in a situation like this. These idiots actually think God is good, in spite of all the evidence to the contrary. They do not deal well in cold, hard facts like he does. They are so stubbornly stupid. Clearly he is going to hurt her, and yet she wants to believe he is not.

"I like you," he tells her, just to see how such words contort her face.

Jason Flynn is so on fire, he is almost as on fire as Martin was. He grins like the devil, because this is pleasure, this is living, this is life. Making people do things they did not realize they were going to have to do. He rapes her. Everywhere. Her eyes close tightly because she can't stand to look at the open eyes of her dead friend while Jason Flynn drills his body into hers the way you drill for oil. In every hole, without compassion. He needs what she has, her innocence, her stupidity, he needs to wipe himself on it, to scar it, to stain it, to mark his fucking territory for God in her flesh because she is the living embodiment of the foolish sheepish damned. As she sobs in her final moments, as he sinks the knife into her kidneys, one at a time, savoring her suffering, he whispers to let her know how lucky she is.

"God was here, precious," he tells her. "You've been saved."

In all, Jason Flynn will be in Aruba for three weeks. During that time, four more women will die. Then he will spend a week visiting Cancun, Mexico City, New Orleans, and, finally, he will go to Houston. In all, three more women will lose their lives, and he is confident no one will miss any of them.

Practice makes perfect. And at last, he is ready for Lauren, because she has a lesson to learn and its name is humility.

After a month away from Boston, during which time his department has mourned him, and the city has seen him buried, and during which time Martin Bernstein has sent emails saying he has left the country because of fear that the mob will also come after him for having been in cahoots with Jason Flynn, and certain that the police have botched the investigation to such a high degree that they have not yet figured out, and will likely never figure out, the true identity of the man burned to death in the Escalade, Jason Flynn is utterly confident that he has perfected his technique, that he has done his homework, that he is dead to the world, that he has prepared himself for the final moments of Lauren's life.

It is late September when Jason Flynn rents a car in Houston, and drives himself to Quemado, New Mexico,

where he rents a cheap motel room near Lauren.
Very near.
So near, in fact, he smells blood. And it smells good.

LAUREN

I am alone in the house, seated at the computer, and have just finished typing the last word of the last sentence of the first section of my first novel, *Run*. Though I initially wanted to write about my six college friends, a chick lit kind of novel, I realized that the chick lit genre all but died with the vapid materialism of the early 2000s. People want more than that. So I have decided instead to write a thriller about a female reporter from Boston who is being chased by her sociopathic ex-boyfriend, a police detective. I know, I know. People will know it's about me. But all the writing journals say you ought to write what you know, and trust me, I know all about this now. With Jason Flynn gone, I know that it is safe to write about him in fictionalized form. I also know that there will be a hunger for the story in New England, where people have now started Facebook groups trying to figure out what happened to me. I will surface again in a year or two, with this book, and then everyone will know the truth. It will be big news. Until then, I'm just enjoying the quiet life here in the country. Actually, I am enjoying it more than I thought I might. I guess that even for all my years in Boston, I am a backwater Southern girl at heart, having been raised in New Orleans, which, yes, is a city, but a city filled with yokels and hicks of the type my mother was drawn to, which is to say the type with tattoos and crack.

I've fallen into a sort of routine here, one that I find very healing and slow. Each morning I wake up at dawn. I tell myself this is because the early bird catches the worm, and all that jive, but in truth I do this because dawn is when John Smith comes out of his house on top of the hill to feed his horses and let his dogs out of their pens. I like to sit on the porch with binoculars, watching him. I know, how stalker-like, right? Well, it's not like he doesn't know I do it. I've told him I like to watch him work. He finds it amusing. He says watching me work is like watching paint dry, and this makes me laugh, because, yes, watching me sit and stare at a computer screen for eight hours a day is not exactly thrilling stuff.

I do believe the man likes to toy with me, just a little.

After I've watched John do his morning chores outside, he usually stops by to share a cup of coffee with me on the porch of the house I have started to think of as my own. I really, *really* like this little house. I can't believe Tio and his wife own it but rarely come here. Some people just have too much money. Then there are those like me, who are running out of their savings with each passing day, with nothing to replenish it. I have plans, though. This book will be huge.

Just watch.

So, anyway, John and I share coffee, and lately I've taken to trying to bake things for him, too. This is because John likes pastries. They are his biggest weakness. Few things seem to make this man lose control, but I have noticed that with baked goods, he can't help himself. He will put away an entire loaf of zucchini bread in one day, with butter on every slice -- and still stay fit and perfect looking because apparently being a cowboy burns up a lot of calories. I like to bake for him because he likes my baking. Plus, with fall in the air, and living out on the prairie like some homestead wife, I find myself overcome with a desire to bake and make soups and stews. I share all of these with John Smith, in hopes, I suppose, that he will actually make a move on me one of these days. He hints at it, we dance around it, we flirt, but he has yet to actually do anything about it. He says this is because he doesn't want me to fall for the first guy I meet after the trauma I've been through, something about imprinting and ducklings, I don't know what the hell he's talking about.

If only I were a pastry, then he'd eat me. (Fans self.)

I want to tell him it's too late, that I've fallen for him whether he approves of it or not. But he's right. I really don't need to be rushing into anything right now. I have never, I repeat, *never*, become friends first with a man I wanted sexually. I have always pushed and sped that physical part of things up. Mistake, or so I am told by the myriad dating books I've been reading on my Kindle lately, trying to figure out how to do this thing right once and for all before it's too late. John Smith is quite a catch, and I want to be very careful about how I set the trap this time. Let it drag out, baby. That's my motto. Leave him wanting more.

So, yes, John and I are neighbors, and we see each other almost every day. I read parts of my book out loud to him and he, very well-read in fact, comments with intelligence and insight. I think of him as my free editor at the moment. Turns out that he has been working on a little mystery series of his own. He sends me bits and pieces of it via email sometimes, and I am blown away by how well he writes. He says it's not a big deal, but to me, because I'm a writer, it's a *very* big deal. I mean, yeah, John's physically gorgeous, and he's self-reliant, and a hard-worker, and patriotic, and loves people so much he can't bear to be around them very much because of the hand-basket in which our nation seems to be caroming toward hell, but even if he weren't all of these things I'd still fall for him, because he's a good person who writes beautifully. If the way to a man's heart is through his stomach, the way to my writer's heart is through words. And he's got lots of them, ordered well, sign of a good brain.

After we share coffee, John usually takes off to do whatever it is that he does all day. Pushing cows, checking water lines, making sure the fences are in order. Things that are very foreign to me and seem to be resurrected from some bygone time. He's very, very good with his hands, and they are very large and rough as a result. I like that about them. They are hands unlike mine in every way. They are a man's hands, a real man, unlike the soft and squishy males I've come to know living in the city. I honestly don't think that if I end up with this country boy I will ever be able to go back to a city man. City men are much too girly.

I've gone out on the ATV with him a few times as he repaired various things around his place, and I have been amazed each and every time by his physical stamina, strength, and the way he is able to figure out problems and fix them. He's not afraid to get dirty. He's not slowed down by cuts and scrapes that would make most city boys cry. He wears a cowboy hat and looks amazingly hot in it, as in sexy. He is focused, and pleasant, and mostly still mysterious to me. He's told me a little bit about his childhood out here, and just a tiny bit about his education, but nothing at all about what he did in the military. I haven't pressed, because the dating books suggest that a woman not be too pushy.

Imagine that. I'm taking advice from dating books. Laugh all you want. I don't care. Look, if you'd been as unlucky in love as I have been, you'd do anything to try to fix yourself.

It is noon now, and I can hear John's pickup rattling up the dirt road. He told me he was heading to town this morning, and asked if he could pick up any supplies for me. I'd said no, but here he is anyway. It is strange to live in a place so remote and rural that everything you need must be planned for. You cannot afford to forget ingredients or supplies here, because it's not like you can just walk down the street to the store. That's something important I've learned being out here, all the things we city people take for granted. Like, I just used to assume that meat came in plastic wrap. I mean, I knew where it came from, sure, but it never really hit me until I got out here and saw all these cattle, with their calves, eking out their existence off the grasses of this land. This is real life. Life in the city is one big charade, and people are so disconnected from reality, from the planet, from the seasons and the patterns of things. This is something I have come to really respect and love about John, his connection to the earth, its cycles, to the water and the rain. In the city, you just turn on the tap and boom, there it is, water. But here in the rural desert, where your water comes from an actual well, you are aware of misusing it.

Anyway.

I go out onto the front porch, and watch the pickup

pull into my driveway. Yes, I can call it mine, at least for the duration of my time here. John hops out, smiling, with a brown box in his hand.

"What you got there?" I ask him.

"I was down at the post office, they said this came for you."

For a moment I am afraid. Even though I know Jason Flynn is dead and the risk to my life is greatly diminished, I haven't been able to shake a certain healthy fear that the whole episode planted in me. Gone are the days of the impulsive Lauren who thought herself invincible.

I look at the return address and see that the package is from Usnavys.

"Shampoo, maybe?" asks John, who is aware of the race I'm in with my best friend to see who can get her business idea launched first.

"Oh, yeah! Wanna come in?" I ask.

John says he'd love to, but that he's got a leak down on one of the water lines that he has to go check. "Pressure gauges are all haywire," he explains. "Cow probably got into something and broke it. I gotta fix these fences."

"Okay. Maybe later? I kind of miss talking to you," I say.

"It shouldn't take me more than an hour," he says. "How about this -- I go fix the water line, and you make us some iced tea. When I get back, we'll socialize for a little while before dinner."

"Sounds good," I say.

"Which reminds me," he says, thumbing the air in the direction of the giant cooler in the back of his truck. "I got a couple of good Porterhouse steaks in town, I was thinking of grilling them up later. Too much for me to eat on my own."

"Are you inviting me to dinner at your place, Mister Smith?" I ask, flirtatiously.

"Only if you'll say yes."

"In that case, yes."

"Great! I've got some good red wine, too. And I got arugula and heirloom tomatoes for a salad."

"Fancy."

"You know how we country boys roll," he jokes.

"On an ATV? Through manure?"

"Right." He grins with one side of his mouth only. It is deadly sexy. "See you in a bit, Miz Fernandez."

He smiles at me full-blown now, and I feel my heart soar. Unlike most of the men I have fallen for in my life, this one is uncomplicated. He is also politically conservative, which surprises me. I always went for the liberal types. I can see now where that was probably a mistake. He's rock-solid, compared to them. Reliable, dependable, strong. He is everything a woman secretly hopes a man will be, and I cannot believe my good fortune to have lucked into him as my temporary neighbor. I am also pleased to report that in the month-plus that I've been living here, he's had zero female visitors, other than that bubbly blonde at the start.

I go back inside, and open the package from Usnavys on the kitchen counter, with an Exacto knife. Inside I find ten beautifully packaged, elegant-looking bottles of hair and body products. The labels are white and rose, with dark gray lettering in a beautiful font. Aniat, the labels read. She's had someone design a hell of a logo, something that looks like a modern block print of a rose, almost Picasso-like. For hair, there is shampoo, conditioner, deep conditioning treatment in a little glass pot, straightening and strengthening serum, and something called "heat fix". For skin there is cleanser, moisturizer, spot cream, wrinkle minimizer, and a lip plumping stick. I marvel at their professional presentation, then open them and sniff. Wow. This stuff smells so good! And unlike anything else I've ever smelled, sort of sandy and oceany, very fresh.

She fucking did it. Of course she did. *Sucias* don't give up.

I immediately dial Usnavys at the salon formerly known as House of Hair.

"Aniat," she answers. "This is Ms. Rivera."

I gush about how great the products are, and Usnavys soaks it in. She tells me she has a bunch of meetings next week with some of the buyers for the top department stores in town. She says the one from Bloomingdales is already in love with the products, and she's working on a meeting with the national office for the stores.

"Looks like you might win our little race," I say.

"Girl, I done *told* you I got it like that."

"Yes, I know."

"You fuck that cowboy yet?" she asks. I laugh.

"No. Not yet."

"Damn, Lauren! Speed that shit up a little bit right there. I know you think you're all playing hard to get and whatnot and what-have-you, but enough is enough. Basta, ya, it's time."

"Why do you care?"

"Because, for the first time in my life I'm not getting me any boom-boom, and so I rely on my friends to regale me with tales of their exotic foreign conquests."

"He's an American."

"Okay, but may I remind you that I am from Boston and the closest I ever been to a cowboy is watching Harry Connick on the damned cable in the middle of the night?"

"You watched *Hope Floats* again?"

"That movie makes me cry, girl."

I laugh. "John says that character isn't a cowboy. He says just because you put on a tutu, that doesn't make you a ballerina. He says cowboy is an actual profession, and he hates how people everywhere in the country stereotype his kind."

"Touchy little cowboy, ain't he?"

"I'd like to touch *him*," I muse. "You should see his mouth. It's...it's the most incredible mouth I have ever seen."

"Just do it, *m'ija*. Because I'm getting sick of hearing about your crush. And take notes. And tell me everything."

"We'll see. He invited me over for dinner at his place later."

"And?"

"And I'm going. Steak and red wine, with arugula

salad. And heirloom tomatoes."

"Just make sure you drink you enough wine to jump his bones, okay nena? Guzzle that vino, baby. Get all loosey goosey, girl."

I can't stop laughing. She hasn't changed at all since college. "I'll be sure to be a perfect lady," I say.

"Since when the fuck *when*?"

"Anyway, I just wanted to call to say how beautiful it all looks. You did a good job."

She thanks me, and tells me that she had a court-mediated appointment with her kids and Juan earlier in the day, and that the judge decided to let Usnavys have her children half the week for now, until the divorce is finalized.

"You know what the judge lady told me?"

"No," I say. "But I should say that 'judge lady' is exactly what Sonia Sotomayor insists on being called these days. Very classy."

"Shut the fuck up and listen, loca."

"Sorry. Go on."

"She said that half this damn country is broke as shit right now, and that if mismanaging money were a reason to take someone's kids away, then most Americans -- and everyone at Bank of America -- wouldn't have their kids at all. We'd be a big orphanage up in here."

"Amen," I say. "But that still doesn't mean you can go blowing all your money again, right?"

"I signed up for a money management class," she brags.

"Good for you!"

"It's through Taina's church."

"Really?"

"I joined the church too."

"What?"

"Girl, this church is like a whole little city. They got everything you need. It's a class for women about money, they call it Shopaholics Anonymous."

"Perfect!" I cry, and it is.

"Hard as all this time has been on me, girl, I'm glad I

went through it."

"Good. What doesn't kill us makes us stronger, right?"

"Got that right. It's funny, too, girl, because now I see Juan, and I don't feel anything for him like a woman feels for a man anymore. I just see him as a friend I had me for a long time, and I still love him as the father of my kids, but I don't think I need him anymore."

"People move apart sometimes. It happens."

"That doesn't mean I won't want him back someday, right?"

"Right. You never know what the future holds."

"But for now, I am honestly happy just focused on this little Aniat line. Besides, when I do find me a man again, he's going to be a Christian."

"If that's what you want."

"Listen to me, here's something I'm figuring out. Them Christian men? They're the biggest freaks in bed, girl."

"What?"

"Serious! The more reasons you give a man to think something's dirty, the better he likes it and the harder he chases it. I want me a gentleman on the street, a freak in the sheets. So next time, I'm going full-on former Altar Boy."

"Wow. Okay."

"You'll see, nena. A year from now, I'll be back in the money, and I'll find me a God-fearing man."

"I have no doubt he'll be afraid of *something*."

"I'll be all fancy at your book release party, with some papi chulo on my arm with his born-again *santo* face on."

"It's a date," I say. "I'm holding you to it."

We say goodbye, and I hang up. I feel happy. I shower and use the Aniat products, and love them. I mean, *love* them. My hair has never smelled so good or so easily been smoothed down. Then I get dressed, in jeans and a white tank top with a dark gray silk cardigan open over the top. I do my hair and makeup, and wait for John to come back from checking the water lines. I do a little extra mascara and eyeliner because I want him to notice me. Usnavys is right. I need to seduce this man tonight. It's time. Or at the very least, kiss him.

I wander the house a bit, not sure what to do with myself. I mix up a pitcher of instant iced tea. Then I go back to the study to edit a little. I check the news on the Internet. I go to Facebook and lurk on my friends' pages, and see what they're up to. I have some very glamorous friends. I am pleased to see that our rock star friend Cuicatl is already pumping up Aniat products on her Twitter feed, which, I should add, has more than 1 million followers.

I go back to the kitchen to check the tea chilling in the refrigerator, and to get some tall glasses down to fill with ice. John should be here any minute now, I think, and at that moment I hear a knock on the the screen door. I smile to myself, because I am almost completely sure that today is going to be the day that John and I finally press our lips together. I didn't hear the ATV or the truck, but he could have been out on horseback, as he sometimes is. I pour the tea into the glasses, and try to calm my heart down enough so that I won't do something stupid, like ask him to take me right here, right now.

"Be right there!" I call out cheerfully. I put the glasses on a tray, and turn around to walk toward the front door. I don't get far though. I am stopped dead in my tracks, and I drop the tray on the floor, because it isn't John Smith, the new love of my life, whom I find standing on the front porch smiling at me in his perfect three-piece suit with the yellow tie, a shiny black pistol in his city-boy hand, pointed directly at my head.

It is my dead ex-boyfriend, Boston Police detective Jason Flynn.

JASON

Jason Flynn steps into the great room of the quaint home in the middle of nowhere, careful to lift his expensively shod feet in their Italian loafers up and over the spilled tea and broken glass. Lauren looks at him, he thinks with amusement, as though she has seen a ghost. Of course, in her small and feeble sheepish mind, she has. She, like everyone else, assumes he's dead. Idiots. A man like Jason Flynn does not get himself *killed*. He is too careful, too smart, too holy. Too chosen.

"What are you doing here?" she asks, her eyes wide with horror, fear, and surprise. Good, he thinks. This is exactly how he expected her to look when he finally paid her this visit, and she has not disappointed him. The terror in her eyes excites him, and the excitement inflates his sword against the fabric of his suit pants.

"It was Martin Bernstein," he says, happy to finally be able to brag to someone about his handiwork.

"Who? What are you talking about?" She is backing up from him now, her hands out in front of her protectively. Why do the sheep-people always do that? Put their hands in front of them when a gun is pointed at them, as though frail fleshy human hands were going to stop a 9-millimeter bullet traveling at approximately 1100 feet per *second*. Idiots.

"In my Escalade. It was Bernstein. Young detective, decent-looking. Polite, hard working. You *do* remember him, don't you?"

"Oh, my God." Lauren is moving away from him, away from him, and Jason Flynn has had just about enough of that.

"Stop," he commands her.

"Why are you here?"

"Stop moving. Now. Stand still. Don't make me chase you."

"Okay," she says, obediently. Ah, yes. That was one of the traits Jason Flynn liked most about Lauren, in the early days of their dating. She was pliant. She always adjusted when he changed plans on her, and she never complained. He used to make promises just to break them, to test her. She knew that she wasn't worth a man's reliability and follow-through. He tested her mightily and for a long time on that trait, and she passed with flying colors, until the end when she decided that she knew too much and she tried to get strong on him. Then, he'd had enough.

"Have you missed me?" Jason Flynn asks her. Lauren does not answer because she is too busy being afraid. He softens his voice, makes it sound like a school guidance counselor who actually gives a shit. "Hey, calm down. Don't worry. It's okay, I'm not going to hurt you."

Lauren actually laughs when he says this. She does not believe him, and this angers Jason Flynn. Usually women in this position believe whatever you tell them, because the power of denial is the greatest power there is, other than the power over life and death that Jason Flynn carries within himself.

"Come here," he orders her.

"No can do." Lauren smirks. She is flippant. She thinks she has a right to be in control.

Jason Flynn's nostrils flare at her defiance. "I *told* you to come *here*."

"I heard you."

Lauren begins to move away from him again, faster this time, toward the kitchen. She lunges for a drawer, and pulls out a long, sharp butcher's knife. This annoys Jason Flynn, but it certainly doesn't scare him.

"Gun beats knife," he tells her. "Just like rock beats scissors."

"That all depends on who's holding it and how badly they want to live," she answers, mocking him. Her eyes are unusually furious and determined. She has changed, and not for the better. Jason Flynn uses his extraordinary brain to analyze this look on her face, and decides that while it will likely inconvenience him that she is feeling confident and self-protective, it is nothing that he cannot overcome. If he wanted to, he reminds himself, he could simply shoot her dead right now. He is a very good shot. She must know this. Why doesn't she care? Then he remembers. She cares because she is one of them, the sheep.

"Don't be foolish," he tells her. "You want to cooperate with me."

"Why? So you can kill me your way? I don't think so. If I am going to die today, it's going to be my way."

Jason Flynn laughs. "No. I don't think so."

Quick as lightning, Lauren reaches back into the knife drawer and takes out a smaller knife, maybe a steak knife, and hurls it toward Jason Flynn like one of those knife throwers at the circus. This stuns him, and in his astonishment he is slow to react. He ducks to his right, the correct direction, but a second too late. The blade sings across the firm flesh of his left shoulder, and embeds itself in the meaty muscle of his upper chest. Lauren looks as surprised as he did that her projectile found its mark. Jason Flynn remains composed, because pain doesn't bother him all that much, not this kind of pain. In fact, it excites him even more. She is going to be harder to catch than he thought, and this makes her a better adversary. This makes killing her all that much more exciting.

Jason Flynn yanks the knife out with his left hand, and sets it calmly down on the kitchen counter, moving ever closer to Lauren and not revealing any emotion, because he has none. Jason Flynn feels only interest, and envy, and rage. And now, the slight inconvenience of pain.

"Help!" Lauren shrieks. But it is too late. Jason Flynn is upon her now, his blood racing from the wound, his desire to violate her almost too great to bear now that he can smell his own blood. The blood of a God. Nectar.

Jason Flynn wraps his free arm around Lauren's neck, and she begins to slash at him with the butcher's knife. Weak slashes. With the gun pointed to her right temple, he uses his left hand to squeeze her right wrist hard enough to nearly break it. She squeaks like a mouse. Good girl. The knife falls with a clatter to the floor. He is eight inches taller than she is, and fifty pounds heavier. Really, she should have known better.

"Let me go you psycho motherfucker!" she screams, bucking against him.

"Not yet," he says. "Calm down. No need for name-calling. Tsk, tsk."

Lauren's teeth sink into the sinews of Jason Flynn's forearm, and her foot comes up from in back of her, and kicks him in the groin. He is momentarily paused in his motions as the pain from his testicles registers and ups his rage. He points the gun at the wall, and fires to relieve some tension.

Lauren instantly simmers down.

"Do not do that again," he tells her in a calm voice. "From now on, you are going to do as I tell you. Do you understand?"

Lauren nods, losing some of her fight at last, and Jason Flynn feels at peace.

"Remove your clothes," he tells her.

"No," she whines.

"What did I just tell you?"

She doesn't answer.

"I told you to do as I tell you, and you said okay."

"I nodded. I didn't say okay."

"Nitpicking." Jason fires the gun into the wall again. Lauren screams and begins to sob. "Do it now."

And she does. She is trembling as she goes, asking him all sorts of annoying questions about what he plans to do to her and how he found her. He ignores her and begins to whistle the melody to a catchy pop song by Lady Gaga that comes to him now. *Judas, Ju-da-as...* He begins to sing *"I'm just a holy fool, but baby it's so cruel, I'm still in love with Judas, baby..."*

"You're sick," she tells him.

"Tell me something I don't already know, genius. In a truly sick and stupid world, a God will seem sick to the masses."

"Is that what you think you are? A God?"

"I stand at the gates between life and death for you now, and only I can decide which way you travel."

"I hate you."

"Fail. Knew that. Don't care. Try again."

Lauren is naked now. He tells her to turn her back to him, and then he pushes her down, hard, against the countertop. He keeps the gun trained on her temple, and uses his left hand to unbutton his trousers. He is so big, so hard, he is a rocket launcher, a holy arrow. He is readying to push himself into her when she surprises him again by spinning toward him with a wild-animal look on her face, raising a glass fruit bowl into the air and bringing it down with a stinging snap upon the top of his head. Jason Flynn sees stars and nearly blacks out. Why didn't he see the bowl there? He should have been more thorough.

He realizes now that he has given her too much freedom, expected her to be docile because that is how she was before, in their relationship. He did not expect so much fight from a girl who ran away so eagerly. The bowl is up in her hands again, and this time, as Jason Flynn staggers back, his pants fallen around his knees, Lauren brings it down upon his arm, the one with the gun. He holds tightly to the weapon, but she smashes the bowl again and again into his wrist, crushing it between the bowl and the granite of the countertop, and then she's basing it onto his hand, and he lets go of the weapon because he has felt the bones in his hand about to snap. He cannot let that happen. He needs that hand.

Jason Flynn watches this all happen as though in slow motion. He is disappointed in himself, but not discouraged. It is time to recalculate and think this thing through. It is time to understand. The gun has fallen on the other side of the counter, in the breakfast nook area, and Lauren has the heavy glass bowl ready to smash it into his head again. He reaches up and takes the bowl from her, and hurls it across the room. Then he grabs her head in his hands, and wants to badly to twist it, to snap her neck, to kill her right here, but that would be too easy. This is foreplay. He's not ready for the climax yet. He's waited too long. He wants to savor the moment. Slow and easy.

They begin to wrestle. He smashes her back against

the counter, and she bites him. It is a stupid way to fight, he thinks, a girlish match. He enjoys watching himself engage in this animalistic savagery. It turns him on to see her so angry and afraid, bloodied and naked at the same time. It is the perfect combination in a woman. She scrambles up onto the counter, and this surprises him. Then before he knows what's happened, she is dropping onto the floor on the other side, and she is holding the gun now, and it is pointed at his own head.

"Stop," she says, and her breasts quiver. He is overcome with an urge to cut them, to carve them up like Cornish hens.

"You don't have it in you. You feel too much. You are one of the sheep."

And the gun fires. This is surprising, too. Jason Flynn feels nothing, however, and he realizes that Lauren is a terrible shot. How fitting.

"Stop!" she screams, clearly panicked now by her own ineptitude.

"Unlikely," he says. "I've waited a long time for this."

He steps toward her to grab the gun away, and she fires at him again. This time, a bullet penetrates his leg, and he feels the searing pain in his thigh, just a flesh wound, grazed. It energizes him.

"You will pay for that," he tells her simply, and then he leaps towards her, and lets the animal out of himself. He has held back too long now. She has no idea what he is actually capable of. She will learn.

"You fucking disobedient back-stabbing bitch," he says, as his body slams into hers. He takes the gun from her in one swift motion, and begins to strangle her. He hears the gurgling, and lets up because he doesn't want her dead yet. He wants her to live to feel every little thing he plans to do. He lets up. Then he sees something curious.

Quite curious.

The look of despair in Lauren's eyes, that look he has coveted for months, flickers momentarily, as her eyes stray from his face to something behind him. It is almost so fast he's not sure he's seen the shift in her face from despair to hope.

Hope?

Quite curious, indeed.

This is when Jason Flynn hears the faintest of sounds, as though someone has quietly and carefully closed the front door. His eyes go stone cold as he pretends he hasn't heard it, as he watches Lauren pretending not to watch whomever is behind him. He is alert now, intrigued, excited. He is not afraid. He has never been afraid of anything. Gods are not afraid. His excellent ears detect the slightest clicking of someone's aging knee cartilage in motion close behind him. Quietly, with a cool and steady hand, Jason Flynn cocks the hammer of his revolver, and prepares himself, mentally, to understand this newest challenge to his well-designed plans.

JOHN

John has put his horse in the corral at Tio's place, thinking that after iced tea he would sweep the beautiful and intelligent Lauren Fernandez off her size 8 feet, literally, and take her on horseback up to his house, where he has dinner marinating. He notices little things, like people's clothing sizes. She is a women's size 8 in clothing, 8 in shoes. She wears a B-cup bra, and brown eye shadow from Mac.

This attention to detail is why, by the time he got to dirt walkway leading to the front door of her house, John knew something was very, very wrong. He is attuned to little things other people don't notice, by virtue of the kinds of jobs he has held in his life, and this includes footprints. There are new ones here, new since he left an hour ago, and they belong to a man.

They are Italian loafers, new. And the stride is long and determined. Mob shoes.

This in mind, John was careful and quiet as he ascended the steps to the front porch. He has had training in moving silently across creaking wooden surfaces. He knows stealth. He knows how to search, what to look for, and how to handle yourself. It is second nature now. In this way, he was able to see the broken tea glasses, the spilled tea, and he was able to hear the struggle inside. He did not have to think about it very hard at all to understand that someone was here, and they were after the woman he has come, to his enormous surprise, to love over the past month.

John enters the room quietly, and she spots him. He is mortified by what he sees. The woman he loves is stripped naked, bleeding and bruised, with a very tall, very strong man on top of her, holding a gun, with his pants around his knees. John puts a finger to his lips to silence Lauren, and he hopes that nothing in her face has given him away to her attacker. Before he has time to even complete the next thought in his mind, the attacker turns on him, and opens fire.

John's reflexes are quick, as quick as they come, and he dodges the shot with enough time to avoid a mortal wound. The shooter aimed for his chest, but the bullet pierces the flesh of his left biceps. It feels like a clean shot, in one side and out the other. Just a little pain, he tells himself. Nothing he can't handle. John reacts instantly, firing his own weapon from his right hand, but not to kill. He has sworn to himself that he won't do any of that anymore. He aims for the legs, the arms, the hands.

Lauren is screaming now, and John tells her to run, to get out of there. The attacker is hit, but not debilitated, and John watches as though in slow motion as the man grabs Lauren by the ankle as she tries to get away, and slams her body to the ground. This is almost too much for John to handle, and he is on the edge of losing control and killing this man. The attacker turns again, and fires on John once more, this time missing altogether because Lauren has kicked the man in the arm and hand and thrown the shot off. The man is angry, and begins to backhand Lauren, beating her in the head with the gun.

John has had enough. To hell with promises to himself.

He is up instantly, and charging toward the attacker, who is so wrapped up in his rage and so confident he has wounded John that he no longer seems to even know the other man is there. He beats Lauren savagely, and when John is two steps away, aims the gun at her head.

John lunges forward, using all of the skills he has learned in his training. His left arm wraps with snakelike precision about the man's thick neck, cutting off his air supply. John's right arm comes up and around, and chops the attacker's arm hard enough to knock the gun out of his hand. He then hoists this man, who is roughly his own size and quite muscle-bound besides, up so that he is kneeling. John uses his right fist now to deliver two sickeningly brutal, nearly fatal blows, one to each kidney. These knock the attacker's wind out of him, and drop him like a rock. His body is heavy, but there is still fight in him. John can feel it simmering beneath the surface.

"Move, baby," he tells Lauren. "Get back. This is going to be ugly."

Lauren, poor Lauren, bleeding and hurt, scrambles away on the floor, and stops herself in the corner of the kitchen, pulls her knees up in a fetal position, and watches in horror.

"Who are you?" John demands of the man, who is now completely under his control.

"Fuck you," the man says. "I am your worst nightmare."

"He's Jason Flynn," Lauren says, in a voice that is calmer than John would have expected. "He's not dead. He set another guy up. He's still alive. He came to kill me."

John Smith smiles. He can tell this scares Lauren. He doesn't wish to scare her, but there is no way she can understand why this news pleases him.

"I was hoping I'd get to meet you," John tells Jason. "I guess my prayers were answered today."

Jason begins to fight back, spewing insults about Lauren. This only focuses John more.

"I've had about enough of you," says John. "This is about to end."

"Fuck you," says Jason again.

John kicks him silent. Then he looks at Lauren to ask permission, and she nods. Taking it as his cue, John grabs the killer's head in both hands. Then, quick as can be, and thrusts the head sharply to the right, once. A loud crack snaps the neck, and Jason Flynn's body goes limp.

"I don't like bullies," John whispers in Jason's ear, as he places two fingers on the killer's carotid artery, to check for a pulse. Surprisingly, Jason Flynn is still alive, though likely paralyzed from the neck down for the rest of his cursed life. John had intended to kill him. Perhaps he's lost his tough. Jason's eyes roll frantically as he tries to understand what has happened to him, and John looks into them for a long moment, trying to understand what it must be like to be a psychopath.

Then, with a calm that can only come from decades of

secret military training, and from the singular focus that a man feels when he is called to defend the life and honor of the woman he loves, John Smith removes his own shirt, wincing against the growing pain in his damaged left arm, and hands it to Lauren to cover herself up. He helps her over to the sofa, and brings her a glass of cold water. She is trembling, crying, and keeps looking at the man on the floor as though he might rise and walk again.

"It's over," John tells her, planting a small, steady kiss on her cheek. "It's okay now. He can't hurt you anymore."

On the floor, Jason Flynn begins to make wet noises as he struggles to breathe. John Smith listens for a moment, then walks to the telephone, picks it up, and dials 911.

"Hello, yes. This is John Smith calling. We're going to need a Med flight chopper out at the Yellow Dog Ranch, outside Quemado. No, ma'am, there's been no accident. A woman's been badly beaten. My name's John Smith, I'm a neighbor, and I've been shot. I've broken the neck of a man named Jason Flynn, from Boston, who was here attempting to murder a writer named Lauren Fernandez. Even though he doesn't deserve it, he could probably use some help."

LAUREN

Two hours ago, a very paralyzed Jason Flynn was flown away from Tio's ranch in a helicopter ambulance. John stayed behind, as did I, after being checked by paramedics and both of us patched up enough to wait for the ground ambulance to arrive over the rough road. I was well enough to get dressed in a set of loose-fitting sweats. We sit on a couple of chairs on the front porch now, waiting, watching the police cars and ambulances come bumping up the road. I cannot stop trembling, and John uses his good hand to hold mine. In spite of his own injuries, he tells me it's over, it's finally over, that everything is going to be all right now, and I believe him.

John has been shot through the biceps, but no major artery or vein was hit. I'm bruised and cut up a little bit, but, incredibly, basically unharmed. This is because Jason was waiting to hurt me slowly, I know it. John agrees with me about this. He tells me that he meant to kill Jason, but is glad he didn't.

"It's almost better this way," he says. "He'll be paralyzed and likely in prison. Not much he can do to anyone like that."

"Where did you learn to snap people's necks?" I ask him.

"Military."

"Yeah, but most average people in the military aren't so precise. You...you seem like a professional killer."

John's blue eyes connect with mine. He squeezes my hand. "Can you keep a couple of secrets, Lauren?" he asks.

"Yes."

"I grew up shooting rifles. And roping. That's just what a boy does on a place like this, it's part of the life. I had to have good aim, and my parents instilled in me good values. Those things, plus discipline and self-control, go a long way in the military, especially when you're ambitious and smart."

"What sort of long way?"

"I'm a sniper. I was."

"What does that mean, exactly?"

"It means I am one of the best-trained assassins in the world. It was my job. It was my calling. I did it to protect people. God knows how many American lives we save by taking key people out."

"Wow." I can't think of anything better to say, but my heart and mind are filled with emotions. Usnavys has been telling me that God doesn't make mistakes, that everything happens for a reason, and I cannot help but marvel at my good fortune to have landed next door to this remarkable man who saved my life.

"I was singled out as having great potential, and I rose as high as you could in that field."

"I am so lucky," I say, overcome with an urge to embrace him. I know. I'm always wanting to shack up with killers. But at least this one is on my side.

"I'm lucky, too," he says, holding my gaze. "I've been hoping to find a woman like you for a long time."

"Whatever."

"Lauren," he says, and I look away. He uses his good hand to gently turn my face back toward him. "Look at me."

"What?" I have a hard time holding his gaze, because it is so naked, raw and intense.

"Why do you think so little of yourself?"

I shrug. "I don't."

"Yes, you do. You don't seem to have any idea how good you are."

I swallow, hard, and say nothing. He's right.

"You're smart, you're pretty, you're funny, you're talented. You have so much to offer, but somehow, for some reason, you don't get it."

"Thank you."

He smiles kindly at me, and it almost seems as though there are tears about to form in his eyes, tears he holds back through sheer force of will. "You know, I was actually planning on making a move on you tonight, after dinner."

"Really? Because I was sort of hoping you might."

"Guess we'll have to take a rain check on that now."

"I guess," I say, noting that he is moving his mouth toward mine.

"Or," he says, planting a single, gentle kiss on my lips, with such tenderness that it is almost impossible to believe this man is a sharpshooter. "I could just do it now. While you're injured and defenseless."

"Assumption."

He smiles. "Did I mention you're a wise-ass, and I love that about you?"

I kiss him again, and it is incredible. All the pain I've felt drains out of me, pushed away by this new electricity and longing.

"Thank you," I say when I come up for air. He answers with a smile that I can only describe as sweet, almost boyish.

The cops and ambulances park, and come to us, asking lots of questions.

John knows some of the firefighter paramedics from the area, and some of the cops. They know him. A young policeman with a baby face takes down a report of what has happened, his eyes working overtime not to betray his astonishment that such a huge crime has fallen into his lap here in the middle of nowhere.

John is taken in one ambulance, and I in the other. He has requested that once we get to the hospital in the town of Socorro, that we be placed in the same room. I miss him instantly. I am completely in shock, numb, during the entire hour-plus ride, as the paramedics start in IV with saline, and check my wounds. They ask me what happened, and I tell them, almost unable to believe the story as it comes out of my mouth.

I am done, I think, with drama. I'm getting too old for this crap.

At the hospital, I am wheeled on the stretcher into a room occupied also by John Smith. He's on his stretcher, and a nurse is cleaning and dressing his wound. Police detectives come to take reports, and to get contact phone numbers, and an enterprising young reporter from the paper in Albuquerque shows up, sniffing around. I commend her on her drive, and tell her what I know. She is over the moon with her inside scoop, and I realize that by the morning much of Boston will probably have heard about this. I will be big news, indeed. Too bad it couldn't have waited until I finished the novel, but all publicity is good publicity -- or so they say. We'll see.

John and I are both patched up and deemed okay to leave within four hours. I've called Tio to tell him about the events at his house, and he, naturally, told Rebecca, who, true to her role as one of the best friends I've ever had, has called to tell me she is driving to Socorro to pick us up, take us back home, and to stay with me for a few days or as long as I need her. John invites her to join us for dinner at his place, and I marvel at how quickly he can just go back to his regular life. He has probably seen many more gruesome scenes than the one that unfolded today.

It is nearly eight o'clock by the time Rebecca pulls up to Tio's house in her big, fancy SUV. We've already dropped John off at his house, with an invitation for the two of us to join him for dinner later. Rebecca has insisted that she head up to his place to prepare the meal while I get cleaned up. John said he could cook with one arm, but Rebecca wouldn't hear of it. She helps me clean up the mess left by the struggles in the house earlier, and she holds my hands and together we say a prayer of cleansing, to set my mind at ease. Rebecca pulls me into a long embrace afterwards, and tells me the same things John has been saying -- that everything is going to be all right now.

I ask Rebecca about her own situation at home. She fills me in on the latest -- that her mother and father are divorcing, that her father has moved in with the other woman, that Rebecca doesn't know if she can ever trust her father again, or speak to him again, that she has mixed feelings about his other children, but has forged a tentative friendship with the daughter, Jennifer, who is her own age and very good with autistic children.

"It's a blessing, in a way," I say, sounding like

Usnavys now.

"What is?" she asks.

"Jennifer coming into your life. To help you with Connor. Maybe it was meant to be."

"That's a very positive way of looking at this," she says.

"And Andre?" I ask her.

She tells me that she and Andre are going to counseling, because the whole thing with her father had made her start to doubt him in ways she never did before.

"He's not your dad," I tell her.

"But I was drawn to him because he had so many of the same qualities of leadership that my dad has."

"That doesn't make Andre a bad guy."

"I know. We'll get through this. There's more to it, but that's another story for another time. You could write a book about it."

"I might."

She shakes her head. "You better not!"

"I'm a novelist now. You know what they say. Never be friends with a novelist."

"Let's not worry about it right now. Let's just get you cleaned up and fed, okay?"

There are tears in Rebecca's eyes. I grab her now, and embrace her, and I tell her that no matter what life throws at us, no matter how hard and scary things get, that we will always have each other. We will always be the dirty girls of Boston University, no matter how old we get or where we live. We will always, no matter what men come and go, no matter what tragedies and joys befall us, have the sucias, and each other. Without this dirty girl right here, and the other one in Boston, I realize, I might not have survived at all.

"That's what keeps me going," she says, crying. "I am so grateful that I have you, and Usnavys, and Sara, and Amber and Elizabeth. All of you."

"Friends are the family we choose," I say.

"Indeed."

Then, she leaves me to my shower and various post-shower rituals, with the following statement. "I don't want to stick my nose where it doesn't belong, but that John guy is a good find. If you let him get away, I will know you're hopeless in love."

"He's hot, right?" I ask.

"Lauren, he's more than that. He's the first real *man* you've ever dated. He's an actual grownup *man*, and he really likes you."

I let her go up to his place, and I take my time with the shower, letting the hot water roll over me, letting it take away my past, my pain, my mistakes. This is a new life, a new chance, before me. I'm not going to mess it up.

I drive myself to John's house in Tio's big pickup truck, enjoying the sense of being a country girl, and am once again struck by the beauty of his home. As I pull up to it in the dark of early night, the lights are on and the shades are all open, because there is no one to see inside except for me and John has nothing to hide from me anymore. The house is solid, large, beautiful, the house of a man with money, yes, but more than that -- a man with strength, and values.

And steak.

John stands over the grill on the front porch, a large set of tongs in his good hand. Rebecca sits on a rustic stuffed deck chair nearby, with a glass of red wine. The steaks grilling smell absolutely lovely, and perfect. John smiles as I walk up, and waves me over. He embraces me, and kisses me, in full view of my friend.

"You look nice," he says.

"Thank you."

Rebecca brings me a glass of wine of my own, and I am more than ready for it. John removes the steaks to a platter, and we all head inside, where the table has clearly been set by my overachieving friend. There are candles, and there is salad, and crusty bread, and butter, and fine stoneware dishes. Everything is beautiful. The house is incredibly perfect, and I realize with a shudder that I am already starting to feel at home here. I could, I think, spend the rest of my life in this place. In this house. With this man. It would be a fine place to raise a family. And he would be a fine father to my children. Not that I'm thinking about any of that. I haven't even slept with the guy yet. For all I know, he could suck in bed. Given how well he uses his hands and body in everything else, though, I seriously doubt it.

We take our seats. We eat dinner and make small talk. The food is excellent, and I am calming down, but I cannot help obsessing on my earlier kisses with John. I want more. And he seems to as well, from the hungry looks he gives me from time to time. They send chills down my spine. Rebecca, no slouch, seems to notice John and my desire for one another, and excuses herself from the table, clearing her dishes to the kitchen.

"I need to head back to your place for a minute," she tells me. "I left my phone there, and I've got a conference call this evening with a writer in...uhm, Australia. Right. I almost forgot."

I give her a look to let her know I see through her lie. She winks at me. John sees it all, and pretends not to notice.

"I might be back later," she says. "But the call might go late. If I stay away, don't wait up for me."

"Rebecca," I say. "You don't have to..."

She silences me with a stern look, and then thanks John for all he's done for me. "It was a pleasure meeting you," she tells him. John gets up, and opens the front door for her, hugging her before she goes. I join him, and together we watch her get into her car and drive away.

"Subtlety's not her strong suit, is it?" John asks, turning toward me and kissing me again. There is such strength and beauty in his kiss, I almost can't control myself. I want him. I am dying to know what it will be like to make love with this man.

"She's a good friend," I say. "She's usually more subtle than that."

"I think she likes us," he tells me, between kisses, each kiss more intense and more passionate than the last.

"Us?"

"The idea of an us. Me and you, as a unit. A couple."

"She does. She said as much."

"What do *you* think of that idea?" he asks, stroking my cheek with his fingers. "A big-shot city girl like you, coupled up with a simple cowboy from the middle of nowhere."

"I hardly think that's an accurate description of you."

"Did you ever, in your entire life, imagine you'd end up with a guy like me?" he asks.

"Probably about as much as you imagined you'd end up with someone like me."

He grins. "I always hoped I'd end up with someone like you. Not a lot of those out there, though."

"I never thought I *deserved* anyone like you," I say, burying my face in his chest. Even now, I think, I cannot really believe a man like this would want *me*. He is the type to want prettier women, better women.

He crinkles his brow, in concern, and then relaxes it in compassion. "You deserve the best life has, Lauren. You need to learn to see yourself the way others see you. That's going to be my number one job from now on, to help you see your true self, the way you look to the rest of the world."

He kisses me again, and our bodies press hard against each other.

"Tell me, what do you think of the idea of an us?" he asks, in a whisper.

"I think I like it a lot," I whisper back.

He leads me by the hand back to table, grabs his wine glass and raises it. "To us, then," he says.

"To us," I repeat, clinking my own glass with his.

Prologue

Thank you for reading this book! I hope you were on the edge of your seat as much reading it as I was writing it!

If you are older than 18 and wish to read what happened next between Lauren and John, please visit amazon.com to purchase the X-rated Very Dirty Chapter by Alisa Valdes-Rodriguez, for $2.00. I so wanted to include it in this book, but did not want to offend any sensitive readers with the quite graphic content. I couldn't write Lauren and John having sex for the first time any other way but in a deeply erotic style. Maybe it was because I spent the whole novel trying to keep them apart. By the time I finally let them get naked in bed together, pues. It was all over, girl!

To find out what happened with Usnavys and Rebecca next, be on the lookout for two new Dirty Girls novels in the next year, one focused on Rebecca and the other focused on Usnavys. There are big changes coming for both of them, because that's life. If there's still interest in these characters after that, we might just visit the other three in their lives, too.

Love you guys lots. You are the reason I do what I do.

Thanks again for your support,

Alisa Valdes-Rodriguez
www.alisavaldesrodriguez.com
valdes.alisa@gmail.com